# PRAISE FOR
# *THE BEAUTIFUL AMERICAN*

"*The Beautiful American* will transport you to expat Paris and from there take you on a journey through the complexities of a friendship as it is inflected through the various lenses of nostalgia, pity, celebrity, jealousy, and—ultimately—love. Jeanne Mackin breathes new life into such luminaries as Man Ray, Picasso, and, of course, the titular character, Lee Miller, while at the same time offering up a wonderfully human and sympathetic protagonist in Nora Tours."

—Suzanne Rindell, author of *The Other Typist*

"Jeanne Mackin's portrait of Europe in the years encompassing the Second World War is achingly beautiful and utterly mesmerizing, and her vividly drawn characters, the legendary Lee Miller among them, come heartbreakingly alive in their obsessions, tragedies, and triumphs. *The Beautiful American* is sure to appeal to fans of Paula McLain's *The Paris Wife* and Erika Robuck's *Call Me Zelda*, or indeed to anyone with a taste for impeccably researched and beautifully written historical fiction."

—Jennifer Robson, author of *Somewhere in France*

"From Poughkeepsie to Paris, from the razzmatazz of the twenties to the turmoil of World War Two and the perfume factories of Grasse, Mackin draws you into the world of expatriate artists and photographers and tells a story of love, betrayal, survival, and friendship. As complex as the fragrances Mackin writes about, *The Beautiful American* is an engaging and unforgettable novel. I couldn't put it down."

—Renée Rosen, author of *Doll Face*

*continued . . .*

"An exquisitely imagined and beautifully rendered story of the talented, tragic, gorgeous Lee Miller."

—Becky E. Conekin, author of *Lee Miller in Fashion*

"Jeanne Mackin blends a tale as intoxicating as the finest fragrance. Spanning wars both personal and global, *The Beautiful American* leaves its essence of love, loss, regret, and hope long after the novel concludes."

—Erika Robuck, author of *Call Me Zelda* and *Fallen Beauty*

"Jeanne Mackin's luminous novel about Man Ray and his model-mistress, Lee Miller, evokes the iridescence of 1920s Paris when youth and artistic freedom and sexual excess were all that mattered. *The Beautiful American*, which readers will rank right up there with *The Paris Wife*, takes readers from the giddiness of the flapper era to the grittiness of World War II. It is a brilliant, beautifully written literary masterpiece. I love this book!"

—Sandra Dallas, *New York Times* bestselling author of *Fallen Women*

## PRAISE FOR THE OTHER NOVELS OF JEANNE MACKIN

"I read this novel in two sittings, eager to learn how the lives and love stories turned out. . . . Before I realized it, I was swept up in Maggie and Helen's intersecting worlds. . . . One of the book's many charms is how wisely it reveals the values and passions of two women from very different eras who, nonetheless, have everything in common."

—Diane Ackerman, author of *The Zookeeper's Wife*

"[Mackin's] narrator, while asserting that she is no 'hagiographer of spurious mystics,' is an engaging woman, solid in her station, widely conversant with the deeper reaches of the paranormal, and magically involved with her quest. Here she leads the mind in a chase as she finds herself tempted to believe in the return of departed spirits, in a prose that is as amiable to read as the palm of a hand. A haunting book in every way. Masterly and fervent." —Paul West, author of *The Secret Lives of Words*

"Jeanne Mackin has written a multilayered, multigenerational story of a spirited encounter with the spirit world."

—Nicholas Delbanco, author of *What Remains*

"A sensitive, affectionate, and appealing portrait of [Maggie Fox], the uneducated girl who at fourteen escaped rural poverty and a drunken abusive father to become America's first and most famous Spiritualist medium."

—Alison Lurie, Pulitzer Prize–winning author of *Foreign Affairs*

"Plenty of romance and intrigue, vital characters and exquisite details of both period and place ensure a vigorous and satisfying read." —*Publishers Weekly*

"The author of *The Frenchwoman* again imaginatively samples French history and here constructs a witty, lightly satirical, entertaining amalgam of murder, greed, and revenge . . . a richly intelligent and charming spellbinder." —*Kirkus Reviews*

"Rich in detail, from descriptions of food and attire to historical personages, this first novel is well written and entirely believable. Mackin is positioned to join the ranks of popular historical novelists." —*Library Journal*

Other Novels by Jeanne Mackin

*The Sweet By and By*

*Dreams of Empire*

*The Queen's War*

*The Frenchwoman*

# THE BEAUTIFUL AMERICAN

JEANNE MACKIN

NEW AMERICAN LIBRARY

New American Library
Published by the Penguin Group
Penguin Group (USA) LLC, 375 Hudson Street,
New York, New York 10014

USA | Canada | UK | Ireland | Australia | New Zealand | India | South Africa | China
penguin.com
A Penguin Random House Company

First published by New American Library,
a division of Penguin Group (USA) LLC

First Printing, June 2014



LIBRARY OF CONGRESS CATALOGING-IN-PUBLICATION DATA:

Mackin, Jeanne.
The beautiful american/Jeanne Mackin.
p. cm.
ISBN 978-0-451-46582-5
1. Female friendship—Fiction. 2. Missing children—Fiction. 3. Americans—France—Fiction. 4. Aliens—Europe—Fiction. 5. World War, 1939–1945—Fiction. I. Title.
PS3563.A3169B43 2014
813'.54—dc23 2013049784

Printed in the United States of America
10 9 8 7 6 5 4 3 2 1

Set in Adobe Garamond
Designed by Spring Hoteling

PUBLISHER'S NOTE
This is a work of fiction. Names, characters, places, and incidents either are the product of the author's imagination or are used fictitiously, and any resemblance to actual persons, living or dead, business establishments, events, or locales is entirely coincidental.

For my husband, Steve Poleskie, as always

# ACKNOWLEDGMENTS

Many thanks to the friends and colleagues who helped get this story to the page: fellow writer Nancy Holzner for her gentle but prodding encouragement—our conversations were my life raft; Ellen Edwards for her gracious and perceptive editorial guidance, and the others at New American Library: cover designer Anthony Ramondo; Courtney Landi, Craig Burke and Jodi Rosoff in marketing; editorial assistant Elizabeth Bistrow; publisher Kara Welsh and editorial director Claire Zion. Thanks to literary representative Kevan Lyon, and friends Alison Lurie, Diane Ackerman, Charlotte Greenspan and Natasha Tall who gave support, insight and the occasional French verb. Very special thanks to Tom Newton and Mary Kay Clapp, who helped me through this book and the ones that came before. Their friendship and encouragement are a great blessing. Thanks to Barbara Adams, the intrepid and extraordinarily patient traveling companion who accompanied me to Grasse and Nice. Finally, I owe a debt to artist Mary Frey, who, years ago when we were young and living happily in Boston attics, patiently encouraged me to look, really look, at photographs.

# THE BEAUTIFUL AMERICAN

# PROLOGUE
# DÉPART

The very first hint of fragrance, experienced when the perfume bottle is first opened, before the fragrance is in direct contact with the skin, the nose, and the heart. Similar, really, to a book opened but not yet read . . . or, perhaps, a door opened to a visitor not yet visible, one who lurks in shadow. The *départ* begins the journey of the perfume and its wearer.

—From the notebooks of N. Tours

In the ornate doorway of Harrods' perfume hall people rushed past me as I stood, frozen.

A radio played somewhere, Churchill's voice rising over the crowd, commending the English again for surviving the storm-beaten voyage. The war was over; we were picking up the pieces and carefully, slowly putting our lives back together. But my daughter was lost, in her own way another war casualty. The grief struck me anew and I was immobile in a doorway, unable to go forward or backward, unmoored by grief.

A summer afternoon long ago Jamie and I went to Upton Lake to swim and make love, and there had been a boat, abandoned by rich summer people who didn't know how to tie a knot, and the boat had bobbed in the waves, turning this way and that as a storm stalked over the lake. I was that boat.

"Move on!" the doorman shouted at me, but my legs wouldn't work. I was exhausted. When I walked, there was a chant in my head, Dahlia is gone, Dahlia is gone, over and over, a syllable with every step, so that I hated to move. People pushed past me, some smiling in sympathy, some merely irritated. Their string shopping bags and brown-wrapped boxes jostled me; their elbows poked.

The doorman frowned. He took me by the arm and pulled me out of that flood of people. "Look, dearie," he said, "are you coming or going?"

"I don't know," I admitted.

His expression softened. He was an older man with a deeply lined face, pale eyes sunk into their sockets, and there was an authority to him that went beyond his doorman's uniform. Probably during the war he had been an air raid warden. He would have been too old to be a soldier.

"Well, then," he said, "why don't you go in? That's always a good starting point. There you go." He turned me around, gently, and gave me a little push, back to that threshold, where I suddenly remembered I wanted to enter, to continue the search for my daughter.

I moved through the doorway, overwhelmed by the synthetic florals and citruses of the postwar perfumes. They enter the nose aggressively, fighting for attention like unruly schoolchildren. What I most remembered about my own child was how the long braid she wore down her back smelled of lavender, a single note of innocence. My lost child.

Seventeen years ago, I ran away. And now, my daughter had, too, or at least I hoped she had, for the other possibilities were unthinkable. But after months of searching, I hadn't found Dahlia in any of those places where a young girl might find shelter: not in the homes of friends in southern France; not in Paris in the narrow streets of Montparnasse, the cafés and gardens and boulevards of those years with Jamie; not in the orphanages that sheltered children whose parents had not survived. She had left no trace.

So I had come, finally, to London, to the almost-beginning. Beginnings are like endings, never completely finished, simply receding like the horizon. Here, in the doorway of Harrods, one rainy morning almost two decades ago, Jamie and I had agreed that we would leave England and go to Paris, and that if all went well, we would marry and begin our family. I had told Dahlia that story, how I had dreamed of her years before she was born.

I had already been in London for three days, walking the streets, asking hotel clerks and checking registers at shelters, looking for her, fighting down panic and dread. The boardinghouse where Jamie and I had stayed had been bombed and so had the little pub where we had had our noon fish-and-chips and pint. There was destruction everywhere. St. Paul's Cathedral had been bombed, St. James's Palace, the Houses of Parliament. Half the population of London had been made homeless. This was no place for a young girl on her own, even one with papers and a little cash, for her papers and her savings had disappeared with her.

Dahlia is sixteen, I kept reminding myself. She was tall and strong and sensible. She spoke French and English fluently and could get by in Italian and German. She had good common sense. She had what she needed to survive, if her luck held.

How had I produced such a child, me, the gardener's daughter from Poughkeepsie? Dahlia was a wonder to me, but in my dread I didn't think of her as strong and competent, but as a lost child crying for her mother.

My lost child. Would I be returning home without her again? I had gone back and forth from Paris to Grasse for months, always leaving home with hope, returning in despair. Home again, without Dahlia. The thought kept me motionless inside that doorway.

"Hey!" a voice muttered. "Move on." A woman, tall, burdened with an armful of parcels, almost knocked me over in her haste to get out the door.

"Watch yourself!" I snapped back. The woman looked at me over the top of her packages.

"Oh my God," she said.

Once she had lowered her arms and I could see her face, I knew her immediately. Lee Miller.

The very famous and beautiful Lee Miller, the *Vogue* model, the muse for the artist Man Ray, who had made of her lips an iconic image of a woman's mouth floating in the sky. She had gone on to become a famous photographer—the only woman photographer who covered battles, not just field hospital follow-ups and stories about the war nurses. She had photographed the London Blitz, the siege of Saint-Malo, the Alsace campaign, the camps in Germany. Nightmare photos.

Lee was heavier than I remembered, and there was a puffiness around the eyes and in the cheeks that drinkers sometimes got. But nothing, not war, alcoholism, or middle age, could mar that perfect nose and those cheekbones, the thick wavy blond hair now worn postwar-style, falling over one eye. Those oh-so-famous lips.

We stood for a long while, staring at each other in disbelief. It's not often that you run smack into your own past.

# PART ONE
# NOTE DE TÊTE

Top note: the fragrance first released when the perfume achieves initial contact with the skin of the wearer, predominating in the olfactory sense for approximately fifteen minutes. Quite often these first notes of fragrance remind the wearer of a certain day in childhood, the smell of a chamomile lawn or a spice cake, or a sunny day at a picnic spot. The top note is the first station on the journey, where the decision of yes or no must be made.

—From the notebooks of N. Tours

In the kingdom of smells, everything is either bliss or torture.

—Colette

# CHAPTER ONE

"You!" she said, and a few of her top parcels fell, as if in emphasis. The old doorman saluted and bent to retrieve them. Lee straightened her hat with a preoccupied gesture. She wore an expensive suit, well cut of real Scottish tweed, but it had seen better days. "I haven't seen you since . . ." She paused, thinking.

"Paris. Nineteen thirty-two," I supplied.

"Yes. Paris." Her face softened. With the help of the doorman, she balanced her packages in a way that allowed her to extend her gloved hand.

Lee shook hands like a man, with a strong grip and a pumping action. You had to stand your ground or her handshake could knock you off-balance.

"You are dressing much better," she said. "I like the jacket. Good lines."

It was one of Dahlia's jackets, made for her by Omar's housekeeper. Omar was my dear friend in Grasse, but I didn't say that, because then I would have to talk about Dahlia and explain who Omar was and it would be difficult to end all the explanations.

Seventeen years is a long time, even longer when a war stalks through them. Sixteen years could not be condensed to casual chit-chat in the doorway of Harrods. "I like your suit," I said, settling for the predictable.

"I still feel more comfortable in trousers and combat boots." Lee hesitated, considering. Perhaps she was pursuing phantoms as well.

"Can you come for tea with me?" she asked. She hadn't lost her startling spontaneity.

"I have an appointment," I lied.

"Please. Just for a few minutes. I'd love the company. I just bought a new hat and really don't know if it works or not. I need another woman's opinion." The hat was just an excuse, of course.

"Okay," I agreed reluctantly.

She laughed with delight. "Okay!" she echoed. "That beautiful American word. Oh, how wonderful to talk with another American. Follow me."

We dodged between jammed and honking cars, splashing through puddles, to a tearoom across the street. Without waiting for the hostess, Lee took the best available table, by the center window.

"Can't get over the traffic," she said with a sigh. "You take your life in your hands just trying to cross the street. During the war there wasn't a car in sight, most afternoons. Certainly not at night, during the blackout."

When she took off her coat and draped it over the chair between us, her perfume tingled in my nostrils, expensive and slightly burning from a note of geranium oil. The scent of geranium swept me back to Grasse, to the dark mixing room, the shelves of bottles, the locked safe where the formula was kept. Jamais de la Vie was an expensive perfume, still made by the enfleurage method, each flower petal hand pressed into a sheet of lard to capture its fragrance. Lee was wearing the equivalent of a hundred roses and jasmine flowers.

She leaned closer. "Were you here for the bombing, or did you go back to the States?"

I still wasn't used to the openness with which some people spoke of those years. For me, they were locked boxes. I was also taken aback by how much I knew about Lee, and how very little she knew about me. Friends and family had made sure that, for years, I knew of Lee's doings, her work and travel, her lovers. Obviously no one had thought to give her news of me. But that is the nature of fame, isn't it? Lee was famous.

Lee ordered tea and a large pot soon arrived, and a plate of pastries. We sat at our lace-covered table and poured Earl Grey into china teacups. Lee took a silver flask from her purse and poured a healthy shot into her tea. I thought somehow it was all a mad dream, it couldn't be real; Man Ray would walk in at any moment, demanding attention, asking Lee where she'd been, and Jamie would be just behind Man, looking anxious. No, that was years ago. The world now, after the destruction, was made of hot water flavored with burned-grain fake coffee, and all the teacups had been broken.

Lee bit into an éclair and the cream oozed out, smearing her crimson mouth. She laughed and flicked her tongue out to the corners. "Real cream," she said with delight. "I shouldn't be eating this. Impossible to lose weight these days. Didn't I hear you were in France during the war?"

"I heard you were all over Europe, often in two or three places at the same time," I said, avoiding her question. "I saw some of your photos."

An edition of British *Vogue* had made its way to the zinc counter of Omar's café, there in my little village in the hills of southern France. The war photos had been almost surreal in their horror. I had thought at the time, leafing through that dog-eared magazine, that our years in Paris, the experiments in surrealism, had somehow been a training ground for what was to come: the violence, the disconnection.

Man Ray, her lover, protector, and promoter during those prewar Paris years, had once made a sculpture of Lee with a single eye representing the entire body of the woman he adored. He had constructed another image in which he had slit her neck, making a crimson gash like an extra mouth. The body had been reduced to separate parts. We were none of us whole. Maybe that was how we had survived, in parts, like pages torn out of a book so that the story could not be read but only guessed at.

Lee sneezed and coughed into a handkerchief. "Wretched cold," she complained. "Had it for weeks. So what did you think of my photos?"

I came back to the moment, to the teacup in my hand, the plate of cakes with their sensual promise of cream and vanilla. Lee wanted me to praise her photos. It was easy to do.

"They were magnificent. Dozens of gray tones." I had remembered that much about photography. A rich photograph had as much color as the real world, except all the colors were some variant of gray. In some ways, perfumes were like black-and-white photographs. Most people will say of a scent "That is floral" or "That is citrus" when, in fact, the perfume has dozens, perhaps a hundred, different components. Art is all subtle variation.

"You remembered our discussions. I'm flattered." Lee preened slightly, tilting her head and smiling more broadly, still dabbing at her nose.

"And the light in the photographs," I said. "You made natural light seem precise, even staged, like in a painting."

"Light," she said quietly. "That's always the most important element, isn't it?" The smile disappeared. She looked out the window at the wet, dismal street. "During the blackouts I thought there would never again be enough light in the world, that it could never fall with a promise of grace instead of a threat. Have you seen Pablo's *Le charnier—The Charnel House*? All black and white and gray, like *Guernica*. For a while the whole world seemed black and white and gray. Even the battlefields. The blood turned gray. Did you see the exhibition in Paris, 'Art and Resistance'? How come I didn't see you there?"

Lee's fingers tapped nervously on the table.

"I wasn't there," I said.

We finished our tea, carefully speaking only of what did not matter. The weather. The new fashions, new movies. She never mentioned Jamie, nor did I.

"I hear back in the States they have invented color television," Lee said.

"Have they?" I didn't have or want a television. All I wanted to see of the world was just outside my window in Grasse. I wanted to see the lavender fields, and I wanted to hold my daughter. At the table next to us, a little girl began to wail that she wanted her dolly and her mother leaned over and whispered in her ear. The child stopped wailing, but sobbed those awful silent tears of a bereft child.

"Has your father bought one? A color television?" I asked, distracted by the little girl. Mr. Miller had been keen on new gadgets, often buying things for the joy of taking them apart and putting them back together. Lee had inherited her mechanical ability from him. From my own father, Mr. Miller's yardman and gardener, I had inherited what in Grasse they called "a good nose." I had been tested and could pick out three thousand different scents; most people could pick out only a few hundred.

"He'll probably try to build his own." Lee laughed. "And do it." We fell silent, overwhelmed.

"Look." She stood and pulled on her gloves. "Can you come to us this weekend? Come meet Roland. I married, you know. Twice, to be precise. Aziz and I married after you left Paris, but it didn't last. God, Cairo was so boring. But I think this one will last. Come meet the husband, and little Anthony. Yes, I have a child. A boy. The most beautiful little boy in the world. I'm absolutely besotted."

Pain knifed my chest. "I didn't plan a long stay," I said, trying to sound a touch careless, a little preoccupied with all the things I had to do. "And I didn't bring evening clothes. In fact, I am wearing my entire travel wardrobe."

It was a silly excuse but one that would do when the truth was too painful. I didn't want to see Lee holding her child. Lee, who had never wanted to marry, to have children, now had both husband and son. And my child was lost; her father, the man who should have been my husband, was an ocean away, living with a different wife, a different family.

Lee laughed. "Darling, that doesn't matter. Wear a sheet if you must. It will be like the old days. Do come! On Friday, take the afternoon train to Lewes and we'll pick you up at the station. On Sunday, we'll drive you to Newhaven and you can catch the ferry to France."

She stood and reached for the bill, signing it rather than leaving cash. I read her signature upside down. Lady Penrose of Poughkeepsie, it said. Lee still had a sense of humor.

I hadn't yet agreed to the weekend, so she played her strongest card.

"Pablo will be there," she said, and was out the door before I could say no.

Pablo. When I had to leave Paris, Pablo Picasso had been the one to help me, not because we were close—we were not—or because he was particularly kind to young girls in trouble—he was not. It had merely been one of those life-forming coincidences. That day, as I stood on the Pont Neuf wondering where I would go, what I would do, he had come toward me on his way to somewhere. There was just enough kindness in his voice when he asked, *"Ça va?"* that I sobbed my story out to him. He had already known, of course. That's the sad truth of betrayal. It makes a poor secret except to the betrayed.

He paused, then gave me a piece of paper on which he'd written the name of a friend who would take me in. He would write to her the very next day, he promised, and I fled to his friend, Madame Hughes, in Grasse. Seventeen years ago. A war ago. A child ago. A lifetime ago.

Lee had introduced me to Pablo, and to many others. She had given, and she had taken. I looked out the window and watched Lee cross the street with that determined stride of hers. She waved, grinned, and disappeared into the crowd.

I stared at the card, wondering how much the train to Lewes would cost. No one ever said no to Lee Miller, and if she thought they might, she simply never asked the question. Of course, there was always a first time. Why should I interrupt my search for Dahlia to play houseguest for the woman who had, years before, derailed my dreams? Because the search is over, a dark voice said in my head. There is nowhere else to look.

I rose to leave the restaurant, walking in the wake of Lee's perfume. I smelled it, then, that bottom note I hadn't noticed before. Camphor, eucalyptus, and the salty, acrid bottom note of merbromin. Medicine. The smell carried me backward.

Scents are memories' bid for immortality; they keep the past alive.

The waitress came and cleared away the teapot and plates as I watched Lee through the window of the tearoom, balancing her parcels and flagging down a cab. There was a look in her eyes that hadn't been there before, and all during tea her fingers had drummed nervously on the table. Dread. That sleepwalking sense that though the immediate danger might be over, who knew what was hiding behind that door, around that corner?

I returned to Harrods, to finish my search of the store. That was all I did, all I had done for six months: search. One by one, I had gone to all the places I had mentioned to my daughter, and I had told her the story of how Jamie and I had stood in front of Harrods one day and decided to go to Paris. I climbed the stairs to the top floor and worked my way down. There were lots of tall girls, some laughing, some serious. None was my daughter.

I bought a hat for Dahlia, a little knit cloche with flowers embroidered on the side. It would go into the box I kept filled with all the gifts I would shower upon my child when she was back home. Buying those gifts had become my religion: if I bought that hat, that book of poems, the painted jewelry box for her earrings, then she was certain to be found.

In the dress section I caught an image of myself passing a full-length mirror and for a moment did not know who that too-thin middle-aged woman with the dead eyes was, and I saw myself as Lee had just seen me. No wonder she had offered to buy me tea. I looked pathetic.

You would, too, I told the mirror, if you had lost your daughter.

In the women's cocktail section one dress caught my eye, calf-length silk with a tight bodice and swirling skirt, green the color of spring leaves, pale and glowing. I stood before it, transfixed by all that shimmering green. It was Dahlia's favorite color.

She had a beret that color, and a matching scarf. All her schoolgirl friends had chosen different colors. They had gone hiking together on Saturday afternoons, arms linked, each girl in her chosen color, a bouquet of pinks, greens, blues, and magentas, bobbing and laughing down the cobbled streets of Grasse. That had been before the war.

"Would you like to try it on? I'm sure we have your size." A saleslady broke the memory.

An hour later, back in my small hotel room, I opened my purse and let the bills and coins spill out onto the bed. I shouldn't have bought the dress. But I saw myself wearing it, showing it off for Dahlia. It was another talisman. I let the dress drop back down onto the bed and thought about prewar things . . . Jamie, those long afternoons in Paris, the all-night parties in artists' studios, Lee and Man Ray presiding over the scene like a goddess and god descended from Olympus, my first tastes of pâté and escargots and rich café au lait, the yeasty smell of the boulevards just after a rain. They seemed to be from a different lifetime. Before Dahlia.

By Friday the London sky had cleared, but I had entered a new state of mourning for my daughter. I had not found her in London, not in the homes and orphanages set up for lost children; not in any police records; not, thank God, in morgue descriptions of unclaimed bodies.

My feet were blistered from wandering the streets, but I felt nothing. For the first time I faced the possibility that she might be gone forever and it was like staring into the mouth of a beast ready to swallow me whole. I would let it. Without Dahlia, there was no point in going on. I might as well be dead and buried.

I purchased a train ticket for Lewes in the morning for one simple reason: I was afraid to be alone any longer. I did not expect comfort from Lee, or help of any sort, merely distraction. Somehow, I had to find the will to return to Grasse, to my home, my empty home, and decide how to survive the next thirty years; if I was to survive.

I wondered what had driven Lee to take the chances she had during the war. Perhaps I just wanted to round off some of those jagged-edged, piercing fragments of our personal history, perfume them with nostalgia to hide the old odor of regret and blame.

When the train arrived, a porter helped me find a seat. It was jammed full. All trains were, all buses, since gas was still strictly rationed. I shared a compartment with a large family that seemed to be going on holiday. The mother was surrounded by satchels and valises, so many that they filled the overhead rack and spilled onto the floor. Her many children ran excitedly back and forth in the passageway. There would be no more holidays for me. This was just another trip, backward, into the past. What for?

Not forgiveness, I reminded myself. The war had made that word meaningless. Acceptance. Simple acceptance. The simplest things are the hardest to achieve.

Lee met me at the train station, as promised, jogging toward me through misty steam and again balancing parcels, this time baskets of eggs, a recently butchered chicken, some spring peas.

"I've been scavenging," she announced proudly. "The ration card was used up days ago. Thank God for the black market. Things are still a bit basic at the farm, but we won't starve. This way." And she pointed to the station exit with that straight, elegant nose of hers. She wore trousers and combat boots and an old sweater with holes in the elbows, and I could see how pregnancy and childbirth had softened her body, though she was still slender enough to model for *Vogue*, if she wanted.

Roland Penrose, her husband, waited for us beyond the gate and helped Lee carry her packages to the car. He was a solemn, dark-eyed man, older than Lee but not by much, well dressed in country tweeds with slightly frayed cuffs on the jacket, just enough to suggest taste and tradition. He was a man who knew the difference between casual and black tie, town and country, all the things Jamie had tried to learn. Roland Penrose had the best "eye" in England and Europe, and the friends and contacts needed to acquire art. His art collection was second only perhaps to the Guggenheim woman's, according to a magazine article about him I had seen in the British edition of *Vogue*.

He greeted me with gentlemanly graciousness, though he was plainly puzzled. Where had his wife found this stray? I wondered what Lee had told him, what she herself remembered. Our friendship, if that was the accurate term, had been brief and intermittent, though for me, at least, momentous.

Roland drove fast, rattling around potholes and fallen branches from the storm of a few days before. I had to hold on to my hat, and when Lee laughed, I laughed as well, to hide the fact that I was weeping. Dahlia had loved fast cars, speeding trips through the countryside. When we rounded the corner and their new country home came into view, Lee looked at me and rolled her eyes. I laughed so hard I could barely catch my breath. If Omar had been there, he would have given me a gentle slap to break the hysteria.

Farley Farm was a huge, ramshackle place with broken windowpanes, faded, peeling paint, and stray cows grazing in an old, weedy flower bed. Lo, how the mighty are fallen, I thought, and it was my mother's voice speaking the words, and I was standing next to her, outside the Miller farmhouse in Poughkeepsie, New York, watching the pretty daughter of the house, Elizabeth, not yet known as Lee, step off the porch in her white summer dress.

"We've no furniture," Lee said, still laughing, climbing out of the car. "Most of it was used as firewood. It will be a bit like camping out. But some of the rooms are actually dry, if it should rain. And there's a stove and plenty of brandy. We'll be warm."

"Look at this," Roland said. Holding the dead chicken in one hand, he took my arm with the other. "We have our own good-luck omen." He turned me to face south, toward the Channel, where a gentle breeze stirred the grasses. Far below us, cut into the turf, was an ancient chalk outline.

"The Long Man of Wilmington," Roland said. "The house lines up with it during the summer solstice."

"Probably this was an ancient place of bloody sacrifice," Lee said. "We appease the gods with frequent libations and lots of parties." Lee took my hand and guided me into the house.

Bare wood floors, peeling wallpaper, wild mint thrust into jugs to add color, huge empty rooms with an almost haunted feel to them . . . I hoped they'd gotten a discount price, because Farley Farm was a wreck. The wind blew through the walls so that the whole house seemed to vibrate with frustration and loss, and the beams creaked ominously.

"We can't make repairs yet because of the shortages." Lee shut a door and it immediately blew open again. "Poor Roland spent an entire day trying to scare up a dozen nails. We'll have to wait, like everyone else. Till then, we just huddle around the stove if it gets too cold."

"We have two hundred acres, two barns, and assorted sheds." Roland rocked slightly on his heels with the pride of ownership.

"We are going to make this a working farm," Lee said. And, of course, she would. Lee could still bend events to her will, the way water refracts light.

"Meanwhile, you can sleep here." She opened the door to a small room that was in better shape than most of the others she had shown me. The window was unbroken, and there was a mattress and even a little nightstand with a kerosene lantern. "If you get cold, as you will, come into the downstairs room. We all gather round the stove and tend to sleep in a large heap. It's warmer and friendlier."

She left me to unpack my small valise: pajamas, a toothbrush and hairbrush, a change of underwear, a fresh shirt . . . and that green gown. What had I been thinking? Rubber boots and a fisherman's sweater would have been more appropriate. Could I return the dress to Harrods? No. I wouldn't. I didn't want to. It had already become a promise that I would find my daughter, somehow.

After hanging my few things on wall pegs and splashing a little water on my face from the porcelain pitcher and basin, I found Lee outside on the side lawn, sitting and drinking with the other guests who had arrived before me, probably by car rather than by train. They sat on folding camp chairs in a circle, passing around cigarettes and a bottle of brandy.

Scudding clouds in a crowded sky cast a greenish light over the scene. Shadows danced as the breeze muffled the sounds of conversation and laughter. I stood frozen outside their circle.

"Everybody, this is my friend Nora." Lee saw me and pulled me into the middle. "We met up in Paris years ago, before the world tried to self-destruct. And we're both from Poughkeepsie, as I recall."

Lee had never remembered our childhood days. A convenient lapse, perhaps. Or a pretense. I had never decided which.

One by one, she introduced me to the others, the *Vogue* model Lisa, instantly recognizable for the beauty mark at the corner of her crimson mouth, and the actress Carmen Delgado, whose name I had not yet heard but I would, Lee assured me. There was a writer, Lesley Blanch, with penciled, arched eyebrows over eyes that followed our every move, as if she was about to take out a notebook and start jotting down observations.

"Features editor at British *Vogue*," Lee whispered.

Pablo Picasso was there, wearing his trademark beret and striped sweater. I wondered if he would remember we had met years before, that he had once done me a great favor. If he did, he didn't refer to it. He smiled and nodded and looked at me through narrowed eyes, framing and composing.

"We never have less than six here for the weekend," Lee explained. "It's easier to stay warm in a crowd."

"Are you an artist or a writer?" Lisa asked me, leaning over Pablo as if she might fall into his lap with any encouragement. She was already tipsy and her words slurred a bit.

"Neither," I said.

"A woman of mystery." Roland, with his grave eyes and close-cropped dark hair, had come out to join us, and again he pulled my arm protectively through his. "Make them guess," he told me. "Let it take all weekend. We'll make it a game."

"Sorry sort of game," said Lesley Blanch, patting her short, tight curls. "Let the woman have her secrets, if she wants." She winked at me.

"Supper is ready, by the way," Roland announced. "Grilled chicken and spring peas. But don't ask for seconds. There aren't any."

"But first, meet the heir to all this glory!" Lee rose stiffly from her chair, pressing her hand to her knee the way arthritics do. She's not young anymore, I thought. I had somehow believed a woman like Lee Miller would be young forever.

A nurse in a cap and apron came toward us from the house, carrying a squirming toddler, about two, I guessed. Lee hurried to her and scooped the boy up in her arms with a whoop. "Come meet Mummy's friends," she said.

"No," he said, pulling her hair and squirming. I felt a sudden pain to the heart, remembering Dahlia at that age, beautiful as an angel, cranky and fussy.

"Oh, come on, precious." Lee opened his fist and planted a smacking kiss on his palm. There was an opacity to Lee's beauty, a thick pane of protective glass between her and the rest of the world. I wondered if anyone there, other than me, knew the source of that defensiveness. But with her child in her arms, all defenses were gone.

"Nora," she called. "Come meet Anthony."

Reluctantly, I rose from the folding chair Pablo had arranged for me next to him.

The boy's damp fingers closed around mine. As small as his starfish hands were, Dahlia's had been even smaller. Anthony looked straight into my eyes as if he knew all my secrets.

Roland rescued me. "Enough, Lee. Let Nurse put Anthony back to bed, and let's eat. I'm ravenous." His eyes met mine and I saw the questions, the curiosity. Art collectors, the good ones, knew how to see, not just look.

"Where's that promised bottle of brandy?" I said.

What was I doing there, in the middle of an English nowhere, reunited with a woman I hadn't cared about ever meeting again, detoured from my search for my own child?

"You look stricken," Lee said, taking my hand. "Food, and a good strong drink. That's what you need."

# CHAPTER TWO

When I was a child in Poughkeepsie, New York, Lee Miller was my playmate. Except she wasn't Lee yet; she was still Elizabeth to the teachers who sent home the notes complaining about her behavior. To me and her family she was Li Li.

We were born a few days apart in the spring of 1907. Her father gave my father a cigar to celebrate. It was easy enough to do. My father, the gardener, was pruning a yew outside Mr. Miller's office window. Mr. Miller merely reached through that window, saying "Success!" He already had a son, and he and his wife, Florence, had set their hearts on a girl.

"My missus had a girl, too," my father is reported to have said. "Weeping now to beat the band." Eventually I realized my mother hadn't wept because she had wanted a boy but because she hadn't really wanted children at all. The factory manager and his gardener puffed away together, that April afternoon, and it was probably the first and last private conversation they ever had, aside from instructions for the garden.

But that connection was strong enough that after a second son had been born and Mrs. Miller decided her reckless, tomboyish daughter needed a gentle, feminine little playmate, I was drafted for the job. My mother put me in my Sunday dress, told me to be on my best behavior, and then rode beside me in the backseat of the car that Mr. Miller sent to fetch me.

She thought that was the proper thing to do, and she would sit in the car, smoking cigarette after cigarette and reading a movie magazine, as Elizabeth and I played. She was hoping that Mrs. Miller would invite her in for a cup of coffee, but that never happened. My mother was married to the hired help.

Momma thought I would "learn to imitate my betters." Her words. In fact, my table manners were already better than Li Li's and her brothers'. The Miller children were not spoiled, but they were allowed a certain latitude to ignore much of the bourgeois adult world—things like grace before meals, combing your hair before sitting at table, not using curse words, standing up when an adult came into the room; such rules did not exist in the Miller household.

So when I was dropped off at the farm where the three Miller children pretty much ran wild, Elizabeth would politely give my mother a tiny curtsy and smile and ask, "How are you, Mrs. Tours," and butter wouldn't melt in her mouth. And as soon as my mother was gone, she would grab my hand and pull me into her wildness. We made foul and noisy experiments with her chemistry set, chased her brothers, and frightened the hens so much they would stop laying. Once in a while if her father was not at the factory, he would come out and tell us to stop tormenting the animals and the servants, but there would be a twinkle in his eye and we knew he didn't really mind. He was proud of his daughter's reckless bravery.

Mr. Miller was not part of the old river-family society of Poughkeepsie that regularly snubbed Momma at the Christmas charities or the Fourth of July fireworks. Mr. Miller hadn't been born to money; he had earned it. In a way, Theodore Miller represented the true American dream and promise: work hard and you will prosper. And how rarely did that really happen? But there was a dark side, of course. There always is.

"He's a womanizer," my father said one day when my mother, over our supper of potatoes and ham, had sighed over the stylishness of Mrs. Miller's wardrobe and the threadbare quality of her own.

"He's a womanizer of great repute and no conscience. You should hear them talk down at the barbershop," Father insisted, pushing his plate away. "Mr. Miller is very free and open in his private life, and his pretty Canadian wife has to accept it. Do you want that under your roof?"

"Hush," Momma said. "Not in front of the child."

For two years, Li Li and I played together every week. But one day when I was seven and dressing myself for the day to come, Momma came into my room and said, "No. Today you're not going. Not ever again."

"Why?" It was a warm, sunny day, good for running through the orchard, climbing trees, splashing in puddles left from the storm of two days before.

"She will go!" my father shouted from downstairs.

"What if she catches it?" Momma shouted back. Father thundered up the narrow stairs and burst into the room. It was Saturday and his suspenders hung from the waist of his trousers; his shirttails were untucked.

"You foolish woman. It can't be caught. Not that way."

"That's not what I heard." She defied him, hands on her hips.

"You heard wrong. Do you want me to lose my position? If you insult them in this way, they'll soon find another gardener. Is that what you want?"

Momma sat down on the bed, defeated. That was the best way to win any argument with Momma: mention money.

So, I went, totally confused and eager to find out what it was I might catch. I hoped it might be a pony, though their voices had told me it wouldn't be something fun.

One of my earliest memories: a little girl, blue-eyed, blond, dressed in white from top to toe—white bow in hair, white dress, white socks and shoes—stands inside her opened front door, hesitating. Mr. Miller's driver has picked me up once again to play with the daughter of the house, but this time, instead of waiting in the car, my mother gets out and stands next to me, her hand heavy on my shoulder.

Li Li hovers warily in the doorway, looking as if she intends to run back into the house. The scent of mud and lilacs fills the air. There's something else, something acrid, medicinal, a nasty smell coming from that front porch, but I don't know its name yet. Menthol. Eucalyptus. Salt of mercury. Hospital smells.

Momma bends down a little and hisses into my ear, "That little girl is ruined." Momma is holding my hand too tightly. I don't know what she means. Li Li doesn't look at all ruined to me. She looks pretty as ever, though she's holding back in a strange way.

Mrs. Miller gives her daughter a gentle push forward. "Go ahead, Li Li. Go play. Don't be afraid," she repeats.

Li Li afraid? Since when? But it's true. She doesn't want to leave her mother's side, to go through that doorway.

That settles it. I run from my mother and step onto the porch, one step, two. I'm directly in front of Elizabeth, who is half hiding behind her mother's skirt. I reach out my hand.

"Come on," I say. I take her hand in mine and pull her, hard. She pulls back like a dog that doesn't want to be crated, and I pull again, even harder. She stumbles forward with a little gasp and gives me a whack on the head. Not hard, not meant to harm, just in protest.

Better. I whack her back and we both laugh.

"Your dad will bring you home," my mother calls. "Don't get your dress dirty. It's just been washed and ironed. And don't play rough!"

Our favorite game was to climb the highest tree in the yard, to see who could get closest to the top before the fear of falling made us clamber back to solid ground. She always made it to the top, some forty feet up. I never made it more than halfway.

But that day, Elizabeth did not play rough. She hardly played at all, barely spoke. Something had happened while she had been away on a trip, and when we were swinging in a weary way on the old tires her father had suspended from the oak tree, I asked her what was wrong.

"I'm not supposed to talk about it," she said, staring at her shoes.

"I won't say anything, cross my heart."

"He put it in me."

Li Li would say no more. She pushed me off the swing and ran back to the house, slamming the door after her.

"Momma, what does it mean, when a man puts something in a girl?" I asked when I was back home, sitting in front of my plate of fried eggs and peas. Mother's mouth opened with horror. She slapped me and never answered the question, but I pressed my ear to the wall that night and listened to my mother and father talking, and the next day I looked up intercourse in the library encyclopedia, and that other word, rape. Seven-year-old Elizabeth Miller had been raped.

My father knew other servants of the house and I heard later about the treatments Elizabeth received, both at Vassar Hospital and at home; the special baths and acidic irrigations, the cervical swabs, the catheters and douche bags for treating gonorrhea; the regular visits of a head doctor, a psychiatrist.

Li Li and I didn't play together after that. Nothing was ever said. It just stopped by the mutual consent of Mrs. Miller and Momma. That was in 1914, the year the Great War began. Li Li had been raped by a sailor on leave, a friend of the family.

Years later, Li Li became Lee, that one elegant syllable, and stopped being the object for other artists' work and started making her own photographs. A large group of those photos was of interiors, with sharp angles, intense light and shadow, and images blurred by glass or hidden behind partially opened doors. A slightly opened door could be a promise or a threat. Hers were always threats. She could make even a row of perfume bottles look menacing.

Every Christmas, my father gave my mother perfume, tiny vials of Fougère Royale, Le Dandy, Parfum Précieux.

Before wrapping them, he would place one drop on my wrist, and I would be transported. Fougère Royale was the scent of Mary Lennox's Secret Garden in Yorkshire, just discovered and not yet restored to its old glory. Le Dandy made me feel like Marguerite St. Just, the wife of Sir Percy, the dandy who was secretly the heroic Scarlet Pimpernel of revolutionary France. Parfum Précieux was . . .

I couldn't find words for the sensation this perfume created until the afternoon Jamie and I went swimming, nude, on a hot summer day, after he had taken a photograph of me and I had fallen into the lake.

Every year, at Christmas, my mother would open the little gift box from Luckey Platt's department store, take a quick whiff, then screw the cap back on and exile the bottle to a shelf in the bathroom, as wasted as a book never read. She refused to wear scent, and he refused to stop giving it to her. Need I say more about that marriage? I had been conceived too soon for respectability and Mother never really forgave Father or me. There were no more children after me.

When you're a child, such things don't weigh as heavily as they do later. I was happy in my false belief that all children had a mother who rarely spoke and a father who drank. Perhaps in Poughkeepsie it wasn't far from the truth. It was a small town with large ambitions, an often uncomfortable blend, like Mr. Miller, the hard worker with flexible morals, as if the blooming largesse of the century wanted to accommodate all its own contradictions.

The town, for me, was the river, the cliffs with the rich people's houses on them, and the streets below with their Greek Revival banks, palazzo store facades, and Gothic churches. The Young Men's Christian Association building had been designed in the style of an Italian palace. No wonder Lee and I grew up dreaming of real castles in Europe, that promised land whence our families had arisen generations ago and to which we longed to return.

My mother, Adele, whose grandparents had arrived from Alsace-Lorraine full of stamina and good intentions, had worked at the DeLaval Separator company before she married. She had a good head for numbers and was given a job in the payroll department. This had been a source of great pride for her, since the DeLaval

Cream Separator Works was the biggest employer in Poughkeepsie. All that ended with her marriage and my birth.

Perhaps the enforced isolation destroyed more than one dream for her. When I got older, and was mooning over Rudolph Valentino instead of an ice-cream soda, I heard the gossip that Theodore Miller flirted with his factory girls and sometimes it was more than flirting. He was tall, blue-eyed, very good-looking. More than one woman in town was secretly in love with him.

My father's great-grandfather had been a perfumer in Paris, a cousin of the great interior designer Dandrillon, who mixed the scents of violet, jasmine, and rose into his paints to hide the smell of varnish. His fragrances were said to last for years, not months. Dandrillon purchased those floral essences from my great-grandfather, Gerald Thouars. Gerald had to flee France along with his aristocratic clientele when the revolution arrived. That was how my father spoke of that event, as an arrival, like a guest, or a debt collector.

Great-grandfather Gerald Thouars ended up in the forested wilds of New York as Jerry Tours, and took up farming. He was a failure at it, mostly because he spent all his time and money growing flowers and herbs and letting the corn and wheat fend for themselves. But he had the prettiest garden in the state. Even after the city of Poughkeepsie grew up all round the Tours' land, and generations of poverty reduced the holding to a small city plot, it was still the prettiest garden for miles around, showing the bones of the original design in the gravel walks and ancient cherry trees standing sentinel in the corners.

Sometimes, after my father had had his three after-work gins and was working up to the fourth, he would take me outside, into the old garden begun generations before, and we would just stand there, inhaling the fragrance.

When the lilacs and roses and lavender were in bloom, you could close your eyes and imagine you were in Provence, on a terrace overlooking the blue sea, or in a secret garden in the walled city of Peking, where courtesans gossiped, or in a pharmacy in Paris, where a bottle of perfume had been spilled. And then you would open your eyes and you would be in Poughkeepsie, with the next-door neighbor's laundry blowing on the clothesline and dogs barking down the street and smoke from the DeLaval Separator company painting gray strokes in the sky.

Daddy had a special peony, an old Duchesse de Nemours that burst into fragrant clouds of flowers each spring, planted fifty years before by Gerald Tours' son, my great-grandfather. A stone crouched under the leaves of this plant, and under the stone was a tin cigarette box, and every month Daddy added two quarters to the secret savings. "For you," he said. "Something of your own, when it's time to leave."

"How do you know I'll leave?"

"How do you know you won't? You'll want to go look at things in the world. See things I've never seen." And so do parents begin the journeys of their children.

Aside from the good looks of our most popular industrialist, my town, and Lee's, was famous for Vassar College, where moneyed coeds with bobbed hair and short skirts carried around Sinclair Lewis novels. They would fill the train station at every break and we townie girls would go and gawk to see what the new fashions were.

And every June, just as the college girls were leaving for the summer vacation, the town would fill again, this time with moneyed young men arriving for the annual regatta of the Intercollegiate Rowing Association, held on the Hudson and beginning at Poughkeepsie Bridge. Boys from Cornell, Columbia, and as far away as

Stanford, swaggering young men with sunburned faces and straw hats worn at a tilt, filled the town during regatta week. The girls of Poughkeepsie rolled down their stockings and rolled up their skirts, rouging their lips as soon as they were out of sight of their frantic mothers.

And every year, nine months after the regatta, some girl, or perhaps two, would give birth to a baby whose father had long since returned to Ithaca or La Jolla. If the girl was rich, she went "to visit an aunt" as soon as she began to show, and came back after the baby was born and handed over for adoption. If poor, she gave birth at home, and that was that.

Either way, she was ruined. Forced to marry beneath herself or face not marrying at all, the working-class girl married her father's mechanic and the rich girl married an unattractive boy from a family down on its luck, willing to overlook her fall from grace in exchange for currency. For the rest of her life, conversation would cease momentarily when she entered the room. People would whisper; ruder people would point. And the already-poor girl would spend the rest of her life doing laundry for the richer folk.

"I find you messing with those boys, don't expect anything from me," Momma said one Christmas after church, when we heard that Mrs. Charles' daughter, Edith, had gone "to visit her aunt." "Don't expect help or sympathy."

# CHAPTER THREE

Once in a while during my girlhood years, I saw Elizabeth Miller from a distance.

When we were ten, the country entered the war already going on in Europe. Overnight all the shops and facades of Poughkeepsie were draped in flags and patriotic signs. I saw Elizabeth at the Collingwood Opera House, which was also our movie theater. They showed Saturday afternoon matinees of German soldiers looking like hellish fiends in their spiked helmets, raping girls and nuns as the Kaiser laughed.

The next year I saw Elizabeth at the Collingwood when the Divine Sarah Bernhardt recited Portia's speech from *The Merchant of Venice*. Sarah Bernhardt spoke in French and no one knew what she was saying, but it was Portia's speech, and we cheered and stamped like mad.

I glimpsed Elizabeth at the Armistice Parade when the war ended, and later, when she played the White Queen in a stage version of *Alice in Wonderland*. She was already tall by then, very athletic looking. No one would ever guess how much of her childhood had been spent in illness. When she was just entering high school, Elizabeth Miller set tongues wagging when she marched into a barbershop and had her hair bobbed, like the girls in the Fitzgerald story "Bernice Bobs Her Hair." Elizabeth wore short, expensive dresses bought in New York City, had a gramophone, played jazz music, and read *Photoplay* magazine, according to gossip. She was friends with the rich prep girls from Putnam Hall, had tantrums, ran away from home often, used foul language, smoked cigarettes, and drank gin out of a flask.

When I was sixteen, I lost interest in the doings of Miss Elizabeth Miller. Whenever I was in a crowd or at some public event, my eyes were on the lookout for Jamie Sloane. And when I did find him, when our eyes met, I was certain he was the only boy in the world, and I the only girl. Everything else was shadow.

Jamie, the school's star quarterback, who sat behind me in our French and Latin classes, was tall and sandy haired and had a long nose made all the more interesting for having been broken in a football game. The youngest son, the darling of the Sloane family, he had that I-own-the-world self-assurance of beloved children. He was a star on the field, in our Latin and physics classes, on the dance floor, and there was something in his stride that made you want to walk with him, in whatever direction he was going.

When he looked at me, he locked onto my gaze the way big cats in the zoo sometimes lock eyes with you, inviting you to put your hand through the bars and pet them. His eyes were golden brown like a big cat's, and slightly tilted over his sharp cheekbones.

His family owned the Tastes-So-Good Bakery, supplying breads and dinner rolls to restaurants as far away as New York City. They were a part of working town society, not the river families in their cliff mansions, and though Mr. Sloane was one of the first in town to buy a Model T, he still wore overalls, not a suit. Jamie was working his way up the ladder, learning the business, waiting his turn, all those other platitudes fathers tell the youngest sons for whom opportunity is scarce, even in a family business. He made the deliveries, and he always left an extra sweet roll in the box for me. He would bow and pretend to doff and swirl a feathered hat, like John Barrymore in *The Beloved Rogue*.

On Sunday afternoons he would come for me in the bakery's truck, honk the horn, and yell out, "Come on, Nora! Motor's running!" We would roar and clatter up and down the country roads outside Poughkeepsie, drinking a little bathtub gin and shouting out the Burma aftershave signs as we passed them: "Within this vale of toil and sin, your head grows bald, but not your chin! Use Burma-Shave!"

We talked about the places we wanted to see, the things we wanted to do. Jamie wanted a life of adventure, never mind the bakery, never mind Poughkeepsie.

"What do you want, Nora?" he asked.

"I don't know," I said to him. You, I said to myself.

"You watch yourself," my mother said when she saw me walking with Jamie, holding hands. "Don't ruin your life like I did."

When I was seventeen, my father died. Heart, the doctor said. Gin, my mother said. "God forgive him, I won't," she added. "He's at peace," Elizabeth's mother intoned at my father's funeral. The only flowers in the chapel came from the Millers, a wreath of yellow roses and red carnations wrapped in a banner that said "He will be missed." "Not by me," said my mother. I sniffed the wreath and it smelled of dust, not roses.

Of course Momma did miss him, the very next payday, when it occurred to her that drinker though he was, he had been the breadwinner, and had made the difference between working-class skimping and true poverty. Broke, we moved in with her sister, older, never married, who welcomed us coldly and gave us a single room with twin beds.

Mother grew more brittle, more full of complaint, till we stopped speaking to each other completely, because all she could say was "I had such potential," and all I could say was "I hate this." I hate living here, I hate your sister, I hate the stench of cabbage and arthritis liniment and dog piss from that damn poodle.

By then Elizabeth had been expelled from two schools and finally finished high school only by the skin of her teeth. She was acting and dancing in local productions.

Jamie took me to see the Rutherford Dance Studio perform their "music visualizations" of writhing snakes and Cretan peasants, and there was Elizabeth, barely covered by gauze, wiggling and tiptoeing around with her legs bent at strange angles. Jamie thought it was funny and I had to explain that it was interpretive dance like the kind Ruth St. Denis did. Like the kind D. W. Griffith used in his movies. After this performance, Elizabeth danced the hootchy-kootchy in the chorus of a musical comedy, and I thought the eyebrows of the old lady churchgoers of Poughkeepsie would disappear right up into their hairlines and never settle down again.

Elizabeth was also in a performance of *The Girl from the Marsh Croft*, a play by a Swedish woman about a girl who has a child out of wedlock and finally marries a rich boy who admires her courage. Elizabeth played the rich boy's sister, a small role, but she danced a polka onstage and showed a lot of leg.

"It isn't like that," Momma said when we left the theater. Jamie hadn't been able to come with me that evening, so I'd given the ticket to Momma and pretended I had intended it for her all along. She wasn't fooled.

"Like what?" I asked, already knowing.

"Girls who get in trouble don't get rescued by a rich man's son." Momma gave me a stormy look. "They don't buy the cow if they get the milk for free."

Once, I ran into Elizabeth at Lindmark's, the bookstore run by bohemians from New York City. Elizabeth was in the travel section, looking at guidebooks to France.

She had rimmed her eyes with black, making their blue even bluer, skylike. She was wearing perfume, L'Heure Bleue, the twilight hour. The ads said it was for women who wanted everything. It was the last perfume my father had bought for my mother, the smallest bottle available because it was very expensive.

If Elizabeth remembered me, there was no flash of recognition in her eyes. I had become a stranger. Stung, I pretended not to remember her as well.

"I need to get out of P'oke," she said, looking up from a page that showed a photograph of boats on the Seine.

P'oke. That was what she called Poughkeepsie. She made that casual comment to me the way one addresses a stranger, to impress and amuse. She had already forgotten our days of shared childhood. Perhaps it was just as well, I thought, considering how they had ended, that little girl in her white dress smelling of sharp medicines and ointments; my mother, like a member of a Greek chorus, whispering "ruined" in my ear.

"Where do you want to go?" I asked, looking over Lee's shoulder and standing close enough to smell the gin and tobacco of her jacket.

"There." She jabbed at the photo of the river, banked with bookstalls and strollers, the great church of Notre-Dame rising in the distance. "The Left Bank. Paris." She looked up at me. "What a strange hat you're wearing. I think I like it."

It was one of my father's old gardening caps. I had washed it, trimmed it with ribbon, and wore it slightly tilted over one eye.

"Can I buy it from you?" she asked.

"No. You can have it. Here."

She put it on, tilting it deeply over her right eye, almost concealing it.

"Thanks. Here, take these. We'll trade." She gave me her nicotine-stained gloves.

When I finished high school in 1925, the year I learned how to dance the Charleston, the year I first read Gertrude Stein, I got a job at Luckey Platt's department store, at the glove and perfume counter. I wore a pink smock with matching cap and spent my day dusting bottles and sorting gloves by size into their proper bins. When no one was looking, I would test the perfumes on my own wrist, inhaling foreign places, exotic lives.

The same year I was snitching perfume and reading romances under the counter at Platt's, a German politician, Adolf Hitler, had organized his new Nazi party, but no one was really paying attention. Not yet. That year, Elizabeth went to France, supposedly to finishing school in Nice.

I looked it up on a map and there it was, a dot in southern France, on the Riviera, a dot that to a girl from Poughkeepsie represented all the sophistication and beauty the world could offer. "Oldest and largest town between Marseille and Genoa," the encyclopedia in the library said. "A popular summer home for royalty and the fashionable world. Named by early Greek settlers for Nikea, the goddess of victory."

"Finishing school? What do they finish?" Jamie sneered, and handed me the flask of gin. It was an August night, so hot my clothes steamed next to my skin and even the backs of my hands were sweating. Jamie had taken off his shirt and lay flat in the grass at the lake park, looking up at the stars. Moonlight reflected off his chest and I couldn't look away. Jamie was good-looking, but it had never occurred to me that he might actually be beautiful in a Greek-statue kind of way.

"They learn about the different kinds of fish forks," I said, "and how to discuss art in various languages, and how to seat people at table—you know, where the countess goes and how to address a bishop. Probably a bit of flower arranging thrown in. Nice is famous for its flower market in the Cours Saleya," I said, quoting the encyclopedia. "And the Promenade des Anglais, a four-mile boardwalk along the ocean."

"I hear she's fast," Jamie said. "She'll be teaching those French boys a thing or two. Maybe she'll dance the hootchy-kootchy for them."

I slugged his shoulder. Hard. "Shouldn't talk about a girl like that." I had never told Jamie that Elizabeth and I had once been friends. Never told him about that day on her porch, the white dress, the smell of medicines, the gossip about the rape. There was always plenty of talk about Elizabeth in Poughkeepsie, but no one ever talked about that and I had come to realize almost nobody knew. It was better that way, and I wasn't about to break the silence. Not even a rich girl would survive such gossip, small-town pity and judgment.

"That hurt! Penalty. Now you have to kiss me." Jamie sat up.

That wasn't a penalty, of course, and it was a game I was willing to play.

Elizabeth never made it to finishing school in Nice. As soon as she arrived in Paris, she fired her chaperone, cashed in her train ticket to Nice, and wired home to her father that she intended to stay in Paris and study art. So much for fish forks and bishops.

Seven months after Elizabeth's departure, Mr. Brennan, the butcher who filled Mrs. Miller's kitchen orders for lamb chops and roasts, told me Elizabeth was back home. Her mother had fetched her, kicking and screaming was his understanding, back from Paris. Speculation on what exactly Elizabeth had done to end her studies abroad ranged from smoking opium to a stint as a white sex slave.

"Emancipated," my mother muttered. "She probably had sexual intercourse with half of Paris."

"Sounds like fun," I said, and Momma slapped me.

Elizabeth, dragged back home, didn't stay put for long. She toyed in theater studies at Vassar College, got bored, and went to live in Greenwich Village before I even had a chance to bump into her again at the bookstore. We heard she was dancing in a chorus until illness drove her home to P'oke. For several years local gossip trailed her as she went back and forth, New York to P'oke, P'oke to New York, her moodiness and fragile health making it impossible for her to stay long in one place, stick with one idea.

Her face was already appearing in magazines, though. She had begun a modeling career. Girls like Elizabeth Miller didn't settle down like the rest of us were expected to do. They made names for themselves. They thumbed their noses at that convention called reputation.

Elizabeth Miller took classes at the Art Students League in New York; she modeled lingerie at Stewart's department store. One day, as she was crossing Fifth Avenue, she stepped into the path of an oncoming car and was rescued by a stranger who pulled her back onto the sidewalk.

The stranger was Condé Nast himself. Yes, that one, the head of the huge publishing empire. Mr. Nast took in Elizabeth's slender height, her long neck and blue eyes, the dress she had purchased in Paris the year before, and within months she was a *Vogue* cover girl, beginning the climb to fame. This was the legend of Lee Miller. How much was truth, how much rumor or invention, I'd never know.

The larger question: do they matter, simple facts? America was in love with celebrities, the photographers and flappers with their short bobs and sexual daring. The world was already in love with Lee and all she represented: the new woman, brave and bold, matching men in sexual freedom, and carrying secrets. They were like their own photographs, full of dark and light, heavy with shadows.

# CHAPTER FOUR

"Stand still," Jamie shouted. "Don't smile. Try and look mysterious."

Jamie had purchased a camera, a little black Leica, and when we went for our Sunday walks, he photographed me sitting under a tree looking into the distance, propped against a doorway trying to look sophisticated, leaning closely into the camera, weeping. The tears were fake, squirted onto my cheeks from an eyedropper of tap water. He carried a copy of *Photoplay* magazine in his back pocket and referred to it when posing me in various ways.

That was the problem, really. It was all an imitation.

"Stop moving!" he shouted, aiming the Leica at me. "Look mysterious!"

"Fat chance," I shouted back, balancing on the public dock at Upton Lake and trying to make my very contrived placement look natural. I was supposed to pose with my right arm across my forehead in a despairing gesture, imitating a Louise Brooks publicity shot, but it was a sultry August day, I was dizzy with heat, and Jamie had made me stand at the very edge of the dock, my heels already hanging in thin air.

I fell off the dock a second after Jamie took the shot.

What did not get photographed: me rising from the water, gasping and streaming like a mermaid. Jamie jumping in after me, laughing and pushing the wet hair out of my face, his fingers tracing a pattern on my cheek. That long gaze shared by two people who know they are about to become lovers.

We crossed that line between childhood and what comes after, the sweetness of flesh against flesh. Jamie took me by the hand and led me to the bakery delivery truck, and we lay down in the back, the truck bed's cold ridges pressing into our bare flesh, leaving marks on our legs and backs after we had slowly, clumsily undressed each other.

"What's that?" I asked warily.

"A rubber." Jamie blushed violently.

"Jesus. Where'd you get it?" We all knew about them, how the soldiers coming home from France after the war had brought condoms back with them. They were hard to come by, though; you had to get your doctor to write you a slip and then convince the pharmacist that you were using them so you wouldn't catch a disease.

"From my brother. He uses them all the time."

"Let me see."

"Want to help?" Jamie wasn't blushing anymore.

"Absolutely," I said.

I lost my virginity in the swirling stale scent of vanilla and yeast and sugar. Afterward, when the sun started to slide down toward the horizon, Jamie wrapped his arms around me and said, "Let's run away together."

It made sense. We had just reinvented the world, and could now be anywhere, as long as we were with each other.

"Where?" It was just a question to answer him, a way to make him say more so that he would continue whispering in my ear. All I needed in my newness was to hear his voice and smell the mossy sweetness of his skin. I would have followed him to Tahiti or Timbuktu. Jamie was more practical.

"New York. We'll have an apartment with a studio in it so I can do indoor shots. I'll get a gallery. P'oke is nowhere, Nora." I had told him that when I ran into Elizabeth Miller at the bookstore, she had called our town P'oke, and Jamie had been calling it that ever since.

"I can't stay here, Nora." He sat up and stuck a piece of grass between his lips, chewed it moodily. "Knowing what I'll be doing every day for the rest of my life."

By that time I was pretty much acting as a maid at my aunt's house, ironing and cleaning and cooking for all three of us when I wasn't working the perfume counter at Platt's. Momma and Aunt Betty would spend all day smoking, listening to the radio, talking about their girlhoods, the men they could have married. Aunt Betty's boyfriend had been killed in the war and there had been no one after that. She had inherited a little money from her father and had never worked, just grew old and dusty and as unused as the silver tea set she kept wrapped in tissue on the formal dining table.

I smelled dust all day long, a peppery, irritating odor of frustration, and some days, some nights, my impatience with life was so unbearable I thought I would burst through my own skin. Something needed to happen. Anything. One night I sat on the stoop of the house and watched people walk by, or bicycle by, or drive by in the occasional car, and my eagerness to join that parade almost made me jump up and run. The direction didn't seem to matter. All that mattered was the possibility of movement and escape.

Momma didn't notice my unhappiness any more than she had paid attention to my father's. She had gone deeper into her own regrets.

"Look at my legs," she said petulantly one day, pulling up her dress. "They're still as good as a girl's." And they were, slender and strong and shapely. "I could have been a dancer in New York." She tapped out a couple of steps, then collapsed onto the sofa. "Bring me a glass of cold tea, Nora. And turn on the radio."

There was money in the world, in those years, and lots of ways to spend it. People were buying Model Ts, radios, clothes, taking weekend trips to Niagara Falls, going out to restaurants where some waiters put two fingers of gin in your glass if you ordered "milk." Life had become a kind of party, and Momma hadn't been invited.

"If only I hadn't gotten pregnant," she would sigh. "I had such potential."

"Okeydoke," I said after Jamie asked me to go away with him a second time. "But shouldn't we get married first?"

"Artists don't get married," Jamie explained somewhat grandly. "We're going to be bohemians, Nora."

"That's a quarterback bootleg," I said, using the only football term I knew. It meant a fake play. "It's your family." I had never been invited over for Sunday lunch, never formally met them. They thought I wasn't good enough for their boy.

"I promised my dad I wouldn't get married till I was twenty-five," Jamie admitted. "If I do, well, he'll be pretty mad and disappointed. He might cut me out completely. You'll come away with me anyway? You know you're the only girl for me."

I pretended to have to think about it. Let's see. The choice was to stay in Poughkeepsie, cleaning up poodle piss and listening to my mother and aunt complain about how unfair life was, or run away to New York with the man I loved.

"Give me a couple of weeks," I said. This was, I knew even then, an irrevocable decision. Once a girl ran off with a boy, or even spent a single night with him, her reputation was ruined forever. I would be as bad as one of the summer regatta girls, doomed to being snubbed on the street, whispered about, no longer thought good enough to be invited into the homes of respectable people. But I didn't care. If Jamie was going, I was going with him. But how?

Jamie and I were making love one night in the backseat of the delivery van when I remembered Daddy's tin box buried under the peony bush. I had forgotten about it and left it behind when we moved into my aunt's house. *For when you want to leave,* he had said. He had known.

"What's wrong?" Jamie sat up next to me, alarmed. "Was I hurting you?"

"I know where I can get some money. At least, I hope it's still there."

"Later, honey," he said, nuzzling my neck.

"Now. This won't wait."

We straightened our clothing, Jamie muttering all the while, and drove to my old neighborhood. Jamie parked the van across the street from the house and switched off the engine. Crickets chirped and a dog barked down the street in the darkness, and I sat there, fighting tears because I missed my father. The house had been painted a cheap pastel blue over its original gray. Daddy would have hated the color. The new owners had torn out the honeysuckle that had twined on the front porch. What if they had dug up the peony and found the box?

"Come on," I said, nudging Jamie. "Now or never."

"I just hope they don't have a dog," Jamie said.

We tiptoed like the Katzenjammer Kids up to one of their pranks, arms in front of us, feeling our way through the darkness into the back garden. There were no lights on inside the house, but it was warm enough that the windows were open. I hoped the new owners weren't light sleepers. "No doghouse," Jamie whispered.

The roses were in bloom. I had almost forgotten the nose-tingling clove and nutmeg scents of Souvenir de Malmaison, Tuscany, and Parsons' Pink, all the old roses my father had kept. They were still there in his garden, hundreds of blooms each glowing like a pink full moon in the dark night.

The peony was still there, too, its delicate green stems bent under the weight of the dead blossoms. I knelt and felt for the stone, and when I lifted it, how light it felt compared with its weight during my childhood when I had been small! The tin box was still there as well. I cradled it to my chest, careful not to rattle the money inside. We tiptoed back out of the garden, and I felt less like a Katzenjammer Kid than Eve leaving Eden.

We counted the money later, in the van's backseat. Almost a hundred dollars. "Thank you, Daddy," I said.

I bought a cardboard suitcase to keep in my locker at the employees' lounge. Skirt by skirt, blouse by blouse, I moved my clothes out of the closet in the shared bedroom and into that suitcase.

We took the train into New York on a breezy autumn day. Jamie photographed me leaning out the window, holding on to my hat and smiling straight into the camera. The train hissed and steamed, rumbled and clanged, and it wasn't just a physical movement but one that involved my entire being. Jamie and I were going forward, into our own story. It was 1927, and I was twenty years old.

Five years, I told myself. In five years, I will be Jamie's wife. So what if the honeymoon came first?

Elizabeth, now known as Lee Miller, was also in New York, taking dancing lessons, studying stage design (a skill she'd use effectively later in her photographs), and being photographed by Steichen and Genthe and the other greats. I had seen displayed all over Manhattan a *Vogue* cover with her face on it. I had stood in front of a drugstore magazine rack admiring the sophisticated gown she wore, the upswept hair, trying to see the little girl who had climbed to the top of the tallest tree. She was there, in the eyes.

I bought a copy to show Jamie and he propped it up on our table, stopping several times a day to admire it.

"See what you can achieve with a little daring?" he said. "A girl from Poughkeepsie on the cover of *Vogue*. Think we'll maybe run into her?"

"Not unless we're invited to a party at the Whitney or the opera."

"Anything is possible," Jamie insisted.

Jamie earned some money by chasing ambulances and photographing accidents, crime scenes, dance contests, and baby beauty pageants for the glossies. His father, understanding that the Tastes-So-Good Bakery did not really require three sons to oversee it, sent him a little money every month, the allowance he would have had in Poughkeepsie.

I knew that Daddy Sloane was being understanding, playing the boys-will-be-boys card with his youngest son. Daddy Sloane thought I was Jamie's wild oats.

The Tastes-So-Good Bakery was doing better than ever, expanding and hiring more employees since Mr. Sloane had bought stocks on margin. I think even my mother bought a few shares in a mining company, that year. Everyone was investing, buying stocks with unsecured loans.

So Mr. Sloane turned a blind eye to his son's peccadilloes—me—and in the letters he sent I could read the hope father and son shared: fame as Jamie—no, as James Sloane, photographer. Baking was a living, but photography . . . well, that was the future. That was art and maybe fame, and nothing was too good for the baby of the family, the youngest son.

Momma knew within a matter of weeks that I hadn't gone off alone, of course. So-and-so heard that Jamie Sloane and the Tours girl had been seen kissing in public in the Metropolitan Museum, right in front of the medieval hall, and this was reported to another so-and-so, and in the roundabout way of gossip the story made its way to my mother's door.

She got my address from Jamie's father and wrote saying only, "Best you don't come back to Poughkeepsie, Nora. That bridge is burned, and there's been too much talk."

"Don't worry, Nora," Jamie said. "I'll take care of you. I'll always take care of you."

I worked in a typing pool, tenth floor in a Midtown building, fifteen minutes for lunch, and in my free afternoon I went to the perfume counter at Macy's and pretended I was going to purchase a bottle. Billet Doux had become my new favorite, a scent of carnation with hints of moss, reminding me of afternoons in the garden with Daddy.

I was happy. I was in love, and newly free. Quite honestly, living in sin suited me just fine for the time being. But there was always a sense of horizon in my life with Jamie, a need to be elsewhere.

Jamie received a couple of invitations to art gallery openings by sheer perseverance. He discovered which afternoon of the month the invitations were mailed out and then sauntered into the gallery, charming the girls who worked there, showing enough knowledge of cameras and darkrooms, light and shadow, to be acknowledged as a fledgling artist.

One afternoon he even met the great Alfred Stieglitz, who by then was bald and gray and as fierce looking as an eagle. Stieglitz had opened "the Intimate Room" art gallery downtown, and was putting up regular shows of new American art, works by people like his beautiful wife, Georgia O'Keeffe, and the photographer Paul Strand. Jamie wanted his photographs to hang at one of those exhibits.

I went with him the day he brought his portfolio to Stieglitz, sat at that great wooden desk and waited, barely breathing, as Stieglitz leafed through Jamie's photographs, pausing at some, peering closely once in a while, but finally folding the portfolio, placing it on the desk between himself and Jamie, and saying, "Perhaps next year, young man."

We went back to our little apartment, not speaking, and Jamie rolled into a ball and stayed that way for a day.

Jamie couldn't get his photographs accepted by one of the uptown or downtown galleries, couldn't find a patron or collectors interested in his photographs, not even the nudes.

The nudes were of me, since he couldn't afford a model. Gradually, persistently, he had worn down my shy reluctance. I had developed a technique of pretending my body was there, but I wasn't. My arms and legs and breasts became alien objects. I could look at the contact sheet and see shadows and light, black and white and gray, not myself. I never wore perfume when I posed for Jamie. I needed to be as colorless and scentless as the photos.

"There are good galleries in London," Jamie said one afternoon when he was photographing my hands. He had blocked off the top half of me with a black board, so that my hands looked very white and fragile, almost corpselike and disembodied. "New York is nowhere," he said. "London is the place to be."

We had burned bridges at our backs, but the whole world lay in front of us. When you are that young, all movement is forward. And so in 1928, we took a steamer to London, third-class, and danced our way across the Atlantic.

We became part of that great reverse migration, from America across the ocean, west to east, heading back to places our ancestors had left a hundred years before; not for any purpose more serious than to play, to see what there was to see, and to achieve what there was to achieve. Great-grandfather Thouars fled to save his life. I made the return trip for him.

Jamie and I stayed in London for three months, moving regularly to less expensive digs till we were in the cheapest bedsit we could find. London was cold and gray and too expensive. His portfolio, banged and stained and dented by then, did not impress the gallery owners nor did his awards from the Poughkeepsie Photography Club, or his photos of New York car crashes, though there was a good one of a new Model T and an old carriage horse, nose to nose, each demanding right of way. The old and the new, Jamie called it, and we had nicknamed the horse P'oke and the Model T Paris, as if we had known all along where we would finally end up.

We went to Harrods one day to see the famous food court and maybe buy a treat for our supper. We hovered in the doorway in our rumpled clothes, streams of people pushing past us, perfumes from the counter teasing my nose, the jasmine of Jamais de la Vie, the rose and amber of Amour, the lavender and moss of Adieu Sagesse all mixing together.

A nanny pushed between us, gloved hands firmly gripping a perambulator with its precious burden. I stooped to look at the red-faced infant, who stared back at me with perfectly round, unblinking eyes.

"Adorable," I said, meaning it, inhaling deeply the talcum and milk smell. The nanny nodded and continued on her way.

Jamie's hair stuck up strangely in back because I had cut it myself to save money. No matter how often I licked my palm and pressed it down over that lock of hair, it stood up like a flag of surrender. I reached up then and smoothed it down and kissed his cheek. "Let's have a baby," I whispered. That's how much I loved him. That's how young and unmoored I was.

"In a couple of years. But for now, let's get out of here," Jamie said, and I knew he didn't just mean Harrods.

Two days later we were in Paris, unpacked in a fleabag hotel on Île de la Cité, and the fleas were worth it, because outside my attic window was Notre-Dame cathedral.

Maybe it was all those bottles of French perfume, or my father, who after a fourth shot of gin would whisper to me, *We'll go to Paris one day, just you and me.* A year after I had arrived, a friend told me about reincarnation and how people traveled to get to where they had once been happy in some other life. Whatever the cause, I was immediately happy in Paris, more buoyant and optimistic than I had ever been in my life. It was like stepping out of a closed dark room and into the fresh air.

Paris was cheaper than London, and even if Jamie did not find a gallery and make money from sales, his allowance would cover us, if we lived frugally. We could go to bars and cafés for meals and drinks, and spend our afternoons walking along the Seine, Jamie always pointing his camera in some direction.

We walked the cobblestone streets of the Latin Quarter, peered through grilled gates at private courtyards with their playing fountains and flower-filled urns. We picnicked in the Luxembourg Gardens, where the writer Hemingway had hunted pigeons for his lunch. We spent a week's worth of cash at the Folies Bergère to see Josephine Baker dance in her banana skirt . . . Josephine, whose favorite fragrance was jasmine, the flower that gave the name to the new music, jazz. We ate sugar crepes from street stalls, and walked up and down rue de Fleurus, hoping to get a glance of Gertrude Stein.

As foreign as the city was, it was hard to be homesick in Paris. It was filled with Americans, all come for the same reasons as Jamie and me, to be elsewhere, to soak up the wonderful exoticness of a place not home. In Café de Flore, the gossip was in American, full of Southern drawls and clipped New England vowels. When you went to the races at Auteuil—and who did not?—the women wore afternoon costumes purchased at Bergdorf's and the men wore Texas brimmed hats.

The gardens, parks, and avenues of the city were lined with young Americans sitting in front of their easels, painting oils and watercolors of Notre-Dame, horse chestnut trees, and French schoolchildren escorted by nuns—all to be sent back home, to Chicago or Memphis or Boston.

Paris had become the center of gravity. It drew in anyone not nailed to the ground by a different reality, and it had drawn in Lee Miller as well, who had left New York and returned to Paris about the time Jamie and I went there.

A few times I thought I saw her. I'd glimpse the back of a tall blonde strolling the Champs-Élysées, or a profile of a woman sitting in a café with Lee's long, elegant nose. I had no idea how to find her . . . or, for that matter, why I would want to. We had gone our separate ways. Childhood felt long ago.

Jamie and I soon established a routine for ourselves. He took photographs in the morning, haunting the streets during the precious early morning light, and I went with him, holding his camera case, cleaning lenses, scouting ahead for interesting shots, for lovers kissing under bridges, lean dogs sleeping in private courtyards, old men smoking in front of a tobacco shop, women scrubbing the household linen at a municipal washing trough.

After a café lunch of ham and cheese, wine, coffee, we went back to our room and made love, and then slept wrapped in each other's arms. I had not known that such happiness existed, being full of Jamie, full of Paris and the light and smells and tastes of that city. I was light-headed with joy. I even loved the smell of the exhaust from the cars, when rainy days trapped the air close to the ground.

In the later afternoon we strolled down the Champs-Élysées, or explored the Roman catacombs running much of the Left Bank, or took the metro to Odéon to sit on a bench at the Luxembourg Gardens. We stopped for coffee or a little glass of brandy when we grew tired, ate bread and cheese when we were hungry, and then when it was dark, went to a bar or café to drink for hours with friends we quickly made, tripping home in the early morning, singing, making love back in our room.

A month, three months, six months passed and Jamie's portfolio thickened with photographs and he needed to purchase a second, then a third portfolio to hold them all. He had met some other young American artists, none of whom had yet a dealer or a gallery, but it was just a question of time, wasn't it? The world could not hold out against them forever; soon they would have an exhibit, and they would sit drinking in the evening, thinking up names for the exhibit: The Outlaws, The Stoics, The Pont Neuf Exiles.

"We are going to rent a hall," Jamie said one summer evening. We were sitting at the little table in our new room in Montparnasse. Even a fleabag hotel had become too expensive and we had moved to a single room. We didn't have an indoor toilet or hot water, and the walls were so thin we heard the quarrels going on all around us in the other flats, but those things just added to the romance of it all, that's how young we were.

It was so hot that night that we sat wrapped in dampened towels, and I had poured water over my head to cool it. Drops of water dripped into my eyes so that when I looked at Jamie, he seemed to be underwater.

"A hall?"

"For an exhibit. We'll put it up ourselves. One painter, one photographer, one sculptor, and a poet who will read his work at selected times."

"Sounds swell, Jamie." I wondered how much it would cost, and if his allowance from home would cover the expense of a hall in addition to our rent and meals. "I was thinking. Maybe I should try to get some work."

Jamie laughed. "What could you do?"

I decided to consider it a challenge. "You'll see."

The next morning, when he rose early to go in search of shots, I did not go with him. Sometime during that sleepless night, I had decided that I would be very good at floral arrangement, and I spent the next morning scouring the florist shops of Montparnasse and Montmartre, offering my services.

None of the business owners I spoke with agreed that they needed an American with bad French to arrange their bouquets. Refusing to acknowledge defeat, I bought a pail of red carnations, the entire thing, and walked past the Eiffel Tower to the Allée des Cygnes, where there was a miniature copy of the Statue of Liberty. I set my bucket down and, with a single red carnation between my teeth, smiled and waved at the passing tourists. I had sold half the bucket, earning about the equivalent of three dollars, when a strolling gendarme stopped and asked to see my license.

"But I don't have one!" I said, smiling even more largely.

"Ah. Then I must give you a ticket," said the young man.

I tried to weep for effect, but when you are young, in love, in good health, and it is a sunny day in Paris, tears do not come easily.

"Maybe just a warning?" I pleaded. I went home with a huge bouquet of the remaining carnations for our own table, and the three dollars still in my pocket, and the warm memory of that gendarme's smile as he warned the "little American" to read the laws before she tried to set up a business again, even on a street corner.

"You don't need to work," Jamie said that evening after I told him about my day. "I'll take care of us. I missed you, working by myself. Come here and give me the kiss that policeman probably expected and didn't get. Did he? No? Then it is mine."

Such happiness does not last. The half-life of a good, strong perfume is usually three hours. The half-life of love is measured in years, if you are lucky, not hours. But it is measured just the same.

I was in Café de Flore, drinking coffee and talking with a friend, Madeline from Albany, when the man sitting next to us put down the paper he had been reading, stood so quickly that he was unsteady on his feet, and rushed out the door.

"He's in a hurry," Madeline commented. She had a high-pitched voice that carried quite a distance, and the other diners looked up as well. Our waiter pursed his lips and blew through them, making the familiar sound of Parisian disdain. He took away the half-drunk coffee, the untasted ham and cheese baguette, but before the waiter could take the paper, I reached for it.

It was the *New York Times*, the Tuesday, October 29, edition.

" 'Stock Prices Slump Fourteen Billion Dollars in Nation-Wide Stampede to Unload,' " I read.

"Daddy must be so upset," Madeline said, looking over my shoulder. "Poor old thing. Bet he's going to cut my allowance. And I just ordered a dozen new frocks."

"Just a dip. It'll right itself," Jamie said, back in our room on rue Froidevaux, across from the old cemetery. "Dad must be nervous, though," he admitted, after he had thought about it for a moment. "I can't go back yet, Nora. We're okay." When we made love that afternoon, rolling naked in the warmth of the early autumn weather, Jamie seemed a little preoccupied. "Don't worry," he repeated so often that I began to worry.

Soon after, Jamie had a letter from his father explaining that his monthly income would have to be reduced a little, but otherwise all was well. People would always buy bread. A month later there was another letter, saying that the Tastes-So-Good Bakery had almost defaulted on a loan and staff were being laid off.

"Come home," his father wrote. "It's time." Jamie grimaced and tugged at his ear, the way he did when he was upset. "No," he said back to the letter.

We were sitting on a bench in the Tuileries gardens, feeding to pigeons the crumbs of our leftover lunch. It was two days before Christmas and the gardens were browned and empty of color and scent. Jamie hadn't received his money from home for the month and we had enough cash to last one more month, if we were very careful.

The planned exhibit of the Pont Neuf Exiles had already been called off for lack of funds, and the sculptor had taken a boat back to the States. Jamie wasn't smiling as often as he used to.

"What else does your father say?" I asked.

"Here. Read it for yourself." Jamie thrust the letter at me, and stood to pace on the graveled path, smoothing back his thick blond hair with the palm of his hand. He had grown it longer, so that it grazed his shirt collar and waved over his ears, like an artist's.

I read the letter. There was a one-way ticket waiting for him at the steamer office, his father had written. Jamie was to sail immediately.

"Just one ticket," I said weakly.

"Don't worry, Nora." He stopped pacing in front of me and leaned down to give me a quick kiss. "I'm not leaving. I'm not leaving you. I'll find work."

"You've already tried," I pointed out. It had been the same story in Paris as in London and New York. The galleries weren't interested in his photographs, and the newspapers, even when they bought one or two, did not pay enough to live on.

"Maybe he's right. Let's go home," I said. "I'll find money for my ticket." For the first time since leaving Poughkeepsie I felt afraid. Something seemed to be coming, something bad, something you couldn't fight. It was much more than the sense of a party ending; it was the sense of an ending to be followed by something menacing and unknown.

"Let's get married and go home," I said, throwing out the last of the crumbs. Pigeons cooed and pushed one another at my feet, black and white and gray birds pecking at crumbs on a gray and white path, as monochromatic as a photograph.

Of course we couldn't go back without being married, without telling lies and saying we had been married all along, ever since running away to New York. Lee Miller could do something like that, live with a man "in sin," but not me.

"Soon as I'm twenty-five," Jamie said.

"Your family will understand if you jump it a couple of years," I said. "Won't they?"

Jamie didn't answer. His father had sent one return ticket, not two. I was still just the gardener's daughter.

# CHAPTER FIVE

A month later, our funds exhausted, both of us were numbly aware of that single ticket for the steamer back to New York, waiting for Jamie to pick it up.

"We've got enough for a dinner and a couple of drinks," Jamie said. "Let's go out. Put on your prettiest dress, Nora. That one with the red flowers on it. I've got a feeling something good is going to happen."

I dressed. We went out. Although we knew Paris quite well by then, we might have been experiencing it for the first time, that night. I wondered if that meant we would leave soon, that we had gone back to the beginning only to find it was an ending.

Montparnasse was quiet that evening. It was January, cold. The festivities of Christmas and New Year's were over and now it was just winter with nothing to look forward to but a spring you didn't really believe in. People were inside, huddled for warmth. It wasn't until we reached the larger boulevards that we found that pleasant sense of being in a sympathetic crowd, heard the soft voices of other conversations going on around us.

It began to snow. Large, feathery flakes hovered in the yellow circles of the streetlamps, undecided which way to float, and then disappeared before they landed on the cobbles. We turned off the Champs-Élysées and walked a bit longer until we stood in front of the Jockey Club on rue Rabelais. Light flooded from its windows into the surrounding darkness. We heard laughter, and music.

"We can't afford this place," I said, peering in the window at the mass of people inside. I had cut my straight, black hair and hanks of it kept falling into my eyes. "Jamie, look at the pearls that woman is wearing."

The Jockey was a bar where people like James Joyce and Hemingway drank, the already famous, and even if they weren't rich, they were surrounded by rich people, and their credit was good. Ours wasn't.

"You've got to think big," Jamie said. "Straighten your hat, Nora. We can sit at the bar and have a beer. Just one."

I hesitated in the doorway. And as I did, a group of six people approached, laughing loudly and shouting back and forth in French and English and German. It was Lee Miller with her friends.

Lee had the good looks you never confused with a different person, a different face; she had style and daring. That evening, she wore trousers and a coat of white cashmere, and a white cap tight around her head so that she almost looked like a boy, except for her mouth, which was painted bright red, and the smoky kohl circling her blue eyes.

When she saw me, she paused and there was a second of confusion in her perfect features.

"I know you," Lee said.

"Yes," I said. "When we were . . ." I was going to remind her that we had once been playmates, but she spoke over me, interrupting.

"The girl from the bookstore. You gave me your hat. Man," she said, "come see. Another girl from P'oke. And she gave me a hat once. Isn't she fabulous?"

Her escort moved closer to us. He was several inches shorter than Lee, dark haired, stern looking, carefully and expensively dressed in a charcoal pinstripe suit and camel hair coat. I had seen his photos in newspapers and magazines. Man Ray, the artist and photographer.

Man Ray and I shook hands. Jamie had frozen the way a hunter freezes when a stag crosses his path. He was a businessman's son. He knew opportunity. Gently, his hand pressed into my back, he pushed me slightly forward, closer to Lee and Man Ray.

"She looks like Clara Bow, doesn't she?" Man said. The four others with them circled round me and stared.

Lee reached up and brushed snow off my bangs. "Were you going in? Come have a drink with us."

"Thanks." Jamie stepped forward, took his cap off, and tipped his head at her, like a delivery boy would, and then at her escort. "Mr. Man Ray, I know your work. I'm a photographer, too."

"Of course," Man said in a bored voice. His five-o'clock shadow made his face look blue in the lamplight. Man was looking at Lee, who was looking at Jamie.

Jamie still looked like what he had been: a high school football hero, a heartthrob. He had sandy blond hair and seductive brown eyes and the shyness evident in his posture, that frequent downcasting of his eyes and the way his head often tilted to one side during a conversation, all that boyishness made him even more appealing.

Lee and Jamie had never met before, not even in our small town. She had gone to private schools, partied with a different crowd; they were two kids from Poughkeepsie finally meeting in Paris.

A moment, frozen in my memory like a photograph: a winter night on rue Rabelais outside the Jockey Club, where two girls from Poughkeepsie bumped into each other, each clinging to her beau's arm; the four of us in the falling snow, music from the club wafting out with the smell of tobacco, perfume, whiskey; each of us looking in a different direction—me at Jamie, Jamie and Lee at each other, Man at Lee. The memory stops there, holds its breath. All is silence and stillness, encroaching shadow. And then we move into the doorway.

Thresholds seemed to be my meeting place with Lee.

Man made that palms-up gesture that men of means make, ushering us out of the cold dark into the overheated club, smiling benignly at us and carefully avoiding standing next to Jamie, who was so much taller than he was. Lee guided us through the crowd at the bar to a quieter table in the back and we sat, the eight of us, left to make our own introductions since Lee and Man were furiously whispering together, Lee rolling her eyes, Man once pounding the table with the flat of his hand.

The two other couples were a German art collector and his wife, Herr and Frau Abetz, and a photographer's model with her husband. Frau Abetz was already very drunk and when she introduced herself—"Call me Trudie, my dears"—her words slurred. Her lipstick was smeared; her white blond hair, lighter even than Lee's, had fallen out of its chignon and dangled over her red cheeks. She had the kind of full, voluptuous figure that would turn to fat if she wasn't careful.

Her husband was busily, almost industriously, flirting with the model—black-haired, pouty-mouthed, wearing a beaded dress cut low at the neck and high at the knee. His hand pounced on hers and held it prisoner; the bouncing motion of his knee pressing into her thigh pulled at the rumpled tablecloth.

Lee and Man's whispered conversation seemed to end in Lee's favor, for she resumed smiling and he did not.

Trudie, calmly ignoring how her husband was now nuzzling the model's long neck, leaned over toward me and whispered, "Six months. Then Miss Miller will leave him. Want to wager? Poor Herr Ray. He's Jewish, you know."

Jamie sat next to me, listening, watching. He was normally full of energy, always in movement except for the moments it took to hold his camera steady, and now he was as still as a cat waiting to pounce.

Man went to find a waiter and Lee smiled at Jamie. He smiled back.

"I'm from P'oke, too," he said.

"Really?" She leaned toward him in the kind of gesture that is meant to exclude others from what has become a private conversation. "Let's not talk about P'oke. What do you do now? Why are you in Paris? Most of the others have left like rats leaving a ship. You'd think the world was ending just because the market dipped a bit."

"I'm working," he said. "Trying to work. I'm a photographer."

"What's your name?" the German art collector asked, removing his right hand from whatever it had been doing under the table and pointing at Jamie for emphasis.

"James Sloane."

"Never heard of you." He turned his attention back to the black-haired girl.

Lee's brows met in a little furrow of thoughtfulness.

Violin music wafted to us from the front of the club, and the smell of old campfires. Gypsies had arrived to play. Most club owners wouldn't let them in, but the Jockey liked to be daring, liked to be the exception.

"Do you tango?" the model's husband asked me. I looked at Jamie. He was talking with Lee. "Yes," I lied.

There wasn't much room to dance, so he—I think his name was Charles—put his arm tight around my waist and swayed me back and forth in time to the music. We did a few quick turns, a few marching steps, then more swaying, more of that movement that suggests lovemaking. I smiled over my shoulder at Jamie, relieved to see he finally was watching. He winked back.

"Didn't know you could tango," he said, when I returned to the table.

"Neither did I."

Man came back from the direction of the kitchen and sat again next to Lee, so Jamie had to pull his chair closer to mine. A trio of black-suited, white-aproned waiters followed Man, carrying pitchers, bottles, trays.

"Finally! Eat, drink, and be merry!" Lee ordered.

We drank a lot that night, French champagne mixed with American cocktails, and we ate, dish after dish brought to the table: smoked trout, cucumber salad, potato salad, little sausages served with their own special mustard.

I hadn't realized how hungry I was, had been for days, until those sausages arrived, sizzling and smelling of garlic and grease. Jamie put three on his plate at once, with a huge dab of yellow mustard next to them, and leaned back to smile at me again. Aren't we lucky? his gaze said. He forced himself to eat slowly, taking thoughtful bites, chewing even more thoughtfully, pretending to be listening to the conversations around us when I knew he was occupied, totally occupied, with the exploding flavors in his mouth. As was I.

Lee and Man and the German collector talked about an exhibit they had visited the day before at a gallery on boulevard Haussmann. Herr Abetz hadn't liked the work, thought it contrived and a little sentimental. Man was defending the artist, saying his work linked the old impressionists and the new surrealists.

*"Nein,"* the collector argued back, thumping his beer mug on the table. "That Spaniard, that Picasso, he is the link. I buy Picasso."

"He buys everything," Lee whispered to me. "Frightfully rich. Related to the Kaiser or some such thing."

Sometime close to midnight, Lee, who had been slumped and giggling to herself, sat up a little straighter and gave Man a gentle poke in the ribs. "Since Jamie's a photographer," she said, "couldn't you use him in the studio? You need a new assistant." Lee had spoken loudly enough for all of us to hear. If Man said no, he would look miserly or ungracious or, worse, jealous.

"Certainly," he said, smiling tightly. "Good idea. More champagne, then, to settle the deal."

Jamie gently kicked me under the table. *We're in,* he mouthed. He looked like a kid at Christmas.

Couple by couple, group by group, the club began to empty as night turned to a newly arriving day, and still we ate and drank until we were the last ones there and the waiters stood yawning around us, looking at the clock on the wall.

Lee stood. "Home," she said, tottering on her high heels. "I need my beauty sleep."

Outside, the snow had been falling more heavily and there was a white carpet over the streets, catching the lamplight and sparkling like rhinestones on white satin.

"I wish I had my camera with me." Jamie yawned and stretched his arms over his head, then held his hands in front of his eyes, making a frame of them. Man shot him a glance that said much. The shot wouldn't work. Jamie was too young. Too romantic.

"Come," Man said. "Let's put these fine Germans into a taxi and walk back. The air will do us good."

The fine Germans were barely awake, having eaten and drunk too much, so Man told the driver to take them to the Ritz on the place Vendôme, the classy hotel where all collectors stayed when in Paris. If it was the wrong hotel, then they could get a room there for the night and return to the other one in the morning. The model and her husband, locked in a tottering embrace, tangoed to the street corner and waved good night.

"Where are you staying?" Lee asked me. "We'll walk you there."

"Rue Boissonade, near the convent." Their bees had flown in and out of windows on those mild days when we raised the sash. The nuns made honey to help support themselves.

Lee put her arm through mine and laughed. "You're kidding! Man and I are just two blocks away!"

Jamie and I lived within shouting distance of Lee Miller . . . and never bumped into her. And then, just as we were about to give up, to go back home, we ran into her outside a club, and like a fairy godmother, she got Jamie work and offered to take us under her wing.

"Aren't we lucky?" Jamie beamed.

The next morning, the same morning really, since we hadn't gotten to bed until around three a.m., I woke to the sound of gravel being thrown against the window.

I rolled out from under Jamie's arm and pulled his discarded shirt around me. He was still snoring as gently, sweetly as a sleeping cat.

Lee was down in the street, grinning up at the window. She put her hands to her mouth as if to shout, then mouthed, "Come down," and beckoned me with her little finger. "Alone," she added. How did I read all that from a third-floor window? Or did I just imagine it?

It was barely dawn, but Lee's grin was irresistible. She hadn't been to bed yet, or at least she hadn't washed the lipstick and mascara from her face, but she had changed her clothes and wore trousers, a man's wool peacoat, a beret. Her camera hung around her neck and a leather kit of supplies was strapped across her chest.

"Where to?" I asked five minutes later, having splashed cold water on my face, run my fingers through my hair, and dashed down into the street. We left crunching tracks in the snow as she turned right and pointed me in that direction.

"Rue du Louvre," she said.

"For?"

"Shadows."

Lee was almost a foot taller than I was, and when she put her arm around my shoulder, I felt like someone's kid sister.

Fifteen, rue du Louvre, Lee's destination that morning, was one of Blondel's apartment buildings, large enough to need two separate entrances, one of metal and one of stone. Blondel had been a polymath, fascinated by numbers, and this building was about the number two. Lee led us to the stone entrance, a double arch flanked by two huge busts of muscled, bearded water gods. It felt quintessentially Parisian to me, with the rich stone carvings of male torsos, garlands, wreaths, the balconies and neoclassical supporting columns. It felt very far from Poughkeepsie, and that felt grand.

"He looks cranky, doesn't he?" Lee pointed to the Atlas on the right, and in fact, his arm was raised to his forehead as if he had a pounding hangover. His left arm was pressed against his hip, a gesture of impatience.

"Wouldn't you, if you knew your entire kingdom was going to sink beneath the ocean?"

"Guess that would ruin your day," Lee admitted. "But how come the sculptor made two busts of the same god? Why not a pretty nymph on the other side of the arches?"

"Atlas was a twin. The second bust is probably his brother, Gadeirus. Together they ruled all the land the gods gave Poseidon, until it sank forever." The second bust had one hand raised slightly over his eyes, as if he was looking into the distance. His other hand was poised protectively over his stomach, a defensive gesture.

Lee gave me a knowing smirk. "Well. Someone did her schoolwork. God, I was a rotten student. And it shows, sometimes. Twins, hey. Wonder what it feels like to have a twin, a same-sex twin. I never wanted a sister, did you? Much prefer the company of men."

"A sister would have been fun," I said. "I was an only child."

"Ah. Poor little rich girl, all alone in a big house with, let me guess, lots and lots of books for company."

"Something like that." Amazing, isn't it, the conclusions people leap to? That day, I was wearing a blouse I'd bought in a secondhand shop, cream silk with hand stitching. I wore my father's gold watch. Silk and gold do give off the whiff of money, I suppose, even secondhand.

"The best thing about Atlantis," I continued, needing to show off, "is that its palace was built of amber. Plato called it orichalc, but it was white and yellow amber. Imagine how Atlantis must have smelled." I inhaled, trying to envision walking through a city made entirely of amber, that sweet, resinous fragrance that is the smell of preserved sunlight.

"Isn't there a palace of amber somewhere in Russia?" Lee was fidgeting with her camera, preoccupied.

"It's a single room. In the Catherine Palace in Leningrad. Walls and walls of carved amber and gold leaf, made in the eighteenth century." Just a few short years later that amber room would disappear as completely and mysteriously as Atlantis, not destroyed by earthquake or tsunami but looted by the Nazis.

"Move over there, Nora," Lee said, no longer interested in history or the scent of amber. "You're blocking the light."

I felt certain we were there to photograph the busts, but instead, when she was ready, Lee aimed the camera at the paving stones. She waited, barely breathing. Second by second, the morning sun climbed the invisible staircase over the Paris skyline, and as I watched, shadows began to appear, nothing definite, nothing definable, only lines and angles thrown against the uneven cobbles. Lee moved slowly in a circle, camera held to her face, pressing the shutter, cranking the film.

"It's about the light," she said once. "And where it falls. Everything else is superfluous."

She took maybe a dozen snapshots, and when the sun had become a firm reality rather than a suggestion and the shadows lost their mystery, she packed the camera into its case and took me by the arm.

"Breakfast," she said. "And a chat. I think we're going to be good friends."

"How come you didn't take any photographs of Atlas or his brother?"

"They're only good for postcards for tourists. If you want one, I'll make one for you."

"No, thanks."

We found a little café and sat inside at a table, though it cost more. We were both shivering by then because the morning sun hadn't brought any significant warmth. Lee ordered for us, coffee with milk, rolls, bread, butter. Slices of ham.

"Don't give in to this French way of eating only bread in the morning," she warned. "You'll go to fat."

Slender as an athletic schoolgirl, she looked as if she knew what she was talking about. I followed her example and slipped some ham into my roll and ignored the pot of jam.

"So," she said, when we had finished our coffee and sandwiches. "Tell me."

"Tell you what?"

"About yourself, of course. What brings you to this neck of the woods?"

The very American phrase made me laugh.

Lee lit a cigarette and offered one to me. We sat there, two girls from Poughkeepsie, smoking heady Gauloises in a Parisian café on a Parisian morning, and I know what I was thinking. My whole body was a tingling thank-you to whatever gods and destiny had brought me there—though, of course, I had no idea what Lee was thinking.

There was no easy answer I could give her. Jamie wanted to be an artist and this was where artists came. (Why did I never, in my thoughts, think Jamie *was* an artist?) I had been bored and unhappy in Poughkeepsie. So who wasn't? And for that matter, what did I want, other than to be wherever Jamie was?

We were the same age, but I suddenly felt younger, even childish next to the great nuanced worldliness of Lee Miller, who was living with an older, famous man, who had already made a name for herself as a model and now was also working as a photographer.

"Where else should I be?" was my feeble reply. Rearranging the same perfume bottles over and over in Platt's department store? Cleaning poodle piss off my aunt's carpet?

Lee laughed and lit another cigarette.

"Exactly," she said.

We talked more easily after that, chitchat about where I'd gone to school (public as opposed to her series of private schools), where I had lived in Poughkeepsie (she guessed from my aunt's address that we were different classes and didn't falsely argue that there were no classes in Poughkeepsie; of course there were), and what we had left behind back home. For me, a mother, an aunt, a deadly boring job.

"So, not poor little rich girl. Poor little poor girl. Even more romantic," she said. "I had a big house and plenty of moola. Friends whose names get in the paper, society column or police blotter of minor offenses, all the same. And brothers. I miss them sometimes, but not P'oke."

As we talked, in my mind's eye I saw my old playmate, that little girl in her white dress, hesitating on the porch, smelling of events and medicines that should have no place in a child's innocent life.

The temptation to remind her of our moments of shared childhood flitted in and out of my conversation. It was so long ago, and it had been such a miserable nightmare for her. Maybe she had forgotten that as well, that morning on the porch. But sometimes I thought I saw it in her eyes, in the shadows around them. She just refused to allow the memories into the daylight.

What I couldn't guess was whether she remembered me as a

part of that event, the little girl asking her to come off the porch, to play. That morning, as we sat drinking coffee and smoking, I made the decision not to remind her. We had the future. What did the past matter?

"Good," Lee said, when the second cigarette was finished. What exactly did she mean by that one single comment? "Time to go. Man will be furious if I'm away too long. I didn't leave a note and he does worry." She wrinkled her nose. "Is Jamie possessive?"

The question was delivered lightly and took me by surprise. I didn't have an answer because I didn't know. Since becoming lovers, we'd had little opportunity to test his capacity for jealousy. Nor did I want to. Never had I questioned my own potential for jealousy because that would mean thinking about Jamie as a possible betrayer, and he wasn't. He was as true and faithful as the North Star.

When I got back to our room, Jamie was gone. He had left a note: "At Man Ray's studio. Meet me for lunch."

He had underlined "studio" three times. I read between the lines: I'm in!

Man Ray, raised Emmanuel Radnitzky in Brooklyn, New York, was almost twenty years older than Lee, and had a face, a posture, that looked even older. More than once, in our time together in Paris, I would see a waiter or barmaid mistake him for mademoiselle's *père*, see the grimace on Man's face, the teasing satisfaction on Lee's. Sometimes, seeing them walking side by side, I got the impression that a short, stocky, aging mortal had somehow captured a goddess and held her captive with some invisible golden rope.

Man Ray encouraged that image. One day, he and Lee walked down the Champs-Élysées together, Lee wearing a leather collar and leash he had put on her. A girlfriend told me that story a few years later, I can't remember who, and she laughed because Man, so proud of his conquest, had looked like a puppy being walked by his mistress owner, not vice versa.

By the time Jamie and I met up with them, Lee and Man had been living together for more than a year, and the story of their meeting was already the stuff of legend among the Parisian artistic set. Lee had decided he would be her mentor. When Lee made a decision like that, it happened. She made it happen. So, fresh off the boat from New York for the second time (no chaperone in tow), she had gone to the studio of the famous Man Ray to introduce herself and announce their relationship, as she envisioned it. But the concierge blocked her path and said Man wasn't there; he had left for the summer.

Lee went to the café across the street and ordered a Pernod to think over. Or did she already know the next step?

Man, who *was* there, who had been watching from an upstairs window, followed the tall, slender blonde and asked her what she wanted. Lee was completely irresistible. He didn't really have a choice.

Man was on the verge of leaving town for the season; he didn't want to be disturbed, he didn't want a student, he didn't want a woman in his life, at least not that kind of woman, the kind that requires attention and care and moments of actual hard work. Moments of suffering. His previous mistress, Kiki de Montparnasse, had left him the year before and he was still licking his wounds and letting the many lovely prostitutes of the quarter meet his needs for ten francs a toss.

But here was this beautiful American, coolly, with absolute presence of mind, sipping Pernod in his neighborhood café, patiently explaining to him that she was going with him, and she was his new student, his protégée. It was too hot to argue.

They drove down to Biarritz in his Voisin sports car, Man stopping frequently to photograph his beautiful new traveling companion, already smitten with her boyish haircut, her swanlike neck, and her long slender legs, those beautiful, perfect lips. He wore a black beret and black linen jacket; she wore a white beret and sweater. They were already a complementary image, a couple.

They spent the summer together, and when they returned to Paris, Lee took a studio just a few minutes away from his, more for appearance's sake than any other reason, though later the room, and the rare moments of privacy it provided, would become important in another way.

The rest was history, as they say.

# CHAPTER SIX

I went to Man Ray's studio at one, thinking Jamie and I would go to the corner café and have a cheese sandwich and black coffee, but Lee had other plans.

She appeared to have slept for a couple of hours, and looked fresh and neat in tailored tweed trousers and a black sweater, her washed hair still damp and brushed smoothly back.

"Lunch together," she announced as soon as I opened the door. "Deux Magots. On me."

"Close that door!" Man shouted. "It's affecting the light. Jamie, move that vase, it's casting a shadow on his face. More to the right. I said more!"

Man was the son of a tailor and sometimes this still showed in the precision of his movements. He wasted no gestures and it was easy to imagine those long, slender fingers of his making twenty stitches to the inch, as good tailors did, as his father must have done.

He was a strange combination of practicality and dream—the foundation of his art, his surrealism. Take a real object and make it do something unreal. Make lips float in a sky, make a pear hold up a cloud, make a woman become a coat stand.

The viewer was supposed to reappraise each object, learn it anew. But sometimes I stood in front of his photographs and paintings and wondered what was so lacking in reality that the world had to be disfigured and reconfigured. That, of course, was the response of a happy person who had not yet received a great and never-healed sorrow, who did not yet need to reconfigure reality.

Fortunately for Jamie, Man also did a lot of portraiture. In fact, he paid the rent that way and so Jamie was given the task of setting up the studio on portrait days—preparing the camera, the backdrops, and then the chemical baths, waiting in the background as Man posed the subject, set up the stage, and took the photographs.

That first day, a heavy scent of sandalwood and spices filled the air. Man's sitter was a middle-aged man of exotic complexion, looking stiff and uncomfortable in formal evening dress, with white gloves placed casually over his black-trousered knees and a top hat tilted slightly on his head. His black-shadowed eyes were on Lee and never left her face.

"The Maharaja of Indore," Lee whispered to me. "Filthy rich. See that emerald on his left pinkie? It's real. Man is to make his portrait, to send off to his fiancée. Then he's going out to the stables to photograph his horses."

"Quiet," Man growled. "Or leave."

When we were a foursome, Man was polite and mildly aloof, the generous man who orders more wine even when you insist you're drunk enough, thank you. His hands, quite lovely, really, were always fluttering around Lee, smoothing her hair, picking off lint, touching, touching, till she grimaced with impatience.

But in his studio when there was a sitter, he liked to play the bully. Jamie was already alert to the game. He moved the vase and winked at me.

Lee shrugged her shoulders and went to a side room and shut the door. I found a stool in a corner, very out of the way, and watched the session.

When Jamie took photographs, he moved constantly, checking the light meter, adjusting the focus, dancing left and right to find the best angle. Man seemed to barely move at all, so economical and concentrated were his movements. When he finally clicked the shutter, it was as if he were actually stopping time for the length of the photograph.

As he worked, taking some dozen shots of the maharaja, I let my eyes wander around the studio. It was artfully disarranged with books piled on the floor, paisley shawls tossed casually over cane-seated sofas and chairs, and a whiskey bar with crystal glasses set up on an eighteenth-century writing desk. Chess pieces, wooden cubes and pyramids like children's toys, bits of mannequins—a hand here, a headless torso there—created strange surrealist still lifes on the tabletops.

Portraits hung on the walls, leaned against the furniture, lurked behind doors. Man still had hanging by a window his 1924 portrait of his mistress Kiki, *Violon d'Ingres*. Kiki with her short black hair wrapped in a turban, her naked back to the viewer and painted on that very famous back the f-holes of a violin, so that her body became an instrument.

I wondered how Lee felt about that piece, seeing her predecessor in such prominent display, and then I wondered if that was why Man had left the photo there, as a reminder to Lee. See. Other women have loved me.

A formal portrait of Erik Satie had been hung opposite Kiki,

Mr. Satie looking more like a philosopher in some German academy than a musician of the avant-garde, and next to the whiskey bar was a portrait of James Joyce, his hands folded, his eyes opaque behind the thick lenses of his glasses.

There were other people I couldn't identify: bejeweled older women dressed in fancy ball costumes, intense young men who glared out challengingly, here and there friendly faces—the elite of Paris, of the world really, since Paris was the center of the world.

Not bad for a girl from Poughkeepsie, I thought, sitting in Man Ray's studio in Paris and wondering if that portrait of James Joyce was hanging a little crookedly.

Man used his balcony as a darkroom, with heavy shutters he could draw to shut out the light, and porcelain basins for the developing fixing baths. During the sittings, the shutters were opened to admit as much light as possible.

On a gray day, as that day was, the natural light was inadequate, so Man had set up lights in big aluminum reflectors. But as soon as he turned them on, there was a brief popping explosion and the studio went dark again. The old Paris buildings had been too quickly, too inefficiently fitted with electric, so the fuses blew constantly.

"Fuse," Man growled, and Jamie was out the door, new fuse in hand.

"I said, 'Are you living near, miss?'" The Maharaja of Indore was speaking to me. He had shifted his position so he could look at me and I could tell by the set of Man's shoulders that he was not pleased about this.

I moved closer to the window and the maharaja's eyes followed me, restoring him to the position Man preferred.

Man actually smiled at me. "Perfect," he said. "Stay there till we're finished."

"I do live near here," I answered the maharaja.

"It is a pleasant neighborhood?"

His voice was higher than I had expected, and ended on an up note, like an upbeat jazz tune, something Josephine Baker might sing.

"Very." I already knew where this conversation was heading. He would ask to visit. And if the visit was amusing enough, he might offer to move me to a better neighborhood, rent free, or at least paid by him. I had already had two such offers from businessmen. Women were to them a commodity like jewels, like fine wines and racehorses.

"May I see your rooms?" the maharaja asked.

"Only when my husband is there," I said. And in came Jamie, as if cued by Noël Coward.

"Ready," he told Man.

The maharaja wagged his finger at me and smiled. "Such a very young husband," he said. "This will not do. Young men must be planting wild oats. He will leave you, miss."

Man took the shot just then, as the maharaja was leering at me, finger still pointed in the air. I saw it a few days later and Lee joked that Man should "accidentally" send this one to the fiancée, not the more formal portrait. Man didn't think it was funny. He was still photographing the maharaja's horses and stables and didn't want to lose the money. Fame got you credit, but at the end of the month it didn't pay the tab.

And so began the dance that was the foursome of Man and Lee, Nora and Jamie. Our lazy days were behind us and with great earnestness we became expats rather than mere tourists. Jamie worked nine and ten hours a day, assisting Man and developing prints. He came back to me exhausted and exhilarated, convinced that this was his way to the fame he desired for himself.

"But if you don't have time to take photographs for yourself, what will you have to show when there is a chance for an exhibit?" I asked.

"Wet blanket. There's always Sunday. I'll get up earlier, take some photographs before I go to the studio."

"And when will I see you?"

"Nora, the vacation is over. Remember, Berenice Abbott worked for Man for three years and learned enough to open her own studio. And she didn't know anything about photography when she started! To be an assistant to Man Ray . . . that's the beginning of a real career."

Lee, too, was working, modeling for Paris *Vogue*, gowns by Patou, day costumes by Chanel. As the discovery and protégée of Condé Nast himself, Lee could get modeling work whenever she wanted. But it wasn't all about connections, not with Lee. There was her beauty to recommend her, that startling cap of blond hair, the slender legginess that would make even a hopsack dress look elegant. And she had personality; it showed even in photographs.

One particularly stunning photo I remember from that time shows Lee in a floor-length sleeveless black dress with a neckline cut almost to the waist and a big flower pinned on it. She leans against a wall, staring at something the viewer can't see, and her expression is one of impatience and discontent. Because of the angle of the shot, her shadow on the wall behind her shows a seemingly different posture, straighter, more formal. It was as if Lee and her own shadow lived two different lives. Duality. There was the Lee you saw, and the secret Lee you could not see. The Lee you knew, and the Lee no one would ever really know.

Lovely women were a dime a dozen, but Lee knew how to hold back, to make the viewer want and need more of her. It was this very quality that drove Man, possessive and insecure, mad. Lee could not be contained, controlled, or even embraced for very long, and the more she evaded you, the more you tried to pin her down.

Lee was already tired of modeling, though, of being the object of fantasy for men who desired her, and for women who wanted her face, her figure. But the Depression was cutting into Man's portrait work and they needed the money Lee earned.

She took me to one of her modeling sessions at Paris *Vogue* (she called it *P'rogue,* of course, just as Poughkeepsie was P'oke, as if all situations could be reduced to a single syllable). The photographer was Huene, a wild-haired Estonian with an accent so thick you could spread it on bread. He obviously adored Lee. He barked orders at everyone else, but with Lee he was polite, even obsequious. "Lean back a little more, darling. No, the smile is too big. Mystery, mystery. Lift up the elbow a little, dearest, turn—sideways."

When his back was turned, Lee would make faces at him, then return to her stonelike stance in a split second. The Estonian could never figure out what I was laughing at. He probably thought I was simpleminded.

"Take a photo of my friend," she said, near the end of the session.

"Too short. No legs," the Estonian said.

"Spoilsport. She's smallish but well proportioned," Lee argued. "I'll fix the hem, you'll see, she'll look fine."

Without asking my opinion or permission, Lee selected a gown from the rack, a red silk jersey with a plunging neckline. "Put it on," she said. "Quick, quick." She found a pair of high heels that added four inches of height, and then took three books from the bookcase.

(They had been shooting at-home loungewear, and so had created a kind of library in the studio.) "Stand on these," she said. "I'll drape the gown over them."

This is what it feels like to have a camera pointed at you, to know that others will see that picture and judge everything about you, to the smallest detail: miserable. I couldn't smile properly. "Too many teeth!" the Estonian groaned. I couldn't pose naturally. "She looks like she has a backache," he complained to Lee.

"How do you do this?" I asked, giving up and pulling the fake pearl earrings off my ears.

"I pretend I'm elsewhere," she said. "For a few minutes someone has power over me, and in my thoughts I just leave. I learned the trick early in life." A metallic quality crept into her voice, and I knew what she was remembering.

Huene, ignoring us, became angry in earnest as he rummaged through the trunk his assistant had set up for that day's shoot. Red satin shoes, rhinestone tiaras, an old-fashioned corset, all went flying.

"Numskull," he yelled at his assistant, a nameless and easily cowed young man with slightly crossed eyes. "Where is the Chanel bag? It must be shown with the next ensemble!"

"They didn't send it over," he said.

"Then go get it!" Huene's hair was standing on end. "Do you think I have all day? No, wait. I need you here. You." He turned and pointed at me. "You go get it. This isn't a playground. Here, we work. Twenty-nine, rue du Faubourg Saint-Honoré. You can find it? Go. Run. Tell the housekeeper Huene has sent you for the new red bag and she is to give it to you."

Lee, grinning, handed me my coat and hat. "Don't worry," she said. "He will tip you for the errand. Well. I'll see to it."

I ran all the way to the Champs-Élysées, not stopping till I came to the corner of rue du Faubourg Saint-Honoré, where I paused for a second to catch my breath and smooth down my hair. I knocked at number twenty-nine, and a little maid opened the door and showed me into a hallway painted beige and white, no hint of color or pastel.

"Yes?" A young woman, but very beautiful, very stylishly dressed in a jacket and trousers and a string of pearls wound many times around her throat, came into the hall. "Coco is not here. What do you want, please?"

"Monsieur Huene sent me, from *Vogue*. He says the red bag was not sent with the clothes for the shoot."

"Ah. I will see if I can find it." She smiled at me and left. I took a few steps forward and looked into the room on my immediate right. It was painted in beige and chocolate, and the sofas and chairs were upholstered in white. The windows at the end of the room looked over a manicured garden that stretched all the way to the next street. Because it was February, the garden was all brown and white, like the apartment. I wished I could see it in the summer, see what roses bloomed there. In the corner of the room stood a dress-maker's dummy in an incomplete Harlequin costume. Chanel was also, at that time, helping to design ballet costumes for Diaghilev.

"Do you like it?" The pretty young woman in the man's suit had returned. "Nijinsky himself will wear it." She handed me a small wrapped parcel.

"It's swell," I said. "But he may trip on that bit of lace at the back."

She laughed loudly, throwing her head back. "You are right and brave to say so. I told her the very same thing. It will be adjusted. Do you like perfume? Wait one more moment. Huene will still be there when you return." She left again, and this time came back carrying a small square flacon of Chanel No. 5. "For you. Wear it in joy and health." She kissed me on both cheeks, and then pushed me back out onto the street.

"Misia," said Lee knowingly when I was back in the studio. "Chanel's special friend. Isn't she gorgeous? And you've done well for yourself today."

I had done very well. A bottle of Chanel perfume and a large tip from Huene, large enough to pay our rent for the week, and Huene had asked me to come to other shoots in case he needed me to run errands.

"You are so young and so helpless looking, perhaps even a little not bright looking, if you don't mind my saying," he explained. "They will give you anything you ask for." I wasn't flattered by this explanation, but at least I would be earning a bit all those days when Jamie was working so hard for Man.

After Lee was finished, we went out for coffee and a brandy. Her gay mood had passed and she was subdued, tired.

"Modeling got me out of P'oke," she said finally. "And it still pays the rent," she said in answer to a question I hadn't asked. "So, what do you do, my friend, when we are all so earnestly earning a living? Are you dancing the tango in some café, praying at Notre-Dame?" She learned forward and smiled mischievously at me. "Tell me, what is your favorite place in Paris?"

"If you have time, I'll show you." I had been startlingly moved by that photo shoot. I had assumed that Lee was taking me there to show off. Just the opposite. She had wanted me to see her powerless, objectified, not Lee the woman but just a woman with no identity of her own. I wanted to give her something back.

"I'm all yours for the rest of the afternoon," she said. "I'll just tell Man the shoot took longer than I had thought." We finished our brandy and headed to the Left Bank to the Jardin des Plantes, which was both a garden—rather, a series of gardens of all types—and a zoo. During the French Revolution, just about the time my ancestor the perfumer Thouars was packing his bags for the New World, some softhearted revolutionary took pity on all the animals being abandoned by the aristocratic houses, many of whom had private menageries of tigers, elephants, and monkeys. And so the zoo had been created to rescue and house the animals.

"Clever," Lee said when she saw our destination. "The zoo. Free, and open all year."

I took her on a roundabout tour of the places I had discovered, the alpine garden filled with small hills and gravel paths where tiny-leaved plants clung close to the wintry ground, waiting for spring, when they burst into brilliant carpets of red and yellow; the neoclassical elephant house; the ornate aviary for pheasants.

When we arrived at the long line of cages holding the big cats, I led Lee right up to the panther's cage. Our shoes crunched over the frosted gravel and we could hear children shouting from a merry-go-round, yet in front of these cages it seemed still, silent, as if all the wildness of the world had been captured and rendered mute in those cages.

He was there, long and sleek and black as a midnight shadow, lying on his belly, paws stretched out, amber eyes staring out of that perfectly black, shining face. His eyes caught mine and I felt the pull of his majesty.

The panther, my father had told me, was the only animal that was said to have a sweet scent of its own. It killed and ate, and then slept for three days, like Christ in the tomb, and when it wakened, it yawned and its breath gave off such a sweet odor that any fawn or antelope nearby followed that scented trail to its source. Then the panther killed and ate, and the cycle began all over again.

"Rilke's poem about the panther was one of my father's favorites," I told Lee. "About an animal caged so long it moves in circles and doesn't remember the world before it was seen through bars."

"I know how it feels," Lee said.

The panther slowly, with mesmerizing grace, stood and began to pace, back and forth, back and forth, its eyes now on Lee.

She had stepped nearer to the cage, so near she could press her face to the bars if she leaned forward another inch or two. The panther stopped pacing directly in front of Lee, and they stared at each other, both panting, waiting.

"You're standing too close," I warned her.

"Look at the flesh on my arms," Lee whispered. Between her gloves and coat I could see the gooseflesh rising. "So thrilling," she breathed. "How do you know you're alive if there is absolutely no danger?"

I had a quick, terrifying image of the panther's claw slashing through the bars and into Lee's beautiful face. Just as I thought it, the panther crouched and showed its teeth in a snarl.

"I promised my father that if I came to Paris, I would come and see the panther. Step back a little, Lee. You're standing too close to the cage."

"It is like childhood," Lee said. "Cages and bars. God, some of those days . . ." But instead of stepping back, she moved even closer. She must have been able to feel the panther's breath on her skin—she was that close.

She was on the verge of speaking of it, that day on the porch, the early days of a childhood friendship when she wore a white dress and smelled not a panther's breath but her own acrid smell of medicines, the lingering sourness of a hospital ward, the day I stretched my hand to hers and called her away from whatever she was remembering, whatever still frightened her.

The panther snarled a second time.

I pulled harder on Lee's hand. I was feeling really sorry that I had brought her here, but this time Lee stepped back, out of reach of that great black claw. She laughed.

"What a coat she'd make! I wonder," Lee said, "if the zoo would let us do a photographic shoot here. Huene would love it."

She lit a cigarette and turned in a circle, trying to decide which direction she wanted to take, if she wanted to head to where the children had gone to find a carousel, or back toward the monkey or reptile house. "Lots of great places for photographs," she said. "So, how are you and Jamie doing?"

The question took me by surprise. "Great. Jamie loves Paris. He never wants to leave."

"And what do you want?' Lee puffed out a circle of smoke and pulled a piece of tobacco off her lip.

"What Jamie wants, because I want Jamie. For always."

"Never tempted, Nora? Never feel an impulse to stray, to discover how some other man makes love to you?"

"Never. I have the one I want."

"I wish I could be that simple. For me, love and sex are two different things. Love is, well, you want to protect that person, help him, share with him. But sex. That's just an urge, an itch. Scratch it, and it's gone, and good riddance. On to the next itch."

Her philosophy seemed cold to me and, ultimately, defeatist, in the order of "all cats are gray at night." There are ginger cats and tabbies, friendly and feral. House cats and caged panthers in a zoo, and lions roaming free on an African savanna. There are cats, and cats. There is sex, and then there is what Jamie and I had, in our little creaking bed in Montparnasse, that making the world new and exciting every time we touched flesh to flesh.

"You mean that, Lee?"

"I do. It's what my daddy taught me, and I think he was right."

That comment haunted my idle moments. How could a father tell his daughter such a thing? And then I realized. This had been part of Lee's treatment after the rape, the philosophy that had helped her survive. The body and the heart were separate and sex was just an activity, perhaps not so different from a strenuous game of tennis. This was the survival skill her father had given her, to disassociate sex from love, as surely as the surrealists, in their paintings and photographs, cut off limbs or put eyes on shoulders rather than faces.

In that way, Lee was much more authentic than the surrealist artists. They made objects of their philosophies. She lived it.

We went to a café for brandy and cigarettes before beginning the walk home. It was late afternoon and the sun had disappeared, leaving Paris in a gray twilight. When we passed a corner newsstand, Lee stopped and rifled through the magazines, looking at the covers, flipping through pages to see the photo layouts, until the old man who ran the stand grabbed one from her hands and said to buy or leave, no free reading.

"I'll buy it for her," a man standing behind us said. I hadn't heard him approach. He was American, well dressed, big diamond pinkie ring on his right hand. When he offered Lee a cigarette, he produced a silver case, all engraved. Money didn't impress Lee. She was more liable to make fun of wealth too obviously displayed. But this man had looks and an impressive refined elegance.

"You're Lee Miller, aren't you?" He made a little mock bow. "I saw you at de Brunhoff's table at the Jockey last week. The brute refused to introduce me."

Michel de Brunhoff was the editor of Paris *Vogue*, the man who had hired Lee to model Patou and Chanel gowns.

"And you are?" Lee extended her hand.

"Let me tell you over dinner. Are you hungry?"

"Famished," Lee said, winking at me over her shoulder.

I walked back to Montparnasse alone. Lee and her admirer went off in the opposite direction.

# CHAPTER SEVEN

"What is that perfume you are wearing?" Jamie came home late the day that Lee and I visited the zoo. He was out of sorts, frowning and in no mood for the kiss I longed to give him. Instead, he gave me a quick peck on the cheek, threw his damp coat on our bed, and slumped into his chair by the window.

"Well, hello to you, my love," I said, determined to be cheerful. "It's Chanel No. 5."

"Sounds expensive."

"It is. Very."

"I thought we had agreed . . ."

I put my finger to his lips to stop him. "It was a gift."

"A gift?" Both his eyebrows went up. "Who gave you an expensive gift? Why did you accept it?"

"Jamie, you are starting to sound like my mother." I told him the story of my day with Lee, the photo shoot, the errand of the red bag, the zoo, the promise of more work from Huene. I left out the panther and the man with the silver cigarette case.

"The zoo!" He laughed. "That's why Lee didn't show up. At the studio," he added. "Man was furious. Shouted at me all afternoon. Come here. Let me smell that perfume again." He burrowed his nose into my neck, tickling me.

"First there is the scent of ylang-ylang, from the Comoros Islands," I breathed, remembering what my father had said about No. 5 in 1922, the Christmas he bought a very small bottle for Momma. "Next comes the scent of jasmine from Grasse. That's in the south of France." I could barely finish the sentence. Jamie's mouth was moving south and had reached my breasts. His hands were moving north, up from my knees. "Then, there is the scent of sandalwood from India. Yes," I breathed. "Yes. If you can't go to Mysore, the bed will do nicely."

Two weeks later I was picking Jamie up from the studio at the usual time, seven at night, when Lee opened the door. She had her own photography studio across the street, but still spent most of her time at Man's. "I've got a surprise for you," she said, tilting her head.

Man looked up from the table where he had been examining contact sheets with a magnifying glass. Jamie was crouched next to Man and, as usual, looked worried. Man was demanding and Jamie's confidence seemed to be shrinking rather than growing.

"Not sure it's a good idea," Man said, not bothering to say hello to me. "You know how he feels about privacy."

"It's a grand idea," Lee said. "And high time. Come on, Nora, you're going to meet Pablo."

"Pablo?" Jamie asked, his eyebrows moving toward his hairline.

"Yes. That one. Put on your coat."

Evidently it had all been arranged beforehand, because when we arrived at Picasso's rather grand house on rue la Boétie, a Champs-Élysées neighborhood with ritzy clothing stores and art and antiquities dealers, we were expected. A maid opened the door and led us to a sitting room where the great artist Picasso and his wife, Olga, rose to greet us.

"Man. Lee. And the American," Pablo said to me.

"The other American," I corrected.

When Picasso looked at me, I felt, well, truly looked at. Some glances are cool and superficial; some are mere nods of the head with the eyes never engaged at all. But Picasso . . . his eyes locked onto yours and peered through to your innermost being. It was like being naked in a crowd, his gaze was so intense. And then his gaze would move slowly over your face, your body, not in a sexual way—well, at least not always in a sexual way—and you would feel as if he had taken you down to your slightest measurement, as if he could tell the length of each eyelash and which foot, in tight high heels, was hurting most.

It was like being locked in the panther's gaze. You couldn't look away until he did.

"And her young man." Picasso extended his hand to Jamie.

Lee gave me a sideways glance. Is it everything you expected? her look seemed to ask.

It was not. Pablo wore a tailored suit and his graying hair was combed smartly back. He looked more like a banker than an artist. The furnishings in the room looked even more formal, more expensive than his suit. The sitting room, and I assumed the other rooms of the apartment, were done in Regency style, with delicate curved-leg tables and sofas, pink and yellow cushions, patterned wallpapers, gilt mirrors.

Jamie looked disappointed. We were used to the bohemian, often run-down but interesting studios and apartments of the artists in Montparnasse. This room would have impressed my mother.

When we were formally introduced to Madame Picasso, I understood. The home, the furniture, were chosen by her and they were a statement of intention: respectability, invitations to and from the right people, not the lowlife.

Olga was still very beautiful with her slender dancer's body and dark eyes and hair. She had been in Diaghilev's Ballets Russes when Picasso met her, and ten years ago she had given up her dancing career for the more ambitious prospect of being Picasso's wife.

Ten years is a long time in some marriages. Olga, when I met her, was a furious woman. She suspected what everyone else already knew and the suspicion of her husband's infidelity had frozen her beautiful Russian face into a permanent expression of jealousy and bitterness. Even when she forced a smile, there was a deep line between her eyebrows, an aggressive jutting of the chin. She looked like a woman about to throw something, and when she walked, there was a suggestion of violence in her footsteps. I wondered which roles she had been assigned when she had danced with Diaghilev's ballet troupe, to match that quiet and intense sense of a building storm.

Their son, Paulo, was there that night as well, though he was sent to boarding school soon after. Nine years old, he had the same blazing eyes of his father, the same barely restrained drama in his movements as his mother. In other words, he wasn't a child as I imagined children to be, but a smaller, sweeter-faced man-boy who seemed already to suspect he would never measure up to his father.

"Drinks," Olga said, and I imagined someone could have said "screw you" in the same tone of voice, except with a Russian accent.

A maid appeared, carrying a tray.

Lee looked at me over Man's shoulder. Her smile was that of a teenage girl who has nailed her brother's shoe to the floor. What fun, her eyes seemed to say.

Jamie stalked through the room, studying the paintings on the wall, the sculptures on the floor and tables. There were photos of Olga and Paulo set into silver frames and in them I recognized various corners of Man Ray's studio. Every once in a while Jamie glanced my way, eyebrows still raised after examining a Matisse or a Braque, and I found myself wishing he did not impress so easily. He seemed so young compared with Man and Picasso. He *was* so young. And young things often got hurt.

I sat carefully on a settee, self-conscious about the run in my stocking and wishing Lee had not sprung this event as a surprise. For someone like Olga, now sitting ramrod straight in a Louis Quinze chair, one should at least comb one's hair, refresh one's lipstick. I felt like a child at a grown-ups' party.

In one corner, an electric train had been set up for Paulo and several times I caught Olga giving that messy train set the kind of look a hostess gives a stray dog that wanders into a formal garden. She did not want it there. I decided I would spend the evening playing with Paulo and his train.

Picasso stood smiling in the middle of this battle of wills, perfectly at ease, the sun around which everyone else in the room revolved. (Lee explained later that his real studio, his working studio, was upstairs in a different part of the building, and no one, absolutely no one, not even Olga, was allowed into it. No one except his mistress, Marie-Thérèse, that was.)

Lee sat on a settee opposite Olga, and Man sat next to her, so close their elbows rubbed.

"Lee," Picasso said, "are you still wasting your time with those fashion photographers?" He looked at her from under graying but still thick lashes. He tugged at his long, straight forelock and smoothed it back, a gesture he repeated frequently that evening. It was a gesture I had seen in other men, usually those proud of their thick hair, an emblem of youth, but in Picasso the gesture was so exaggerated it seemed more a ritual, a superstition, than simple vanity.

"Fashion pays the bills," Lee said. "Cheers." She drained her glass and held it out for a refill.

"My portraits pay the bills," Man said darkly.

"And you, young man, are the new assistant?" Picasso turned to Jamie. "Man doesn't usually take male assistants, only young girls."

"He did it as a favor to me," Lee said, finishing her second cocktail. "I thought it would be fun to have a young man around." She turned white, realizing what she had just said, and that it could not be taken back. Trying to make it mean something else would only underline what she had actually meant. So she went forward. "Besides, he's taller," she said, slipping her arm through Man's. "Finally, I can make you jealous." And that was the perfect ploy. His ego was flattered. His mistress longed for his jealousy.

It was dark outside, and my stomach was rattling with hunger. Olga's sardine hors d'oeuvres were small and she, in good frugal housewife fashion, had portioned only one each. I wondered where we would be going for dinner—Jockey, Taverna, or even just the local bistro for beer and plates of sausage.

First, though, must come the shoptalk: what dealer was doing well, who was going out of business, which collector had paid what price, what museums were scheduling group exhibits of which school; which mistress was being unfaithful to her artist lover. Jamie sat and listened as Man and Picasso quipped back and forth in a coded language of commerce and art.

Lee and Olga gossiped quietly about the wives of various collectors, people I didn't know. I pushed Paulo's toy locomotive around the tracks and rearranged the miniature cows grazing alongside it.

After a half hour and another round of cocktails, Paulo was taken away by a nanny for his bedtime, and Pablo rose.

"Don't wait up," he instructed Olga. "We may be late." Exeunt husband and friends, leaving behind angry, suspicious wife.

Outside, I took a deep breath and slowly exhaled.

"Well?" Lee asked.

"Warn me next time," I said.

"Then this is a warning. There's more to come." She slipped her arm through mine. "Having fun?"

Pablo's mistress was already at Trianon, waiting for us. Pablo had kissed Olga good night on the cheek. He greeted Marie-Thérèse Walter with a long kiss on the lips.

Marie-Thérèse was blond compared with Olga's darkness, athletic and strong compared with Olga's slender fragility. Her smile was warm and open, compared with Olga's closed face.

"So you are the American," she said, shaking my hand and repeating exactly Pablo's greeting to me. That was how I knew Jamie and I had been discussed. What had been the point of the discussions?

Marie-Thérèse slid over on the banquette, making room for me next to her. Pablo sat next to me, and Lee, Man, and Jamie sat on the other side, Lee in the middle, looking very pleased with herself. I looked at the trio and thought how lucky I was to have beautiful Jamie as my darling rather than sour, angry Man.

"Poughk*ee*psie?" Marie-Thérèse asked, emphasizing the long *e*'s so that my hometown sounded almost exotic. "Like Lee?"

"But we didn't really know each other there," Lee said, not looking up from the menu. "We met in a bookstore, didn't we, Nora? You were wearing that funny hat. I wonder how the sole is tonight, and if there are oysters."

Pablo ordered four bottles of a good crisp rosé for the table, but when it arrived, he poured none for himself, just as he had refused cocktails when Olga served them. So Jamie and I drank his share for him. Man and Pablo relaxed finally, and Lee and Marie-Thérèse and I talked about skirt lengths and movies and the cold weather.

Pablo's mistress was sweet and earnest and very young. I felt sophisticated, even old next to her, though there wasn't that much age difference, really. Lee gave me the details on Marie-Thérèse later: Pablo had seen her coming out of the Galeries Lafayette three years before, and walked right up to her, offering to do her portrait. The poor kid had no idea who he was, knew nothing about art and less about a man called Picasso, but she liked his face and his manners and agreed to meet him the next day. She was only seventeen, jailbait, so they had to lie about when they had actually met and when the affair began, placing it officially a year later.

"And now, you're his muse," Lee said to the girl, pouring more wine and raising her glass. "Pablo says his work has never been more creative, more filled with genius. To you!"

Marie-Thérèse blushed that intense, allover red that blondes with porcelain skin give off. "I just sit or stand as he tells me to," she said.

"Well, then, here's to obedience and patience. May they never cloud my door." Lee emptied her glass. "I hate being told how to pose. Man has resorted to photographing me when I'm asleep. He moves my arms and legs and shoots away."

That wasn't completely true. Between photo sessions with *Vogue,* she still worked as Man's model. I'd seen the photos he had taken of her the week before. There had been a new vaudeville show in town and he had hired three midgets to pose with Lee, one dressed as a harem dancer standing between Lee's open legs. It was bizarre, perhaps humorous, but it made me a little queasy, looking at it, seeing Lee reduced to a pair of lovely extra-long legs. A different photo Man called "Prayer" was of Lee on her knees, naked backside submissively facing the camera.

I remembered how modestly Jamie posed me at Upton Lake. Jamie and Man were two very different kinds of men and I knew which kind I preferred.

Lee played with the oyster shells and murmured something about Olga, but her eyes were on a table across the room, on another couple, a slender middle-aged man with a thin mustache underneath a prominent nose, a woman with dark hair piled on top of her head and too much makeup on her exquisite face.

"Odd-looking couple," said Lee. "But her dress is very expensive. Mainbocher, I'd say."

They seemed foreign even in a city filled with foreigners and I strained to hear some of their conversation, to pick up their accent or language.

"Bey," Man said quietly, his eyes following Lee's. "His name is Aziz Eloui Bey. Egyptian. Spends half the year in Cairo, and the other half in Paris. The woman is his wife, Nimet."

Aziz Eloui Bey looked up from his plate, where he had been precisely dissecting a duck breast with orange sauce. He smiled at us.

"What an awful-looking man," Lee said, not returning his smile.

"Yes. But very wealthy," Man said. "I plan to do their portraits."

..............................

"So what did you and Man and Picasso talk about tonight, when I was playing choo-choo with Junior?" It was two in the morning and Jamie and I were in bed in our little room in Montparnasse. I was lying absolutely still, but the room kept circling around me.

"Pablo said he will find some work for me. Photographing works in progress, children's first Communions, that kind of thing. Do we have any bromide, Nora? I think I'm going to be sick. Do you think those oysters were off?"

"Work that doesn't get exhibited just goes into files and folders," I said. "There are tablets in the pocket of my jacket. Get one for me, too."

"Wet blanket. Work that pays bills and makes connections. We're on our way, Nora. This time next year I'll have a solo exhibit. I'm certain of it."

He didn't even have a gallery yet, poor kid, and he was planning his first one-man show.

"Well, before you buy your tuxedo and top hat, come give me a kiss. Forget the bromide."

Jamie came back to bed and hovered over me, his eyes looking amber-colored in the dim light of a single candle.

"My beautiful boy," I whispered.

"Man showed me some obscene photographs at the studio this afternoon," Jamie said, smiling down at me.

"You mean girls and donkeys and the other tourist-postcard naughtiness?"

"No. Real stuff. Photographs they couldn't use in the October issue of their surrealism magazine, the one dedicated to the Marquis de Sade. Some pretty strange stuff."

"I bet. Who were the models?"

"Not Lee. Girls I didn't know."

"Well, that's some relief." I remembered then, Lee had told me about that issue, how Man and his surrealist friends were aligning themselves with the Communist International and Sade. "Can't see the connection," Lee had said. "Do you?" "Maybe they think Sade epitomized freedom. For men," I had said. "He liked his women in chains."

"Get off me," I told Jamie. "You're leering."

"Sorry." He rolled over to his side. And then we started laughing, and we made love in our old way, gently and sweetly.

Pablo did find some work for Jamie, so in addition to helping Man in the studio, my beautiful boy was traveling all over Paris, photographing children and gardens and amateur play productions, the kind of event that the people involved want to have recorded, while no one else will ever, ever care enough to want to see the photographs.

But as Jamie said, it paid the bills and paying the bills was a key ambition in those days. Paying the bills was something many people were no longer able to do. When Man had said he wanted to make portraits of the rich Egyptian couple, he wasn't being greedy; he was being practical.

Man was busy earning money with commercial work and didn't have quite as much time for his art photographs and his models, and I was spending more and more time running errands for Huene. (I knew Paris better than the back of my hand by then, including the rich hotels on the grand boulevards, the alleys of the Marais, the cellars of the Louvre, all the nooks where a photographer might want to shoot, or find interesting objects for a layout.) So, Lee found herself with a little free time on her hands.

"Even Jamie is too busy," she complained one afternoon. "He used to take me out for coffee in the afternoon after he finished in the studio. Only for ten minutes," she added. "He was always in such a hurry to get back to his rooms with you."

Lee decided to make use of her free time. The year before, she had acted in Jean Cocteau's film *The Blood of a Poet*. Was "act" the correct word? Mostly she wandered around like a statuesque sleepwalker in a Grecian robe, a strange effect made stranger by having eyes painted on her closed eyelids. That winter, 1931, Lee decided to step behind the camera. She accepted a job with Paramount to film an English version of *Stamboul*. Lee was not to act or even model in it, but to film the set backgrounds and other images, and take publicity photos. It required her to spend a good part of that winter in London, and when she did come back to Paris, all she wanted to talk about was the film, not communism or surrealism or Sade.

Part of the plan was to get away from Man as well, to have a little freedom across the Channel, as she put it to me one day. We were in Man's studio, in the small bedroom alcove, waiting for Man to finish a sitting and for Jamie to come back. He had been hired to photograph an anniversary party. Lee was just fresh from a week in London, doing the publicity shots for Margot Grahame, the platinum blonde who played the countess in the movie.

"She's actually quite lovely," Lee said, loudly enough for Man to hear through the closed door. "Even if she does bleach her hair." Lee's hair was naturally blond. Almost white when she was a child, it had darkened to a streaked honey. She had wanted to lighten it, and Man had accused her of being bourgeois and vain.

"Well, I am. Bourgeois and vain," she said to me, drinking straight from the bottle of whiskey Man kept in the studio. It was a very cold afternoon and the studio wasn't well heated, so we had thrown all the bedcovers over us and we lay there, still shivering and trying to steal a little warmth from the whiskey.

"That's how I've made my progress in this world, by being bourgeois and vain," she said, knocking back another large gulp and then shaking her head the way a dog does when worrying a bone. "Why does he throw it up to me now? Do you think he would have taken up with me if I had been plain and simple and shy? Or even poor? Daddy's money helps support me, you know. Man can boast all he wants about paying the bills."

It was the longest complaint she had ever made about Man. There was a thud from the other room, Man banging something, and the sound of the sitter's voice, a woman, asking in French, "What is she saying?"

"Nothing," Man said. *"Rien."*

Man finished the portrait sitting, Jamie came back from photographing the anniversary party, and we went out to dinner, the four of us, back to the Jockey, where we had met the winter before.

That evening Lee was full of chatter about London and the film and the people she was meeting, the gowns and the bedroom gossip, the budgets for the shoots, the new designers setting up fitting rooms in Harrods.

I could see Man getting tenser by the moment. When the waiter came, Lee ordered steak and asparagus. "It costs a fortune," Man complained. "Can't you wait till spring—you have to have imported asparagus?"

"What will you have?" Lee asked me, ignoring Man.

"I'm not that hungry. Just some soup, I think," I said. Jamie and

I never knew when Man would pick up the check or when we would be paying on our own, so we had learned to order very cheaply, just in case. We usually filled up on bread before going out.

"On me, tonight," Lee said. "I've been paid for the publicity photos. Have a steak, Jamie. You look a little thin. Nora, don't you take care of this man of yours?" It was going to be a rough evening, with claws unsheathed.

"She takes great care of me. And I don't want a steak," Jamie said, putting his arm around my shoulders.

"How sweet," Lee said. "Look at them, Man. Two little lovebirds."

Man slammed his glass down on the table, spilling his wine. "Lee, can't you talk a little less and listen a little more? Be more like Nora."

Damn, I thought. Just when Lee and I were actually starting to get close. No budding friendship could survive a comment like that. I inhaled and didn't exhale, waiting to see what form Lee's revenge would take.

She sipped her wine, but her fingers were tapping on the table.

"Tell me, Nora," she said after a thoughtful moment, "did you accept Pablo's invitation?"

Jamie looked at the white tablecloth and cleared his throat. "What invitation?"

"Didn't Nora tell you? Pablo told me he was going to ask our little Nora here to pose for him. To be his model. To see inside his studio . . ."

"We get it," Man said. "Shut up, Lee."

"He did send a note asking me to pose. A couple of weeks ago. And no, I did not accept his invitation." I forced a dismissive smile.

"Do you think that was wise?" Jamie asked. His arm dropped

from my shoulders. "Maybe I will have a steak, Lee. Let's call the waiter back."

That, I thought, was a particularly mean revenge and I shot Lee an angry look but she ignored it.

We drank a lot, spoke little, and ate even less, once the food arrived. Man was angry with Lee, she was angry with Man and me, I was angry with her, and Jamie was angry with me. Not a brilliant evening.

By the time coffee had arrived, though, Lee had cheered up and was giving Man's hand affectionate little squeezes on the wine-splattered tablecloth. Jamie's arm was back around my shoulders, though I felt a little tension in it. There would be a "discussion" once we got back to the privacy of our room.

Just as we rose to leave, half an hour later, in walked the Egyptian couple, Aziz Eloui Bey and his wife, Nimet. He was dressed in a tuxedo and had probably been to the opera. She was in floor-length red satin with an ermine cape. Nimet wore a heavy, flowery perfume that filled the room when she entered, overpowering even the smell of the cabbage and pork the people at the next table were eating. Aziz and Nimet were the core of a large group of people in formal evening clothes, most of whom seemed to know Man, because there were exclamations and shouts of greeting back and forth. This cheered Man immensely. All artists like public recognition, much as they claim to long for privacy.

Aziz came over and introduced himself. He had exquisite manners, emphasizing his delight at the chance meeting with a little bow, and when he shook Man's hand, he held it for a second, putting his other hand over it in a tight clasp.

Lee gave me a slight poke in the ribs and pressed her lips together, a sign that she was working hard not to laugh.

"Mr. Ray, would you be so kind as to make my wife's portrait? We would be eternally honored." Aziz made another little bow, more a nod of the head, and this homage made Man stand taller.

"I think I can fit you in," Man said.

Aziz stood waiting. He wants you to tell him how beautiful his wife is, I thought. Man, say something. Ingratiate.

"Well," Aziz said, "we will ring the studio and make an appointment."

"Yes," Man said.

"Good evening." Aziz directed the formality to all of us, his eyes making a quick circuit of our table. But they stopped when they rested on Lee. "Good evening," he said again, addressing only her this time.

"What a joker," Lee said, when we were back in the street. "That mustache. Doesn't that Austrian wear one like it?"

"Hitler. His is shorter and thicker," Man said.

"God, I hate mustaches," Lee said. "The only man who looks good with one is James Joyce, and that's because he has no lips."

Man was silent and thoughtful.

# CHAPTER EIGHT

"Okay," Jamie said when we had climbed the four flights of stairs and were in our room. "Tell me."

I didn't bother to light a candle. There was a full moon and plenty enough light for undressing by. Besides, quarrels always seem easier in the dark, don't they? Gentler somehow, for not being able to clearly see the other person's face.

"Two days after we went to Pablo's house and met him and Olga and Paulo, he sent me a note. He asked me to model for him." I rolled down my stockings, slowly. Jamie usually loved to watch me do this, but not that night.

"That much I could figure out from what Lee said." Jamie pulled at his shirt so hard he popped a button. I picked it up and put it on the table so I could sew it back on in the morning.

"Yes," I said. "I'd love to know why she said it, though. Man was the one picking on her, not me." I unbuttoned my dress and let it fall to the floor. We stood face-to-face, Jamie bare-chested and me in just my slip, but he didn't move to put his arms around me. I felt alone, adrift. He was never angry, never cold and distant. That evening, he was. Preoccupied, as well. I thought that if he didn't touch me soon, I would turn to stone.

"Were you planning to keep it secret?" he said, sounding a little too much like Man.

"It was a note to me, not to us," I said, sounding perhaps a bit like Lee.

"And you said no. Why? He pays his models."

"Yes. And sleeps with them as well."

There was a clatter from the alley, cats jumping on garbage bins or perhaps a homeless man—there were more and more of them lately—trying to find a warm sleeping spot for the night.

"Damn cats," Jamie said, drawing the curtain.

"I thought you liked cats."

"He could have helped us."

"You mean helped you."

"Prude. You can take the girl out of Poughkeepsie, but you can't take Poughkeepsie out of the girl."

"Clever," I said. "Did you think of that one all by yourself?"

"If only you were a little more like Lee."

Ah.

It was like a blow, and my knees gave out. I sat on the bed so heavily the springs creaked. Jamie hesitated, then sat next to me.

"Listen to us," I said. "Like an old married couple. Maybe we should."

"Should what?"

"Get married."

Jamie stood up again and ran his fingers through his hair. It reached well past his ears, and curled like a child's before its first haircut.

"Your timing is incredible. Can't you see how busy I am, Nora?

Working ten, twelve hours a day to pay the bills"—more of Man's influence here, I couldn't help but think—"and trying to find time to make my own art, to take a few good photographs, and you want a wedding."

"Not necessarily a wedding. Just a husband. A city hall kind of thing."

"Lee doesn't demand marriage from Man. Or even want it."

"I'm not Lee."

"Did you believe that Egyptian guy? What a creep. Looks like a real wet blanket. I'm tired. I'm going to sleep now." And sleep he did, so far on his side of his bed he almost fell out, till I reached over and pulled him close and we slept in our usual manner, his arm around me, my head on his shoulder.

The next morning, Jamie slept later than usual and I had to tickle him awake.

"You'll be late," I whispered in his ear, throwing my leg over him.

"No work today. Man's going out of town and the studio is closed." He shifted his weight so that I was fully on top of him. "Time to play."

"You're not angry anymore?"

"Well, let's just see." He moved my hand down his belly. "Nope. Not angry anymore."

For the first time in weeks we had a leisurely morning together, lovemaking and coffee and bread, and a talk, a real talk.

"You *are* working too hard," I said. "I'm going to get work as well, more work than Huene is giving me. But not as a model. I mean, did you really want me to come home smelling like one of Pablo's cigarettes?" Do you want me coming home to you from Pablo's bed? was what I meant, but decided not to say.

"No. I don't want you to come home . . . like that. But what work can you do?" Jamie looked skeptical, but good skeptical, like when we were in high school together and I had boasted that I was going to get an A on my Latin final. Proud skeptical. Show-me-because-I-love-you skeptical.

"I'll find something," I insisted. "And then maybe you can just accept work from Pablo and stop slaving in Man's studio." After last night, I had started to think it might be better if we spent a little less time with Lee and Man.

"Impossible. I can't afford to buy all the equipment I need to set up my own studio, so I need to use Man's when he allows me."

"Just don't spill the chemicals," I mimicked. That was Man's mantra in the studio. Jamie had learned immediately what else was not permitted, in addition to not spilling the chemicals: don't look too hard or too long at Lee. In fact, they didn't look at each other when Man was around.

"Besides, Nora, Man is an important connection," Jamie said. "Eventually, he will pass some of the portrait work on to me. Maybe even some of the advertising work he does. He's going to introduce me to people. Important people. The dough is only half-risen. Too soon to bake it."

His father said that. Jamie was quoting his father. Talk about taking the boy out of Poughkeepsie.

That afternoon we traced our favorite walk through the city, arm in arm, laughing like schoolchildren, past the luxury hotels near the Champs-Élysées where harried-looking porters and errand boys walked poodles by the dozen, stopping for an aperitif at Fouquet's, then on to the Luxembourg Gardens.

Jamie had his viewfinder with him and took photographs of facades and iron grilles over windows, of children playing in the street and an organ-grinder with his monkey. He almost took a photograph of a brown wintering bed of rosebushes in the Luxembourg, then stopped himself. "Too romantic," he said. "No interesting shadows."

We had mail waiting for us at the American Express office—a letter from Jamie's father with the same news we'd been getting from home for months. Times were getting harder. He'd had to lay off two more employees. Jamie's brothers were working too hard trying to keep the business afloat. Time for Jamie to come home. There was no check with the letter, but we were already used to that. We were on our own.

I had a letter from my mother, the second one I'd received since I'd come to France, and she said pretty much the same thing, adding that her arthritis was making her life a misery. I was not to come back to Poughkeepsie until Jamie had "done the right thing." "Not that I expect him to," she concluded. "Why should he bother? Have you been to the Folies Bergère?" she wanted to know.

"Do you love me?" I asked Jamie, standing outside the American Express office. The air smelled of burned chestnuts, charcoal smoke, car fumes, and when I looked at Jamie, the odors became a perfume of Paris, of being young and in love.

"Of course."

I flung my arms around him. "Forever," I said. "You and me." I kissed him there on the street, in front of American Express, and an old man in this dusty black beret kissed his fingertips to us.

"My turn!" he shouted, and Jamie waved him away.

"Not a chance," he said. "This one is all mine."

# CHAPTER NINE

That spring was the first time Lee mentioned the name of Julien Levy, the New York art dealer.

"He's looking for photographers to show," she said, crossing her legs at the knees, so that silver silk, as flowing and shiny as water, rose up her thighs to where her garters showed. It was past midnight and the Paris sky revealed just enough moon to make the sequins on the silk wink as Lee moved.

Through the open window we saw a Harlequin in black and white sprint by, chased by a woman wearing a black leather corset and high heels and nothing else.

"Madame Sandro and her new boy. God help him if she catches him, in the mood she's in. That dominatrix outfit has gone to her head." Lee downed her glass of champagne in one toss.

"Speaking of champagne . . ."

Lee and I were having a smoke on the tiny wrought iron balcony, curled up next to the potted red geraniums and ivy. She refilled my glass, dropping her cigarette in her lap as she did so. "Damn. It already burned a hole. Huene will kill me." She was wearing a hand-embroidered slip borrowed from a *Vogue* shoot. She had come to the costume ball dressed as a model in a state of undress, wearing the slip and stockings and nothing else, with her hair disheveled, her makeup smeared. Man had finished the costume by encasing her left arm in a wire cage and putting a dog collar, complete with attached lead, around her neck.

They had dressed me in a tablecloth by cutting a hole in the middle and pulling it over my head. On top of my head, Man had strapped a basket with a live lobster that kept hitting its claw against my forehead. The basket was lined with seaweed, and it dripped salty and pungent down my neck.

"How's the lobster looking?" I asked, lighting another cigarette from the one already in my hand.

"A little tired and listless," Lee said.

"Right. I'll go into the kitchen and have the maid boil it up soon and serve it with butter. Let Man get angry, I'm not going to spend the rest of the evening with a dead lobster on my head."

"You tell 'em," Lee agreed, slurring her words and clinking her glass against mine.

The party, that evening, was in Zizi Svirsky's apartment. Zizi was a Russian émigré, a very handsome concert pianist except that he had bad nerves and could never actually play a concert, so instead he decorated homes for a living. He was much in demand and his parties tended to be large and wild. The love of his life, a Tatiana something or other, had run off to marry someone else, so Zizi gave a lot of parties that spring. Payback by champagne, we called it.

He was the only man I ever met who could dress as an apple tart, complete with piecrust hallowing his head, and not lose an ounce of dignity.

"It's those Russian brains of his," Lee said. "Genius. Great in bed, too."

Ah. No wonder Man had seemed tense. The party was given by one of Lee's lovers. I didn't know exactly how many she had. I expect she didn't either. But who was counting?

Not Lee, certainly. The nightmare experience of the child Li Li Miller of Poughkeepsie had created Lee Miller of Paris. Smoldering beneath her beauty, her talent, her fondness for champagne and the unconventional, was that little girl in the white dress, afraid to step off her own porch. How does a child comprehend such a thing as rape? She doesn't. Instead, she grows up and lets a lover put a dog collar around her throat in revenge because he knows she has many other lovers.

Except Lee was beginning to resist, to take control over what others, men, had previously controlled. That, I knew instinctively, was one reason for the multiple lovers. I belong to me, she was saying. No one else.

Man's career and reputation had taken a beating that winter, while Lee's was all shining ascendancy. His recent exhibit in Cannes had not been a success. Very little of it had sold and Man was having money problems because fewer and fewer sitters were coming to the studio. Not many Americans were left in Paris and those who stayed, like Jamie and me, didn't have the cash for a formal portrait.

Lee, though, had earned more than money by working on the film set in London that winter. Her name had been buzzed about; people were realizing she was more than Man Ray's girlfriend, more than a lovely model: she was an artist herself.

The great Charlie Chaplin himself had come to her Paris studio to be photographed. Lee had posed him immediately under a large chandelier that seemed, in the photograph, to be growing out of his head. The actress Claire Luce came to be photographed with her Siamese cats, one of which had left a long scratch on Lee's hand. Lee hadn't minded because Claire was such fun in the studio, balancing plates on her head and tap-dancing on the table. Claire was another upstate girl, born in Syracuse and full of gossip about a young dancer, Fred Astaire, with whom she was to dance on Broadway.

Man, plainly dispirited, had begun to talk of returning to New York. More, he wanted Lee to "live as his wife." In other words, no playing around. Fidelity. Obedience. The whole ball of wax.

"God," Lee said, slumping against the pots of geranium on Zizi's balcony, "do you really see me frying fish in some miserable flat in Brooklyn?"

"So, tell me more about this Julien Levy," I said, draining the last bubbles from the champagne bottle directly into my mouth. "What kind of photographers is he looking for?"

"Avant-garde, of course. He's asked Man to give him some names."

"He should look at Jamie's photographs." I was pretty drunk—how else could I explain the fact that I had allowed a lobster to sit on my head for the past three hours?—but underneath my dizzy silliness, in that corner of my brain that could step back and watch even when the rest of the brain was soused, there was a tingle of excitement. Maybe Julien Levy was going to give Jamie his big break.

"Sure," Lee agreed. "I'll speak to Man about it."

Zizi stuck his head through the window and handed Lee a just opened bottle of Taittinger's.

"Perfect timing, as always." Lee blew him a kiss.

"It's a bribe, my darling. I want you to come dance with me." Zizi smiled angelically inside his fake piecrust halo.

"To that?" Lee protested.

Zizi had hired a trio of violinists for the evening, portly long-faced fellows in suits that had seen better days. They were playing something sad and slow, and profoundly Russian. They made me want to weep. Or perhaps it was the champagne, or the thought of Jamie. I was more in love than ever, head over heels, over the moon, dizzy with it. Lee stuck her hand through the open window and let Zizi pull her through to the drawing room, where various couples clung together, barely moving.

Zizi had decorated all the rooms in his apartment in different themes. The one inside my window where he and Lee danced was a safari filled with zebra skins on the settees and mounted rhino and lion heads on the walls. The chandelier was made of candles stuck on the ends of twisting horns. "Poor lion," I wept, looking at the head on the wall opposite my window. The trophy was quite old and the occasional moth flew out of it to commit hara-kiri in the chandelier, but once, it had been a majestic beast. It had roared and purred—did lions purr?—and stalked through a distant jungle.

A woman costumed as an aviatrix, in leather jacket and tight little leather cap, crawled through the window and took Lee's place next to me and the geranium pots. Amelia Earhart had just announced she planned to repeat Lucky Lindy's solo flight from Newfoundland to Paris, and stylish Parisian women now wore leather jackets and aviator caps. This particular Amelia handed me her handkerchief, revealing long pointed red nails that I thought the real Earhart would have filed down for the flight.

"I know," she said, patting my shoulder. "I know."

"It's the lion," I wept. "That wonderful, wonderful beast. Come to this."

"There, there." She put her arm around my shoulders. "Chin up. Could be worse. Could be us up there."

"Very tr-true," I hiccuped.

"You're a friend of Lee Miller's, aren't you," the aviatrix said, no question mark in her voice.

"Guilty as charged, Officer."

"I haven't met her yet. Could you introduce us?"

"Sure." I pointed through the window to where Lee and Zizi tried to cling together, her free arm around his neck, her other arm, encased in Man's wire cage, forcing six inches of space between them. Zizi's hand was on her backside. "Lee, meet Amelia. Amelia, meet Lee."

"That's not quite what I meant."

"I know." The lion hadn't sobered me, but this woman did. This was happening more and more frequently, total strangers approaching me, asking for an introduction to my friend Lee Miller. I was starting to feel over my head in the large and crowded swimming pool that was the artists' Paris. I crawled through the window and from the other side promised the fake Amelia that I would introduce her to Lee later.

Jamie was in the second parlor, the one decorated like a harem, with embroidered cloths over all the furniture and carved wooden grilles on the walls. The only light came from little brass lamps shaped like genie bottles from an Aladdin illustration, and the air was sweet and heavy. There was a brass hookah in the middle of the room surrounded by a circle of brightly colored cushions. Jamie and four others sat there in the twilight, passing the mouthpiece around.

"Hash," he said when I sat next to him.

"No thanks."

His eyes were hugely dilated. When I leaned against him, it felt as if his entire body had turned into a feather pillow; he was that relaxed. "I love you," I whispered into his ear.

Lee came in, alone, and took a long inhale off the hookah but did not sit down. Jamie smiled dreamily at her.

"Shall we go cook the lobster?" she said. "I think he's all done in, and I'm famished."

The next day, at Man's studio, we saw the first printing of a brochure Man had been commissioned to do for the Compagnie Parisienne de Distribution d'Électricité, to promote the use of electricity.

"Come see," Lee said, taking my coat and pulling me forward. Man spread open the brochure on the table and Jamie and I stood there, making the appropriate noises of admiration.

My father told me once that Thomas Edison had offered to make Poughkeepsie the first electrified city in the country. But the city fathers had said, "No, thanks. We like Poughkeepsie the way it is, gaslights and all." And Edison had gone to New Jersey instead. Paris, on the other hand, was paying surrealist artists to brag about its plans for electrification.

The suited men of industry who had hired Man Ray got a little more than they had bargained for, though. He had photographed Lee naked and then cropped off her head and legs, making a sort of modern Venus de Milo. Then, he had drawn white lines across her torso, electric rays. I could imagine good bourgeois husbands and wives looking at this pamphlet and wondering if electricity in the house might cause a little madness.

Man had made several other images of a headless Lee Miller torso, and I wondered if Lee was as uncomfortable with it as I was, this reduction of a woman from an identity to a faceless piece of a body, not even a whole body.

Of course, the best piece in the pamphlet was the photograph of the place de la Concorde at night, all lit up like a Christmas scene.

"Can you guess what's wrong here?" Lee asked, grinning. "The place de la Concorde is still lit by gas, not electricity. We didn't find out till after we took the photograph, and decided to use it anyway."

"Good thing it's a limited edition," I said, handing the brochure back. Man gave me a harsh look. He could not stand any criticism, not even as a joke.

Jamie thought the art-brochure was spectacular. He thought most of Man's work was spectacular.

"So who is this Julien Levy?" I asked Man, helping myself to coffee from the pot Lee had put out.

"Got to run," Lee said. "The Duchess of Alba is coming to my studio for a sitting." And she was out the door quick as if a runner's pistol had begun the race. She hadn't said anything to Man, despite her promise, and Man didn't look happy that I even knew the name.

In fact, Man's face looked bereft as the door shut after Lee, and I couldn't help but wonder what he most regretted: that Lee spent quite a bit a time away from him these days, or that the duchess had asked Lee rather than him to take her photograph. Or that I had brought up the art dealer, Julien Levy.

Jamie sipped his coffee and looked at me over the rim of the cup. I held his gaze and he saw exactly what I wanted him to see. Opportunity. Pursue it. Take it. Man was busy setting up a tray of glass plates. For the formal portraits he still preferred a huge old camera that used the plates, not the more modern film cameras.

"Let me do that," Jamie said, putting down his cup.

"Lee said he's here scouting for photographers for an exhibit. Julien Levy," I repeated, in case Man had forgotten the question.

Man looked tired and rumpled. He had put on weight and his tailored shirt was too tight, the cloth pulling at the buttonholes. His curling black hair needed a stern brushing. There were circles under his eyes as shiny and dark as purple eggplants. "Don't you take care of this man of yours?" Lee had asked me months before. Man looked like no one was taking care of him. I wondered if he had seen Lee and Zizi dancing together the night before, Lee swooning at Zizi's neck, his hand on her backside. The obvious intimacy of it.

"Julien is an old friend," Man said, going to a sofa and sinking deeply into it. He pretended to look over his shoulder out the window, but he wasn't really seeing the street, the children playing, the old laundrywoman with her heavy basket. His dark eyes were unfocused, darting back and forth like cats looking for a way to escape a room.

The room was filled with a current of expectation.

Jamie continued to arrange the glass plates in the tray, his strong hands moving swiftly and precisely, revealing the athlete, the high school hero who carries the football over the line, who makes the last winning shot on the court. "So, what's the exhibit?" he asked.

"Just new photographers. No theme other than that." Man's eyes focused now on a photograph tacked to the wall—a portrait of Lee wearing the cage he had designed for her arm. "You know how New York is, as far as art goes. Ten years behind Paris."

"Yeah. I know." Jamie smiled and light caught on his sharp cheekbones.

Man knew what he was supposed to say, what he had to say, since he had taken Jamie into the studio and made him an assistant. This was how it was done. Friends naming friends. Great people helping small people up a bit. "I'll ask him to have a look at some of your photographs before he goes. He's leaving soon."

"That would be great." Jamie had the sense to say it casually, to downplay his thanks. But the electric current that had been building completed itself and there was an invisible arcing of current between Jamie and me. We both knew the importance of that moment.

"I'll bring him round on Wednesday."

That gave us three days to prepare.

There wasn't time for any new photographs, but Jamie spent the next three evenings, almost entire nights, printing up old shots. He didn't sleep except for an hour here and there, and he barely ate. I saw little of him. Man was out of the studio a lot, probably taking Julien Levy around to meet with other artist friends, so Jamie had free use of the studio, the equipment, the chemicals. Lee, to make up for breaking her promise, must have helped him a bit because he showed me some of the prints, explaining, "Lee likes the shadows in this one," or "Here, she likes how the sun seems to be rising out of the man's head," and "She thinks this one might be too naturalistic but I should show it anyway."

My role was to keep out of the way. No problem. Weeks earlier, I had found a job. There was a little chemist's shop down the street, and I had convinced the owner I was just the ticket to increase his sales of perfume. "The nose knows," I had explained to him in English, and he had found that very, very funny, though I wondered if he really knew what I had said. His English was as bad as my French, but we had reached an understanding: I worked on commission only. No sales, no pay. He had nothing to lose.

So, every afternoon I dressed in my best white blouse, dark skirt, high heels, and fake pearls and stood in front of his little perfume counter, pretending to try the various fragrances though I never actually put any on my skin, not until the end of the day when it was time to leave and I could take my scented pulse points home for Jamie to enjoy, whenever he returned.

Our schedule was shot all to pieces, with Jamie spending more and more time with Man in the studio, and some days I didn't see him until he drifted in after midnight, smelling of developing-bath chemicals, too tired for anything but a hug. When we made love, which occurred less and less frequently, it was quick and without tenderness and sometimes even without protection, it began and ended so fast. "Don't worry," Jamie said on those occasions. "I withdrew in time."

"I'm not worried," I said.

At the pharmacy, women would drift in for plasters for their children and bromide for their husbands' indigestion and I, dying of jealousy for their small, wonderful, domestic lives, would open a bottle and spritz a little fragrance their way.

The trick was to make a five-second assessment of the woman and decide which fragrance would most appeal to her. Sophisticated Chanel No. 5? Exotic Shalimar? If she was young and had runs in her stockings, I would pick a little flacon of tuberose and spice from smaller, less famous houses than Chanel or Guerlain.

Perfume must never be sniffed directly from the bottle, but sprayed into the air or, better, on the wrist of the buyer. A quality perfume smells slightly different on everybody, takes on some of the personality of the wearer. Brunettes and blondes may buy the same fragrance, but it will smell like two completely different ones on each wearer. And so when the occasional male customer wandered into the store and stood bemused and confounded over the array of perfume bottles, the first question I asked was her hair color ("natural, please, sir, if you know it") and her weight. The heavier the woman, the lighter the perfume must be.

Had she grown up in the city or the country? Was she quick-tempered? No stimulating scents but rather calming ones with lavender. Passionate or cold? Men would invariably take a step back when I asked that question and look askance. The answer was always whispered.

I had lost some customers with those questions, and other even more personal ones. But I had gained even more customers, almost a kind of following, because the choices I guided the customers to were unerringly right. Nine times out of ten, that was my success rate. And on the very first try. Invariably, the customer would sniff at my choice, express delight in varying degrees, try several others, and then purchase the first one.

Boulet's sales in perfume tripled. After I'd been there only a week, he gave me window space to make a display, a kind of ancient Greek temple made of painted cardboard with perfume bottles as columns. Jamie had photographed statues and fountains from the Tuileries and collaged the photos onto the back wall of the temple, just past the perfume columns. We had thought it rather clever and Monsieur Boulet kissed his fingertips when he saw it.

Two weeks after I'd begun the job, I'd bought a cup of *café crème* at the upstairs salon at Printemps, and been satisfied to overhear a woman at the next table say to her companion that she must, she really must, try the perfume counter at Boulet's. She'd heard there was a charming young woman there who knew perfumes the way some men knew a deck of cards.

Father would have laughed. He'd made me spend hours sniffing garden flowers and herbs with my eyes closed so that I could tell a tea rose from a damask, sage from rue. I had thought it a game, no more. In France, where pleasure and sensuality were esteemed rather than stood in a corner and labeled sin, such training was proving very useful.

The day before Julien Levy was supposed to come to our rooms and look at Jamie's work, I was again at Boulet's, earning my commission. The early afternoon passed quickly. Two hours at the perfume counter, then a break during which I bought a little cup of coffee from the café at the corner and drank it, shivering, at an outdoor table. The day was damp and windy. Schoolchildren returning home clapped their hats to their heads, and housewives had their aprons blown up into their faces.

I made that little cup of coffee last the full length of my break, so that I could sit and watch the women and men of Paris, some hurrying, some strolling, some silent and stormy faced, others laughing.

Then, back to the perfume counter for another two-hour shift. This shift was always quieter. Most women were home making dinner, or dressing their hair and getting ready to go out for the evening. Streetlamps were shining when the shop bell rang and a final customer entered.

She wore furs, expensive ones, and shoes with heels so high you knew she had a car and driver waiting for her. No woman could walk cobbled streets in such shoes. Her perfume entered before she did. That was always a mistake. Leave a slight trail like a memory behind you, but never let your perfume arrive before you.

Leper bells, my father used to call this heavy-handed application of perfume, after the lepers of olden France who had to wear bells to warn people of their approach. "Here comes Mrs. Brown," he would whisper in church on Sunday morning without turning around to see her. "Smells of lilac and mothballs. Here comes Miss Stoltz." He wouldn't say what she smelled of, but everyone in the neighborhood knew how she spent her Saturday nights. "Not alone," Mother said with tight lips.

This obviously wealthy woman in Boulet's smelled of spice and incense, enough to perfume a dozen churches. The scent was correct: she was a brunette, full-bodied without reaching the point of heaviness. But she simply wore too much.

"I wish a new fragrance," she announced, slapping her little beaded purse onto the glass counter and sitting on the stool Mr. Boulet had placed there, once he saw how I could convince the customers to linger a while, to sniff and eventually purchase. "Miss . . . ?" She looked closely at the name tag I wore on my blouse. "Miss Tours?" She paused. "Do I know you?"

"We met at the Jockey. I was with Miss Lee Miller and Mr. Man Ray."

It was Aziz's wife, Nimet.

"Yes. Now I do remember. Lee is such a funny girl." It was clear exactly what she meant by that: Lee keeping company with a shopgirl. Nimet narrowed her eyes, and the thick kohl around them made it look as if there were two black holes in her face where the eyes should have been.

"I am learning to swim. We will be going to the Riviera," she said. "I wish a new perfume. Something suitable for athletics, yes?"

I didn't think Nimet would be spending much time perfecting her sidestroke. Poolside martinis seemed more her style. But she was the customer and I was there to assist.

"Have you been to the Eiffel Tower?" I asked, trying to make conversation as I studied my artillery of perfume samples.

"So boring," Nimet said. "If I want to climb something high, I go to the pyramids." Was she laughing at me? Her face was so heavily made-up it was difficult to read her expression. Sitting there before me, Nimet made me aware that her name had popped up in several conversations with Lee, thrown in with the other trivia I hadn't paid that much attention to. Paris was filled with names of artists and celebrities and their mistresses and wives; if you paid attention to all of them, you'd probably have surrealist nightmares.

Lee had laughed at both Nimet and her husband, Aziz: she with her overblown beauty and strong Egyptian accent, he with the promise of a potbelly to come and the hand gestures of a spoiled prince. He snapped his fingers all the time, at waiters, barbers, chauffeurs, Lee had said. He tapped the side of his nose when he wanted to appear cunning. He templed his hands in front of his face when he wanted to look thoughtful. So transparent.

How was I remembering all this now, with Nimet there in front of me? Lee must have talked about him much more than I had noticed.

"What perfume do you wear now?" I asked Nimet, though I already knew, had known from the very first night at the Jockey when she had walked into the restaurant in her private mist of fragrance. Nubian Amber. A pleasant enough fragrance if appropriately worn, though too heavily weighted with musk, in my opinion. It had a kind of leftover "party from the night before" aura to it, no freshness.

"I don't remember," she lied, testing me. "I have heard the little countergirl at Boulet's knows her fragrances. Choose one for me."

"Madame is wearing Nubian Amber," I answered mildly. "You like spice and incense. May I suggest Enigma from Lubin?" I took a bottle from the shelf. "Your wrist, please. Let it dry completely before you smell it."

Enigma was one of the older perfumes and still very popular. It seemed designed for Nimet, the way you sometimes found a book written before you were born and yet that book was about you. Even the advertising used for Enigma shouted "Nimet!" with its sphinx and winged green Egyptian scarab surrounded by art nouveau flowers.

After I applied a single drop, Nimet vigorously waved her hand in the air to dry it. As soon as it began to dry, I smelled heat and sand and the cooling water of the Nile.

"So you know Miss Lee Miller," she said casually, still vigorously waving her hand as if flies plagued her. Her heavy gold bangles clanged together. The emerald and diamond ring she wore caught the light and sent it back against the dark walls of the shop, prisms of shiny wealth alighting on jars of cheap face cream, boxes of stale candy and shaving soaps.

"I have the honor. Does Madame like the perfume?"

She sniffed tentatively, bringing that lovely nose with its flaring nostrils to her bangle-weighted wrist. "No. It is too mannish. Try another. Something womanly. Flowers. Spices."

Enigma was one of the strongest florals, so I knew Nimet was stalling; she was there for something other than perfume.

Monsieur Boulet, meanwhile, was watching us from his mezzanine office window. He had observed Madame's furs, the emerald ring and gold bracelets, and his eyes looked like they were going to pop out of his head. He had smoothed his curly hair down with a palm of spit and straightened an otherwise always crooked tie. We didn't normally have clientele like Nimet Eloui Bey. Housewives and shopgirls were more our crowd. Was this the beginning of a trend? Was his little shop to become fashionable? Stranger things had happened, stranger fortunes made. Chanel, after all, had started out stitching straight seams in another woman's workshop.

I smiled at him, hoping his heart was strong enough for this, and returned my attention to my extensive display of samples. I chose Bouquet Manon Lescaut out of meanness. It was dated, too overwhelming even for women who liked to overwhelm with their scent, and it was named for a very unhappy love affair and the woman who died because of her infidelity. Even just sitting on the shelf, the flacon seemed dangerous to me. I had often considered throwing it away. Perhaps I had saved it just for this moment. I did not like being pumped for information about the famous Lee Miller.

"Try this," I said sweetly. "Other wrist. Mustn't blend scents." The *départ* of Bouquet Manon Lescaut spoke of tragedy, with its funereal scent of carnation and incense. Sadness washed over me as soon as I opened the bottle. When I applied a single drop to Madame's wrist, she again flapped her hand for a few moments with a great clanging of bangles, then sniffed. The top notes deepened the tragedy, with a hint of smoke and burning cedar, as if a million funeral wreaths had been set afire. (These were just my impressions. Some women, happy women, were pleased with the scent. They were of stronger constitution than myself.)

Nimet sniffed her wrist. "Perhaps," she said.

"Shall I wrap it? The medium or large bottle?" Time for this little transaction to end.

"Large bottle. Please give your friend a message. My husband detests her."

"Righto," I agreed, though of course I would deliver no such message. I smiled as I said it, because Monsieur Boulet was still watching us. "Anything else, madame?"

# CHAPTER TEN

When I saw Lee that evening, we spoke of many things, but I hadn't had a chance to mention Nimet and her visit. Charlie Chaplin had visited her studio again, and she had spent all afternoon with him, "horsing around," as she expressed it. We were sitting outside the Dôme, side by side in the folding chairs of the café, drinking brandies and dining on a bowl of nuts as we huddled inside our coats. Across the street, a performer was leading his trained goats up and down a ladder. A little spotted one bleated with annoyance and had to be tapped on her backside before she scrambled up.

"Wonder why goats don't like to climb ladders," Lee mused, finally distracted from the evening's topic of the Little Tramp, who, in real life, was devastatingly attractive. "I mean, why is this supposed to be entertaining?"

"Maybe the goats know there's no food at the top, so what's the point?" I suggested.

"So young, and so cynical." Lee signaled to the waiter to bring two more brandies. Man came down the street just then, appearing in the quivering light of a streetlamp. He hadn't seen us yet, so we had a moment to study him. He looked defeated to me, round-shouldered, long-faced, heavy-footed, all those clichés that suggested a losing boxer stumbling out of the ring. He hadn't sold anything in weeks and the sittings were more infrequent. It had been a while since I had heard him boast that he paid the bills.

"Thank God for Julien Levy," Lee mumbled quietly, watching him. "He's agreed to give Man a solo show in New York next year. Maybe he'll sell work and build up his bank account."

There was real tenderness in Lee's voice that evening. Underneath the tension, the spats, his jealousy, and her need for freedom, underneath even the professional competition, Lee and Man truly cared for each other. For Man, unfortunately, it was love, aching, can't-live-without-her love. I'm not certain what it was for Lee, except that night there was tenderness in her voice.

Man, still making his way down the street, saw us. He smiled and waved. The smile was forced. When he was up close, I saw shadows around his eyes.

"Brandy, darling. That's what you need." As soon as he sat down, Lee put her glass to his lips. He tipped his head back and swallowed greedily.

"Another," he agreed. "Several others. I spent the entire day with Julien, who insisted on walking rather than taking cabs. We must have covered ten miles."

"Whose studios did you take him to?" Lee smiled at a passing waiter, who ignored the table he had been heading toward to take her order instead. She had that effect on men.

Man rattled off a list of names, some of which I had heard before, some of which were completely new to me. Lee signaled the waiter again, and when he came with the bottle of brandy, she took it from his hand and thumped it onto the table. "Leave it, please," she said, and because she was very beautiful, dressed all in white and with lamplight shining in her blond hair, the waiter smiled and backed away as if she were the queen of France.

"Where's Jamie?" Man asked after a third brandy.

"In the studio, getting ready for Julien's visit tomorrow," I answered. "There are a couple of prints he wants to redo."

Lee and Man stared intensely in the distance, at nothing.

"What's up? Spill the beans." I put down my brandy glass.

"Julien has decided to leave a day early," Man said, not looking at me. "First thing tomorrow morning. Can't be helped."

And I was the one chosen to carry this news to Jamie. The cowards. Lee must have known all along. All that evening as we sat drinking and munching nuts and watching goats climb ladders, she had known Jamie wasn't going to get his chance. I stood and my knees almost gave way, I was so angry.

"I'll go get Jamie," I said. "No point in him spending another night working in the studio." I turned to leave, but over my shoulder I had a parting remark for Lee.

"That Egyptian's wife came into Boulet's today," I shouted louder than necessary. "She seems to think you are flirting with her husband."

The other café patrons turned their heads in Lee's direction. There were smirks, raised eyebrows. Lee sat up straighter than ever.

"Touché," she shouted back gaily. Man reached for the brandy bottle.

I went to Man's studio and banged at the door, forcing Jamie to answer it. Our agreement was that I did not interrupt his work for anything other than an emergency, so when he unlocked the door and opened it, he looked angry.

"Nora, what are you doing here? I've got hours' more work to do."

"No, you don't," I said.

Jamie put down the glass jar of developing chemicals he had been carrying, placing it carefully on the middle of a table. "What do you mean?"

"I mean Julien Levy is leaving first thing in the morning. He isn't coming to see your work. Man just told me."

Jamie's mouth opened, then closed. I heard his quick, forceful exhalation and then it seemed he stopped breathing, stopped moving, stood there like a statue, half-turned away from me. His hands had curled into fists.

"Come home with me," I said. "It's late."

"Lee didn't say anything about it," he muttered. "She didn't tell me."

"I think she just found out today," I said.

"No, she would have known even before Man found out. The bitch."

"Hey!" I said.

Jamie smiled and I wished he hadn't. It was the kind of smile that means trouble, that means something has happened, a crossroads or turning point has arrived, and things will never be the same.

"You watch yourself, Nora," he said. "She's nobody's friend, that one."

His mood changed after he said that. His hands released their fisted tension, and he even tried a smile, a real one. "I'll clean up here. Then we'll walk home. I don't feel like going out to a café tonight."

It was almost midnight by the time we reached our apartment, our bed.

Jamie flung himself onto it, exhausted. I would have screamed and wept with frustration and fury, but Jamie merely put his arm over his eyes, as if the light from the bare bulb overhead hurt them.

"There will be other opportunities," I told him.

"Sure." He sat up and lit a cigarette, taking a long, harsh drag and slowly blowing out the smoke. "Sure there will."

I poured two glasses of whiskey, big ones. I sat next to him, leaning my head on his shoulder. I could hear the couple upstairs arguing about the new dress she had just purchased even though the rent wasn't paid, their voices crackling like a faulty radio through the flaking plaster walls. Across the hall, the gray-haired nameless sculptor who lived in that single room had put a record on the phonograph to dull the noise of the upstairs quarrel—Josephine Baker singing "J'ai deux amours." He had played it so often the hissing scratches obscured Josephine's voice in some phrases.

"Sure there will," Jamie repeated.

Julien may or may not have been called back to the States a day early, but even so, why had Man left Jamie's name at the very bottom of the must-visit list? Stupidly, I said it aloud.

"Because no one has ever heard of me," Jamie explained.

"But then what's the point of discovering a new artist if everyone already knows about him?" I complained, raising my voice over the muffled music and the quarreling neighbors, wondering if this was how Mozart had developed his songs for four voices—a combination of anger, frustration, lyricism, and thin walls. "Damn Man. Damn Julien Levy." I said it because Jamie would not.

"Right," Jamie agreed, slugging back more whiskey. His mouth worked in a funny way, the way children's do when they are trying not to cry. He sucked on his bottom lip to stop the quivering, then jumped up and pulled me into his arms, and we danced to the scratchy music coming from across the hall, that other expatriate

American, Josephine, singing that she loved two places, her home and Paris.

"Ever wonder if we did the right thing, coming here?" Jamie asked, staring at the ceiling. "We were having fun in New York, weren't we?"

I didn't remind him that we had left New York because he hadn't been able to get a gallery. Or that we left London because he couldn't get a gallery there either. We had washed up in Paris to look for a gallery. Well, "washed up" wasn't fair. Paris was its own delightful, gravitating reason; we didn't need an excuse to want to be there. But the three years since our arrival had been a search for Jamie's success, a success that seemed as elusive here as it had in good old P'oke.

I knew no more about photography than Lee and Jamie had taught me, yet even I suspected that Jamie's photographs were somehow lacking. When he tried to be a surrealist, he merely imitated. If Man photographed Lee wearing a cage on her arm, he asked me to pose with my leg wrapped in chains and my head cropped off. If Man photographed an apple with clock hands on it, Jamie photographed a pineapple wearing a hat.

The prints were good, technically. Everyone agreed on that. But. With Jamie's work there was always a but.

The photographs that moved me, that seemed exceptional, were his unstaged street shots: children playing in piles of leaves in a fenced school yard, maids still in uniform daydreaming in front of a fancy shopwindow in the place de la Concorde, men playing *boules* in the alley next to a butcher's shop in Les Halles. He had a feel for those images, more than Man had, or even Lee, because he had a feel for the people, the real people, not the names, the celebrities, the leftover aristocrats—for the people who survived the events, not the people who created them.

Such images, though, were not fashionable. Atget and Brassaï had already taken those images years before, and now they were merely romantic, good for a local paper back home to show people who had never been abroad what Paris looked like at dawn, how the children played, what young women wore on their hats. But not good enough for a gallery.

That November, the textile factories in France starting going bankrupt. Beggars appeared at the outdoor cafés, caps in hand, only to be chased away by waiters. Some of them were children. Guilt tingled my scalp whenever I sat outside and tried to enjoy a *café crème*, a brandy, a quick sandwich.

"Something very bad is coming," Lee said. "I can feel it." We were at the Dôme again, but had decided to sit inside. Because of the cold, we agreed, but it wasn't the only reason. Watching the newly unemployed walk up and down the boulevards, their faces haunted and haunting, was not a pleasant pastime.

It was November 25, and I had woken up with the phantom memory of a taste of turkey dinner, the closest thing to homesickness I had experienced since I had been away. Lee had suggested we go to the Dôme and see if they had prepared any *dinde* for the Americans.

We had made up the quarrel by then, Lee insisting that she hadn't known Julien Levy was leaving a day early. Man hadn't bothered to tell her, so how could she tell us? I believed her. I wanted to believe her, though I still felt a clinch of distaste and anger every time I met Man, and that was almost daily.

Jamie had sent a batch of photos home—postcards, he had called them, sneering at his own work—and his father had sold them to the Poughkeepsie papers. We were back to square one. "Don't tell Lee," he had instructed me, his face burning. The P'oke paper offered more for a spread of four photos than Man had paid him in a month of servitude.

That night, that November 25, Jamie had received the check from the Poughkeepsie paper, so when he joined Lee and Man and me at the Dôme, he was in a good mood. He shook Man's hand, a real grasp of a shake that pumped Man's arm all the way up to his shoulder. He gave Lee a kiss on the cheek. "Other one," she said, turning her face for the second kiss. Jamie hesitated and kissed her on that cheek as well.

"We are hoping they have turkey," I told Jamie, making room for him next to me.

"Don't get your hopes up," Lee said darkly. "I already asked. They didn't cook any turkey today. Not enough Americans left to bother. I really wanted turkey and gravy and cranberry sauce."

"Then go back to Poughkeepsie," Man said. "Run back to Daddy." From his voice, you could tell that was exactly the opposite of what he wanted Lee to do. In fact, it was his fear of what she might do . . . leave him.

"Let's eat ham and sausages like we usually do. When in Rome," Jamie said. "Brrr. I think it's warmer outside than in."

"Maybe I will go back home," Lee said.

The waiter came, the white dish towel tied around his waist stained with mustard and tomato sauce, his black shoes dusty and scuffed. Standards were slipping. He lit the candle on our table, then stood morosely as only jaded Parisian waiters could, and waited.

"Sausages," Man ordered. "Four orders. Boiled potatoes with parsley. Green salad. Rosé wine, the Cresci."

"No, I want chicken," Lee said.

The waiter stood there, looking like Job with a new rash to plague him. He knew that Man placed the orders for all of us, yet Lee had changed the order of things. What to do? Man was obviously the authority, the head of the table, yet Lee was, well . . . no one said no to Lee. The waiter considered, wiped his forehead on the stained cloth, then turned on his worn-down heel without answering.

Fifteen minutes of our very stilted conversation later, he returned with a platter of sausages and stuffed chicken legs that looked like sausage. If only all situations could be so easily solved. By the third bottle of Cresci we were laughing again, chatting loudly and shouting over one another. Lee and Man were holding hands on the wine-stained cloth and Jamie had his arm around my shoulders. When he thought no one was looking, his hand slipped beneath my blouse and he brushed his fingertips over the bare skin, making me shiver like meadow grasses stirred by a breeze.

The old men at the table next to us were watching, though, and raised their glass to Jamie.

I wish I had a photograph of that night, that moment, when there was nothing we couldn't overcome, nothing we couldn't ultimately laugh at. Life was a bowl of cherries and weren't we just Yankee Doodly Dum, looking swell on the sunny side of the street.

In December, Lee bought new ski pants and a fur hat and went with the fashionable crowd, skiing in St. Moritz. Man didn't go. Too busy, he lied. Too expensive, I knew. He couldn't afford it, while Lee was earning money hand over fist, and there was always Daddy's allowance to see her through any tight spots.

Man and Jamie and I saw Lee off at the train station, waving forlornly like children not taken on holiday. "I'll be back soon!" Lee called brightly out the window, her breath steaming in the cold air. She looked very happy. Perhaps, I thought, looking sideways at Man's darkening face, too happy.

At the resort, Lee met up with Charlie Chaplin and his friends. She sent me some photos taken with her little folding Kodak: Chaplin at a formal restaurant with a napkin on his head, a spoonful of mashed potatoes playfully splattered on his cheek; next to him, Gloria Swanson looking vampish; and on Chaplin's other side, Gary Cooper brooding handsomely into the camera.

*Vogue* also published photographs of the season, since St. Moritz was the most fashionable place to be on the planet, once snow blanketed the ground. I thumbed through the magazine at Boulet's shop so that I wouldn't have to buy a copy, and was studying the new fashions for that season, the ever shorter skirts, smaller hats with turned-up brims tilted over one eye, the fur trim on jacket sleeves, wide-legged velvet trousers. Not that I would be wearing any of them. I bought my clothes at a secondhand store and they were always three or four years out-of-date.

There was one dress, though, that turned me green with covetousness. I flipped the page to see if there was a second photograph of it, flipped right to a page spread with the St. Moritz crowd, the Prince of Wales sloshing down the slopes in less-than-princely manner, the bediamonded celebrities taking tea in the pseudo-quaint shops, Lee and Charlie Chaplin dancing friskily in a nightclub, his mouth open in a shriek of Little Tramp delight, his arms positioned over his head like semaphore flags, Lee vamping over her shoulder for the camera. Another photo: Lee and Charlie and Gary and Gloria at dinner in some swank chandeliered dining room, candlelight making the photo a little hazy in some places.

Next to Lee sat Aziz Eloui Bey.

Lee looked . . . it was hard to think of the right word. Peaceful. Serene. There was an uncommon openness to her face. This was what Lee looked like when she was unguarded, I thought. Maybe Man was always photographing her in cages and traps because he sensed the invisible protective cage she wore around herself in Paris.

Aziz looked like the little boy who had caught the brass ring on the merry-go-round. And his wife, Nimet, smoldered next to him, looking as if she were about to catch fire and burn the whole place down.

# CHAPTER ELEVEN

A week later, Lee was still in St. Moritz and as usual I went to Man's studio to meet Jamie so we could go to a café for dinner together. Jamie wasn't there. Man was.

"There's a sitting tomorrow, so I sent him out to buy some more glass plates," Man said, opening the door to me. "Come in. Want a drink?" He brushed snow off my hair and shoulders. He smiled. "Come in," he said again.

I had walked into that studio a hundred times without hesitation. That night, I hesitated, the way my aunt's poodle had when it was time for a flea bath, wanting to obey, to not give trouble, yet not wanting to come out from under the sofa because of what lay in wait. Man had smiled more at me in one minute than he had in the past year.

"What's up?" I said, stepping over the threshold. My boots left damp footprints on the old Oriental carpet.

"Nothing. Just thought we might have a drink together. Get to know each other a bit." Man helped me out of my coat and guided me to the worn sofa. "Sit on that side," he said. "It's closer to the stove. You look cold. That's a pretty dress you're wearing. Very flattering."

He looked exhausted, but not from physical exertion. Troubles in the soul, my father would have said.

"Missing Lee?" I asked, accepting a glass of whiskey.

"Not at all," he lied. "She has her life, I have mine."

Man and I had never been alone together before. We had never had a reason to be. Now there was no one else to look at, no other face on which to focus, so I studied his face, the wiry black eyebrows, the squarish Edward G. Robinson–style jaw (no coincidence there, Edward G. being another Emanuel, another son, like Man, of Eastern European immigrants). The broad W of Man's hairline over his sloping forehead looked dangerous. He smelled of acrid photography chemicals and underneath that of bay rum aftershave.

He was an attractive man who dressed well and carried himself with confidence. Lee's feelings for him had been very genuine and not merely opportunistic, as some had suggested. But nothing lasts, especially not love. Wrong, I told myself, clutching the glass of whiskey Man had given me. Me and Jamie. We're going to last. I felt that, knew it to be true with every bone in my body.

It was already night and dark. Man had turned off the electric light that hung from the ceiling and we sat in the uneasy dark, illuminated only by the streetlight shining in through the window. The night was very quiet in the way that snowy nights can be, all sounds muffled. Once in a while a taxi honked.

Man started to hum a tune under his breath. That, Lee had told me once, was his cue that he was feeling romantic, and that was how I knew Man had seen the photos, too, of Lee sitting next to Aziz with that strange, unfamiliar glow on her face.

I knew what was coming and why, but I wouldn't be used that

way, as a tawdry revenge on a straying mistress. Curiosity kept me seated, though, inhaling the dust of the sofa, the bay rum aftershave. When he slid close to me and put his arm around my shoulders, I held my breath.

"You're a very pretty girl," Man said, putting his face close to mine. "Jamie is a lucky guy."

"Very." I stood. "When Jamie comes back, tell him I'll meet him at the Dôme." Then, realizing that I couldn't be rude to Jamie's boss, I added, "Want to have dinner with us?"

Man stood as well. "No. I'm meeting with Pablo."

"Give him my regards. And Olga as well."

Man gave me a long look and there was something of the panther's gaze in his eyes, that longing for freedom, knowing all the while that if the cage door were opened, he might not want to cross the threshold after all. It was lonely out there. "I wish Lee were more like you," he said. "Loyal. Devoted. Easy to be with."

"You make me sound like a cocker spaniel."

Man didn't laugh.

Lee came back from St. Moritz in time for Christmas and the four of us celebrated together, decorating a potted palm with cutout gilt-paper stars and exchanging gifts on Christmas morning, in Man's studio. I gave Lee a sample bottle of perfume from Boulet's. She gave me a Hermès scarf, Jamie got gloves from Hermès, and Man got an umbrella and bowler hat from Hermès.

"I never really liked shopping," she explained, wrapping the scarf around my neck and tying it in a floppy silk bow. "Easier to shop all in one place." She kissed me on the cheek. "Merry Christmas, Nora," she said.

We were sitting on the floor around the potted palm, drinking coffee corrected with large doses of whiskey. Snow fell outside the windows, giving the room a bluish, underwater quality. There were no shadows that day, no strong contrasts, only different shades of water with occasional accents peeking through—Man's green and gray tie, Lee's blue eye shadow, Jamie's bold striped socks, knitted by his mother and sent over for Christmas.

They were hideous, those socks, the kind of garment a toddler would be dressed in to cuten him up, but Jamie had worn them thinking that Man would find them funny, perhaps even surreal.

Bad misjudgment. Man dressed well and never confused his own wardrobe with artwork, unlike his friend Salvador Dalí, who a few years later would arrive in the States with a loaf of bread tied to his head. Puns in attire, Man thought, were for his models, not himself. So when he saw those socks blazing out between Jamie's cuff and shoe top, he gave a kind of sneer rather than a laugh.

"Oh, come on! You know they're funny," Jamie insisted.

"You're funny," Lee said, and she leaned over the piles of discarded wrapping paper and gave Jamie a kiss on the lips. Not a long one. Not a sexy one, the kind of kiss a girl would give a younger brother.

Man glared anyway.

Lee had a new quality about her, a soft wistfulness that counterbalanced her more acerbic moments and comments. After having partied in some of the fanciest restaurants in the world, with some of the swankiest people, she returned to us seeming less confident, not more. And Man, with that junkyard dog courage of his, became even more bullying, more possessive.

To keep the peace, Lee leaned over and kissed Man as well, on the lips with open mouth. He closed his eyes. Lee kept hers open.

Uh-oh, I thought.

That Christmas, that Hermès Christmas, as we were clearing up the mess from the unwrapping of presents we heard singing in the streets. A crowd marched down the boulevard, carrying placards: France for the French, and Down with Communists.

"They're wearing black shirts. Like Mussolini's boys," Man said, leaning out the window and looking down into the street. The snow had stopped and the air was clear and bright and cold. The boys' cheeks were red, and their hands, when they raised them in a fist salute, showed chapped knuckles.

They were workers' hands, thick and callused and now mostly unemployed, and yet these young men and a few women as well were marching for the right to give up their rights, we thought, to do away with the prime minister and his Socialists, what the unemployed workers and nationalists called their bleeding hearts and their tax-and-spend policies. In one of Mussolini's speeches, reprinted in one of the Far Right newspapers, he had said, "Fascism should more appropriately be called Corporatism because it is a merger of state and corporate power." That's what those unemployed workers demonstrated for—the bankers and the factory owners.

We watched in silence, all sense of Christmas celebration washed away.

"Maybe it's time to go home," Man said, when the crowd had turned a distant corner and was out of sight. "Back to New York." He looked at Lee, but she would not meet his gaze.

"Come on, Nora," she said. "Let's be useful and make some sandwiches or something. I'm starving."

..............................

In January, Julien Levy's art exhibit went up in New York, with works by Man, Dalí, Picasso, Cocteau, Atget, and others I didn't know. Julien sent Man copies of the reviews in the New York papers, and for the first time, I saw the image Man had in the show that would become so famous, or so infamous, the *Boule de neige*: a glass paperweight with a cutout image of Lee's eye floating in it. One of the papers had included a photograph of it and I almost dropped the paper when I saw that photo; it was so disturbing, a single eye floating like a fish in a bowl.

If the whole point of surrealism was to free repressed urges through unrepressed images, I did not want to imagine what had urged Man to make that paperweight, the violence he had imagined, perhaps wished for.

Lee seemed to take it in stride. There was always a touch of cruelty in the worship of beauty, those crippled bound feet, suffocating whalebone corsets, poisonous lead face paints of previous times. Wasn't the most beautiful woman in the world that armless, defenseless Venus de Milo? As a fashion model and photographer's model Lee perhaps had grown used to seeing her body, at least images of it, dissected in various ways: legs cut off at the knees, torso without the head attached. She herself, when she had done some freelance photography work for the Sorbonne medical school, had walked from the Left Bank to the *Vogue* offices carrying an actual severed breast on a dinner plate, remnants of a mastectomy. She had photographed it with salt and pepper shakers.

The editors, of course, had been totally scandalized. How dare she be so disrespectful, so brazen, with the female body? But wasn't that Lee's point, though perhaps taken a bit too far? Didn't they, every month in their issues, take women apart and put them back together again, as if women were so much meat?

And there was that other Lee, seven-year-old Li Li Miller, already tainted with the knowledge of the brutality men could do to the female body, the little girl only I knew, since I was certain Lee had never told Man about the rape, nor anyone else.

Honestly, I think that's why Jamie's work never really took off. There wasn't an ounce of cruelty in him. He lived in a world where pretty women were safe from sadists, where men opened doors for them and lit their cigarettes and said "Yes, ma'am" if they were older, and "Sure, sweetheart" if they were young; where men liked or at least accepted them just the way they were, no adjustment needed except a little perfume and lipstick for dress-up occasions.

There is imagination, and there is imagination. Jamie's imagination lingered on lovely and natural things, not angles where a cropping knife might cut.

Man's imagination went into dark places and took his women there as well. That darkness had appealed to the darkness in Lee when she first met him. But it was a difficult thing to live with, that danger, that darkness, that suggestion that life is frail and to love means to always be vulnerable. Lee had learned too young and too thoroughly how vulnerable the female body could be, and soon Man's imagination began to close in on her. She hated closed doors where she could be held prisoner, and Man was trying to close them.

No wonder she began to daydream about a place filled with light and open space, and the man who could take her there.

After that time, whenever I saw photos of the *Boule de neige*, of Lee's eye floating in a paperweight—and it was reproduced surprisingly often—I heard those *Front National* marching shouts in my head. They seemed to me all of a piece, though whether the surrealist movement was prophetic or somehow an early imitation of what was to follow, no one will ever know.

Nineteen thirty-two was a year of encroaching shadow. Everyone felt it, that darkness beginning to fall. Momma wrote a letter, long for her, telling about the Hooverville camp springing up outside Poughkeepsie, where the unemployed and homeless camped. The U.S. Depression, that father of breadlines, had rooted itself deeply in Europe as well.

The French newspapers cheerfully pointed out that six million Germans had already lost their jobs, but I didn't see that France was doing much better.

In Paris, the street traffic thinned as more and more Americans returned home to try to piece things back together. Four apartments in our building emptied in one month, so that our landlady offered to move us into a larger room without increasing our rent. She was nervous, thinking probably of those times when we had asked for more coal, more hot water, and her reply had been sharp, her prices high. Would we abandon her as well?

I put my arm around her shoulder and assured her we had no intention of leaving and she almost sobbed with relief. Jamie moved us into the larger room, and that soon seemed a mistake. We never felt at home in it, the way we had felt at home in our small familiar room.

Shops began to reduce their hours and then closed altogether, and burn barrels appeared on street corners to warm the newly homeless. The unions, those people still with jobs, began to strike in protest, leaving the city without transportation, sanitation services, mail, and schools, for days on end. "Broke" wasn't what happened to vases and windows; it was what happened to people, to cities.

But the economy, the newly shuttered shops and cafés, wasn't the only omen of disaster to come. In March, the baby son of Lucky Lindy, the aviator hero of France, was kidnapped. Even the Parisians, normally indifferent to American woes (until those woes crossed the ocean), were appalled and saddened. Lucky Lindy had been their hero as well; he had chosen to end his transatlantic flight in Paris, not London or some other European city. It was difficult to find papers on days when there were updates; they sold out immediately.

Personally, I couldn't think of anything worse than having your child stolen from you.

In Germany, the little man with the ridiculous mustache, Herr Adolf Hitler, ran against von Hindenburg in the presidential elections, and though he came in second, many thought that he would win the next election.

"Impossible," Man said. "The man's an idiot."

"Stupid like a fox about to break into the chicken coop," Lee said. "He never smiles in his photos. That's not a face to trust."

Troubles began to pile up like a train wreck. Spring rain ran in torrents down the cobbles, leaked through roofs, soaked our clothes and shoes. Man was short-tempered and fiercely possessive, stopping Lee with a "Where are you going?" and "When are you coming back?" every time she went out the door. As trees began to leaf out, Jamie grew thin-lipped. My Jamie? Could it be that he was homesick?

I asked him.

"No," he said. It was Sunday, a long free day of ringing church bells, a day free of Man's demands and errands, and there Jamie was, sitting by the window nursing a cup of cold coffee.

"Then why aren't you out taking photographs?" I had already taken a walk, alone, down the Champs-Élysées, and pawed through racks of used books in the stalls along the Seine. And Jamie wasn't even dressed yet.

"What's the point? I'll never show them anywhere. I mean, how many boxes of prints should I fill up and stack in the corner before I admit I'm a washout?"

It was hard to argue that one. I decided on the simplest, most truthful argument I could come up with. "I believe in you," I said, sitting in the chair opposite him. "You take great photographs. Not stylish, but that's the thing with style, isn't it? It doesn't last. A new style will come and another and another. What's important is that you photograph what you see, not what Man or Lee or anyone else sees."

Jamie wasn't convinced. He looked at me the way I had seen him look at his father in Poughkeepsie, with love but also a kind of distance, as if we didn't share a common language.

"I'm starving," I said. "Let's go eat."

"Go without me. I've got to think."

This was the first time I had ever seen Jamie in such a black mood, the first time he couldn't pack up his troubles in his old kit bag and smile, smile, smile. We were turning a corner and I didn't know what was at the end of this street. Oddly enough, I thought instead of Lucky Lindy, let my heart swell with his sorrow, the hellish pain of losing a child. I thought a lot about children those days, walking out of my way to pass school yards and playgrounds where they played, wondering when Jamie would, as my mother said, do right by me. He would be twenty-five, soon.

There was a café on our corner, a nameless little place with a sandy wooden floor and dented zinc bar and a calendar on the wall from 1928. Normally, I avoided this café. It smelled of cabbage and vinegary wine and the clientele seemed unwashed and uncaring.

One old woman in particular scared the hell out of me. She had a deeply lined face, and she painted her mouth as large and red as a clown's. Her frizzy hair had been hennaed to the color of a Christmas stocking and her ancient fur coat had patches of mange. She always sat at the same table, and no one ever sat with her. She seemed, to me, to epitomize the words "old and unloved."

That afternoon I ate alone at the café, trying on various futures the way Lee tried on different evening dresses. Jamie's black mood had infected me as well, and for the first time I considered the possibility that . . . I couldn't finish the sentence, not even to myself. Of course he loves me, I told myself.

The old woman and I eyed each other over our omelets and glasses of sour wine. When I put a fork of egg to my mouth, she did the same. When I lifted my wineglass, so did she. I fled the café without finishing my solitary meal. She cackled with delight.

The next day I worked only half a shift at Boulet's. My sales technique had improved so much that any woman who ventured near my display counter left that store with a bottle of perfume, whether she had planned to buy it or not. But customers were fewer and fewer and I couldn't exactly lasso them in off the street corner. Boulet was disappointed, perhaps even a little angry, that the visit from the bejeweled and befurred Nimet Eloui Bey hadn't put his place on the map. Our clientele were still shopgirls wanting a cheap lipstick and housewives needing sticking plasters.

I spent my free morning at the zoological garden, visiting the panther. When I was near his cage, I felt near to my father. When I had asked Jamie if he was homesick, the question had been for myself as well. I wasn't. But the sense of loss was there for something I couldn't name.

The rain had finally stopped and the morning was all warm sun and fresh breezes, keeping the skin alert to possibility, to the joy of touch. Trees showed delicate new green leaves and the air smelled of muddy resurrection, as if the world was being newly shaped. The park was filled with mothers and children, feeding my new obsession with the various nuances of wails after skinned knees, high-pitched midget shouts of anger and joy, the strange way little boys ran, with their feet and elbows all at different angles.

A group of children had gathered in front of the panther's cage when I arrived, boys in short pants and girls in frilly pinafores, a swirling mass of screaming tots daring one another to get closer to the cage, and their mothers and nannies, looking monstrously huge next to their tiny wards, flailing and yelling to keep the children at a safe distance.

The panther himself looked bored. He yawned and I wondered, if I got close enough, would that yawn smell of the ancient amber walls of Atlantis? What exactly was the magical sweet fragrance of a panther's breath that according to legend could so easily lure his victims?

This was the fifth or sixth time I had visited him, and every time it had been this same ritual: his initial boredom. Then he would lock his gaze onto my face, rise, and begin to pace, never breaking our eye contact. It gave me a thrill of both fear and recognition. I knew this animal couldn't possibly be the same panther that the poet Rilke had visited and written about, yet there was something immortal about the beast, a sense that no matter what happened outside his cage, this panther would be here always.

That's how wrong we sometimes are. But that day, the panther still had his immortality.

The children ran back and forth in front of the cage and then, in groups of twos and threes, they wandered away with their mothers, as bored as the beast himself, looking for new excitement or perhaps an ice cream. They left a scented trail of candy and shampoo and powder.

"Hi, Nora."

I hadn't seen her sitting under the opposite tree, smoking a cigarette, looking like a photograph of a woman sitting under a tree, smoking.

"This is a surprise. Come here often?" I sat next to Lee and accepted one of her cigarettes. It was an Egyptian brand, flavored with clove.

"Not often. Only when I need to be quiet, to think. Never one of my favorite activities." Lee laughed and there was a hint of wistfulness in her voice.

"So, what did you come here to think about?" I asked her.

"You can guess. Lunch on me if you get it right the first time."

"Aziz."

"Bingo." Lee tossed her cigarette and stretched out one long, elegant leg to crush the butt into the gravel. "I think it's serious, Nora." Lee said it the way a girl just invited to the prom would say, "He likes me!"

"How serious?"

"Love and marriage and baby-carriage serious."

"Oh, God."

Lee laughed again. "My feelings exactly. I mean, I could not have chosen a more complicated situation, could I? If you had sent me on a scavenger hunt to find the most unworkable romance possible, this would be it. Man is beside himself, of course. We haven't discussed it, but he knows, I'm certain he knows."

How could he not know? Since she had returned from St. Moritz, Lee had been walking on tiptoe, humming to herself, gazing dreamy-eyed into some horizon we didn't see.

"Does Nimet know?" I already knew the answer to that question, but I wondered if Lee did.

"Don't think so." She pulled another cigarette out of her purse and lit it with a new silver Ronson lighter. It had been engraved, but her thumb was over the inscription.

"So what's the plan?" I took a cigarette when she offered it, more because I wanted to read that inscription than inhale Egyptian clove, and it was what I thought: *A to L. With love.*

"No plan. Day by day."

"Why tell me? How do I come into this?"

Lee looked into my eyes with the panther's steady, fearless gaze. "I need to talk about him. Even when I'm not with him, I just need to talk about him, to feel him with me. Nora, have you ever felt like this? Why didn't someone tell me? Jesus. It's laughing and crying, feeling young and old, safe and lost at sea, all at the same time. It's every opposite meeting head-on and thumping into your heart. I'm delighted. I'm terrified. And you're the only person I can tell this to."

She took my hand then, held it as if she were going underwater and I could pull her back up.

"Okay," I said. "Talk. Tell me about his tailor, his education, his hobbies. Is he good on skis?"

That was a very long morning. Is there anything more boring than listening to a girl in love go on and on about her beloved? Lee wasn't at all bored, of course. She was ecstatic. I'd never seen her like that, soft and vulnerable just from saying a man's name.

"Thanks," she said, an hour and far too much detail later. I think I knew more about Aziz than his mother did at that point, about his favorite professors in Liverpool where he had studied engineering; about the glass models of eyes in his doctor father's study and how he had played marbles with them; his early chaperoned dates with Nimet; his favorite Savile Row tailor and Cairo terrace bar; the songs he sang in the shower. He loved Cole Porter.

"Got to go now," Lee said, standing, run-down and out of words like a windup doll. "Nimet is coming to my studio for a sitting."

I stood as well. "You're doing Nimet's portrait?"

"Yeah. She asked me to. How could I say no?"

"It's easy. You say no. This is a bad idea, Lee."

"No, it's a great idea. I don't want Man to know. Not yet. Why act guilty?"

Because you are? And then I heard Jamie's voice in my head. You can take the girl out of Poughkeepsie . . . No use judging Lee by P'oke standards. And it wasn't as if Man were holy Mr. Faithful. There was a code of honor of sorts in all this, but I hadn't figured it out yet.

Several days later, Lee showed me her portrait of Nimet. Aziz's wife looked straight into the camera, her eyelids slightly lowered over her huge black eyes. Her mouth had a suggestion of a smile but no more than that. Lee had costumed her in a turban and flowing velvet robe, a nod to Nimet's Circassian ancestors, to emphasize her exotic beauty. It was, when all was said and done, a very generous portrait for a woman to make of her lover's wife.

"She's beautiful," I said, handing the photo back to Lee. We were in Lee's studio, alone. Lee used the studio for her sittings and to store her personal things and to hide in, once in a while, when Man was in a sulk. And, let's be honest, she took men there, men who stayed for an hour, who were interesting and passionate and either too much in a hurry to get a hotel room or too broke to afford one.

Man never visited it. He hated it, hated that Lee kept it, because he knew why she did, that it wasn't just for sittings and shoots. On the surface, her reason for having the studio was for respectability.

Lee and Man were not married and a lady never used the same address as her lover. Appearances had to be kept up, even when the whole world knew the truth of the situation. But Man knew.

That day, though, the studio felt different, almost cozy, the way a room gets when two people in love inhabit it. The sofa pillows were scattered on the floor and a blanket had been bunched up as a pillow, with a half-empty bottle of whiskey next to it. A man's scarf was draped over a chair. It wasn't one I had ever seen Man wear.

Lee followed my glance. She grabbed up the scarf and folded it lovingly, then stuck it in a drawer.

"Nimet should be lovely," Lee said. "Aziz says she spends half the day soaking in a Vichy water bath and the other half putting on her makeup. They live in separate apartments, you know."

"And what does Nimet say?"

"Not much." And that was all Lee would say of the sitting. I wondered if the wife and mistress had been able to make small talk. Have you tried the lobster bisque at the new restaurant on rue Soufflot? Who does your hair? Love your shoes, where did you get them? Oh, and by the way, I'm in love with your husband. Smile! Don't move!

# CHAPTER TWELVE

Lee disappeared into a protective silence. After that morning in front of the panther cage, when she had rhapsodized about Aziz, love, and life in a way that would have embarrassed even a schoolgirl, she never said his name again, at least not when I was with her and certainly not when Man was around. She hadn't decided what to do yet, and silence, secrecy, were needed for the making of plans. One of the first lessons photographers learn in common with comedians is this: timing is everything. Lee was timing her exit.

Looking back on it, I can find motives other than self-protection and deception in her silence. Don't some doctors lie to their patients and say, "Don't worry. You'll be fine," even as they are planning the amputation? Lee's silence was meant as a reassurance, an admittance that Man could only handle so much bad news at once.

Because there was more bad news, and Lee had sensed it was coming. In March, Julien Levy had shown the work of both Lee and Man in a New York gallery. When he sent the reviews, we passed them around for a reading, Jamie and me, Lee and Man, all together at the Dôme, sipping coffee and whiskey. Mistake. Lee's work had received better reviews than Man's. Man, deeply upset but unwilling to show it, saved face by claiming he had a portrait sitting and storming off.

"At six o'clock on a Sunday evening? I don't think so," Lee said, when he was gone. "He can't take a little competition from the girlfriend. Sore loser."

"Lay off, Lee," Jamie said, for once siding with Man. "Leave the guy a little pride." They glared at each other, Jamie looking almost as stormy as Man had, Lee with a crooked half smile of triumph.

In fact, her photo, reproduced in the paper, was technically magnificent and emotionally a kind of last word to surrealism. Lee had photographed the back of a woman's head, one hand resting on top of short, tight blond curls. Her fingernails were painted and filed talon-sharp; the collar of her white blouse was buttoned tightly and high on the neck. There was a suggestion of danger and bondage, but no tricks, no gimmicks. It was life as we saw it, not as we had invented it.

Man realized that he was losing control, and for a man, for an artist, that was a kind of death. He went on a severe diet, a cleansing diet he called it. Food, he could control.

Later that spring, Julien Levy gave Man his first American one-man show, and the reviews again were not good. One magazine called the show an assortment of "nuts and nudes" and described Man as a "kinky-haired photographer." The reviewer made not-so-sly innuendos about Man's Jewish background, and salacious comments about the bits and pieces of Lee's body in the photographs.

Maybe in Paris anything goes, but New Yorkers were not amused by the surrealists' viewpoint, their irreverent attitude toward the various parts of female anatomy with the underlying suggestions of violence. If surrealism were a perfume, the *départ* would be surprise, the top note amusement, and the middle note the kind of sigh a sleeper breathes out during a nightmare.

Nor was Lee's father, back home in Poughkeepsie, amused by the reviewers' lascivious references to his daughter's navel; he sued for libel over the damaging comments about Lee. She had a reputation to protect, never mind that for several years Man had been photographing her in various stages of undress or that a few years before, Lee had modeled for the first ad for Kotex, creating a very public scandal with this reference to the great unmentionable: menstruation.

Six months earlier Lee would have laughed at the crude references to her anatomy. But suddenly she was very concerned about her reputation. I saw the influence of Aziz in this.

Man, meanwhile, had lost a good fifteen pounds and was looking fit and lean, but not particularly happy. Around this time, somewhere in the emotional labyrinth of that spring, as Lee hummed and tiptoed through her love-hazed days, Man began to carry a pistol.

"Man bought a gun," Jamie said. "He keeps it in a drawer in the studio." Jamie finished the second half of his drink and signaled the waiter for another. We were sitting at one of the outdoor tables at the Dôme, watching the setting sun turn the sky behind the Hôtel des Invalides different shades of turquoise and magenta. Our conversations had begun to grow a little stilted and they were mostly about Lee and Man, as if "we" was a topic no longer of concern. I thought this was because Jamie and I had grown so close, knew each other so well.

It was June by then, a month of early suffocating heat that left us irritable and lethargic. When we went out in the evenings, where heavy air simmered over the heated pavements, Jamie drank gin with tonic, not wine. This was new.

All the time we had been in Paris, Jamie had drunk wine or whiskey. Gin, he had said on occasion, was so P'oke. Drinking wine became one of those expatriate gestures that made us feel even farther from home than we were, made Poughkeepsie seem like a colony on the dark side of the moon, while we were on the light side, where the natives spoke French and drank wine and rolled their *r*'s in the backs of their throats.

"And does he say what this gun is for?' I put my hand on top of Jamie's and stroked the skin there, enjoying its texture, smooth and tough.

"To shoot his rivals."

"Jesus. You're kidding. That would include half of Paris, wouldn't it?" If I had thought that Lee's overwhelming infatuation with Aziz would slow her down in the sexual arena, I had been wrong. Aziz and Nimet had, several weeks before, returned to Egypt for the six months that they spent there every year. And Lee now was spending many nights and often days and nights away from Man, holed up in her own studio, not answering the door if anyone knocked. But if you pressed your ear to the door and waited, listening, as I did once out of curiosity, you could hear Lee and a man speaking, laughing, and the sound of glasses clinking.

I saw her once through a café window, sitting opposite a man I didn't know, leaning back, laughing, inviting him to light her cigarette and then leaning in closer, whispering.

Lee was testing her theory that sex and love were two different things, and she could have both . . . separately. Every time I met her, she seemed to have the remnants of a different aftershave on her.

And now Man was carrying a pistol.

“This is not a joking matter,” said Jamie, irritated. “I don’t think he really plans to shoot anyone. But when Lee comes into his studio now, I don’t dare even look at her. I’ve known some jealous men before, and women.” A knowing glance at me interrupted the thought. “But Man . . . he’s a whole other story.” Jamie held the cold glass of gin and tonic to his forehead.

The café was crowded that night, filled with people eager to be out of their stuffy, hot apartments and sitting in the somewhat cooler air of the boulevards.

“Did you look at Lee much before?” I asked, wondering, if I hadn’t been there, which girl in the café Jamie might find tempting. The redhead wearing the blue hat or the little dark one who was reading a book and never once looked up? He had never openly flirted with anyone, not even during the wildest, hard-drinking evenings. But sometimes he looked wistfully at passing women. And then he always pressed his hand on mine, or put his arm around my shoulders and teased me a little about my jealousy.

I *was* jealous, even though I had no cause. I was more in love with Jamie than ever. Time hadn’t dulled the passion or even the fun, and when he was busy and elsewhere, which was more and more often the case, I thought of him constantly and found myself hoping that the bride or birthday girl he had been sent to photograph wasn’t pretty.

“Look at Lee? Of course not.” He sounded even more annoyed and impatient. “God, Nora, talk about jealous.”

“Just asked. That’s all.”

He finished his drink and sat back in his chair, far enough away that our hands no longer met on the table.

Julien Levy is on your mind, I thought, and did not say. Julien was back in Paris, scouting for more artists for another show. We knew he had returned because Lee and Man were having dinner with him that night. We hadn't been asked to come along. Not a good sign. Now Man wasn't even making empty promises of bringing Julien along to look at Jamie's photographs.

Perhaps Man had described the work in a way that guaranteed Julien would not be interested. Maybe Jamie *had* looked at Lee a little too often, a little too long. Lee certainly had looked at him. The two of them seemed almost like brother and sister, physically, with their slender height, their high cheekbones, their straight light hair brushed back from wide foreheads. I had looked at the two of them, drinking together in a café or studying a contact sheet in the studio, and thought what pretty babies they could make together, and the thought made me dizzy with jealousy.

"Thank God Aziz has gone back to Cairo," I said. I didn't know how much Man knew about Lee's meetings with other men, but he did know about Aziz, and Aziz was the real threat, not the onetime Charlies. Lee believed she was in love with Aziz, whatever that meant.

Lee herself had told Man about Aziz and little by little she was removing her personal things—an old cardigan she wore in the morning, slippers, her spare toothbrush—from Man's place and moving them to hers. Piece by piece, she was leaving Man.

"Good timing for both of them," Jamie agreed. "Clever of Man to get a pistol only after Aziz has already left. Great stage directions, there." Jamie, not usually cruel, laughed and began to hum the tune we had heard Bricktop sing only last week—"Miss Otis Regrets," about a woman who shoots her straying lover and then is herself lynched by an angry mob. Lee, who knew about such things, said Cole Porter had written that song especially for Bricktop, the flaming-red-haired American singer who owned a popular club on place Pigalle.

"I don't think Man would like a lynch mob." Jamie signaled to the waiter for another gin and tonic.

"I'd better tell Lee about the gun." I finished my wine and gave the empty glass to our waiter, indicating I wanted a refill.

"She already knows," Jamie said. "He showed it to her. Took it out of the drawer and pointed it at her."

"Damn. What did Lee do?"

"The worst thing possible. She laughed at him. Wonder where they took Julien Levy for dinner tonight. Probably the Jockey." Jamie started humming "Miss Otis Regrets" again, and smiled one of the saddest smiles I'd ever seen.

That summer, our last summer, after Aziz had left, Lee spent quite a bit of time with Julien Levy, and I think Julien was one of the men who occasionally holed up in her apartment with her behind the locked door. Lee and Julien and Man made a rough threesome, and Jamie and I laughed about it, since Man would never shoot his own art dealer. Jealousy and love counted for only so much among artists. A woman could be replaced, but a good art dealer was hard to find.

Lee even managed to get Julien over to our rooms to look at Jamie's photographs before Julien sailed back to America, and so I finally met him, this dealer Man had for weeks kept as unavailable and busy as a princeling not allowed to mix with the hoi polloi. That was me and Jamie. The hoi polloi, the workers, the outsiders.

Julien looked a lot like Man. They both had thick dark hair, intense and opaque brown eyes, a tendency to haggardness in the face if they were not well fed and well rested. Julien also dressed impeccably, suit and tie and hat, even to visit the hoi polloi. He came to our rooms on a Monday night and I could tell by his steps on the stairs, heavy and a little slow, and by the way he kept looking at Lee over his shoulder, that he had come to see Jamie's work as a favor to her.

We did everything wrong, of course. Jamie tried to look artistic, with his long hair and old shirt unbuttoned at collar and cuff, his bare feet in cheap sandals bought at a street market. Instead of artistic he looked down-and-out. Unpromising. I served a tray of fancy hors d'oeuvres bought very expensively at a shop I normally wouldn't even go into because of their prices. They were fussy little things, toothpicks overladen with pineapple and bacon, soggy pastry boats filled with overcooked creamed vegetables. And sherry. My God. Did I think I was setting up a tea at an English girls' sorority?

Julien accepted one or two canapés out of politeness and praised our apartment—"Such a splendid view of the old cemetery." He admired the way I had strung lights with paper lanterns from the ceiling, approved my dress, and, in fact, commented on everything except Jamie's photographs.

When the soggy hors d'oeuvres and too-sweet sherry had been set aside, Jamie spread open his portfolio on the bare table. Lee and I took the two chairs and sat in a corner, like children trying to behave as the grown-ups talked. Lee held my hand and tried too hard to make interesting conversation. I didn't hear a word she was saying, all of my attention focused on Julien.

Julien looked at Jamie's photographs, one by one, his expression never changing, his rhythm never varying. Right thumb and forefinger to right corner of photo. Pause. Run eyes up and down, left and right. Turn photo facedown on left side of portfolio. Right thumb and forefinger to right corner of next photo. Over and over, without a single spark of interest in those opaque brown eyes.

Jamie seemed to shrink an inch, then two inches, then three, till he was slumped and round-shouldered in defeat.

"You know, those street shots are very good," Julien finally said, when the last photo had been turned facedown. "You have a feel for that kind of thing. Unfortunately, I can't sell it right now. The market's not there, people still want Atgets for that kind of thing. But maybe next year. That's the only sure thing in the art world, you know. It keeps changing."

Maybe next year. The same thing Jamie had heard in New York and London. Where would we go next? Paris had been the goal, the destination, and now it, too, was a failure.

Lee squeezed my hand hard. She rose and went and put an arm around Jamie's shoulders.

"Next year would be just fine," she said. "But of course you'll want to put him in a group show first." Lee's cheerfulness was about as real as the pearl necklace our landlady wore. You could see the hard falseness in it a mile away.

"Of course. Thank you, young man." Julien put his hat back on.

Damn. He didn't even remember Jamie's name.

Julien was out the door far too quickly. Lee lingered, blew me a kiss, whispered something to Jamie; then she, too, was gone. We heard their footsteps going down the stairs, Lee's light high-heeled clicks and Julien's heavier leather-soled thuds. At the bottom of the stairs, before they pushed open the door into the street, we heard laughter.

Jamie got drunk that night, and the next. He didn't come back to our room after working in Man's studio, and when I asked him where he had been, he wouldn't answer.

"Don't crowd him," Lee advised. "Let him lick his wounds." She had come into Boulet's to say hello, and leaned against my display counter, aiming her camera at the perfume bottles, trying various angles but never clicking the shutter. "Too dark in here. God, Nora, no wonder you're so pale. We need to get you into the fresh air."

Her concern touched me. Lee was not prone to noticing how other people were doing, if the truth be told. Like many artists, she could be on the self-absorbed side.

"I'm worried about Jamie," I said. "That visit from Julien really depressed him."

Lee fidgeted with the sample bottles, turning them this way and that to see if she could make them catch any light. "It takes time," she murmured.

"How much time? We left Poughkeepsie five years ago, and Jamie hasn't had a single show. Anywhere. I think he's giving up."

"I'll talk to him. Do you have a small size of this?" She held up the sample of Nubian Amber. "It reminds me of Aziz."

"That's because it's Nimet's fragrance."

Lee dropped the bottle back on the counter and stared at it as if it had suddenly become dangerous. Monsieur Boulet, sitting in his mezzanine office, heard the loud clank and peered out his window, made an exaggerated Gallic shrug, and returned to his newspaper.

"How do you know her perfume?" Lee looked at me with suspicion.

"Because she came in here once. Trying to get information about you. I told you."

"Did you? I must not have been paying attention."

"Always a possibility."

"And what is that supposed to mean?"

"Lee, you do know that Man is carrying a pistol?"

"Of course I know. So what? You think he would actually use

it?" She laughed. She put her hand up, straight-armed, and made a gun barrel of her forefinger, as children do. "Bang," she said. "Maybe I'll shoot him."

"That's not funny."

"No. It's not. But it is ever so slightly boring. Such a cliché."

# CHAPTER THIRTEEN

Over that long, hot summer our lives returned to a kind of normalcy. Jamie worked for Man, I sold perfumes at Boulet's, Lee either posed for *Vogue* modeling shoots or wandered the city with her folding Kodak, taking photographs of shadows, anything menacing that caught her eye. We became a foursome again, meeting at cafés in the evening, making small talk that passed the hours. Lee, perhaps out of pity for Man, spent more time with him and less time "adventuring," as she called it in our whispered conversations.

The summer heat eviscerated us till we were no more than working, sweating, drinking shells who sometimes couldn't even be roused to go to the Dôme for a plate of potato salad and cold sausage.

Jamie and I grew closer than ever. He was so tender in bed he sometimes reduced me to tears. Before Julien came to the studio and thumbed so listlessly through Jamie's work, our lovemaking had grown routine and infrequent. Now, after Julien, it was as if Jamie couldn't get enough of me. Nor I of him. We clung together, shipwreck survivors sharing the same plank, only I hadn't noticed yet that there had been a shipwreck. I was happy, and nothing in the world can make you oblivious to your surroundings like happiness.

That morning, the morning of the day when I had to look, and look hard, Jamie woke me by gently poking his elbow into my ribs. "Listen," he whispered. "They are going at it again."

Unwillingly, I opened my eyes to the new day, squinting and yawning, then rolled even closer to Jamie so that our bodies met at chest, hips, thighs, and knees. From next door, through the thin walls of our apartment, I could hear Madame Blancard screeching at her husband, who had apparently just come home from a very long evening out. It was six thirty in the morning and the sky was streaked with lavender and coral over the red tile roofs of Paris.

Jamie and I, clinging to each other, giggled like schoolchildren as the missus called her husband every name in the book: louse, worm, maggot, mule—this was how we had learned our zoology terms in our chosen language. Then, the sins: fornicator, philanderer, liar, deceiver.

"What was that last one?" I whispered, catching a word I did not know.

"I think she just called him a eunuch."

"Ah. Then the quarrel will end soon and we can go back to sleep." We had been at the Jockey until midnight, and then spent another three hours in Lee's studio, drinking. Fatigue pressed me heavily into the mattress and I wanted only to sleep longer.

Next door, Monsieur Blancard exploded with rage. There was the sound of flesh violently meeting flesh. Weeping. A change in atmosphere, perceivable even through the walls. Sounds of cooing, then the creak, creak of bedsprings. It was how all their arguments were settled, with insults, a blow or two, then lovemaking.

"Let's quarrel," Jamie said. "Then we can make up."

"Let's make up without quarreling. And then let me sleep."

When I awoke the second time, Jamie had already left for Man's studio. Man himself wouldn't be there till later in the morning, but Jamie was expected to show up early, tidying, sorting, labeling, setting up the chemical baths in the developing room, so that when Man arrived, he could start immediately to work.

On our little table, Jamie had set a place for me with bread and jam, milk and coffee. Jamie was thoughtful that way. There had been only brothers in his family, no sisters, and he still seemed a bit in awe of women in general and of me in particular. I liked it that way. When he looked at me, I felt bathed in a golden light, the way saints are on holy cards.

He had become even more attentive that summer and I could feel something building up, an electricity in the air. I was certain he was going to say we should get married. Married, and then that return trip to New York, because as much as I loved Paris, I knew it was temporary, knew a moment would come when we would both feel we had overstayed our welcome and it was time to go home. Departure was in the air, a smell of smoke and grit and baker's yeast, the damp smell of leaves before they drop in the autumn.

I took my bread and coffee and sat by the open window, filled with the sense of being loved by Jamie

"Hey! Daydreamer! Throw me the key!"

Lee was down in the street, shouting up at me. She still wore her dress of the night before, a short sheath printed with tiger stripes. Her blond hair stood around her head like a mane and her ruined mascara made dark circles around her eyes. She hadn't been home yet.

"Key?" she shouted again. Lee was hard to take, first thing in the morning. She brought a turbulence that seemed to set everything about her in motion.

I preferred my mornings calm. We lived hard, dancing and drinking late into the night, rising early, busy all day, trying to earn money, to make contacts, to see everything that was to be seen, and of course to be seen. There was a frenzy to life that Lee exacerbated, though it never really went away . . . except for my moments enfolded in Jamie's arms.

Those first few minutes of the day, when Jamie had left for the studio and I did not yet have to leave for my job, I could sit in the stillness that allowed the senses to expand and explore, to really notice the world, and how it smelled and how the floor, when you crossed it with your bare feet, was gritty with the sand the little cleaning girl used to scrub it. All the colors, the red carnations on the table, the green and yellow pâtisserie sign across the street, the blue uniforms of the schoolchildren, seemed so much brighter than they had before, and when I thought of Jamie, the colors grew even brighter.

For several weeks my senses had been sharpening, my tongue picking up on flavors I hadn't noticed before till I could barely eat; everything tasted so strongly. And the smells. The world had become all fragrance, amber and lily and dog shit in the street mixing with Monsieur Boulet's aftershave and our landlady's lunches of fried fish and boiled cabbage, an alchemy that made me want to sit still, barely breathing, my hand on my belly rising and falling with shallow breaths.

That morning, I wanted to sit, quiet and alone, wrapped in wonder, but I reached for the door key hanging on its nail and threw it down to Lee.

A moment later she banged up the stairs, shoeless. "My feet are killing me." She threw her expensive heels into the corner and took the chair opposite me, the only upholstered, somewhat comfortable chair in our room. Jamie's chair.

"You didn't go home last night," I said. Her expensive dress and silk jacket were as pleated with wrinkles as a lampshade, and stained with red wine.

"No. After you and Jamie left the café, Man went back to the studio and I went to a party. Aziz wouldn't mind. He wouldn't want me to be sad and lonely."

"I'm pretty certain Man doesn't feel that way about it."

"Man." She laughed, not happily. "Don't worry. He's not the shooting type. Any coffee and bread for a hungry friend?" Several times, Lee had made jokes about Man's pistol. She refused to take it seriously.

"Is there a type?" I gave her my second cup of coffee and the bread I had saved for my lunch.

"If I wanted someone keeping track of me, I'd have stayed home in Poughkeepsie," Lee muttered, biting angrily into the roll, leaving red lipstick marks on the bitten edge. "Come to think of it, Papa was more freethinking than Man and less of a nag."

Bells started to ring, calling the neighborhood to prayer. It wasn't Sunday, so there was either a funeral or a wedding and I thought how strange it was that we marked both events with such similar fashion: bells, flowers, a gathering, a liturgy.

"Can't stand that racket," Lee said, forcing the last bit of roll into her mouth and covering her eyes.

"I like them. . . ."

"You were going to say they remind you of home, I bet." She grinned wickedly, brushing hair out of her eyes. She had let her bobbed hair grow a little longer and curled it. Perhaps Aziz hadn't liked it as short as she normally wore it.

"No, I wasn't. I was going to say that they sound the way pine needles smell."

Lee raised one eyebrow. "You mean like Christmas morning. Too bad you bobbed your hair. If it were long, you could sell it and buy a present for Jamie. You know, 'Gift of the Magi.' You probably adore O. Henry. So sentimental."

"I wonder what Man will buy you for your birthday," I countered. "Maybe a chastity belt."

"He won't get the chance." Lee finished her coffee and put the cup down.

There was a smear of red lipstick on her cheek. I considered wiping it off for her, but decided against it.

"He must be wondering where you are. Jamie left for the studio half an hour ago and they will have begun work by now."

"Let Man wonder. I don't have any jobs today and I feel like being lazy." Lee rose and paced around the room, touching the books on our single shelf, the lamp next to the still-rumpled bed, the tattered muslin curtain of the privacy screen closing off our washing and dressing area. She had been there several times, including that disastrous night she had brought Julien, but that morning she seemed to be seeing it for the first time. "Do you get homesick?" Lee asked, turning back to me.

"You mean, do I miss American plumbing? Oh, yes."

"No. I mean home." Lee sat on the bed twisting the ring on her finger. It was an emerald, a good one. From Aziz, I assumed, since Man couldn't have afforded such a thing.

"Home is people, isn't it?" I said, not wanting to answer her question directly. I was still filled with that glowing sense of Jamie, and a question and promise of forever, and not in a mood to share that knowledge with Lee.

"People. Yes. Did you have a lover back in Poughkeepsie? You did. I can see it in your face. Do tell."

"Don't have to. He's with me here, in Paris."

"But no one loves you like your own father," Lee mused, talking more to herself than to me. "God, sometimes I really miss my father. Do you?"

"My father died years ago."

Lee, never a hypocrite, cut to the chase and didn't waste words on false sympathy.

"Did he leave you any money?" she asked.

"Only enough for a single boat ticket."

"You poor kid. My father. Well." She leaned back, clasped her hands around her knees, and smiled wickedly. "Plenty of moola. Big house, servants. But Daddy has good principles. Made us play with the workers' children so that we wouldn't think we were better than they were."

Shame is the most corrosive emotion. I could have told Lee then that we shared a certain childhood memory. I was one of those workers' children.

But I didn't tell her. In the expat community class was vague, even nonexistent. It was one of the things we all loved about being expats: identity became a form of self-creation when there was no family, no shared past, no definition forced on us by anything other than our own skills and needs. The past was all tucked in, asleep.

What would have happened if I had reminded Lee of those days we shared, the tire swing in her yard, chasing the chickens, that day she had stood on the porch in her white dress? Would it have changed anything?

The silence was a charm protecting both of us, Lee from the memory of rape and its aftermath, me from the memory of class stigma, and I did not want to lose the protection.

"It's raining. That will break the heat." Lee opened the window and extended her hand, letting the heavy drops splatter into her palm. "Can't stand reminiscing. I came to ask you to a party. Tonight. My studio, not Man's. Can you come? You and Jamie? Both of you. It's important."

"Of course both of us," I said. After the party, I thought, I would tell Jamie. He would be twenty-five in a few months. The promise to his family not to marry young ended on this birthday. Just in time.

Lee's party was the largest one of the season, all arranged at the last minute and perfect down to the last detail, despite the lack of agonized planning. She had a knack for that sort of thing, knew how to find the perfect caterer, the best wine sold at discount by the crate, flowers out of season from florists no one else had ever heard of. She must have spent a small fortune on orchids and shrimp canapés . . . and mirrors, because that was how she had decorated the studio, with mirrors all over the place, on the walls, freestanding on the floor, propped onto easels.

"You did all this in one day?" I asked when Jamie and I arrived promptly at nine. A girl hired for the evening took my coat. A waiter arrived from nowhere with a tray of champagne flutes.

I turned and saw my reflection, dozens of reflections, back-and-forth and into-infinity reflections, illuminated by flickering, disorienting candlelight.

The studio was already packed. No one ever missed one of Lee's parties—or Man's, for that matter—but that evening Lee seemed to have invited everyone she knew, and they had all come. Lady so-and-so and Maharani this and Lord that . . . all of Lee's sitters, all her artist friends, all the society people. It was like a who's who of Lee Miller's life in Paris: the poet Breton, the surrealist filmmaker Jean Cocteau, the Russian director Dimitri Buchowetski, his star actress Margot Grahame, the failed pianist turned decorator Zizi Svirsky, the publisher Donald Friede . . . all present and accounted for.

Pablo elbowed through the crowd to say hello. He looked unhappy because he did not like parties, and he hadn't brought either his wife or his mistress. But he gave me a friendly hug in greeting, then stepped back and looked hard at me, running his eyes up and down my figure. His large black eyes grew even larger and I knew he saw what no one else had yet seen.

Man was stewing in a corner, drinking whiskey rather than champagne, and his gaze never left Lee but darted around the room, following her every movement. I wondered what the hell was going on and wished I hadn't come except how could I have not come? If you saw a car careen out of control and head toward a cliff, would you really be able to look away?

It was so crowded we could barely move, much less dance, yet various couples clung together in one area of the studio, two-stepping to a soft ballad coming from the gramophone, filling the air with a scratchy sweetness. The dancers were reflected in a circle of mirrors, doubling and tripling their numbers, and I realized that evening was Lee's salute to surrealism, the way the mirrors doubled us, or cut us off at the legs or reflected some torsos as headless, depending on how the mirrors had been hung. It was a fun house for grown-ups, for artists.

Jamie disappeared a few minutes after we arrived, probably looking for the corner where a hash pipe was being passed around. The sweet exotic odor of it, stronger even than the thick smoke of French cigarettes, had greeted us at the door and already clung to my clothes and hair.

"What do you think?" Lee found me in a corner where I had retreated to wait and watch.

"Gorgeous. And a little frightening. Seven years of bad luck if one of these gets broken."

"No more bad luck for me, kiddo. To hell with that." Without looking at Man, she raised her glass in his direction. She knew he was watching, glaring, unblinking, from his own corner. "He was good to me, in his way. But that's not the same as love, is it?" She shouldered a path into the crowd and danced, by herself, eyes closed, face all dreamy and soft. I couldn't bear to look at Man, to see what he thought of this little performance.

Jamie appeared at my side. "Hey, Nora, why the wallflower? Walls will stand up by themselves, you know." He was drunk, high, carefree as he rarely was those days in sobriety. "Have a drink." He offered a bottle.

"No." The very thought of whiskey, or even champagne, made me want to gag. Soon, very soon, I would have to tell Jamie what I had suspected for several weeks.

"Spoilsport." Ah. One of Lee's terms. Over the course of the year, he had picked up quite a few of Lee's turns of phrase.

"Do you ever get tired of this?" I asked Jamie, putting my arm around his waist.

"Tired of what? Champagne I can't afford? The pickpockets at the Eiffel Tower? Snotty waiters? Man's treating me like a lackey? How could I get tired of all that? Here, have a drink."

"No!" I pushed the bottle so hard its contents sloshed over both of us.

"No need to waste it," Jamie said, wiping at my dress.

"We need to talk. Someplace quiet."

"Yes," he agreed. "We do. But let's dance first." The music on the gramophone had changed. It was an American tune, slow and sweet and wordless, the sentiment climbing up and down on clarinet notes soft as smoke. Jamie nuzzled his head into my shoulder, pressed me close to him, and I thought maybe we didn't really need to talk, maybe we could just go on and on like that, close, moving together, as sure and silent as animals without language.

At the end of the song, the electric lights were switched on, and we were bathed in the harsh reflected light ricocheting back and forth from the dozens of mirrors. People squinted as if the sun were in their eyes; they twisted their heads trying to avoid the glare.

Lee stood on a chair, banging a spoon against a glass. "I have an announcement," she shouted. "Hey! *Attention, s'il vous plaît!*"

Someone took the needle off the record. The dancing came to a standstill, conversations halted. Everyone turned in Lee's direction. Jamie dropped his arm from my waist and he, too, looked up at Lee. I saw something in his face that took me so by surprise that I fell back a little, as if I had been struck. Oh no, I thought. Not Jamie.

Lee saluted the crowd. "This is good-bye, folks. I'm going back to New York."

Everyone in the room had been politely silent before the announcement; now they were stonily so. You could have proclaimed that Greta Garbo had just flown to the moon or that France had declared an American-style prohibition, and people would not have been more dazed, though I saw satisfaction on the faces of some of the women who had been upstaged by the beautiful Lee Miller. I could think only of the expression I had seen on Jamie's face when he thought I wasn't looking.

Man still sulked in his corner, more than a little drunk by now. The room was no longer silent. It was filling with the murmur of whispers and surprised exclamations as people turned from Lee to look at Man.

The pistol was in Man's hand. He raised it. He pointed it at Lee. The gesture, so small in description, seemed to take three days, not three seconds; three days, the amount of time a panther sleeps before it lures its next victim with the sweetness of its breath.

Someone gasped. Someone pointed. Everyone saw it by then, that gleaming black pistol. Lee had gone white. Even under the red lipstick, chapped in some places, her lips were ashen.

Man took careful aim, squinting, moving the pistol slightly to the right. He was the only person in the room moving; everyone else had turned to stone. He pulled the trigger.

I heard the click and it seemed to take years for that bullet to reach its destination. To Lee's left, far too close to her, a mirror shattered.

It takes broken glass a hundred years to fall to the ground, and when it does, the noise is like an explosion. Cocteau was there that night, and years later when I saw his movie *Beauty and the Beast*, with all the breaking, flying mirrors, I wondered if he was thinking of the night when Man fired at Lee.

When it was over, there was a different sound. Lee was—whooping with laughter.

"Feel better, Man?" she shouted at him.

"Much better!" He laughed back.

Other people around me started to laugh, too, falsely, tentatively. Perhaps this was a prank. The surrealists, they go too far, *n'est-ce pas*?

Jamie thought otherwise. He dropped the whiskey bottle and lunged at Man. They grappled and Jamie ended up on top, obviously on his way to a bloody victory, when Pablo and some other man I didn't know pulled him off and separated the two.

"You damn coward!" Jamie shouted at Man.

"You absolute fool," Man said, calmly. "I missed on purpose." He used a pristine handkerchief to wipe blood from his split lip, and I knew our days in Paris were over.

Lee stepped off the chair and went to stand between Man and Jamie. She put a hand on Jamie's shoulder and whispered something to him. Jamie turned away. When he raised his head, his eyes looked directly into mine though we were separated by the length of the crowded room. In his gaze I saw everything I had most dreaded. His mouth opened as if he would say something, but instead he looked away. My heart broke with the realization.

The party ended soon after by mutual unspoken understanding. The party was well and truly over. One by one, couples disappeared from Lee's studio that night, no one bothering to say good night, just disappearing like cast members leaving a failed rehearsal.

As the revelers shuffled away in various stages of intoxication, Lee smiled often at Man, but kept a distance from him, and he, still dabbing the now rusty-stained handkerchief at his lip, stayed away from her.

Not knowing what to do, only that I had to do something, I went to where Lee had stood on her chair to make the announcement, and studied the spot. Glass, sharp-pointed shards, had fallen just a foot or two from her. She could have been injured, even if Man had purposely missed. Glass could have flown into that beautiful, perfect face of hers and ruined it forever. I remembered how she had stood close to the panther's cage, too close, tempting whatever fates had bestowed such vulnerable beauty on her, and I wished the panther had slashed her.

Lee and Jamie were standing together, not speaking. If they had been whispering, acting slyly, I think it would have been easier. Instead, they just stood there, intimacy written large on their faces. God, how tired I suddenly felt.

I dug my coat out from the pile on Lee's bed. Jamie met me at the door. "I'm going to stay a while. Make sure she's okay," he said.

"Sure," I said, shivering though it was a hot night. And then, as an afterthought: "What about me?"

"You only have to walk down the street. You'll be fine, Nora. Damn, Man just tried to shoot Lee. I don't want to leave her alone with him." There was such anguish in his look I almost felt sorry for him. Almost.

"He wasn't really going to shoot her, you know. It was just another act, a spectacle."

"I'm not so certain." He walked me to the door and then closed it on me.

I walked home alone, rehearsing lines in my head. Jamie, I'm pregnant. Think you're ready for a family yet, my darling? Think you can be ready in say, eight months' time? And what are we going to do about Lee?

By three in the morning, Jamie still hadn't come home. I knew what the next step was, the next act in this particular drama. I put my coat on and walked back down the street to Lee's studio. It was dark and silent. She hadn't locked her door. Crackers and pretzels crunched underfoot, so they heard me coming. When I pulled back the curtain on the small alcove where she kept a bed, Jamie and Lee blinked up at me, their arms wrapped around each other. None of us said anything. What could words express that the look in Jamie's face did not?

I stood there for what felt like an eternity. They stared back and our speechlessness thickened our tongues and our wits, reduced us to animals incapable of language. I could have roared or whimpered. That was all. Silence was better. Stupidly, I bent over and picked up a bottle that had fallen off Lee's table. Perfume. The room stank of attar of rose. I put the bottle back in its place and turned to go.

I wandered the streets, after that, watching the dawn turn the eastern sky a dingy gray as the early laborers made their way to bakery shops, the stalls of Les Halles, and the few construction areas still being worked on in Depression-quieted Paris.

When I finally returned, exhausted, to our room, Jamie was stepping out from behind the screen where we kept the towels and soap and washbasin. His sandy hair was tousled, his skin damp and pink from a scrubbing. The morning light sculpted deep shadows under his cheekbones. He had never looked more beautiful and I had never loved him more than I did in that moment just before it was all to end.

"Say something," he said. "Don't just stand there, all silent and wounded."

"I am wounded. But I will say something, since you asked me to. A question or two. How long?"

He knew exactly what I meant. "A few months."

"How many is a few?" I needed a certain specificity, needed the incision to be clean and sharp as he cut out my heart.

Jamie sat on the bed and rubbed his damp hair with the towel. I used to do that. Dry his hair for him.

"After Lee came back from St. Moritz. That's when it started."

Christmas. New Year's. The day at the zoo when Lee had gone on and on about Aziz, in front of the panther's cage. All that time she had been sleeping with Jamie.

"Your idea or hers?"

"Why does that matter?" He threw the wet towel on the floor and stared at it.

"It does."

"One night in the studio when Man was out with Picasso, Lee started to cry. Something had happened that day, she wouldn't say what, but it made her sad. She was crying, for God's sake, Nora."

"You poor sap," I said. I sat next to him, feeling numb except for that strange ache in my stomach, that beginning of a new life. Jamie stood up and stepped into his trousers, turning sideways to zip up in that strangely coy manner men seem to reserve for that one single gesture.

"I have a shoot this morning. I'm going to work."

"And then what? Me or Lee. You can't have both."

"It's not that easy," he said, buttoning his creased shirt.

"Yes, it is."

Realizing that he was not going to answer quickly, that he was not going to open his arms and beg forgiveness, swear singular and undying love, was more painful than finding him in bed with Lee had been.

"You have to think about it. That's an answer in itself." I slumped onto our bed. My knees were quaking; the floor, the formerly solid, all-too-hard floor, had turned to liquid beneath my feet.

I had planned, this morning, to tell him about my pregnancy. Now I saw I could not. Jamie would do the right thing, I knew. He would marry me. And grow to resent me, perhaps hate me.

"Let's talk later," he said. On his way out the door he stopped and patted my shoulder, as if I were a child who had dropped her ice-cream cone.

"Me or Lee," I called after him.

I got my answer later that day, when I went to Lee's studio looking for him. The door was locked. I knocked on it until Lee answered. She was wearing Jamie's shirt, nothing else. There was a look on her face, a hardness, a kind of challenge, that reminded me of the little girl who always climbed to the very top of the tree. Who always won the race. Over her shoulder, I could see Jamie still in her bed. She hadn't pulled shut the curtain on the alcove.

"Good," I said, and not even I knew what I meant by that.

Jamie did speak, that time. "Damn," he said.

Lee put her hand on my arm. "It doesn't mean anything," she said.

"It may not mean anything to you, but it does to me. And it will to him."

The room still stank of attar of rose.

Next act: abandoned, lovelorn woman wanders down a darkening street. If this were a photograph, it would have been a distance shot, showing the woman dwarfed by the looming buildings of a city not her own. When Lee betrayed me, I lost Paris as well as Jamie.

I went back to the room I had shared with Jamie, threw my clothes into my suitcase, and walked down the three flights of stairs for the last time, with no idea of where I was going or what I would do. I knew only I could not go back to Poughkeepsie, become a regatta girl with a fatherless child, the focus of gossip; the girl who brought silence and raised eyebrows into every room she entered. Nor could I force Jamie into a shotgun marriage. We both deserved better than long years of a marriage in which resentment eventually filled the days and nights, the wife feeling wasted, the husband trapped. A marriage like the one my mother and father had. I wouldn't marry Jamie knowing he was now in love with Lee.

That was when I ran into Pablo.

I was crossing the Pont Neuf and he was going in the opposite direction, so we met in the middle. He didn't kiss my cheek or even greet me, yet he saw the situation for what it was. The suitcase was a giveaway. We stood there together, leaning over the bridge and staring into the rippling gray water of the Seine, not saying anything for a long while. Pablo puffed on a cigarette and I worked to keep my eyes dry.

"You didn't tell him," Pablo said. "That you're pregnant. Don't look so surprised. That's what artists do. They see things. That's why Jamie wasn't a very good artist. He saw only what he wanted to see."

"No. I didn't tell him."

More silence. Pablo coughed. He nodded at my suitcase, then took out a little scrap of paper and wrote down a name, an address, a phone number.

"I have a friend," he said. "I knew her husband. She's old, lives alone. She would be glad for company. Go there, and have your baby. I'll call her and tell her you're coming."

The address was in Grasse. The south. Where they made perfume.

"Okay. Thanks." I took the scrap of paper.

Pablo patted my shoulder. "Courage," he said.

He left, and I was alone. Bereft. Heartbroken. You can go back to the room, I told myself. Pretend this hasn't happened. Wait for

Jamie to wake up, to see what Lee really is, that he is just another toss to her. You can ask Man for the name of an obliging doctor to take care of this.

No. I couldn't. I wasn't the same. Jamie wasn't the same. Our very realities had changed and I couldn't go back to before that moment when I saw the way Jamie looked at Lee.

As for the child I carried, I wanted it. I was filled with curiosity: was it a boy or a girl? I already longed to hold her. A barge motored under the bridge, grays and browns over green water, a country family sitting on the deck, lunching on bread and cheese and wine from a straw-covered bottle. Children scuttled in and out of the barrels and sacks, playing. They waved up at me. I waved back.

# PART TWO

# NOTE DE COEUR

The middle notes, the *notes de coeur*, rise after the *départ* has opened the senses to possibility and the top notes have begun the narrative. The nose loves stories, and while the top notes are the "once upon a time" opening, the middle notes begin to suggest destiny. Is the scent telling a story of passion now or remembered passion? Perhaps of love to come? Jasmine, for example, mixes well with almost any other oil, and at the same time has an almost hypnotic effect, and so can suggest past, present, or future. It must have a companion to define its story. In fact, the real story of modern perfumes is the art of blending, just as the different people who are in it are the real substance of any one life.

—Notebooks of N. Tours

# CHAPTER FOURTEEN

Sometimes I wonder what would have happened if I had stayed instead of run. If I had fought and wept and shouted. Would it have made any difference? Would any of us have been spared what was to come if I had forced that situation to a different conclusion? That's the problem with the finite. You can open only one door at a time, and you'll never know what was behind the door you didn't open.

In October, Lee Miller sailed home, back to the States. I had a letter from Pablo telling me. "Jamie asked for your address, but I did not give it to him, as you requested," Pablo wrote. Jamie could have insisted, I thought. He could have somehow forced Pablo to tell him where I was; he could have come after me. He had not. And that was that.

The rest of Pablo's brief letter was filled with news of Lee and Man. Lee had left him soon after that catastrophic party. Man had walked in the cold autumn rain to the Dôme, sat down next to a friend, and dropped his pistol on the table, saying he wished he were dead. And then he went back to his studio and made a self-portrait of himself with a rope around his neck and the pistol pointed at his own head.

It was very melodramatic. He knew how to create an effect. Love was love, but art was art and though he mixed the two a little, he never confused them.

"Man will survive it, I think," Pablo wrote. "It is mostly his pride that has been injured. Lee is going back to New York. I think Jamie will go with her."

I folded the letter back up and put it in the bottom of my suitcase, feeling as if I were folding up and putting away my own youth. The scent of rose, Jamie's favorite, would become for me a scent of loss. Rose had once been my favorite scent. Lee stole that as well. The envelope from Pablo included a note from Jamie and a wad of folded bills, all our money except the amount he would need for the crossing:

"I'm sorry, Nora. I never meant to hurt you. These things just happen, don't they? Let me know if you need anything. Pablo wouldn't tell me where you were, he said you didn't want him to. I think I understand. I hope someday we can be friends."

And this was the strangest thing of all. Despite the hurt, the anger, the jealousy, the betrayal, if anyone had asked, I would have said, "Yes, Lee is my friend," and "Yes, I love Jamie." Perhaps there is memory beyond experience. Perhaps we all sensed that the violence of Lee's farewell party was a prophecy of things to come, when the bullet would not purposely miss the mark, when survival would be all that mattered, really. Seven years and more of bad luck was on its way. Measured up against simply staying alive despite the odds, everything else was child's play. We had played rough, that was all.

I lost touch with Lee again, after that autumn of '32. In Grasse, in the southern hills high above the Riviera, far from the clubs and cafés and parties of Paris, few people had heard of her, or of Man Ray. And that was fine with me.

My life acquired a new focus: my daughter. Just as Jamie had become my focus when I was sixteen, now his daughter became the center of my life. Lee became something from a different lifetime, sensed in strange ways when a certain breeze picked up or when I woke at three in the morning and didn't know what had awakened me.

"Men!" said Pablo Picasso's friend Natalia Hughes, the first morning I was with her, vomiting wearily into a slop bucket. She wiped my forehead and tsk-tsked in sympathy.

Madame Natalia Hughes was the widow of Eugène Hughes, wine merchant of Grasse, and before that the widow of Senia Alexandrov of St. Petersburg, and daughter of Vladimir and Eugenia Rodyanov, also of St. Petersburg. Outcasts of the revolution. That's what she called her parents, and herself and her first husband. "They drove us from our homes! And when I think of the poor tsar and tsarina and their children . . ." She shook her frizzed, slightly orange curls.

Madame Hughes was seventy when she first opened her door to me, eyed me up and down for several minutes, then said, with her Russian-accented French, "You'd better come in. You don't look well. Come, come."

After a very long day of trains and buses through the foreign south of France, I had arrived in Grasse. It was already late and dark and cold in the way that ancient stone towns can be cold, giving off an accumulated damp chilliness as soon as the sun sets.

Natalia Hughes' house was off the main square, place aux Aires, high up in the center of town, behind a large three-tiered fountain. Her house was ochre, like the other houses, steep and tall with a very austere facade adorned only by peeling pale blue shutters. There was a little terrace off the downstairs sitting room, just large enough for a table and three or four chairs.

I could see for miles from that terrace, down to the other tiny gardens of houses on streets below us, to the lavender fields and olive orchards beyond Grasse, and the slumbering stony hills beyond the fields. When I walked to the other side of town, to the south, I could see all the way down to the ocean, miles and miles away, so steep were the hills. But all of those discoveries were made in the days to come, when I wandered the old city, trying to feel as little as possible, because when emotions did surface, they were anger and fear and more than a touch of simple self-pity. That first evening I was too exhausted for anything but a quick handshake and a sincere thank-you.

"Pablo says you are an intelligent girl," Madame Hughes said, taking my suitcase and carrying it up a narrow, steep flight of stairs, her hair shining like a torch leading the way. "That is important to me, that you are an intelligent girl. And you read nicely? You will read to me. We will keep each other company. Until your baby comes."

"Until my baby comes," I agreed, having no idea what would happen after that.

Perhaps I am making this sound an easy thing for me, this journey to Grasse, to my life as a mother without a husband.

It was not. Some days I did nothing but walk all day, up and down the twisted, narrow streets, feeling like an animal caught in a maze. I missed Paris the way a person is missed, with pain and regret.

I thought often of a plaster death mask I had seen once in Paris, at the Quai du Louvre. This was where *L'Inconnue de la Seine*, the drowned girl fished out of the Seine in the 1880s, had been found.

All the artists of Paris had a copy of her death mask, that lovely sixteen-year-old girl who, fifty years before, had thrown herself into the river. The doctor who had prepared her for burial, after she had been taken back from the river to which she had given herself, had fallen in love with her and made a mask of her face. Her smile was as lovely as that of the Mona Lisa and the surrealists adopted her as a symbol of their own lost loves . . . or perhaps a symbol of the fragility of life and beauty. I thought of *L'Inconnue* often.

But just as my thoughts turned dark during those days of walking the old town, I would turn a corner and see a stone house with potted flowers on the windowsills, bright red geraniums and mossy ferns against gray stone and ochre, and somehow the colors gave me courage . . . the colors of the flowers, and the permeating scents accumulated from the surrounding lavender fields and jasmine farms. Grasse had once been a glove-making city, and because tanning leather is a smelly process at best, it soon also had a few perfumers to scent the gloves. By the nineteenth century, Grasse had become the perfume capital of France.

I had fled to the center of the world my father had told me about, where amber, jasmine, rose, cedarwood, vanilla, geranium, and rosemary and all the lovely scents met in little glass bottles displayed in shopwindows. The perfumes I had sold at Boulet's had mostly come from Grasse. In a way, I had come home.

Grasse, though, was not an easy city to love. Paris had been light and open and festive. Grasse was closed, dark, somber, especially in the shortening autumn days. Paris played and flirted and tempted. Grasse held her secrets dark and close. There were few straight lines in the city, few opportunities to view any expanse longer than half a block ahead, unless I climbed to a high hill to see the landscape or the ocean.

Even time seemed lost. I could walk over tiles set in place a thousand years ago, and then pass a house where a radio was playing Duke Ellington. Time turned and twisted on itself.

As days turned to weeks, I began to feel safe there. Not happy, and also not unhappy. Just existing, in the way that animals exist, eating and sleeping and feeling that new growth in the womb. I found a new rhythm to my life, and new friendships, new thoughts in new mornings.

In exchange for room and board, I was to cook and clean for the two of us, and read to Madame Hughes in the evenings when she did not want to play her piano. I went to the butcher and the greengrocer to get ingredients for our noonday meal. As they simmered away on the stove, I rested, hand on my belly. Madame and I ate together in her tiny dining room, surrounded by lace doilies and statues of the Virgin Mary and dozens of silver-framed photographs topping the side tables and bureau.

Sometimes in the evenings, Madame played her piano. She was a magnificent pianist, her long nimble fingers dancing up and down the keys as she played Chopin and Schubert, Liszt and Borodin.

For Sunday dinners, Madame Hughes invited her oldest friends, Monsieur and Madame LaRosa, to join us. They were a handsome middle-aged couple, he impressive with a full beard just beginning to turn gray, she well rounded in shape and with a quick smile. Her perfume was Guerlain's Parfum des Champs-Élysées and she was in love with all things Parisian, though she had never been there. I thought that was why she liked me: I had lived in Paris. His family was one of the larger landowners in the area, and supplied much of the jasmine and lavender the perfume factories used. His great-grandfather had been invited to meet Queen Victoria when she vacationed in Grasse a hundred years before. People in Grasse did not forget things like that.

Monsieur LaRosa was much amused by my ability to name the different oils in perfumes with just one or two sniffs, and every Sunday he would bring a different sample to test me: old-fashioned Jardin de Mon Curé, smelling much like my father's old garden, full of roses and lavender; the new Arpège with its modern notes of honeysuckle, coriander, and vetiver; Jicky, with its blended notes of bergamot, rose, and coumarin.

Some of his perfumes were quite old, dating to Napoleonic France. His family had made a point of collecting them much the way other people collect fine wines.

"God made Grasse so that the world could have perfume," was his motto, repeated several times each visit.

The other people of Grasse, the shopkeepers, the postman, the local gendarme, were politely formal with me. They were accustomed to having strangers in their midst, the occasional vacationer who wandered south from Paris or north from Nice. Such people did not stay and so did not matter. It seemed I was staying. I was certain there was plenty of speculation and gossip about Madame Hughes' new companion.

Madame Hughes and I soon grew close in the way that women do when there is a great age gap between them: I found her interesting and she found me amusing. She would tell stories of her early years in St. Petersburg, the glittering balls and sable coats, dancing in the style of Isadora Duncan in her short Grecian tunic for the court at the Summer Palace; the time she had given a private piano recital for the tsarina Alexandra and her children, and how the children had spun around and danced when she played "The Flight of the Bumblebee."

Her husband, Senia, had been part of Tsar Nicholas' special guard, an older man devoted to his young wife. And then, the revolution, that terrible leaving behind of all that was known, the flight to safety in a foreign country.

"Never again will I be forced from my home," Madame Hughes would exclaim, waving her long fingers with their many rings. "Sleeping in dirty hotels with bedbugs, depending on strangers and never knowing if you can trust them. No. I came here. Here I stay."

Southern France was spiced with these old Russian émigrés. The men, nodding over their *cafés crèmes* and brandies, could be seen in the cafés; their wives and daughters worked in shops and salons all along the Riviera.

Madame's first husband had been wiser than many of the other Russian émigrés, though, and saw all too clearly that on a permanent basis the seaside would become too popular, too expensive for them, so he bought a little house in Grasse, in the hills, or as the locals called it, the balconies of the Riviera. A song, Madame said. That's what he paid for it. She always fluttered her veined hands at this point in the story, indicating the flaking paint on the yellow walls of her sitting room, the scuffed, unvarnished floor underneath the threadbare Oriental carpets. A year after moving there he collapsed one day while watering a potted lemon tree, and never recovered.

"My poor Senia," she would say. "He was a very passionate man." She would wink. "Perhaps if he had been calmer . . ." Five years later she married Monsieur Eugène Hughes, of Grasse. Monsieur Hughes had been calm, but he died anyway, three years after the wedding.

"I have not had good luck with my marriages," she would conclude, sighing. "Thank heavens Senia left me with my son, Nicky. Eugène and I had no children. I was, you understand, no longer young." Sigh. A shake of the head. A playful smile as she remembered things she did not wish to tell me.

Madame lived frugally, content with her chipped china and moth-damaged curtains and the other possessions that had survived years and events that fragile people had not survived. Her most valued possession was the baby grand piano. She stroked it every time she passed it, murmured words of love and encouragement.

Pablo, in his letter to her, had not told her I was pregnant and she admitted, years later, that her first impulse had been to throw me out, that first morning when she held my head as I vomited into a slop bucket. Madame was not enthusiastic about having a child in the house. All that noise. And the scandal! But I had looked so pitiful, she explained. Far too young to be on my own.

Her one child, now forty-five years old, was a widower who ran a seaside hotel in Nice, and a city hotel in Lyon. That was how she had met Pablo Picasso. He had stayed at the Nice hotel some years ago and Nicky had bought some of Pablo's early works. Those drawings were now worth a pretty penny and Monsieur Picasso wrote to her twice a year, inquiring after her health. *Et voilà!* Again, that fluttering of hands for emphasis.

Picasso, Lee had once told me, kept track of people who owned his works, making sure they did not sell them cheaply or even, sometimes, without his permission. It was one of his methods for controlling his prices and his reputation. "He's clever, that little Spaniard," Lee had said.

In Grasse, Madame and I were both outsiders in a place where families went back for generations. We were part of the great diaspora of people discontented or endangered by their native geography and so forced to inhabit foreign places.

By agreement, the father of my child was never mentioned, not even after my belly grew so big I looked like I had swallowed a watermelon whole. Not being able to talk about Jamie to anyone was like losing him all over again, but it was good preparation for my future as a mother without a husband.

When I went and stood in line under the awning of the greengrocer's to get vegetables for our evening soup, I listened as Madame Casseli complained about her husband's snoring, and Madame Brialy sighed over her husband's gambling. They would mutter together with genuine pleasure, women full with their men, their lives.

"How is Madame Hughes today?" Madame Brialy would ask me. "And the baby? Does the kicking wake you up at night? You look pale." No one asked about my husband. They politely called me madame rather than mademoiselle, but they knew. Scandal has a scent to it that good housewives easily pick up, a tang of history and failed reputation, perhaps like the methane sourness given off by apples gone bad.

The butcher, Monsieur Bonner, did not call me madame or mademoiselle but only Nora, as if we were old friends. He looked at me too long and too hard, and once he put his hand on my belly. I slapped it away. He sneered and the cut of beef he sold me that day was full of gristle.

One night in February when winds rattled the shutters and a damp cold filled the house, I mentioned to Madame Hughes that I had not written to my mother for several months. Madame tsk-tsked and brought down from her desk a pen and inkwell and several sheets of thick cream-colored stationery. "You will tell her," she ordered. "She must know there is to be a grandchild."

It was difficult to write that letter, saying the words that mothers were terrified to hear: a child, no husband. We had never been very close and in Grasse I felt even more distant from her than I had in Paris. Yet Madame was right. Momma had to be told. I wrote the letter and posted it the next day.

My mother wrote back a month later, saying "I told you so," and "don't plan on coming home any time soon." Not till it was sorted out, though what she meant by sorted out I didn't understand. Jamie, she wrote, had come home from Paris and was in New York City, taking photographs for the society columns. "Is he the father?" she wanted to know. "Or did you act like a real tart, there in Paris? Why is Jamie in New York with Lee Miller? I just don't understand you young people."

My mother had enclosed a clipping from the *World-Telegram* showing Lee in her French beret and fur coat, smiling into the camera from the railings of the arriving ship. The reporter had described her as the most beautiful woman in the "cargo of celebrities" on board and Lee herself was quoted as saying she was coming home to photograph Americans, because "everyone here is so good-looking." Behind her, appearing a little lost in the crowd, was Jamie, looking not toward the camera, but at Lee.

Jealousy put a vise around my chest so that it was hard to breathe.

"You know this woman?" Madame Hughes was reading over my shoulder. She leaned close to me and I smelled the lavender of her clothes, the orange water she used to rinse her hair, her perfume heavy with amber and tea rose.

"Yes, I know her."

She took the newspaper clipping and studied it. "Very lovely. But there is trouble in her face." She put the clipping facedown on the table.

I wrote back, denying that Jamie was the father. Let Mother make of it what she would.

She wrote again some months later, including newspaper clippings of the doings of Lee Miller. Salt in the wound. I thought she sensed my trouble and did it on purpose. She sent the clipped and saved pages from *Vogue* showing Lee modeling a sequined evening gown by Lanvin, and ads for Lee's new photography studio on East Forty-eighth Street, extolled as the American branch of the Man Ray School of Photography. Lee had left Man, but not his connections, not his useful reputation.

My child was born in June, when Grasse was filled with the fragrance of blooming roses. It was a difficult birth and the workers who marched down the street carrying baskets of dawn-picked roses for the perfume factories must have been appalled by my screams. The midwife's concerned face terrified me because I thought I saw death in it; the pain was that bad. I fought her for a day and a half, and when the baby was finally put in my arms, I was too exhausted to do anything but count the fingers and toes before I fell into a feathery unconsciousness.

"She's hungry," Madame Hughes said when I woke up. "You must feed her now."

The baby's eyes met mine. She waved her minuscule fists. What I experienced was not so much love, not at first, though of course a mother loves her child, but a sense of being taken over, occupied, much as an army occupies a country. One hopes for a peaceful outcome, but my life was no longer my own.

Thankfully Madame Hughes did not ask me to leave her home. She had been completely won over by the baby. Instead, she opened a larger room for me and equipped it with a new mattress, new curtains, and a cot for Dahlia. When Dahlia was a few months old, she was baptized. Madame Natalia—we were on more familiar terms by then—insisted on this, and she insisted that Monsieur LaRosa and his wife be the godparents. "He is powerful, influential," she said. "People listen to him."

She invited all the neighbors to come and celebrate with us, and fed them chicken and cheeses and fruits. "A great expense!" she wailed with the usual flurry of her ringed hands. "But it must be done. Bad luck if not!" So I stood at the baptismal font, in the ancient Cathédrale Notre-Dame-du-Puy, dizzy from lack of sleep, and watched as the priest dribbled water over Dahlia's tiny pink forehead and pronounced the words that made her a member of the church and the Notre-Dame congregation. I thought perhaps my father, with his old Catholic French heritage, would have been pleased.

Later, I learned that the only reason the priest had agreed to the baptism of the fatherless child was because Monsieur LaRosa, who had agreed to pay for certain repairs to the church, had insisted.

I announced the birth in a letter to my mother, who after several months of angry silence sent me a package with booties and a little cap and a warning that she hadn't mentioned her granddaughter to anyone in Poughkeepsie. She also enclosed new clippings about Lee punctuated with her own gossip. Lee had been ill. Fatigue and overwork and perhaps a little too much drinking and dancing, most people suspected, but I knew better. It was that old lingering poison from her rape, the gonorrhea. When she was stressed or overworked, she had to go to bed for days, sometimes weeks. It had happened once or twice in Paris as well, though we had never discussed the true cause of her illness.

Taken by her father to the Poconos for a recovery, Lee had returned and started a new fad in Poughkeepsie for "Pluto Water," prescribed by Lee's Dr. Hay, for purging and losing weight. My own momma had lost eight pounds and was feeling very young and lively, she wrote.

The clippings included photographs Lee had taken for *Vogue*, advertising perfumes and cosmetics, lovely photos of all the desirables made even more so by good lighting and staged settings. The work looked static, though, as if her imagination had gone to sleep. Lee was bored; I could see it in the pictures. "Her brother Eric is in New York with her, working in her darkroom," Momma wrote. No mention of Jamie in that letter. I wondered if he was working in Lee's darkroom alongside Eric.

And then, just as I studied the last clipping, I heard Dahlia give a little whimper and I went to pick her up, to give her everything of me that others hadn't wanted, or hadn't wanted for long.

From the very start, Dahlia was a possessive child, crying when I left a room, wailing inconsolably if anyone else took her from my arms. She seemed to be saying I belonged only to her, and soon I believed her. Dahlia's huge eyes would follow my every move; she smiled when I smiled, cried if I frowned. I was completely taken over by her.

For Christmas that year, Dahlia's first, Madame Natalia's son came up from Nice to visit. She had warned me he was coming with several admonitions and shakings of her finger.

"He is a charmer," she said. "A real ladies' man. You must resist temptation."

Only mildly curious, I barely brushed my hair, and didn't bother putting on lipstick. I was exhausted from being up most nights, walking with the wailing Dahlia in my arms, but I also did not want to cause Madame concern by appearing to be primping for her son. If he was good-looking, it was of no concern to me. I was done with men.

So when I opened the door, wearing a gravy-stained apron and with my hair falling into my eyes, he was as taken aback as I. The charmer was a stout, middle-aged man with thinning hair.

"Ah," he said, startled. "You are the new companion my mother has written about in her letters." There was disapproval in his voice.

"Call me Nora," I said, extending my hand for a shake. He looked at the food stains on my fingers, sighed, and gallantly, bravely took that hand and kissed it.

"You may call me Monsieur Alexandrov," he said. After an appraising moment, he did something completely unexpected. He brushed my hair out of my eyes and smiled at me. It was a good smile.

From the kitchen, Dahlia, strapped into a cushioned chair, began to wail.

"My child," I said, turning sideways and getting ready to sprint down the hall.

"Yes. She calls. I will go find Mother."

"Sitting room," I said. "At the piano." A chord sounded, the opening notes of "Pomp and Circumstance" in honor of Nicky's arrival.

After dinner, sitting by the little Christmas tree, Monsieur Alexandrov, his collar and vest unbuttoned to accommodate the feast we'd just eaten, entertained us with stories of Nice, of the vacationing moving picture stars and composers, artists, and poets who could be seen in the casinos in the evening and nursing hangovers on the boardwalk in the afternoon. They were especially thick on the ground in February when Carnival began, and Monsieur Alexandrov was already stocking his little hotel with champagne and bags of confetti for the celebrations to come.

Monsieur had a good ear for gossip and a wonderful way of enhancing it in his storytelling. We laughed all evening and I found myself telling him some of my own stories, mostly of parties with Lee and Man, that evening at Zizi's when I had worn a lobster on my head. I did not mention Jamie.

"You must find Grasse boring," he said.

Upstairs, Dahlia wailed. "Not exactly," I said, getting up to go to her.

Monsieur Alexandrov visited irregularly but always for Christmas and the Fête du Jasmin in early August. "He comes to see the girls," Madame Natalia told me that August. "You will see what I mean."

And I did. The jasmine festival began in the afternoon with a parade of floats down the rue du Pays. Topping each float was a duo or trio of pretty young girls dressed as flowers, the stems and petals of which covered only what must absolutely be covered in public. The normally modest young women of Grasse became sirens for the day. They threw baskets and baskets of flowers to the cheering crowd, drenching us in their perfumes. Dahlia shrieked with delight.

Monsieur Alexandrov gave each float a long, appraising glance and occasionally licked his lips wolfishly. Once, he caught me looking at him and again gave me that large, warm smile. There were fireworks after sunset, and we sat on the little terrace, drinking wine and watching them.

"Not too much," Madame Natalia warned me. "Not before the child is weaned." She carefully placed her chair between mine and her son's.

# CHAPTER FIFTEEN

Dahlia had just said her first words—*"Maman, chat, chouchou"*—when I received the letter from my mother saying that Lee Miller had done something very strange. "She's come back to Poughkeepsie from New York with an Egyptian in tow! She has married him! Can you believe it? I wonder if she'll end up living in a tent or a harem."

I thought of Aziz, in his tailored silk suits, his quietly gracious manners . . . with his wife, Nimet, named one of the most beautiful women of the century. I guessed that marriage was officially over. Guessed Jamie was history as well. I put down Dahlia's spoon, still filled with pureed squash, and tested my feelings. A surge of satisfaction made me smile, but only briefly. I didn't want revenge. I had wanted Jamie more than anything in the world, and Lee had discarded him, just as she had discarded so many others. What would Jamie do now?

My child screamed, banging her tiny fists on the table, forcing my attention back to her. I eased the spoon into her mouth, but she angrily spit out the squash and knitted her dark eyebrows at me, threatening a storm.

"That blouse will never be white again," Madame Natalia said, wiping at me with a towel. Dahlia laughed.

"Little devil," I said, tickling her squash-covered chin. "Momma's trying to read a letter."

"No," Dahlia said.

"She is precocious," Madame Natalia said. "That word doesn't usually show up for another year or so."

Several months later Momma sent a newspaper clipping of Lee on the *Conte di Savoia*, leaning over the railing and waving for the cameras, getting ready to sail off to Alexandria, and the clipping from the *New York Times*: "Lee Miller a Bride."

Lee looked radiant, healthy, and full of hope. Aziz, standing next to her, looked a little frightened, I thought. There's an old nursery room puzzle: what do you do when you've caught the tiger by the tail?

"Jamie is back in Poughkeepsie," Momma finished. "Working for his father at the bakery. Still takes those photographs of his. You'd think he'd have given up his little hobby by now."

That could have been my life. Jamie and me in Poughkeepsie, first child born exactly nine months after the wedding and then a married life so long we occasionally found each other boring. Boring. Jamie? No. Sometimes there was a sensation on my shoulder blade where he used to kiss me, a memory burned into my very flesh.

When Dahlia was two, and Madame Natalia offered to watch over her for several hours each day, I decided it was time to work again. And in Grasse, the best work for anyone whose family did not own a bakery or café was in the perfume industry.

Pablo's offer, two and a half years before, of a friend's home in Grasse as a solution to my "predicament" had been more than coincidental. He had given it thought, and arrived at a perfect solution.

During a spring Sunday afternoon dinner I told Monsieur LaRosa how I had sold perfumes in Paris. We had just finished a plate of goat cheese flavored with rosemary and were looking forward to the citron tart. There was a vase of fresh mimosas on the table and Monsieur LaRosa tapped it thoughtfully, considering.

"Would Fragonard do?" he asked. There were dozens of perfumeries in Grasse and I had expected to work at one of the smaller ones; Fragonard was old and large and very famous. The very next week I had a part-time job in their shop, waiting on the American and English tourists who couldn't even say in French, "I'll try that fragrance" or "How much for the larger bottle?" The sales skills I'd practiced in Paris for Monsieur Boulet came in good stead, and I was quickly able to steer women in the direction of a suitable fragrance. Soon I was selling three or four bottles for every single sale the other salesgirls made.

This did not make me popular, but it brought me to the attention of the manager, who began using me in the office as an interpreter, able to handle correspondence in both French and English. I preferred the sales floor to the office, standing amid those glass shelves loaded with gleaming gold and yellow bottles, showing women the proper way to spritz or dab perfume, to test it. When you sell perfume, you sell a hope, a dream. The yearning gleams in the customers' eyes and the fragrance, those top, middle, and bottom notes, become a map to a hoped-for heaven on earth. But the office paid better and I had Dahlia's future to consider.

That summer, I was sent to Nice as a company representative, to bring samples to international clients who did not particularly want to take that long road from the Riviera up to the "balconies" in the hills, who preferred to stay close to the Nice casinos and the girls in the revues.

Dahlia screamed and threw her little water mug when she saw me in my traveling suit, looking so unlike her stained, weary mother. I hugged her and kissed her repeatedly, but she only cried harder. I considered canceling the trip, but that would risk my job, and we needed the money. Eventually, I crept out the door like a thief as Madame Natalia tried to distract her with a toy, and ran to the bus stop with only minutes to spare.

Nice was nowhere as large or varied as Paris, but it was exciting nonetheless, after the quiet life of Grasse. As in Paris, Nice's old cobbled streets of the *Vieille Ville* and the newer paved boulevards lining the ocean or headed uphill to the modern apartments were crowded with foreigners—tourists who still had the money to travel and stay at the large, luxurious hotels lining the Promenade des Anglais along the oceanfront.

Monsieur Alexandrov's little hotel, l'Auberge de l'Opéra, was not one of those expensive, glitzy places. It was situated at the southern end of boulevard Jean Jaurès, around the corner from the promenade and Opera Beach. Only three stories high and painted a bright yellow with turquoise shutters, it was the kind of hotel that elderly gentlewomen from England or financially embarrassed barons from Austria preferred. Quiet. Respectable. No gambling on the premises, no floor show, although those were available just around the corner.

What l'Auberge offered was reasonable rates, quiet, clean, spacious rooms, aging waiters and maids who had worked there for years and remembered you by name, and the owner-manager, Monsieur Alexandrov, who had perfect manners and discretion.

Monsieur did not see me when I first entered his hotel. He was standing to the side, half behind a screen, greeting a customer with old-fashioned side whiskers and a battered suitcase. He bowed frequently, little obsequious gestures that somehow diminished him . . . until he stood straight again, all five feet six inches of him, and I saw the look in his eye. He was nobody's fool and nobody's servant, but he knew how to greet a member of the minor aristocracy. He knew how to keep his customers returning, year after year.

The receptionist, a mousy woman named Solange with faded blond hair and chapped lips, asked if she could be of assistance. Her voice was filled with unasked questions. Judging from the ladies taking tea on the little patio, I was the youngest person there by several decades.

"I would like to speak with Monsieur Alexandrov," I said, putting my suitcase on the floor.

"He is busy at the moment. Will you wait?" Mademoiselle Solange made the required offer with a note of suspicion in her voice.

Just then, Monsieur Alexandrov, finished with the side-whiskered gentleman, saw me.

"Nora," he said, crossing the lobby swiftly and taking my hand. Again, that little kiss just over the knuckles, that old-world gesture that always caught me off guard.

"Nora, what can I do for you? How interesting to find you in Nice." He seemed different from the middle-aged, slightly bored man who visited his mother in Grasse, better-looking, interesting in a man-of-the-world way. Or perhaps I was different. That was our first meeting, really, that afternoon in Nice.

"Business," I said. "Your mother said you would give me a

room. Free," I added in a whisper, handing him the note Madame Natalia had sent with me.

He frowned as he read it. "It says I am to provide you with a good room, and to make no charge. I am also to provide breakfast and dinner in the dining room. Again no charge. This is presumptuous." He bowed slightly so that he could speak very quietly, close to my ear. His breath tickled my neck and his voice at that moment had a slight trace of his mother's Russian accent, a hint of Fabergé jewels and caviar in his vowels and consonants.

"I agree," I whispered back, suppressing the urge to reach up and touch my neck where his breath had warmed it. "But your mother insisted. The factory is not paying my travel expenses."

A long, appraising stare. A smile. "Well. How about this? The room will be without charge if there is an available one. Otherwise, it will be half-price to cover the hotel's expenses. And breakfast will be provided. But not dinner. Not unless you dine with me."

I hesitated, as expected, but not for long. Nicky, admittedly not the most handsome of men, nevertheless gave off charm the way flowers give off their scent . . . naturally and agreeably. And once he was away from his mother's watching eye, it was evident that he could be a ladies' man. With his confidence, his dark eyes, the brilliance of his smile when he flashed it, there was something of Pablo about him. A flirt, a heartbreaker.

I was no longer naive, or trusting. I saw Nicky for what he was, and it was okay by me. I wanted nothing that could be confused with love.

"Agreed."

How easily we came to an understanding. There was none of the foot-shuffling, yes-or-no despair of a teenage romance, none of the soul-searching right or wrong before the jump into the deep end.

Nicky was as different from Jamie as day was from night, and that seemed right. My heart belonged to Dahlia and, if I was honest, still to Jamie, but what I did with my body was my business. "I wish you could be more like Lee," Jamie had said once. Well, I thought, I'll give it a go.

Nicky's marriage, he explained that first night over martinis on the terrace, had been built on love and not good sense. The marriage had faltered. He had mourned, of course, when his wife died ten years ago. He had observed the formalities. But death had merely ended her suffering; the marriage had been long over. Nor would he remarry. Life was so pleasant. There was the sun, the beach, the casinos, the pretty women in summer dresses. Why complicate it? Why risk so much known happiness for the unknown?

"And what of you?" he asked. "You do not seem the type of woman to be alone, without a man."

"I didn't used to think so either," I said.

"An infidelity. A betrayal," Nicky guessed. "That is often how first love ends. Women expect too much."

"Do we?" I tried to feel angry, but found I couldn't. Perhaps it was the martinis. Perhaps it was the warmth of his hand on mine, the beauty of the evening with its sound of waves on the beach, the stars overhead, the gay laughter coming from the casino terraces around the corner. Nice is not a good city to be angry in.

"And, of course, there is Dahlia," he said. "The beautiful if somewhat demanding child. She makes it impossible for you to go back home. What is that strange-sounding city? Poughkeepsie?" The pressure of his hand on mine increased slightly.

"Yes." I was overcome with guilt, blaming an innocent child and realizing that, at that moment, I did not miss her. I was glad to be away from her screams, her neediness.

"It is all right, these feelings," he said, reading my mind. "Did Mother ever tell you how she locked me in a closet one day because I would not stop pestering her? She bought me ice cream for supper and I forgave her immediately, but I think she has never forgiven herself. These things are complicated. Pleasure is not."

Nicky ordered a salad with tuna and olives, iced oysters on the half shell, and a bottle of champagne. No dessert. "It is better not to overindulge, especially not the first night," he explained.

Since first realizing I was pregnant, I had felt older than the oldest church in Paris, not so much in years but in the mind, the heart. With Nicky I was young again, a learner with training wheels on my bicycle.

To feel carefree, though, is as short-lived as the most volatile of scents. The next morning when I woke up in Nicky's bed with bold strips of Nice sun warming my legs through the window shutter, the sense of age returned. I missed Dahlia for the first time in my life. It was no longer a starry evening of champagne and oysters but a new morning and it should have been her voice waking me up. I missed her like I hadn't known a person could be missed. Not even in my strongest moments of love with Jamie had I experienced such a powerful emotion.

Nicky held me as I wept. "There, there," he said, rocking me. He didn't need to ask me why I was crying. It was for that beautiful, if demanding, child of mine back in Grasse. "You will be home again tomorrow," he said, only a slight edge of impatience in his voice.

My business in Nice that afternoon was even more successful than I had hoped. I met with a small group of German businessmen in a tearoom on the Promenade des Anglais, and spread out a little display of perfumes, old and new, explaining the various properties of the fragrances. Only one of the men spoke fluent French and my German was limited at best to words learned very late at night in Paris cafés . . . hardly appropriate phrases for a business meeting.

The one who spoke French translated for his companions but gave me frequent sideways glances. I worried he was flirting. But when the orders had been placed and the deposit checks written out, he took me aside and said, "Don't you remember me, mademoiselle?"

I looked harder at him than I had before. Yes. He was older, dressed much more conservatively, but it was the art collector I had met that first night in Paris with Lee, the customer that wily Man had been wooing, the one who bought only Picassos.

"Herr Abetz. How nice to see you again. How is your wife . . . ?" I couldn't remember her name.

"Trudie. She is well. She stays in Berlin now. Traveling no longer suits her. I am surprised you are in Nice. Did you weary of Paris?"

"Yes," I said. "I wearied of Paris."

He eyed me and I thought he was seeing through that little lie. "Your friend. Miss Miller. How is she? A lovely girl. And your young man. His name escapes me."

"Mr. Sloane," I said stiffly, uncomfortable with how easily he had put those two names together. Had everyone seen but me, even that very first night? I had been so busy showing off with that silly tango performance, perhaps I had missed the first telling signs.

I stood. "So nice to see you again," I said, offering him my hand.

"Yes. I suspect the next time we meet, I will be in uniform. I will be commissioned." He stood as well. "Our chancellor grows restless."

It was 1935 and in Germany Hitler had been elected to replace

President von Hindenburg. Hitler was *Führer und Reichskanzler*—leader and chancellor.

Nicky and I quickly became friends during the day and lovers at night. I understood that when I returned to Grasse, other women would take my place. It didn't matter. He was as elegantly polite as Aziz had been with Lee, and he kept secrets and withheld much, as I suspect Aziz did. With Jamie, love had been all or nothing. With Nicky, it was merely sensual and fun and fit neatly into a little compartment.

There were nights when I had to have dinner with clients, German and American businessmen looking for luxury items for stores and hotels and expecting to be entertained before placing their soap and perfume orders. I wined and dined them; I flattered and even flirted a little. But at the end of the evening, after their purchase orders had been completed, Nicky would send a car and driver to pick them up and take them to the nightclubs of Nice.

Then I would join him in his very lovely rooms on the top floor of l'Auberge de l'Opéra, where white lace curtains floated in the salty breeze and the morning sun warmed my bare legs sticking out from under the coverlet. He fussed with a coffeemaker in his green-tiled kitchenette, and I thought it was quite pleasant to be a woman of the world instead of a lovesick girl.

All of this, of course, we kept secret from his mother. When he made his visits to Grasse, he was once again Monsieur Alexandrov.

I did well in Grasse as a translator and seller. After a couple of years I was able to have my suits and dresses tailor-made. I bought a secondhand red Peugeot 201 and darted up and down the curving hillside roads, through olive groves and into scrubby pine forests and out again into the dazzling light of southern France. Dahlia, growing by leaps and bounds, came with me on short trips to the towns and villages around us, Vence and Pertuis and Apt, picnicking in lavender fields or meadows of wild thyme. Every two or three months I ventured south to Nice, to the perfume buyers and to Nicky.

But sometimes it felt as if I were living someone else's life, and somewhere in the universe there was a different woman with a different life, with a husband with tawny hair and sharp cheekbones who built a swing in the backyard for his daughter.

The day I left Paris, I had split myself in two, like Atlas looking one way while his twin, Gadeirus, looked the other, and neither of them saw the disaster coming. I had been with Lee that day she went to photograph Blondel's building on the rue du Louvre. I had thought she wanted to photograph the magnificent statues, but instead she photographed shadows on the street. *It's all about the light,* she had said. *Everything else is superfluous. I think we're going to be friends,* she said. We had been. And then, she became the disaster I hadn't seen coming.

Dahlia, meanwhile, became a proper little French girl, with a perfect accent. In midafternoon she ate her *goûter*, her bread with chocolate, and when she sang in the bathtub, she sang French nursery songs.

She had my dark hair, but she looked more and more like Jamie, growing tall and leggy for her age, her lightly freckled cheeks stretched over emerging slanting cheekbones. I would look at her and see Jamie looking back at me, and long for the great unknown of that life with him, the life I would never have.

One day when we were sitting on church steps near a park, Dahlia went to play with a friend. I watched bemused at the way children turn a leaf into a saucer, a pebble into a teacup. Had I played at tea? No, Lee and I had climbed trees and chased her brothers; we had been tomboys playing rough and ready. Lee. I half hated her, half missed her.

There were only three pretend place settings on the ground, and Dahlia's little friend, Chantal, looked at her sternly and asked where her setting for her daddy was. "One and one and one and one," Chantal said. "Four. Not three. My daddy is coming for tea."

"I don't have a daddy," Dahlia said.

I waited, not breathing.

"Why not? Everyone has a daddy," said her playmate.

Dahlia stood. "I don't want to play anymore," she said. She came to me and threw her arms around my knees. I tousled her dark hair and my heart did somersaults in my chest.

In 1937, in the spring of the year before I turned thirty, I got a card from my mother, and a note asking me to come home. She was getting married and moving to California and wanted to see me and my daughter. "We'll tell them you're married and widowed," she wrote. "Make up a name."

Pretend I was widowed? As if no one would see through that ploy, I thought. For one month, the planned length of my stay, I could manage the farce. But Jamie would be sure to hear about it. Gossip would flow down the streets of Poughkeepsie like rainwater.

Five years had already passed since I had seen him. Where had the time gone? In diaper washings and bedtime stories, I thought. Evenings in Nice with Nicky. I hadn't heard from Jamie, or tried to contact him. Maybe it was time? And what would I say?

Stop it, I told myself. Do you expect him to run to you, fall on his knees, beg you to marry him? I had seen a silent movie once at the moving picture house in Poughkeepsie, lovers separated by the Great War, the soldier coming home to the girl, to the girl's daughter, born while he had been in the trenches. He had done that. Fallen on his knees, begged. It was only a movie, Nora, I told myself. More likely, you won't see Jamie at all. And if you do . . .

If I did, I wanted the movie version, the happy ending. I would end the silence and tell him everything. We were older, wiser. The betrayal was a long time ago. We could pick up where we left off. Or maybe not. Maybe that chapter was over. But how could it be? As soon as I thought of going back to Poughkeepsie, I thought of Jamie.

Nicky sensed my indecision. "Go back," he said. "You can afford to take a month off. A trip may be just what you need."

"Do I need something, Nicky?" I asked, sitting up on my elbows. He was in the bathroom just off the bedroom, his face covered with shaving cream that made his black eyes even darker, a towel wrapped around his waist. "Is that what you think?"

He put down the razor and looked at me. "I think if you don't go to your mother, you will regret it later. And who wants to live with regrets?"

"And what will you do, all that time?" I already knew.

"Work hard and then find ways to amuse myself, darling. And miss you every minute."

Dahlia and I sailed past the Statue of Liberty on the Fourth of July. The statue hadn't been there when my great-grandfather had fled France and the revolution. I wondered what that great harbor had looked like to him, that bit of rocky real estate jutting into the Atlantic, before it had its skyscrapers and monuments, when New York was still a mud-path village and France, until the guillotine, had been the center of civilization. Roles had reversed. Now I was coming from a quiet hillside village in France to the greater city of Manhattan.

We spent the night in the city, not at the Plaza but at a hotel just one price grade down, and used cabs, not the subway. I had the strange sensation that my older self, the woman wearing the tailored suit and the professionally clipped hair, holding her daughter's hand, might bump into her young self, that poorly dressed, lovesick girl who would follow her guy anywhere.

My child was terrified of the fireworks and the parades and the commotion. She was not normally a fearful little girl, but we led such a quiet, calm life in Grasse. I realized how little English she knew, how for all purposes she was, in fact, a French girl. I looked at her the way I anticipated my mother would and wondered, what am I doing? Shouldn't I bring my daughter home for good, before it is too late?

The question was an awakening. I still thought of Poughkeepsie, or at least the United States, as home. And there was a deadline to my situation. At some point, Dahlia might become irrevocably French. Not a bad thing in itself, but it meant that if I wanted to stay with her, I, too, would have to stay in France.

Momma met us at the Poughkeepsie train station, looking as I had never before seen her look, or at least didn't remember her looking. She seemed younger, not the old woman I had anticipated, and her hair was bleached blond. She was slender and made-up with red lipstick and powder to hide her freckles. When she came toward me, tottering a bit on her heels, forced to take small steps by the tightness of her skirt, Dahlia hid behind my skirt and looked up at me, her eyes large with fear.

"Nora!" Momma shouted, waving. The train was pulling out already and the noise made it impossible to hear each other. I waited till the train had chugged down the tracks, the grinding of metal on metal and the hiss of the steam dying away.

"Hi, Momma," I said.

We looked at each other. We did not hug or kiss, just looked.

"You're older," she said.

"You're younger."

"And who is this?" She crouched down carefully in her tight skirt, her knees twisted to the side, and extended a lace-gloved hand to Dahlia.

"Dahlia, say hello to your grandmother," I said.

Dahlia stepped shyly forward and gave her grandmother a kiss on both cheeks. A French greeting. Momma wiped her face and pecked Dahlia on the mouth. Dahlia wiped her mouth. We're not off to a great start, I thought.

"I still haven't forgiven you," Momma said as the taxi took us to her new apartment. My aunt had died and left the house to Momma, who had promptly sold it along with most of the furnishings. "Leaving like that. No good-bye, no word from you for months on end. And to do what you did . . ."

"Not in front of Dahlia," I said. "And I haven't asked for forgiveness."

Dahlia was sitting on my lap, listening intently. Forgiveness. That was an English word she did not yet know.

Momma's apartment was filled with new furniture from the Sears catalog: an upholstered sofa, a coffee table, swan-neck lamps twisting off the walls like modern gargoyles—lots of chrome and

Bakelite—and in the bedroom, twin beds with Hollywood-style headboards of padded pink satin and bows.

"What happened to the furniture from our house? I thought it was in storage?" I asked. We had had good, solid oak pieces passed through generations.

"I gave it to the Salvation Army. Don't live in the past, Nora. We have to move forward. Coffee? I bought a spice cake from the bakery. You used to love their spice cakes."

Had I? I didn't remember.

"Come on, missy," Momma said, offering her hand to Dahlia. "Let's have some cake."

We sat at the new kitchen table, all metal with folding legs so it could be stored away, Momma eyeing my suit and haircut and nodding approval. Dahlia looked at her cake as if it might bite her, and when she tasted it, she spit it back out onto her plate.

"I want apple cake," she said in French.

Momma's eyes almost fell out. "My God, Nora. My grandchild is French."

I started to laugh. I couldn't help it. Then Momma laughed, and finally Dahlia.

"I just want to warn you," Momma said the next day. Her fiancé, Harold Littlewood, was coming for cocktails, and she had invited a few "close friends" as well. I was in the kitchen stuffing the valleys of celery with cream cheese for the canapé tray. Momma, already wearing a floral sundress, very off the shoulder and short to the knees, was wiping clean a dozen rented sherry glasses.

"Warn me about what?"

"Jamie will be here."

I put the spreading knife, still loaded with cream cheese, on the table.

"Okay?" Momma asked. "His family and I became quite friendly while you were over there in Par-ee kicking up your heels."

Dahlia was sitting on a kitchen chair playing with a doll her grandmother had bought her, braiding its hair and cooing to it in French.

"What's that funny look mean, Nora?" Momma narrowed her eyes. "You said he wasn't the f-a-t-h-e-r, so what's the harm? You didn't lie to me, did you?"

"No harm. It's just been a long time, that's all." Then, quickly, "Dahlia, do you want a cookie? Are you hungry?"

I spent the rest of the afternoon trying to calm myself, to pretend that it would be pleasant to see Jamie, to catch up, but I wasn't sure how I felt about him anymore. In my memory, he was the passion of my life. What was he now, in the present? Perhaps my feelings weren't so much in the past as I had thought, because I caught myself looking in the mirror, brushing back my hair, trying to see myself as he would later that day, hoping that his eyes would light up.

There was also the matter of my daughter. In my mind's eye I saw that pretend tea party on the dusty ground in Grasse, the three settings instead of four because Dahlia did not have a father. The silent movie—"I didn't know about the child, Bess! Please, marry me. Say you'll be my little wife!"—played over and over again in my imagination. Stop it, I kept telling myself. You're not a young girl swooning over the high school hero anymore, or even that expatriate girl in Paris, certain—mistakenly so—that her man was hers alone.

Momma had insisted the sherry hour be formal, so we stood in line to greet her guests—first Momma closest to the door, then Mr. Littlewood, then me. Mr. Littlewood gave my shoulder an occasional pat for reassurance. He, more than Momma, guessed that this event might be painful for me. We had met the evening before, over a fish fry at Stenkel's Grill.

I liked Mr. Littlewood. He was a man of even temper, and he seemed to adore Momma. He was polite to me and had brought a tube of pickup sticks for Dahlia to play with, patiently explaining the game to her, how you had to throw them into a pile and them remove them, one by one, without disturbing the others. He gave her a hairbrush. "Fuller, of course. The best. It will last you all your life, little girl, long as you don't lose it. 'Make it work. Make it last. Guarantee it no matter what.' That's our motto."

Dahlia had looked at him with large, serious eyes and offered a very grave, *"Merci, monsieur."*

"Lordy, lordy," Mr. Littlewood had laughed. "A Frenchy!"

Mr. Littlewood winked at me and forked a piece of fried haddock into his mouth. "In this family, the daughter is as pretty as her momma." He gave Momma's arm an affectionate pinch. "And Dahlia here, well, she's going to be the real beauty, aren't you, little miss?"

The Sloanes were the first to arrive that afternoon, father, mother, two older brothers . . . and Jamie. They made their way down the line, shaking hands, exchanging exclamations about the weather—"excruciatingly hot"—and murmuring "how do you do's" to Mr. Littlewood, who shook their hands and then slipped them a business card.

I concentrated on smiling and giving my handshakes the just-right amount of pressure, but I watched Jamie out of the corner of my eye as he greeted Momma, Mr. Littlewood, and then stood in front of me.

"Hi, Nora," he said. "I heard you were in town. Good to see you." The electricity between us was so strong I thought the room would catch fire. Five years disappeared.

"I wasn't certain you would come," I said.

"Why not?" He was still holding my hand, smiling.

He looked older. Well, so did I. But Jamie also looked defeated, even more so than he had that night Julien Levy had thumbed through his photographs, bored, pretending he would give him a show next year. Jamie's shoulders were slumped. His suit was too tight—those bakery cakes—and his hair too short. He had barbered it back to Poughkeepsie standards, cut away the long waves he had worn in Paris to look artistic. Now he looked just like the man he swore he would never be, the early-up, early-to-bed baker smelling of yeast and stooped from the worktables. My heart pounded against my ribs. Signs of age and mortality added to the tenderness of what I still felt for him. No question about it.

"Staying long?" this new Jamie asked.

"A few weeks. Can I get you a sherry?" God. We were like actors in a bad play.

The other guests arrived—the minister hired to perform the ceremony, the neighbors down the hall, Momma's banker who had helped with the house sale, and a few others. Mr. Littlewood put a record on the phonograph, something with lots of clarinet and soft drums and then a crooner singing about meeting a million-dollar baby in a five-and-ten-cent store. Momma passed a tray of crab cake on crackers and we sat on leatherette chairs and the chrome-legged sofa. We moved as little as possible because it was too hot and crowded. The backs of my legs stuck to the chair and every time I shifted, there was a tearing sound of skin pulling away from the fake leather seat.

The room filled with sour smells and chitchat. Mr. Littlewood took a chair next to mine and asked me dozens of questions about France, mostly about housekeeping there. What did they use to scrub floors? And that, ahem, commode in the washroom? He had done so well as a Fuller Brush salesman in Poughkeepsie that he had been able to buy a larger franchise in Los Angeles.

"Not quite Beverly Hills," he said, "but not too far from it. I intend to expand out that way. Your mother has always wanted to live in California." He winked at me, an exaggerated stage wink for my mother to see.

"Has she? I didn't know that."

"There's probably lots about your mother you don't know. It's like that with mothers and daughters. Fathers and sons as well. We all have secrets." He winked again.

We sipped our too-sweet sherry, and he rose to circulate, told to do just that by a severe nod by Momma. Jamie's mother came and sat next to me, fussing a bit with the pink tulle of her hat. "Well, Nora," she said, and her voice was cool enough to break the heat wave. "How are you, over there in France?" She had begun to dye her brown hair, and gray roots showed at the temples. There were crinkles around her eyes and mouth, and the line of her corset, needed to contain years of sweet rolls and cakes from the bakery turned to fat, showed through the thin silk of her flower-printed dress.

"I'm doing well enough, thank you, Mrs. Sloane."

"Thank the good Lord Jamie had the sense to come home. I wish he'd never taken up with that Miller girl, though. She had him pretty down, there, for a while. I warned him about her, but would he listen? Don't you think he looks well?"

"Yes, indeed." Jamie was standing in a corner, talking to Mr. Littlewood. He sensed we were discussing him. He turned and gave me a smile, the old kind, corners turned up and slightly dimpled, as if he was trying not to laugh.

"We were so glad to get him home again. Can't say that the time in France and then in New York was particularly good for him. We shouldn't have let him go."

I didn't remember that Jamie had asked permission, but that was beside the point.

"On the contrary," I said. "I think it was just what he needed. Especially if it was what he wanted."

"Well, you would say that, wouldn't you?" she said knowingly. I rose and went to talk to the minister.

After a while I moved to the door and looked at Jamie over my shoulder, inviting him to follow me. I couldn't stand being in the same room with him and acting a stranger to him. He put down his sherry and five minutes later we were sitting outdoors, side by side on an iron bench under a chestnut tree.

"Not at all like Paris, is it?" he joked, waving at the smokestacks trailing sooty banners in the jagged skyline over Poughkeepsie.

"No. Don't you wish we were sitting at the Dôme, drinking a cognac? You always took the chair right under the *T* of the *tabac* sign."

"Remember the old waiter who always flirted with you a bit? It's been a long time, Nora. Feels like a lifetime ago."

For me, the years had fallen away and I felt that old excitement and yearning. After five years and that betrayal? How could I? But there it was. During the course of that awful afternoon party, second by second I had grown more aware of him till sometimes it felt we were the only two people in the room. Time and distance had not diminished that old tie between us. Nothing had been forgotten. I had merely been asleep and was waking up once again. He wasn't as young or confident as he had been, but he was still my Jamie, the boy I loved.

"God, it's hot. I thought I was going to melt in there," I said. *I still love you,* I did not say. *Should we give it another go?* I wanted to ask. Planned to ask. For Jamie, I'd even move back to Poughkeepsie.

We sat in silence, keeping a formal foot of space between us, not talking or touching, just watching the pigeons who gathered at our feet assuming bread crumbs were in the offing. I rehearsed in my head the words I needed to say.

Jamie took off his jacket and loosened his tie. Patches of sweat showed through the back of his shirt and his hair was damp and plastered flat. I caught the spicy scent, and all those mornings in our Paris apartment rushed back at me.

You have to tell him about Dahlia, I instructed myself.

"I have to tell—," I started, but he said the exact same words at the same time. We both stopped, startled, laughed nervously.

"You first," I said.

"Okay." Jamie shifted his weight and crossed his legs, turning slightly toward me. "You left Paris without saying good-bye," he said. "I was really upset. Why did you do that, Nora?"

"The last time I saw you, you were in bed with Lee."

"I never meant to hurt you. It just . . . kind of happened."

"Isn't that what you said in Paris? Did you love her, Jamie?"

"I may have thought so at the time. I loved both of you. Different ways. When you left . . . and not even a letter to say where you'd gone. I worried. I didn't find out you were in Grasse until Lee finally heard it from Man, who'd heard it from Picasso. I missed you," he said, shaking his head.

"How did you have time to miss me? I bet Lee kept you pretty busy. In the studio, I mean." No need to be crude, I reminded myself.

Jamie kicked a piece of gravel with the tip of his well-polished shoe. "It only lasted a couple of months. Well, for her, it was all fun and games. In New York, once her brother came to work in the studio, there wasn't that much for me to do. Not enough work for two assistants. So out goes Jamie. I tried to make it on my own again, but it's tough in New York. I had drinks with Julien Levy one night. Remember him? Nothing came of it."

I remembered. All those gallery owners saying maybe next year and meaning never, those days trudging up and down the avenues and side streets, Jamie's portfolios tucked under our arms, all those nos. That nightmarish visit of Julien to our room, his bored thumbing through months and months of Jamie's work.

"I'd had enough," Jamie said softly. "So, here I am. Back in Poughkeepsie. It's not so bad. I just bought a great house with a garage. The bakery is doing well again, and I get jobs photographing weddings and things. No more art shots. No more knocking on gallery doors."

It was early evening and slanting sunlight cast deep shadows under his cheekbones. Dahlia's cheekbones were still just a hint under baby fat, but I already knew she was going to have Jamie's face. "Ever think about coming back to France?" I asked.

"No. I'm done with traveling. I'm settling down." Jamie took my hand for the first time and looked into my eyes. "I'm getting married, Nora. Next month. That's why I bought the house."

I felt an invisible hand punch into my stomach.

"I'm going to be a father," Jamie was saying. "I've told Clara I'll marry her, and I intend to. She's . . . uh. Well, she's going to have a child. Our child. It's time, you know. Past time, as my mother keeps telling me. Other guys have three or four kids by my age."

That invisible punishing hand punched even deeper into my stomach. You *have* a child, I wanted to tell him. But there was no point. He was marrying someone else. I hadn't wanted to force him five years ago, and it was too late to ask him to marry me now.

He laughed and ran his fingers through his too-short hair. "If our baby is a girl, I'll have to make sure she stays away from guys like me. You okay, Nora?" He began to rub my hands as if I were in a faint or something. "I'm such a clod," he said. "I forget your husband died. You poor kid. Who was he, Nora? Anyone I knew back in Paris? Where'd you meet him? Your mother said he was a Frenchman."

I felt turned to stone. "I didn't have a husband, Jamie. That's something my mother made up because I have a daughter."

Jamie opened his mouth, then closed it again. He wiped his hair back, that old gesture, except now his hair was cut short and when he smoothed it down, it revealed a receding hairline. And I loved him all the more for it, Jamie, stumbling out of boyhood toward middle age.

He considered, choosing his words as if one might be poison. "Just a story. Because you have a daughter. Well . . ." He forced a laugh. "You always wanted children." He cleared his throat. "Must be tough. And I understand why your mother did that. She has to live here, after all. And you know how people are. All that gossip, people looking down their noses. Doesn't change how I feel about you, though, Nora. I hope I'll always be your friend. I won't ask who the father is. Not my place to judge. But I'd like to hit him in the nose for not doing the right thing."

I couldn't look at him. I didn't know if I was going to laugh or cry. And I knew I wasn't going to tell him he was the father. He was getting married. Settling down in Poughkeepsie.

He leaned back and put his arm around my shoulders and we sat like that for a long time, the summer heat mixing his sweat with mine through my blouse. I forced myself to breathe slowly, calmly. Did it never occur to him that the child was his? Apparently not. And that made her not his. Dahlia was mine alone.

Crickets began to chirp and dogs barked down the street. The sun was slipping down in the sky as if it hadn't the energy to stay up there, blazing away, and that was how I felt, too. Like sliding away.

"They're saying there's going to be war in Europe," Jamie said. "Maybe it's time for you to come back, too. Stay home."

"Back to what? My mother is moving to California, I have no friends left here in Poughkeepsie, none that ever mattered."

"I'm your friend, Nora."

I stood. "We'd better go back. People will be leaving soon. Momma will want me to say good-bye to her guests."

Everyone left a half hour earlier than the invitations had said the party would end, and Mr. Littlewood kept reassuring Momma it was because of the heat, no other reason; the paper flower decorations had been real pretty, the sherry a good choice, the canapés delicious.

"Even so, it will be good to get out of here. Start up again somewhere new," Momma said, kicking off her heels. "California or bust, right, Harold?"

"No bust for us, Adele," he said, puckering up and kissing her.

"Even so, I thought the Millers might come. Rude of them not to," she said, pouting. "After all, our daughters used to play together. And she was over there in France with you, wasn't she, Nora?"

"You invited the Millers?" I dried a platter Mr. Littlewood had just handed me, and stood on tiptoe to put it on its shelf. Mr. Littlewood was wearing Momma's frilled apron and whistling at the sink.

"Sure I did. Hoped they might bring some of the photographs Lee has been sending from Egypt. She climbed the pyramids. I hear she's settled down now with that Egyptian husband of hers."

Somehow, I didn't think so.

I spent the rest of that month helping Momma pack up the apartment and get ready for the big move to California. The wedding itself was small, a candlelit chapel ceremony with Momma and Mr. Littlewood and me and Dahlia, and her neighbors for witness. Jamie came with his camera and tripod and took photographs for her.

"I'm going to expand my studio, here in Poughkeepsie," he told me. "Bakery half the week, and the studio the other half, a little sideline with portraits, weddings, and class pictures. Maybe even bring in an assistant or two."

"Good for you, Jamie. I'm glad to hear it." I meant it. His best photos had always been of people, not things or places or fragments of dreams as arranged by Man Ray and the other surrealists. Clara came with him, and I recognized her from high school, the girl who had sat on the right side of me in geometry class. Bright, a little bossy, and none too pleased to see me again.

"Going back to France again soon, Nora?" she asked.

Jamie looked at Dahlia, all dressed up in a new polka-dot dress and holding Mr. Littlewood's hand as we waited for the minister. I looked at her, too, trying to see her as Jamie did.

"Cute kid," he said, looking only briefly. Perhaps he saw only the black hair, the baby-round face. He didn't see the eyes, his eyes, so deeply set they almost tilted, or the length of her legs. She would be tall, like he was.

The minister arrived, looking harried and red-faced from the heat, and the few people there sat in a single row of folding chairs as Momma and Mr. Littlewood exchanged vows and rings. When it was over, she threw me her bouquet of white lilies.

"Your dad and me. We had some tough times, but I tried to be a good wife," she said, hugging me. She was wearing perfume, something I didn't recognize. It was poorly blended with too much strong floral and a suggestion of powder. It was a perfume for a young girl and meant to be worn in a single dab, not large splashes. "Your father's been gone for a long time, and you went off," she said. "Now I'm Mrs. Littlewood. Mrs. Littlewood of California." Her voice was a little fierce, as if she was convincing herself as well.

"Don't you worry none about your momma. We'll make it work, make it last. Guarantee it no matter what—right, Adele?" Mr. Littlewood added.

The next day, they were gone. California or bust. My mother had become a laughing bride, almost girlish in her shocking pink travel suit, leaning on Mr. Littlewood's arm and looking up at him from under mascara-darkened lashes. I still hadn't called him Harold. The new reality of her was so different from the remembered one of my childhood, that cold and distant woman, that row of untested perfume bottles on the bathroom windowsill. My father hadn't made her happy, and she hadn't made him happy. And as she had said, that was over. I wondered if Jamie's child, in twenty years, would be saying the same thing about her parents. I tried with all my might to wish them well, to wish them happiness.

Before I left Poughkeepsie, I took Dahlia to Upton Lake, to the same dock where Jamie had photographed me right before we decided to run away together. He had wanted me to look serious and mysterious that day, and I could only laugh because I was so happy just to be with him, to feel that electricity.

Children have a special sense we lose when we grow up. They see what is invisible and hear what is silent. At the lake Dahlia let go of my hand and screamed like she was possessed. She would not be comforted, not by the promise of ice cream or a second bedtime story that evening. When I asked her what was wrong, she wept and jutted out her bottom lip in a mute paroxysm of worry, and then clung to me the way I had seen children do when they had gotten separated from their mother at market day. I think she sensed that I was longing for Jamie, for the past before she was born, and she didn't like it. Who would? To have a mother go back to the time before us?

I didn't see Jamie again before I returned to France. Did I half hope he would rush to the train station, wave at me, shout, "Nora! I love you!" and stop me from going, take me in his arms and kiss me madly as the train steam hissed around us?

I couldn't remember which movie I saw that scene in. But it didn't happen in my life. Jamie was at the bakery, or maybe he was at the tailor's getting a rented tuxedo fitted for his own wedding. I got on the train with Dahlia, and after I found our seats and put our overnight cases on the overhead racks, there was no one to wave to out the window, no one to blow kisses to.

I headed back to France with my daughter, Jamie would marry

his Clara, and that electricity he roused in me, that sense that he was the only man and I the only woman in the world, would go back to sleep.

The next day Dahlia stood on the deck of the ship and waved farewell to the Lady we had greeted while coming into New York Harbor, and I thought about beginnings and endings and all that is lost in between.

# CHAPTER SIXTEEN

"Oh, heavens, I missed you!" Madame Natalia stood at the door of her little house, arms wide. "The trip went well?"

Dahlia dropped the box of gift chocolates she was carrying and ran to her. "I missed you, too," she said, hugging Natalia fiercely. Her pink dress glowed against the faded ochre of the house. She smiled at me over her shoulder, her little face radiant with joy.

I picked up the chocolates and tucked them under my arm and smiled at the two of them. It was good to be back. New York had been noisy and crowded; Poughkeepsie held nothing for me. Every place I had visited—the lake, the movie house, Platt's department store, where I had first sold perfume—had felt lifeless, as if I had been a ghost visiting my own past. Grasse was the present. Grasse was home.

A month after I returned, Jamie sent a letter written on stationery from Tastes-So-Good Bakery. There was a smear of grease at the bottom and I sniffed at it, inhaling the vanilla and cinnamon of childhood. The grease holding the scents had turned rancid during the letter's weeks of travel. Jamie wrote mostly about Lee, who, according to the local gossip, had left Egypt without Aziz, and was to spend the summer in France. She was staying in Paris at the Hôtel Prince de Galles, if I wanted to get in touch.

I didn't. The past had been pushed into a box, and that box pushed into a corner. I wanted it to stay there, and to stay closed. I was worried about Jamie, though. He was getting married soon, yet his letter was all about Lee.

A second letter from Jamie arrived in the autumn. He enclosed a photo of him and Clara in their wedding clothes, she in frothy white with a fishtail hem swirled at her feet, he in a black tuxedo with a too-tight collar, smiling gamely for someone else's camera.

"Who's that?" Dahlia asked, grabbing for the photograph. She was in school for the first time that autumn, and wore the new blue and yellow uniform even when she didn't have to. She loved going to school, just as I had. Children who are unhappy at home frequently prefer school to home. Dahlia was lonely. No siblings, no father, just me and Natalia.

She studied the photograph, squinting a bit at it. I reminded myself to have the doctor check her eyes. "It's the man we met in Poughkeepsie," she said. "At Grandmama's wedding. You went out with him in the afternoon and when you came back, you looked sad. I saw you through the window."

I had left Dahlia with Momma's upstairs neighbor, that day of the party. "I couldn't have been that sad. I was going to see you in a few minutes."

Dahlia just rolled her eyes at me and studied the photograph some more.

"I don't like her dress," she said. "And the man looks stupid." That was her new word. Everything, from her morning mug of milk with a spoonful of coffee mixed in to the story I would tell her at bedtime, was stupid.

"It will pass," Natalia always said, looking up from her knitting. "Nicky went through a similar phase."

We had reached a stage in our friendship where she was simply Natalia, not Madame, and she felt free to criticize me, which she did often but not unkindly. Dahlia had begun calling her Grandmama and Natalia did not discourage her.

In that letter, Jamie also wrote about Lee. She had been in Cannes visiting Picasso that summer. Man Ray had been there, and an artist we hadn't met, an Englishman, Roland Penrose.

"Bet they had a swell time," Jamie had scrawled. "I bet those parties were wild. I wonder if Man Ray had his gun with him."

Lee had been just a few hours away from me, but it might have been the other side of the moon. I had Dahlia, and my work with the perfumers, and the pleasantness of those evenings in Nice with Nicky. If, deep inside, a spark still simmered, a longing for the old friendship with Lee, of that first love with Jamie, for those heady café evenings blue with cigarette smoke when we argued everything from leftist politics to academy painting standards, well, then, I did my best to ignore that spark.

After her stay in Cannes, Lee returned to Cairo and Aziz, to duck shoots on an oasis, trips to souks and pyramids, cocktails at Shepheard's, the women in pearls and black satin, all those very rich and bored people waiting, and not knowing what they were waiting for. Perhaps once in a while they discussed Mussolini's intentions in northern Africa.

One of Lee's more famous photographs from that time is "Portrait of Space," taken during a desert expedition, with her camera shooting out through a torn screen to a distant and empty horizon.

The rip in the screen is shaped like a nomad's tent, bedraggled by wind and heat, and the bare landscape has a menacing quality. Many of the photos Lee took in Egypt are empty of people, suggesting her state of mind: loneliness and discontent. Paris, for both of us, was a long time ago.

Jamie stopped writing. I had no more news from him, no news about Lee, and Momma's letters from California were about the movie stars she had seen on the streets or going by in their chauffeured automobiles: Ann Sheridan, Jack Benny, Joan Crawford, Cary Grant. She underlined Cary Grant three times and added exclamation points. Some days in quiet Grasse I felt isolated and restless. Other days I felt at peace and tired in a healthy way from chasing after my daughter.

Dahlia kept growing ever prettier, ever taller, as seasons passed. With that athletic American build inherited from her father she towered over many of her friends. She looked older than her age and one day I remembered that Lee had been only seven when she was raped. Lee, too, had been taller, prettier. I didn't sleep well after that. For a month I wouldn't let Dahlia out of the house unless I was with her, not even to walk to school.

Finally, Natalia took me aside. "I had a son, not a daughter, but still I know a mother's fear," she said, touching the cross she always wore. "You must protect her, yes. But you cannot suffocate her like this."

"I had a friend. When she was very young, something awful happened to her."

"I understand. Yes, we will be careful. But Dahlia has friends and a protector here in addition to you. Her godfather is Monsieur

LaRosa, remember. Keep her away from the butcher, though. He likes to touch girls. Otherwise, she is safe." Natalia raised her eyebrows. I realized I never saw children in his shop, only lines of unsmiling housewives glaring at the skinned rabbits and legs of pork and lamb hanging from ceiling hooks. They all knew.

"Okay," I said. After that, I let Dahlia go to school and come home alone, as the other children did. But never did I send her to the butcher shop, not even when she was old enough to carry money and run errands.

Just a few months after this conversation, in the late summer of '39, Hitler invaded Poland.

That evening Madame LaRosa unexpectedly and uncharacteristically tapped on a window in our sitting room rather than politely knocking at the door. Natalia gave me a cross look and told me to open the window. She had been listening to a music program on the radio.

Dahlia and I were sitting at the table, struggling with the multiplication tables. I had been trying to reassure my daughter that the multiplication tables could be memorized, it just took time and practice. Dahlia, unconvinced, chewed the eraser end of her pencil and made faces at me. She let her new glasses slip down her little nose and crossed her eyes. She hated the glasses and I didn't like them either. She looked older with them. She was growing so quickly. When I looked at her I wanted to stop the clock, stop the seasons, keep her small and safe.

"Look," Madame LaRosa said through the opened window, holding up a newspaper. "War."

"Come in, Louise," Natalia said. "Don't stand in the street like a hoodlum."

No one could have looked less like a hoodlum than Madame

LaRosa, with her neat chignon pinned at the back of her neck, her sprigged dress with its lace collar. She was flattered by Natalia's suggestion that she might be youthfully dangerous, and when she let herself in through the front door, there was an unusual spring in her step.

"We must make preparations," she said. "Albert says that now Hitler has gone into Poland, France will declare war on Germany." She sat and fanned herself with the newspaper, thinking, and that suggestion of youthful excitement vanished. Her face grew serious, sad. "Thank God my Albert is too old to be called up."

Natalia made the sign of the cross. We were both thinking of Nicky, hoping that he, then fifty-two, would also be too old.

On September 3 France declared war, as Monsieur LaRosa had predicted. Natalia, normally reluctant to use the telephone we had installed in the hall, called Nicky every day for a week and each time it was the same message: No, he hadn't been conscripted. Too old, I could hear him shout over the line.

"We will make preparations," Natalia said the next week, when I was packing for a trip to Nice. "Tomorrow, you will ask Nicky what he thinks."

I had no idea what preparations were made for a war. I knew how to soften and knead together little pieces of soap to make one larger piece and how to thin cream with milk to make it go further and how to line thin-soled shoes with newspaper to make them warmer in cold weather. All children of the Depression knew those things. But war? War was the panther, his mouth open, ready to spring at the throat. How did you prepare for that?

"I think Mother is right," Nicky told me the next day. "Don't trust it. The government thinks they can make this go away by ignoring it. They are wrong."

Nicky and I were sitting in the café of the Hôtel Negresco, his favorite spot when he wanted to get away from his own little hotel, to see what other menus were offering, who was bartending, what the favorite cocktails of the season were. Everyone knew him, everyone gave him special treatment, and our wine was always "on the house."

I had spent the afternoon with a series of clients from department stores in America and Germany who were already ordering for spring shipments. The war was in the north—it hadn't reached us yet—and I couldn't think past the fact that my new heels were too tight and that Nicky looked like he was putting on weight.

Inside, a band was playing a tango. I could hear the clatter of crystal glasses, soft conversation, and women's laughter dance in and out of the notes of the music. The world was all soft air and fragrance and music and the pleasant weight of Nicky's hand on mine. War seemed a different reality altogether, the witch's house in an otherwise beautiful and enchanted forest.

"Buy sacks of flour and sugar," Nicky said, breaking our silence. He was preoccupied that night. "And eiderdowns. Make sure the coal cellar is full. Tell Mama to wall up some of the best wines in the cellar, and her good jewels." He said it casually, as if he were making a list for market day. "Would you like to dance, Nora?"

The tango ended and the band played something slow and sweet. We danced, and his arm was tight around my waist.

"If you want to go home, back to America, this is the time," he said. "Soon, it will be too late."

"Maybe when the school year is finished," I said. "It would be too difficult to take Dahlia out of her classes now. Too upsetting. Besides, this feels like home to me. Mr. and Mrs. Simmons aren't leaving. Why should I?" The Simmonses were an elderly couple who spent half the year in Nice, in Nicky's hotel, and the other half in Paris. Originally from Chicago, they liked to buy me a coffee and have a chat when I was in town and their conversation was full of quaint phrases and gossip from many years before.

"It is different for them," Nicky said. "They are old. You are young, and you have a child to think of."

"My child is happy here. And so am I. We'll stay here. My adopted country."

"Brava," Nicky said, holding me even tighter. "I just thought I should tell you. This will get serious."

The words meant little to me, who had never experienced war except as a horror that happened elsewhere, as shown in the newsreels of the Great War and the Spanish Civil War. It only became real for me when Dahlia came home with a gas mask dangling from her book pack. One had been handed out to every schoolchild in France. My daughter tried it on to show it off and changed from her beautiful child-faced self to a gnome with an insect face. "For when the Bosche gas us," she explained.

"I don't think that will happen in Grasse," I said, trying to reassure myself more than my child. Even so, Natalia and I swept and scoured a portion of the cellar and stored away candles, matches, blankets, a basket of preserved foods, and jugs of water. Our own private bomb shelter.

Natalia selected the best wines from her cellar, some bought many years before when Monsieur Hughes had still been alive, and we bricked them behind a false wall in the shelter. "A song," she sighed, reading the labels and handing me the bottles, one by one. "He bought them for a song. Nicky says that when the war comes, and after, they will be worth much. I can't imagine the vineyards with no one working in them. Nicky says there won't be any grape harvests for a few years. He says there will be nobody to pick the grapes."

We filled the coal bin, stocked up on extra bags of flour and rice when we could get them. Prices had already skyrocketed because others were doing the same.

All that planning for disaster made me want some lightness, for Dahlia if not for myself, so I bought cloth and made a new dress for her, sunshine yellow wool, with flounces at the hem and on the straps. The skirt billowed so much she looked like a flower when she spun around in it. For myself, I bought a copy of *Vogue* for the first time in years, to see what Paris made of all this preparation. And there it was, in black and white, in full-page advertisements: the war as seen by the fashion industry—chocolate boxes shaped like gas masks; dresses shaped like parachutes with dozens of pockets so that you could grab items you might need on your way to the bomb shelter.

Over the next few months, two and a half million other Frenchmen were put into uniform and sent up to the German border. In Grasse, Monsieur Bonner's two eldest sons went. We were glad to see them go. After Natalia's warning I looked harder at that family and thought there was too much of the father in the sons, and judging by the silence and the stern faces of the other customers, they felt the same way.

Pierre Morgan, who was not really quite right in the head and spent his days making strange little drawings on any paper he could find, was also called up. We all wondered how they could ever train addled Pierre to hold a gun instead of a pencil.

Nicky did not come home for Christmas that year. We put up a little tree in our sitting room and set gifts under it, but Nicky called and said he couldn't leave Nice. Too busy. Nor did he come for New Year's. I wondered if there was a new woman, if he had fallen in love with someone, and was startled to experience a strong pang of jealousy. What we had wasn't love, not exclusive love, but still, I had come to depend on him.

"Nora," he said over the phone, after he had finished a call to his mother. "I miss you."

"Do you?" My voice was a little reproachful.

He laughed. "The supreme compliment. You are jealous. After all this time."

"No, I'm not."

"All the times you could have been, you were not. Now that there is truly no reason, you are. Perhaps it is American logic. I have to go to Lyon, Nora. I will be spending a few weeks there."

Weeks. In all the time I had known him, he had never spent more than a few days. He said Lyon was chilly and impersonal compared with the sunny friendliness of Nice, and that the men who stayed in the Lyon hotel cared only about business. "Silk and steel," he complained. "That's all they think about." The guests in the Nice auberge, like him, were pleasure seekers.

"What are you doing in Lyon?" I asked.

"Business," he said brusquely. "My love to Dahlia." He hung up.

"Monsieur Nicky?" Dahlia said, squinting up from her homework. The temper tantrums and tears were things of the past. Dahlia had grown calm, even-tempered, and usually cheerful. She was a happy child, but she did not like sharing her *maman*.

In May, Germany invaded France. They broke through the Maginot Line in the north with such force, such speed, that the French soldiers had no choice but to throw down their arms. Natalia, Madame LaRosa, and myself were sitting around the radio listening to the BBC when they made the announcement. Blitzkrieg.

We heard the word for the first time. It was just dusk and we were sitting in the semidark of Natalia's curtained parlor. All three of us made the same gesture: we dropped our knitting and put our hands over our mouths.

"What is it?" Dahlia came into the room, pushing her glasses back up onto the bridge of her nose.

"The Germans are in France," Natalia said.

Dahlia scratched at a scab on her leg. "Are they coming here?"

"No," I said. "Of course not." Natalia crossed herself. We sat on into the evening, pretending to listen to the music from the radio, Schubert's Unfinished Symphony. When the radio concert ended, Natalia went to the piano and replayed the piece, slowing the pacing of it, making it a dirge.

On the evening of June 10 the BBC announced that the Germans had entered Paris. A swastika flag flew over the Hôtel de Ville. I tried to imagine the Café Dôme filled with German soldiers, armed, sitting where Jamie used to sit, under the *T* of *tabac*.

The week after the Germans marched into Paris, I went to Nice and found the city overflowing. I could barely elbow my way down boulevard Victor Hugo.

Parisians had fled the city by the thousands, heading south. This flood of humanity merged with refugees from Belgium and Holland, and the roads and boulevards had turned to slow-moving parking lots, filled with cars and bicycles and even horse carts piled with pots and mattresses and trunks. I thought of Man Ray and Picasso and wondered if they were somewhere in this tide of humanity and for the first time in many months I wondered where Lee was. Not in Paris, I hoped.

I bumped my way through the crowd and found Nicky in the lobby of the hotel, poring over the register with his desk clerk.

"Tell Madame Lowe she must share her room with another woman. We will find a suitable guest and put a cot in the room," I overheard. "No more singles, everyone must double up. And put two cots in the office as well." He looked up and his face wore an expression I did not recognize. Worry. Fear. Anger. All mixed. Quickly, he thought to smile at me, to reassure me.

"Nora. Go upstairs, darling. I'll be with you soon."

I carried my overnight case and perfume sample case upstairs and waited, glad for Nicky's spacious and quiet rooms at the top of the hotel. I switched on the radio and heard France's new prime minister, Marshal Pétain, saying that the hostilities between France and Germany were ended. It was over. There would be no more war for France.

People were shouting in the streets, dancing without music. When I went back downstairs, bottles of champagne were being passed around in the hotel lobby.

"Better the Germans than the Communists," said old Mr. Simmons, waving his glass at me. "Won't be so bad, I suspect."

"Don't be stupid," Nicky said, appearing at my side. It was the first and last time I heard him be rude to a guest.

Mr. Simmons glared down his long nose and went into the bar to find his wife.

"The old fool," Nicky said. "They'll find our so-called peace carries a high price."

We sat that evening on the Hôtel Negresco patio, not just because it was a warm summer evening, but because the dining room was completely packed. There were so many refugees from the north that eight people were seated at tables meant for four and others ate standing; when they were finished, they went off to sleep in their cars or on the beach because there were no more beds to be had in Nice.

Nicky and I had a private table outdoors through professional courtesy and his having passed a large note to the waiter. That evening was the first and the last time I heard the word "resistance" from Nicholas.

"Listen, Nora," he said. "I need you to pay attention. *Maman* will not understand, and you must pay attention from now on to keep her and Dahlia and yourself safe."

Nicholas signaled to the waiter and ordered a second helping of steak and potatoes. His suit was already tight around his waist and he caught me looking at his vest, where the cloth stretched around the strained buttons.

"Don't worry," he said. "We will all have plenty of opportunity to slenderize in the months to come. Finish your steak. You may not have another one for quite a while." The waiter brought his second plate and Nicky and the waiter exchanged a glance I could not read, even though I was already paying attention.

"He will be gone soon," Nicholas said, "Most of the young men will be. And France will be divided. Eat, Nora."

Just as he was finishing his second helping, he looked up and I followed his gaze to where a man had just stepped onto the patio. He had dark hair combed straight over his forehead and his eyes never stopped moving over the crowd, watching, searching. He saw Nicky and came to our table. In the years to come I would remember this moment, this innocent little wave of greeting: when Jean Moulin, the leader of the French Resistance, came to our table. He wasn't yet wearing the scarf around his neck that would become his trademark, the scarf that would hide the scar from his failed suicide attempt after he had been captured and tortured by the Gestapo the first time. He did not survive the second capture and torture.

"The steak is good?" he asked Nicky, not looking at me.

"Good enough," Nicky said. That was all. The air became electric around them, filled with hundreds of unsaid words. Nicky gave him a packet, and the stranger left as quickly as he came.

"What was that about?" I asked.

"Nothing that need interest you. Let's dance, Nora. Don't talk. Enjoy the music."

I found myself wishing, that evening, that I had never known Jamie, that I had been heart-whole when I had met Nicky. I felt at home in his embrace, safe and wanted. Love isn't really about what we think of the other person, but how we feel about ourselves when we are with that person. With Jamie I had been too young, too naive, too clinging. With Nicky I was confident and content with life as it was. It wasn't a grand passion, but it was a livable one, and perhaps that was better.

But, I told myself, if I hadn't known Jamie, I wouldn't have Dahlia. And life was unimaginable without her.

Soon would come rationing and hunger, bombers flying overhead. German and Italian soldiers, tanks rolling down our streets. Resistance. But that night we were still waiting for those things to come. We drank too much and Nicky whispered words in my ear to make me laugh.

In between his jokes and murmurs he began to give me instructions. Buy as much perfume from the factories as my capital would allow. It, like everything else, would soon be in short supply. There would be a shortage of glass and labor, and without those the perfume industry would be crippled. Were the good wines walled up in the cellar? *Maman*'s pearls hidden? Keep your radio tuned to a German channel at all times. If you listen to the BBC, tune it back to the German channel immediately after. He smiled as he told me these things and anyone looking at us would have thought we were discussing the new summer fashions.

"Why buy perfume?" I asked. "No one can afford it anymore. Who will buy it?"

"Soon, German generals and colonels will come here. They will take French mistresses and will buy gifts for them. Don't overcharge them. They will not forgive or forget. Sell as much as you can, as quickly as you can, because soon they will simply take it and pay nothing."

Blackout was already in effect by then: no lights, not even candles, allowed in case they might be spotted from overheard, or from the ocean. When the last light of the evening was gone, we made our way, in darkness, upstairs to his rooms, hearing laughter and shouts and moans from the street as others made their unlighted way back to rooms, homes, cars, wherever they were spending the night.

"You know," Nicky said that night, as we were undressing in the darkness, "if you weren't such a good mistress, I would be tempted to marry you and make you my wife. Maybe when this is over, you should speak with Dahlia. I know you would want her permission."

"I'll think about it," I said, pressing up against him under the cool sheets.

"Good," he said.

Were we engaged? Was it that simple? It had been so complicated with Jamie and in the end the complications had defeated us, the worries, the jealousies, the betrayals. Maybe, I thought, beginning the slow drift into sleep, this is how it's supposed to be. Easy. Friendly. But was it really enough? Marrying Nicky when I still thought of Jamie seemed like a cheat.

Lee had separated sex and love, I remembered. Perhaps I could separate love and marriage.

.................................

When I returned to Grasse after that June weekend, the boys that had gone off as soldiers to the front had been demobbed and sent back home, the butcher's sons, André and Paulo, among them. The ones just back gathered in listless groups on street corners and in cafés, whispering, waiting, some of them visibly wounded, on crutches, faces puckered with burn scars or emptied pant legs flapping over missing limbs. André and Paulo had not a single wound between the two of them, and there was whispering about that, how they had hidden in the backs of trucks to avoid the fighting.

I followed Nicky's instructions closely in the following months, putting all my cash into perfume and other goods that might eventually be bartered. Other merchants were doing the same, acquiring and selling off stock at a dizzying pace, trying to keep one step ahead of the rationing, the shortages, the eventual outright theft of our goods by the Germans.

The Gypsies called these years the "great disappearing." That was what it was like. Every week something different and vital disappeared from our lives. Our wheat, wine, cheese, fruit, were all sent to Germany. The Nazis forbade the fisherman to take out their boats and fish disappeared from our tables, so that soon we were living on "tomatoes and sunshine," as people bitterly said. Trust among neighbors evaporated like water from salt fields, leaving behind suspicion.

As Nicky had said would happen, the men began to disappear. Some were sent as forced labor to work camps and factories in Germany; others became resistance fighters who went into the hills and forests or the secret cellars of Lyon to fight against the Nazis and against what Vichy France had become: a country of collaborators, who believed better the Germans than the Russians, and this would be over soon, and it wouldn't be that bad, if we just went along.

One evening in 1941, on the Negresco patio, I ran into one of Man's occasional models, a red-haired girl named Marie-Louise. I was not friendly at first—I had spent the day demonstrating perfume samples to my new buyers, all German officers who were sending them to mistresses, French girls in Paris. The experience had left me sour. But Marie-Louise was in a talkative mood and didn't care if I wanted to listen or not.

She spent an hour filling me in. Lee and Aziz were still officially married—Marie-Louise stressed "officially"—but Lee was in England living with the art collector Roland Penrose and Aziz was in Egypt. It was a matter of time before they were divorced, if Lee managed to survive the war.

"Why wouldn't she?" I asked, not liking Marie-Louise's tone.

"She takes awful chances, Man says. Running around with her camera, photographing even when the air raid sirens are going off. Man says she's going to become a war correspondent. She's tired of fashion shoots. She's photographing for *Vogue* again, but taking pictures of the war."

That was Lee. Climbing to the top of the tree, taking every risk that presented itself. I felt a shiver of fear for her. "Where's Man?" I asked.

"Paris. But not for long." Man had left Paris when the Germans entered, but like most of the refugees, he had returned soon after. That was in the early part of the war, before the laws against Jews had been passed, before the trains to the camps began, and when Parisians, even Jews, thought they would be left alone. The next time Man left, it would be many years before he would return to Paris.

Pablo was still in his studio on the rue des Grand Augustins, Marie-Louise reported. In Paris, all the theaters and restaurants were open, but they were filled with Germans. Marie-Louise sighed and downed her whiskey. She herself was trying to get a *laissez-passer* to go back to Paris, where she had been hired to appear in a musical revue, but it was tough; the passes to get through the demarcation line between occupied and Vichy France were not easy to obtain.

"I should never have come to Nice," she complained, and got up to stumble to the bar for another refill. By then the waiters had been replaced by waitresses and the girls of Nice did not give good service to the haughty Parisian girls who were stranded there.

"You were friends with Lee Miller?" Nicky asked, taking Marie-Louise's chair. He had appeared out of nowhere, walking very silently for such a heavyset man. "They say she is taking some very good photographs of the Blitz in London."

"She was always handy with a camera, and in the darkroom," I said, and my tone made Nicky look at me hard and raise an eyebrow.

The ocean was streaked orange and violet with the colors of the sunset. Seagulls called overhead. Even the seagulls looked newly skinny, I thought. "When you go back to Grasse tomorrow, leave the side door unlocked when you go to bed," Nicky said. "Leave what food you can on the table. You will have visitors, two people, and no one, especially *Maman*, is to know about this. They will be gone by the time you get up in the morning. We are moving them to Switzerland."

It happened as he said. The next day, around one in the morning, when Grasse was in darkness, I heard the side door open. Natalia and Dahlia were asleep. I listened, ear to my closed door. Two voices, very soft conversation. A spoon fell once. And in the morning, before dawn, they were gone. I got up earlier than usual to clean up their dishes, to put away the pillows and blankets from the floor of the pantry.

This happened several times in the following months. Nicky never explained; I never asked. Once, in the morning, there was blood on the floor. I cleaned it up as best I could, but it stained the tile, so I made up a lie about cutting my finger on the butcher knife to tell Natalia.

"That was a lot of blood from a little cut," she said, peering at the floor. "Perhaps we should put a rug over the stain. Just in case."

In case the police should get suspicious and decide to search the house, she meant. Nicky's mother was more aware of what was going on than her son gave her credit for.

France was divided, and so were we, in Grasse and in other towns. There were households like ours, which listened to the BBC each evening, reports from London, and from de Gaulle, the leader of the Free French. Ours was not the only home that sheltered faceless midnight visitors. But there were other households that belonged to the right-wing *Parti Populaire Français*, people who attended meetings where they used the Nazi salute as a greeting and who ferreted out names and locations of resistance fighters to give to the police.

Sometimes, when I was standing on line to buy the few eggs or ounces of meat our coupons allowed, a man or a woman would glance at me and look quickly away and I would wonder, is that the person I must not know about for their own safety and mine? Or is that a person of whom I must beware?

Nicky gave me a name, Varian Fry in Marseille. "He is from the Emergency Rescue Committee of New York," Nicholas said. "If anything happens, someone will come to you and give you that name. You can trust them."

Dahlia and I had our first fight, that Christmas.

One morning, I was changing the sheets on Dahlia's bed. The air was cold and I was worried she would catch a winter fever that was going around, and had decided to wrap her pillows in flannel.

Something rustled, and when I shook the pillow, a copy of *Libération* fell out of it. It was a resistance newspaper, and strictly forbidden. That word had new and frightening meanings under the Vichy government.

I burned it in the stove and waited for Dahlia to come home for lunch.

At noon I heard her fling her schoolbag on the table just inside the door.

She came into the kitchen and gave me her usual hug and I could feel her shoulder bones through her sweater, as delicate as a bird's bones. All our children were too thin. The food we grew, the milk and cheese from the cows and sheep we pastured . . . most of it was sent to Germany and we lived on rations.

Because there was no more baby fat on her, Dahlia looked older than her age. Her cheekbones slanted across her face and there were dark hollows under them although she was only eight.

She grew stiff in my embrace, and pulled out of it. "You're angry about something," she said.

"I found the paper hidden in your pillow."

She sat at the table and pulled a hunk of bread from the loaf. The bread was gray with additives, sawdust and who knew what else?

The baker wouldn't say, was afraid to say. He used flour authorized by the military police.

"It's only a paper, Momma," she said.

"A forbidden paper, published by the resistance fighters. Do you know what would happen to you, to us all, if it were found in this house? Do you think they wouldn't question a child? You think they wouldn't?" I raised my hand to slap her for the first time, and stopped just at the last second, when my hand was an inch from her face.

She looked at me, and the separation began, when my child was no longer exclusively mine, when she began to belong to something larger. There was a flicker in her eyes of anger and rebellion, and then a curtain fell over her face. The openness of childhood disappeared. Her face was unreadable.

I was the one who wept, not Dahlia. "Never bring that paper into the house. Promise," I pleaded.

"Can we eat now?" She did not look at me, but out the window. Our neighbor, Madame Orieux, was hanging her quilts to air and stood framed in her own window, looking at us, her head tilted to its good side: she heard better in her left ear than her right.

When Dahlia looked back at me, it was as if we had changed places. See what you've done, her gaze said. Spoken so loudly, so indiscreetly, in front of that woman next door.

"You think I don't know," Dahlia said quietly so we couldn't be overheard. "About the people who come at night and leave before morning. You tell me nothing, and then accuse me of keeping secrets. Why do you never talk about my father?" She stuck out her bottom lip and was again my child, my little one.

She ignored the bowl of soup I put in front of her.

I leaned against the sink, thinking what to say, what not to say.

This was the moment I had dreaded for years and there was no going around it or over it. I had to walk right through it.

"He was an American. A boy I knew. We went to Paris together, before I came here to Grasse."

"Poughkeepsie," she said, remembering our trip there years before. "Why didn't you marry him?"

"He was in love with someone else."

She looked up, confused, still young enough and innocent enough to believe that if you loved someone, he was bound to love you back.

"Does he know about me?" she asked.

"We separated before you were born."

"So I know about him, and he doesn't know about me." She spooned her soup, her eyes thoughtful.

For Christmas, we put up boughs of evergreens and made presents for each other, and I also gave Dahlia her first bottle of cologne, a light fragrance suitable for a young girl.

Dahlia unwrapped it from its brown paper and turned it over and over in her hands, opening the flacon.

"Don't you want to try it, sweetheart?" I coaxed, seeing my daughter but remembering my mother.

"At school, they say you are selling perfume to the Germans," Dahlia said, looking up at me with her huge, serious brown eyes. "Is this one the German officers buy?"

"No. This is one I do not show them." I felt cold, not just because it was December and we had only a small fire in the old tile stove.

"They are recruiting children?" I accused Nicky the next time I saw him, the weekend after New Year's. "This great organization of yours uses children?"

"I didn't give her the papers. Someone from her school must be distributing them."

"Not my child," I said through gritted teeth. Vichy France was thick with police commanded by Germans, Frenchmen in blue uniforms and brown shirts, outcasts from the Far Right and released prisoners who tortured and assassinated those in the resistance.

"Children in occupied France are taking even greater chances," Nicky said. "They cross the demarcation lines on their bicycles to carry messages. They go where adults cannot." He closed the door firmly behind us, because I had accosted him in his office behind the reception desk instead of waiting for a more private moment upstairs.

"Not my child," I said again, pulling on his arm, forcing him to look at me. "She is all I have."

"All?" he said, quietly. "What about me? What about France, this country you said you love so much?"

I didn't have to say it again; he saw it on my face. Dahlia was everything, the reason I worked hard, the reason I sold perfumes to Germans I detested, the reason I had stayed in Grasse where she was growing up safe and protected by me, Natalia, Monsieur and Madame LaRosa. She was my gravity, my center. Nothing mattered but her safety, her happiness.

That night I slept on the far side of his bed, not letting him touch me.

I thought of leaving France, but by then, it was too late. Pearl Harbor had been bombed and the United States had entered the war; I was no longer a member of a neutral nation, no longer able to travel openly. The first convoy of Jewish deportees had been sent from Vichy to Germany and the true horrors were beginning. Even those who had once supported Pétain and the armistice with Germany now feared the future.

"Get us out of here, Nicky," I said the next morning.

"Yes," he agreed. "It is time. I will make arrangements. I will keep your daughter safe, Nora. I promise."

Arrangements took time and there was a priority list of people needing to leave France. Others were in immediate danger: they would be shot if seen on the street, tortured if captured. We had to wait, he said.

# CHAPTER SEVENTEEN

When next I went into Nice a few weeks after telling Nicky I wanted to leave France, there was a "Closed" sign on the door of the hotel and the lobby was filled with German officers. All of his regular guests had been told to find lodgings elsewhere. The Allies had landed in North Africa. Germany, knowing that an Allied invasion into southern France was planned, had sent their troops into Vichy.

"Go upstairs," Nicky said, looking not at me but over my shoulder, watching. "Stay there and don't open the door unless you are certain it is me on the other side of it." I made my way through the lobby, trying to ignore the stares of the officers. Hours passed before Nicky joined me. He looked tired and anxious.

"Are you hungry?" he asked. He carried a tray with bread and a little cheese. "It's all we have. They have emptied the kitchen, and the wine cellar. Go back to Grasse, Nora. Tomorrow. First thing. There is nothing more for you here in Nice. Wait in Grasse."

"You are here," I said almost apologetically, touching his sleeve. At that moment, I did love him. He was kind and charming and gallant in a way Jamie had never been. And there I was again, comparing him to Jamie.

"Thank you for that," he said. For our last night together, we drank a bottle of wine he had hidden from the Germans, and sat and talked nonsense long into the small hours of the morning, telling our stories to each other, filling in the holes of the past. I told him about climbing trees with Lee, the perfume bottles lined up in my mother's bathroom. He told me about his father's gold cuff links, the pearl tie stud he hid in his mouth when they crossed the border out of Russia, the dog he had had as a boy that had been left behind. We gave each other our memories. And in the morning, I went home to Grasse and stayed there, waiting for word.

Natalia and I had three more nighttime visitors that spring. They were no longer announced. I just put food out in the evening, in case, and if it was gone in the morning, if the cups and plates had been moved, the blankets on the floor rumpled, I knew someone had been there. I wondered when our turn would arrive, when we would become nighttime travelers.

"Uncle Nicky didn't call me," Dahlia said the last Sunday evening in May. It was warm and because of blackout regulations we sat in the dark, on the little terrace. Occasionally we heard a plane overhead and the loud, angry buzzing would fill our heads; there would be a moment of fear, and then the sound would begin to fade away, the dangerous humming no louder than a mosquito's, and there would be a moment of pure joy at simply being alive.

"He's probably busy," I said, caught in that moment of temporary bliss when the sound of the plane first died away completely.

"He always calls on Sunday evening," Dahlia said. She sounded frightened.

"Then the lines are down. He'll call tomorrow," I insisted, hiding my own worry.

Roses were blooming and the air was heavy with their scent. When I closed my eyes and inhaled, concentrating on the odor, I was transported back to the night of Lee's last party in Paris, the night Man shot at her. The night I found her in bed with Jamie. The sense of loss and defeat went through me like electricity, as if it had all just happened.

That overwhelming sense of dread told me that Dahlia was right. Attar of rose marked the end of one thing and the beginning of something else. Something was wrong with Nicky. The air blossomed with presentiment.

"What's wrong, Momma?" Dahlia reached for my hand in the darkness.

"We'll be fine," I said, pressing her hand, promising both of us.

Natalia, inside and sitting at her piano, began the gentle chords of a Chopin nocturne. She played from memory, effortlessly, but there was hesitation in some of the notes. She, too, was hoping the phone would ring. It didn't.

The next day, a school day, Dahlia stayed home. We were all three of us waiting. At dusk, at the end of those long hours, Solange, Nicky's receptionist in Nice, knocked on the door.

"Pack a bag. One small valise each," she said. "We leave as soon as it is dark. You, too, Madame Hughes," she said, looking at Natalia. "You must come as well."

Natalia crossed herself and sat heavily, as if her legs couldn't support her. "My God," she whispered several times.

Dahlia, sitting at the table in the parlor, frowning over Latin conjugations, heard us and came into the kitchen. She put her arm around Natalia, and the child tried to comfort the woman. Dahlia didn't weep or show fear. Her face looked so adult at that moment it froze my heart. She's growing up too quickly, I thought. It's the war.

"What does this mean?" I asked. "What is happening?"

Solange smiled. "He told me you would ask questions. He said, 'Tell her it is time to go. Remember Varian in Marseille.' "

Our old code. I could trust Solange.

"Is Nicky coming, too?"

"No."

Natalia began to moan. Quicker than I did, she saw what this meant. She put her hands over her eyes and wept. Dahlia hugged her tighter.

"Where is Nicky?" I asked.

Solange turned me aside and spoke quietly so Natalia couldn't hear. "They have taken him to Lyon. We think to the École de Santé."

Gestapo headquarters. "My God," I said, echoing Nicky's mother.

We did as Solange instructed. We packed a single bag each and left the house as it was, with dishes in the sink, Dahlia's homework spread out over the table. Natalia paused in her sitting room. She closed up the piano, touched it lovingly. We went out into the night and Natalia looked once over her shoulder at the home where she had lived for so many years.

"It happens again," she said bitterly, and her Russian accent, slumbering for so long, made her words thud and growl. "I must flee and leave everything behind. First the Bolsheviks, then the Germans."

I felt numb with fear. Nicky had tried to prepare me, had warned me there were dangers ahead. But to think of him, that pleasure-loving, worldly man, in the bowels of the Gestapo headquarters . . . I couldn't bear it.

Solange and the others who took her place did not lead us to Marseille. The safe house there was already being too closely watched. Instead, we traveled in a northeasterly direction.

Days later, sleeping in a mountain hut somewhere just outside Switzerland, I awoke in darkness, confused. A storm was raging, rattling the windows, blowing rain through a crack in my bedroom in Poughkeepsie. That was how I knew it was a nightmare. Daddy had kept our house in good repair; there had been no cracks in the window. Dahlia moaned and pressed closer to me. I put my arms around her. My daughter, my treasure. Places didn't matter. Only Dahlia did. "Thank you, Nicky," I whispered before falling asleep again, exhausted. He had kept my daughter safe, as he had promised.

# PART THREE
# BASE NOTES

The bottom notes of a fragrance are recognized after approximately thirty minutes of wear, long enough for a woman to fall in or out of love, to remember the happiest or saddest days of childhood, to reminisce about those moments when everything changed. Much can happen in half an hour. The world can change, and so the perfume must change as well, in a way that adds meaning to the notes that have gone before. The base notes are the foundation of the fragrance, the most lasting impression. When a perfume is remembered, it is usually the base notes that leave the strongest memory.

—From the notebooks of N. Tours

. . . after the things are broken and scattered, taste and smell alone . . . remain poised a long time, like souls, remembering, waiting, hoping, amid the ruins . . .

—Proust

# CHAPTER EIGHTEEN

"My God," Natalia said, standing in front of her house, three years later.

The windows were boarded over with Xs of wood; paint had been splattered on the front. The window boxes had been torn away, leaving rusting nails jutting out. A ragged hole in the bottom of the door showed where the hungry cats of the neighborhood had been sleeping for the past few years. Someone had made that hole on purpose. No one can despoil a house worse than a tribe of tomcats.

Natalia dropped her valise and rubbed her eyes as if clearing her vision might restore the house.

Dahlia put her arm around Natalia's shoulders. In the years that we had been gone, Nicky's mother had developed a dowager's hump, and she stood, bowed and comfortless, muttering softly in Russian.

"So, you came back," said a voice behind us.

I turned to look. "Is that you, André?" I asked. The butcher's son leaned against a wall smoking a cigarette. He had the same round-shouldered, chin-lifted attitude he'd had as a boy. I'd never cared for him. He looked too much like his father, spoke like him, eyed the women and girls of the town in the same way, as if they were meat to be hung in the shopwindow.

"Yeah," he said. "Didn't think you'd be back. And is that little four-eyes? You've grown, Dahlia. Not bad looking for an American."

Dahlia pushed her glasses back up her nose and glared at him. "You could help us," she said. "We need to tear down the wood so we can open the door."

"Don't bother," he said. "Side door is already open." He slunk away, his cigarette tip glowing in the dark.

We walked around to the side. The door wasn't just open; it had been taken off the hinges and carted away. We walked cautiously inside, already prepared, we thought, for the worst, already so fatigued by the shock of arrival we expected we couldn't feel much more.

The night we'd left Grasse, it had been moonless and silent. Everyone had stayed in their homes behind tightly closed blackout curtains. No one waved farewell. No one knew we had left until several days later, I suspect, when it would have been noticed I wasn't queuing up for our rations.

The night we returned to Grasse, in 1945, the war was over, or at least the most visible part of it. Men sat outside the café once again, drinking, playing chess. Housewives gossiped loudly in their courtyards or shouted from window to window over the narrow streets. There were no Nazi flags, no German slogans pasted on walls, no soldiers on the streets. The people of Grasse had taken their city back for themselves.

But the end of war does not necessarily mean peace. Coming into town, we had seen a group of young women clustered under a streetlamp on place du Petit Puy. Their heads had been shaved; several looked bruised and beaten. The retributions, the punishments of the collaborators, had begun.

Dahlia saw the women and looked at me, frightened. I wondered if we had left the safety of Switzerland too soon. But the three of us had agreed: it was time to come home.

The Swiss had granted us a tolerance permit, allowing us to reside but not to work, and so we had spent those years in a single attic room in Geneva, living on charity from the Quakers, in a hotel that had been converted into a hostel for war refugees. Dahlia had been allowed to attend school, and Natalia had been allowed to play the piano in the ballroom, which had been converted into a mess hall for the refugees.

Those had been lost years, for me, unable to work, unable to return to either Grasse or Poughkeepsie, unable to do anything but live with regret and fear. When I thought about Nicky, a blackness came over me. We hadn't heard from him or about him. We hoped he had been sent to a labor camp, because we had heard you could survive the forced labor. But there were other places you did not survive, were not meant to survive.

Those good years, the happy years in Paris and then Grasse, were a lifetime away. Some days, walking along the shore of Lake Geneva with nothing to do but wait, I missed even Lee, and then I would remember Lee in bed with Jamie, her arms around his neck, that strange little smile on her face.

And as I remembered, it seemed so long ago, so irrelevant. Survival mattered. Nothing less.

"We have survived," Dahlia said, that night of our return to Grasse. She was twelve years old and it seemed strange for my little girl to sound so grown-up.

I was glad to be home for many reasons, but she was the main one. This was where she had been born, where she had spent happy years of childhood, and no matter where I might live in the future, Grasse would be beloved to me because it had been beloved to Dahlia. I reached over and tousled her hair.

"We survived. The house hasn't," Natalia muttered.

We walked wordlessly from damaged room to damaged room. The kitchen had been scavenged of dishes and pots and pans; the rugs and curtains had disappeared. Upstairs, clothes we had left behind no longer hung in the old wardrobes.

"It was the war," Natalia said. "People needed them." But betrayal made her voice tremble.

The devastation went beyond theft: flowered wallpaper hung in damp strips and a heavy smell of rot and cat piss filled the air. A thick layer of dust coated everything. Although much of the furniture had been taken away, probably to be burned as fuel when coal ran short, Natalia's piano was there, out of tune but intact. She ran her fingers over the keys, tried a chord, then shut the lid.

Dahlia's school uniform still hung on the back of a chair. She picked it up and shook the dust off it, laughing at how small it was.

Natalia wandered aimlessly, picking things off the floor, running her hand over dusty sills, tilting her head, listening. She had hoped Nicky would be there, waiting for us, but the silence in the house was absolute.

"I'll go to Nice and see if there's any word of him," I promised her. Those who had fled during the war were returning to their homes, but we knew many would not be coming back.

We slept on the floor that first night, on mildewed cushions. The next day we began putting the house to rights. We carried mattresses out onto the terrace for an airing, scrubbed the floors, made arrangements for new strong doors and shutters. I went out to scour the shops for what I could find: a bar of soap, a few pots, some cloth for curtains, a handful of potatoes, a single slice of ham.

When I returned home after hours of standing in lines and haggling, Madame LaRosa was sitting with Natalia on the old sofa. When Madame LaRosa saw me, she sprang to her feet and we hugged for a long time, each fighting back tears.

"The police came looking for you the day after you left," she said, dabbing at her eyes with a lacy handkerchief. "That was how we found out you had gone. They came and asked us if we knew where you were. They came several times. I can't think about what would have happened if you had still been here." She did not ask why we had had to leave. We hadn't been the only household sheltering fugitives.

Madame LaRosa had brought us soup and a cake and we ate together at the dining room table that afternoon. Like old times, Natalia said, though several dining room chairs, the carpet, and the old paintings had been taken and the room felt too large because of its new emptiness.

"I think I like the room like this," Dahlia said. "Nice and open and sunny."

"Very modern," Natalia agreed, smiling bravely.

After lunch we went into the cobwebbed cellar, carefully carrying a single candle so that the old dry beams wouldn't be set ablaze. I found a heavy stone and hammered away at the false brick wall. The wine we had stored was still there, safe. Natalia selected a bottle and back upstairs, we toasted our health, our homecoming, and the end of the war. Dahlia finished an entire glass and asked for more, but I wouldn't give it to her. "Momma!" she complained.

"It will strengthen her blood," Madame LaRosa said. "A second glass, just today. And then no more until you are sixteen." She wagged her finger at us.

Dahlia giggled and snuggled close to me on the cat-smelling sofa. Natalia looked at us, and did not smile. There was hunger in her mother's eyes, hunger for her own child.

The third day of our return I took the bus to Nice.

The city looked worse for the poverty and neglect of the war years. On avenue Jean Médecin many of the shops were boarded and closed. Nicholas' hotel, l'Auberge de l'Opéra, needed fresh paint and new shutters. The wood floors were stained and scuffed, and the menu posted on the board out front offered only seafood stew or sausages. Nicky would have been furious.

No one from the earlier years was working there. They were all strangers to me, and when I asked about the owner, they shrugged, they knew nothing. The hotel had changed hands.

One woman was kind enough to ask my name, and when I told her, recognition flared in her eyes. "Wait," she said. "When I began to work in the office last year, there was some old mail on the desk. I think one of the letters was for you. I'll go get it."

A letter from Nicky. I'm safe, he would say. I'm in Portugal or Zurich. My hopes began to rise like morning mist steaming off a roof. I could feel a smile beginning to take shape on my face.

She went into the back room behind the counter . . . the same one Nicky used to emerge from, wiping coffee from his mustache with a pristine hotel napkin. When she returned and handed me the envelope with my name written in unfamiliar handwriting, those hopes that had begun to rise fell once again.

It was only an unpaid bill from my seamstress.

. . . . . . . . . . . . . . . . . . . . . . . . . . . . . . .

It was too painful to stay at Nicky's hotel, so I took a room in a private house—everyone had "rooms for rent" signs up, trying to bring in a little money—and for two days I walked up and down the oceanfront, unwilling to go home to Grasse, to tell Natalia there was no word from her son. Nice was once again full of Americans and French, many still in uniform, but no more elderly gentlewomen from England, and certainly no Austrian barons. On the second day I ran into one of Nicky's old waiters, Jean Carles. He was sitting on a bench, watching the waves roll in and out and break up the three-toed claw prints the seagulls left in the sand. Jean's hands were jammed into the pockets of an old, frayed coat and he hadn't shaved.

Those were the easiest changes to observe, because the younger Jean had been handsome and vain and well dressed. Now he was thin and dull-eyed. I sat next to him and after a few minutes he roused enough curiosity to look at me. He recognized me.

"He won't be coming back," he said. "They shot him, at the École de Santé in Lyon. They said he fell from a window, but that was a lie. They executed him because he wouldn't give names."

Nicky, my lover, my friend. To die like that. Alone. I couldn't let myself think too much of what he had gone through before that final bullet ended the pain.

Jean and I sat together for a while, watching the waves and seagulls, not talking. I wouldn't be seeing Nicky again and the sadness was overpowering.

I rehearsed in my head what I would say to Natalia, realizing there were no soft words, no gentle way, to announce the death of a son.

..............................

After events such as those, life does not return to normal. You must create a new existence, one full of holes and regrets. If grief were a perfume, it would be all top notes with nothing to follow. Bottle by bottle, we sold the wine Nicky had told us to store before the war. We lined up for ration coupons; we planted tomatoes on the terrace. I sewed curtains and a new school uniform for my child. We had the piano tuned and encouraged Natalia to try to play it, but the music was dead for her. When my daughter laughed, she did it behind her hands, as if in secret, because the laughter was gone.

You go on, and you walk with ghosts beside you.

The perfume factories woke up from the enforced slumber of war shortages and began production in earnest, trying to fill an already-waiting market eager for pleasure and luxury. I easily found work in the factories as a translator, an office girl. I also worked in the lavender fields, moving down the rows of plants, snipping flower heads and laying them carefully in baskets. The physical strain of that labor felt good, felt right. It felt good to go home with an aching back, too tired to speak. Natalia had already fled into her own private silence. Her grief became a wordless, stony one. The stories she used to tell disappeared, and the music as well. She sat by the window looking out into the street, refusing to give up the wait for the son who would never again come up that path and knock on that door.

Now begins the saddest story I know, how a mother loses her daughter, how a war never really ends but ripples through the rest of your life in ways you may not expect.

Natalia had lived for hope, and once she knew Nicky was dead, she gave up that hope. She died the next year, of a weak heart. Her last words were in Russian, and I heard her say "Nicky" several times. When she was in her bed, struggling for breath, she looked through me into corners of the room, seeing things I couldn't see. Her fingers moved over the covers as if she were playing a waltz, and then her breath rattled in her throat and the fingers lay still.

Dahlia seemed to come to an end of her resilience, with the death of the woman who had been a grandmother to her. She wept inconsolably and would not return to school or her studies for weeks, not until I reminded her that Natalia had hoped she would go on to university and study languages or music. Only then did Dahlia agree to go back to the school in Grasse and begin to make up for the lost time during our exile in Switzerland and the disruptions of the war, working at the dining room table from late afternoon until midnight.

I would sit on the sofa opposite the double doors to the dining room and glance at my child, my lovely child, looking pale and somehow saintly, like a church painting of the Virgin, her face lit by the single lantern she used, all else in dark shadows.

My knitting needles would clack the way Natalia's once had; I had found bags of wool stashed in Natalia's dresser, good prewar wool that had somehow been left behind during the scavenging years. Dahlia took an occasional break from her work, to stretch and talk for a few minutes. She began again to ask questions about her father. What foods had he liked? Was he a good dancer?

I searched for and found stuck in the back of a desk drawer the old photos Lee had taken in Paris. The edges were mouse-chewed and damp, but there were Jamie and me at the Dôme; Jamie in Man Ray's studio setting up the lights, black cords twisted around his hands; Jamie and me mugging for the camera outside the Closerie des Lilas, where years before Hemingway had liked to drink.

Ah, that youth, that freedom.

"He was handsome," Dahlia said, holding the photos close to her face and squinting.

"Very," I agreed.

"I would like to meet him. Can we go back to Poughkeepsie, just for a visit?"

Travel was still difficult then, and expensive. "I have to save up a bit," I said. "It will take a while." Natalia had left me the use of her house for as long as I wanted, and then it would go to a distant cousin. Meanwhile, there were taxes, repair bills, all more than the small salary I was earning.

Was Jamie even alive? The thought, not a new one, clenched my chest with fear and loss. Once the States had entered the war, he would have been certain to enlist, to do his bit. More than once during those years in Switzerland, I had worried about Jamie, and then felt guilty because I should have been thinking of Nicky.

"Tell me about my father," Dahlia said one evening, sitting next to me.

I pulled her close and brushed back her hair, noticing the recent change in its texture. When she was little, her dark hair had been so fine that ribbons and bands would fall out of it a minute after being tied, as if the hair had a rebellious life of its own. Now, though glossy, it could be held back with pins and ribbons; it was obedient, subdued. They had to come, I supposed, those first days of womanhood for my child, but if I could have delayed them, I would have; I would have kept her small and safe forever.

"He was a baker's son," I said. "And an athlete. A high school football hero. And he wanted to be an artist. A photographer."

"Why not a painter or a musician?"

"I don't know. Maybe he wanted to take pictures of things as they were, not reinvent them."

"Maybe I'll study photography."

"They don't teach it in colleges. You'd have to apprentice to someone who already has a studio and work like a slave. You wouldn't like that," I added, remembering Man Ray's studio: the nude models, some of whom were prostitutes, the alcohol, the drugs, the sex. "I thought you wanted to study art history. Vermeer, wasn't it? The old Dutch masters?"

"Tell me more about Jamie," she said. I did. All the stories I thought she might want: the ambulance chases in New York for those tabloid photos, the boat across the Atlantic, nights of dancing the Charleston, his sadness in London when the galleries didn't want his work. Our years in Paris: the cafés, the panther in the zoo. "And then he fell in love with someone else," I ended.

"I think I'll start reading the American writers," Dahlia announced the next week. "I'm tired of Balzac and Verlaine."

Dahlia was getting ready to leave me, to leave France, but I missed the signals. I think the war was partly to blame. Even people native to France wanted to leave; there were too many difficult memories and still too much hardship, and even when the war was over, it wasn't really over.

There was, primarily, the question of collaboration and the trials of the collaborators. Who had worked with the Germans and who had merely done what they could to survive, and where was the dividing line?

Was it collaboration to maintain one's old work of selling perfumes, once all the customers were German? When one sold perfume to the German officers vacationing in Nice, was one also selling possible information? When did survival become collaboration, and collaboration treason?

I began to worry that they would come for me, and I had reason to worry. Tens of thousands of people were arrested and questioned—store owners, mechanics, wine sellers, doctors, priests, hairdressers, as well as Philippe Pétain, head of the Vichy state during the war. Pétain had been tried and found guilty and sentenced to death, though that was changed to life imprisonment.

News of the trials, one after another, dozens a day, filled our newspapers. But the secret justice was most feared: in the street, in cafés, in their own homes. Pistols put to the head, triggers pulled.

"You'd think people would want to put it behind them," Madame LaRosa said one evening. "This need for revenge will do no good." She didn't visit as frequently once Natalia was gone, and we no longer shared Sunday afternoon dinners. Monsieur LaRosa had had a stroke and did not leave the house. "And if we all sought revenge for everything that had happened . . ." She put down the newspaper she had been reading and stared thoughtfully into the dining room, where Dahlia sat with her books and papers.

"Things happened here, when the war was ending, when the chaos seemed even worse than the war," she said quietly. "To the women and the girls. Housewives sold themselves for a bar of soap, a loaf of bread. Young girls gave themselves for a pair of nylons or a chocolate bar. We didn't talk about it. And there was worse, girls taken right out of their houses or stopped while going about their business."

Madame LaRosa turned down the radio. We'd been listening to a music program, popular songs about homecomings and bluebirds. End-of-war music that for a few minutes allowed the listener to believe in happy endings.

"Sentimental, aren't they?" Madame LaRosa said. She cleared her throat. "It wasn't always soldiers," she said quietly. "It wasn't always soldiers and strangers."

A second memory of that homecoming night: André Bonner, the butcher's son, leaning against a wall, waiting, followed quickly by the old memory of Lee in her white dress, stepping off her front porch.

In the dining room, Dahlia sighed and closed her book with a thump. "I hate Greek," she said, smiling, pushing her glasses back up her nose. "Can I come sit with you?"

"Yes." She was old enough. She should hear whatever Madame LaRosa had to say.

"Why didn't they stop them?" I asked. "The police, the fathers and brothers."

"Because the men involved had friends who would protect them from accusations. It was war. There were more important things to worry about. That was what they said."

"Accusations of what?" Dahlia said.

"Rape." The word hung in the air like a sword.

On an evening in May I returned from a day of work at the perfume factory. Dahlia was in the kitchen, nibbling a pencil and frowning over the hated Greek translation she had yet to complete. Soon she would have to take her exams and decide where and what to study. I hoped she would be admitted to the Sorbonne, but Dahlia seemed indifferent to the possibility of living and studying in Paris.

"Momma, there's a letter from Poughkeepsie," she said, pushing the mail toward me over the table. "Open it, quickly." She brushed the hair out of her eyes and looked at me. She was already several inches taller than I was and to see this almost-grown child looking up, her face as shining as it had been on her first school day, undid me.

"Who is it from?" Dahlia stood and tried to read over my shoulder.

"Your father." I had to sit down, quickly. It was an unseasonably hot day and my hands still smelled of jasmine, an almost overpowering smell in that still, closed room.

Dahlia sat, too, her mouth a round O of surprise.

Jamie's handwriting had changed. It had a wobble, a tilt, a sense of rush.

> Dear Nora,
> I've been thinking about you. Showed some old photos to Clara yesterday and the one of you at the lake slipped out of the album. Remember that day you fell in? Clara could tell from my face that more than a dunking happened that day. I remember what happened afterwards. No more need be said. I wrote to your mother in Los Angeles and she says you spent the war in France and Switzerland. Why didn't you come home, Nora? Is it because of what happened between us? That was so long ago. You shouldn't stay away. Not because of that.
>
> I was with the U.S. Sixth Army Group in '44 when they invaded southern France. I was probably just miles away from you. Got a little shrapnel in my shoulder, but nothing serious. After the ar-

> mistice I went up to Paris for a bit but didn't stay long. Was homesick for Poughkeepsie, believe it or not. There were times in Paris, Nora, when we were there together, that I thought I'd never want to be anywhere else. Things change, don't they?
>
> I hope you don't mind that I wrote to you. I was just wondering how you were. Write, if you get the chance.

Jamie had written the letter on stationery from Tastes-So-Good Bakery and my mouth flooded with the remembered taste of vanilla and cinnamon and the smell of the floor of the van where we first made love.

Dahlia took the letter from me and held it almost reverently.

Then, she folded the letter carefully and gave it back to me. She stood and put a pot of water on the old coal-burning stove, beginning supper preparations. She moved strangely, like someone in an unfamiliar place who doesn't know where the sharp corners are, the dangerous steps up or down. Her world had been reconfigured in the space of one letter, a few sentences.

"You must write to him," she said, peeling a potato. "You must tell him about me."

"Yes," I agreed. She looked so much like him. The old hurt was still there, that betrayal and rejection when he chose Lee, not me. But a stronger feeling overwhelmed it, and that was my love for Dahlia. If she wanted the moon, I would pull it down for her. If she wanted her father, she would have him. With Nicky and Natalia gone, her family in Grasse had shrunk to only me and she needed more.

"I'll write to him tomorrow," I said.

"When I come home from school, maybe I'll add a P.S. before you post it. That will surprise him. 'Dear Father.' " Dahlia grinned.

But Dahlia didn't come home from school the next day.

Her usual arrival time came and went and she didn't show up. I was surprised. She was usually punctual. Children who grow up in wartime know better than to let their whereabouts go unaccounted for. Then dusk came. No Dahlia. I was angry. My serious child was becoming a little flighty, staring into mirrors when she thought I didn't see, fussing over clothes, daydreaming over her homework. I wondered if she had a beau and hadn't told me.

But when it turned dark and she still wasn't home, anger turned to fear. I put on a cardigan because the spring night had turned chilly, and walked to the places where I thought she might be: the café where she and her friends sometimes ate cakes after their classes; the bookstore, which was already closed and dark inside. I walked toward her school, thinking she had been hurt, had twisted her ankle or fallen on the steep cobbled street; perhaps she was waiting for me and crying in pain, but I couldn't find her.

"I will wake up from this," I began to tell myself. "It's only a bad dream." But it wasn't a dream.

I broke into a run, but she was not on any street where I might have expected to find her. By the time I made it to Madame LaRosa's house, I was sobbing and incoherent. Pale with fright, she went upstairs to make sure her husband was safely asleep, then came out into the night with me. We searched the narrow streets of Grasse for hours, calling Dahlia's name. Around midnight Madame LaRosa took me by the hand. "There is nowhere else to look. You must go home and wait," she said.

The thought of stepping into that house, emptied of Natalia, of Nicky, and now of Dahlia, filled me with horror.

"Perhaps she is already there waiting for you," Madame LaRosa said. "Come, I'll go with you. I won't leave you alone."

As soon as we entered, we heard the weeping. Dahlia was upstairs in her room. I went up the steps two at a time. She was curled up on her bed, still in her clothes. I turned on the light.

"No," she whimpered. "Turn it off."

I had already seen the torn blouse, the blood on her legs running into her socks, the bruise on her face. I went to her and rocked her, folding her small and safe into my embrace, darkness filling my chest.

"I'll go get the doctor," said Madame LaRosa.

The doctor, a young man fresh from medical studies in Paris, gave Dahlia a brief examination, cleaned her wounds, and then gave her tablets to make her sleep.

"There shouldn't be lasting damage," he said confidently, and I had to press my fists against my stomach to keep from hitting him. It wasn't his child in there, still crying in her sleep. "If signs of infection show up in a couple of weeks, call me."

I thought of Lee on the porch, smelling of chemicals. Not my child. "I'll need a written statement for the police," I said, the blackness in my chest giving way to fury.

"Are you sure?" He looked at me with pity but also with impatience. "Do you want to put your daughter through that?"

He and Madame LaRosa exchanged glances. "Think about it," he said. "If you want a report, I'll have it ready in a couple of days."

I sat by Dahlia all the rest of that night and the next day. She slept for a full twenty-four hours, waking only around midnight, stretching and yawning and then, immediately, the memory of it making her turn on her side, knees pulled up to her chest. When I tried to leave for a few minutes, she whimpered in fear.

"I shouldn't have been out that late," she said the next day, when she had recovered enough to drink a bowl of coffee with milk.

"No," I said. "This is not your fault. You did nothing wrong. I'm going to the police this afternoon. Madame LaRosa will come and sit with you."

"No!" she cried in terror. "Don't tell anyone! Please!" Her eyes widened with fear and horror. "He said if I told anyone, it . . . it would happen again."

"Who?"

Dahlia clamped her mouth shut and tried to turn away from me.

"Was it André Bonner?"

Her silence was the answer.

That afternoon after Madame LaRosa came to sit with Dahlia, I went out, slamming the front door behind me. I could feel the eyes of people watching as I passed houses and stores. Curtains stirred open and shut. People who had been standing in groups talking grew silent. They knew.

When I went into Bonner's butcher shop, the other customers parted to let me through. I went to the counter and tried not to gag on my fury, mixed now with the metallic smell of blood from freshly butchered rabbits.

Father and son were working side by side, skinning the rabbits. There was a pail of heads and feet and blood and fur. Monsieur Bonner looked up. His son did not. André was almost middle-aged by then, married to a little mouse of a woman who bore him a child every year and a half. When he stood next to his father in the shop, though, he still had the look of a frightened boy.

"You already used up your coupons," Monsieur Bonner said. "What do you want?"

"Ask him what he did to my daughter," I said, pointing at André.

"On Tuesday night? My boy was here with me. All night. Weren't you, boy?" Father and son grinned at each other. The other customers left the shop, the doorbell jingling with each hurried departure.

"If he ever touches her again, I'll kill him," I said.

Monsieur Bonner put down his cleaver and leaned closer to me over the counter. "That's a threat. I'll have to tell the police about that."

"And maybe I'll tell them about those rabbits. Black market, aren't they? You've been selling black market for years, and maybe more than rabbits and chickens." Madame LaRosa had told me that the townspeople thought the Bonner men had sold information. Nicky had died rather than give names and the Bonners had sold them.

There was a momentary fear in the butcher's eyes.

"Get out of my shop," he said. "Foreigners." He spit on his own floor.

Dahlia would sleep only with a light on. She alternated between seeming younger, a child with a mild lisp, and older, silent and forlorn, aware of things no girl should know. For weeks she wouldn't leave the house, not to go to her classes, not to sit in the sun near the fountain, not to visit Madame LaRosa or go with me to the greengrocer's and bakery. Neither of us could stand the thought of entering the butcher's shop. Because I would no longer buy meat from the butcher, other families also began to boycott him: families with pretty daughters, I noticed. There was an acrid odor of ill will in the town, small and large acts of vandalism. Paint was splashed against my front door. The neighbor's cat went missing. This, too, was part of the war that did not end even after the treaties were signed.

There were strong winds that summer and autumn, hot and dusty currents that came in from northern Africa. When Dahlia began going to her school again, and returned in the evening to her studies at the dining room table, her papers had to be weighted down with plates so they wouldn't blow away. She was there in the morning when I left, and there in the evening when I returned. She didn't visit her friends or join in any of their activities.

I worried, sometimes, that she shared my thought: if I had gone home to Poughkeepsie instead of running away to Grasse, she would have been born and raised there; the rape would not have happened. It was my fault. The guilt sickened me, but then I would think, there would have been other horrors. She, illegitimate, would have been ostracized, a girl with no father with a mother who would have been the focus of a town's gossip and hate. Dahlia's fear and misery crept into me.

I was glad work was busy at the factory; it distracted me from my worry about Dahlia. The tourists had returned to the Riviera and we now had more of them than before the war, GIs still in uniform, demobbed soldiers, English and American couples on a European vacation. Once summer ended, the south of France filled with people escaping the cold weather of Paris.

I was busy and exhausted when I returned home that evening, my hair stiffened by the dusty breeze.

Dahlia had dinner ready for us, potato stew with tomatoes and chickpeas and basil. She had just ladled it into bowls and carried them to the table when we heard a knock on the door.

"Madame LaRosa," I said, but I already knew it wasn't she. She would never drop in at dinnertime without an invitation. Dahlia's face turned white with fear.

When I opened the door, three men in police uniform were standing there, strangers not from Grasse.

"Madame Tours?" The shortest man checked a paper in his hand.

"Yes."

"You are to come with us. You have been named as a collaborator."

"You must be mistaken."

All three of them smiled. They had heard that often enough, their expressions said. "No mistake," said the one with the paper.

"It was Monsieur Bonner." Dahlia came and stood next to me. "He did this to get revenge. This is my fault."

"Was it Bonner?" I asked.

"Can't say," said the short man, but I saw yes in his eyes.

"And did he tell you his son raped my daughter?"

"Momma." Dahlia took my hand.

"Come along. This will be sorted out soon," said the tallest. He had a hard look in his eyes. He seemed almost bored.

"What about my child?"

All three men looked at Dahlia, appraising her. "She's old enough to stay on her own," said the shortest.

"Go to Madame LaRosa," I told her. "I'll be home soon."

"This is my fault," Dahlia said again, dropping my hand and taking a step backward.

"It's not. Dahlia, Dahlia, it's not your fault! Go to your godmother. Stay there."

Perhaps that was the fatal error, those words, "stay there." They have such a ring of finality.

They took me to police headquarters in Lyon. It was not the same building where Nicky had been held. They were not the same people. The war had been won; the questioners had been changed. But the cells were the same, I thought, small and damp and dark. I slept on a cot crawling with bugs and when I woke up, a woman in uniform came and led me to a room with a single bulb, a straight-back chair in front of a desk, and two men in uniform behind the desk.

"You sold perfume during the war. To the Germans. Is this correct?"

"Yes. Early in the war. I had to earn my living."

A room with a single bulb, me smelling of sweat and fear seated in front of two men in pristine uniforms . . . the stuff of nightmares. Nothing in my life had prepared me for such a thing.

"We think you sold information to the Germans," said one man.

"That is a lie," I said.

A half hour passed of accusations and my denials of them. It ended suddenly. One man looked at his watch. The two of them rose, their chair legs screaming against the bare wood floor. I was led back to my cell and kept there for three days, three days of judging time by the degree of darkness within the cell, because there were no windows. Night was lighter; they turned on a bare bulb in the hall outside the cell at night. Six meals: stale bread and cold coffee for breakfast; thin vegetable soup and more stale bread for supper.

I was left alone, and that was enough to terrify me, because alone I had time to think of what had been done to Nicky by the Germans. My jailors weren't German, but they thought me guilty of a crime, and guilty people are at the mercy of judges who often feel no mercy.

The real nightmare, though, was thinking of Dahlia, her stricken face, and what she had suffered, was suffering. Madame LaRosa could be cold and formal. I hoped she was holding my daughter, comforting her, telling her everything would be all right.

On the fourth morning I was led back to the questioning room. I was so desperate to return to Dahlia I had decided to say anything that might get me back home. But that was the puzzle: if I confessed to their charges, I would never see her again. If I didn't confess, I had no idea how long they would keep me.

Immediately after the war these interrogations happened quickly. Trials were brief and judgment followed close behind, like a dog trained to heel properly. Even Pétain's trial for collaboration had taken only a few weeks. But the trials had ended; people wanted to forget the war years. It would be more convenient for them to simply forget about me as well, perhaps to leave me there until I said what they wanted me to say.

I was pushed back down in the chair. The short one, the bully, offered me a cigarette. I refused it. His partner leaned back in his chair, arms folded across his chest. The questions again began. Did I tell so-and-so the names of the men of Grasse who had joined the resistance? No. Did I tell the Germans where the freedom fighters had hidden arms? No. A whole list of accusations, each one more elaborate and impossible than the next. I knew nothing.

"Madame, what did you tell them?" the short one asked finally, exasperated.

"How to select a perfume for their wife or mistress," I said.

Both looked at me in disbelief. The quiet one almost laughed. The corners of his mouth twitched and he busied himself with papers on the desk. I hadn't slept, and when I blinked at that bare bulb, I saw a halo around it.

A third man entered the room. He whispered something into the ear of the man who seemed to be in charge, the man sitting directly in front of me who had sat back, listening and watching, as his partner fired questions at me.

This time he spoke. "Is it true, madame, that you arranged for a delivery of perfume to a Mademoiselle Simon in Lyon, in the fall of 'forty-one?"

I remembered it. A stocky little German had insisted I send four bottles of Chanel No. 5, not just one, for her birthday. Nicky had laughed when I told him about it. He had asked for the address and the date it was to be delivered. It had struck me as unusual at the time, even more so now. Nicky. What were you up to, Nicky? It wasn't just about the perfume, was it?

"Yes," I said.

The three men whispered together again. I heard the name, "Alexandrov. Nicholas."

"It is safe to admit such things now," said the third man. "Did you also shelter refugees?"

"Yes."

"Bring her some coffee. Hot coffee, with milk and sugar." To me he said, "You are free to go, madame. The driver will take you back home."

When I rose, they did as well, in new respect.

"He was a very brave man, your Nicholas," said the man in charge. "I met him once, before he was taken by the Germans."

I had thought I had merely aided people who needed to leave France. Thanks to Nicky, I had done more. I had given addresses, dates, names of Germans, for the resistance to do with as they needed.

None of that mattered anymore. Only Dahlia mattered.

When I got back to Grasse, it was dark and Natalia's house was empty. I went to Madame LaRosa's, and her house was dark and empty as well. Confused, I went back home to wait.

The dry, dusty wind was still blowing when I went to bed, but I did not fall asleep. The next day I went back to Madame LaRosa's, thinking she and Dahlia would have returned from wherever they had spent the night, that Dahlia would burst out the door and hug me in greeting. But the house was still locked up and empty.

"Monsieur and Madame have gone to Normandy," said a passerby who saw me peering in a window. "Her sister sent for her."

"Did they take a young girl with them?"

"No. It was just the two of them. There was no young girl with them."

That was how I met Omar, who became my friend, who kept me going, taught me to hope. He was passing on the walk, his arms full of freshly cleaned tablecloths for the café. He dropped the cloths and caught me as I collapsed.

To suddenly live in a world where you can no longer find your daughter, where you no longer know where she is, or if she is . . . it was worse than any other disaster of my life, worse than all of them put together. I would have endured any of them, all of them, a thousand times over, rather than hear those words: *There was no young girl with them.* The world went black when I heard those words. Where was Dahlia?

"Come. I'll take you home," said the man who helped me back to my feet.

# CHAPTER NINETEEN

It was six months since I'd been questioned. Six months since my daughter had disappeared, and now I was at Farley Farm in England, and Lee was pouring a very long shot of whiskey into my glass. I drank it in two long gulps, coughing after I swallowed, and Lee gave me a knowing glance. Roland pointed at the door and gestured like a traffic cop, his arms windmilling us into the drafty dining room for supper.

There really wasn't enough chicken to go around, but hunger wasn't a bother. Those of us who had spent the war years in Europe had learned to ignore the rumbling hollowness of our stomachs. There was plenty of alcohol. Dinner was noisy with laughter, the clattering of knives and forks on chipped china, and the constant, slightly underwater sound of wine or stronger stuff being poured, sipped, guzzled.

I thought of my father coming home to his supper, still wearing his gardener's overalls, so that my mother yelled and called him a lout and hurled other insults. She had had aspirations, my mother. She wanted her husband to come to table in a tie and jacket, to speak of the avant-garde art exhibit at the armory, or one of the new books reviewed in the Sunday *Times*. Daddy had been content to trim hedges, to water the seedlings in the greenhouse, to read his same grimy anthology of poetry over and over.

After supper, he fell asleep in his easy chair, and Mother would jab angrily at a piece of embroidery. He would wake up from a dream and put his arm around my shoulders and whisper, "Someday we'll go to France and see the great gardens. Just you and me. We'll see that panther in the Paris zoological gardens."

"Isn't Anthony precious?" Lee had changed seats and sat beside me, pouring more garnet red wine into my emptied glass. Her hand shook a little.

"Yes, he's a beautiful child."

"I had a tough time with him. Days in bed, getting stitched up after. Never got my figure back. Never will, I guess." Lee put the bottle back on the table. She had spoken a little loudly and the two young women had leaned closer to us to listen. Lee laughed, a sound like breaking glass, and went back to sit beside Roland. If I had somehow thought this was going to be an intimate weekend with Lee Miller, I had been very mistaken.

After dinner we went back outside, wrapped in blankets against the chill.

I listened to the night, to the wind in the leaves, to Lee telling a story about her travels in Budapest immediately after the war, the newly homeless aristocrats, the starving peasants. "The streets were full of oxcarts and American cars," she said. "I photographed the graves of the American boys who died in the raids there. Grass had barely begun to grow over them, and the American and Brit oil companies were already there negotiating for rights." She picked up a stone and threw it at a tree. It plunked and fell to the ground.

The spring light slowly evolved from misty green to a soft gray that blurred outlines, and I was drunk, too. Jamie would walk through the door at any minute; Dahlia had not yet rooted in my belly, changing everything.

Lee brought out candles and lanterns when it was fully dark and we sat there, finally exhausted and silent, locked in private memories as stars appeared, one by one; and when the moon rose, we gathered a second energy and started again. Roland went into the house and came out with another armload of bottles. They clinked as he walked, making the same sound as perfume bottles being boxed in the factory.

We built a bonfire and we arranged our chairs around it, silenced by that ancient gesture of seeking fire in the midst of cold darkness. Sparks flew up into the dark sky, shooting stars in reverse.

"I knew you in Paris." Pablo sat next to me, putting his hand over mine, puffing pipe smoke in my face. The dark had enlarged his black eyes, and he seemed like a beautiful bird of prey, all beak and shining orbs.

"We did. I didn't think you would remember."

"The eyes," he said. "And no from a pretty girl. I never forget that, either. I wanted you to model for me, and you said no." The constellation Orion was visible over his shoulder, Orion, the sign of the hunter.

I had said no to Pablo that first time Lee took us up to his studio, and Jamie had been furious. *Think of what he could do for me. Do you always have to think of yourself, your own small-town morality?* It had been the first of many wounds I had received in Paris, the city of delight.

Two days later I had gone to Pablo's studio and hiked that long flight of stairs, each step a hesitation and the decision made anew, to tell him yes, I would pose. But he wasn't there, and when we did meet again, on the weekend, he didn't repeat the request.

Lisa, who had been flirting with Pablo all night, stood and began to dance, hiking up her skirt to show her thighs and an occasional glimpse of garters and pink pantie. Roland beat out a rhythm on the table and Lee banged a spoon against an empty bottle.

"Don't sit under the apple tree with anyone else but me! Anyone else but me, anyone else but me!" they shouted tunelessly into the night, over and over, till one by one we rose and wandered into the house, to the heat of the promised stove, the pillows and blankets spread out on the floor.

I was the last to leave the circle of the dying fire. The stars had begun to disappear into the gray dawn, as if they were as tired of the night and the English countryside as I was.

Instead of seeking the animal warmth and companionship of the shipwrecked group sleeping on the floor in front of the stove, I went to the room Lee had allotted me and wrapped the mildewed blanket around me. Wooden slats covered half the window, a remnant of the blackout years, but now they looked like prison bars.

Dionysus, the god of wine and merriment, liked to ride on the back of a panther. And the medieval bestiaries of rare animals all said the same thing: the panther was the only animal with a sweet scent of its own. I fell asleep, remembering the lavender scent of my daughter's hair.

I awoke with a raging headache and in complete, devastating confusion, all the beds of my life—my childhood bed in Poughkeepsie, the hard mattress of my room in Paris with Jamie, the oversoft feather mattress in my room in Grasse—all mixing together. But I was in none of them.

A guest bed, in a guest room. Lee's house in England. A child was crying and I thought it was another of my nightmares, that if I pulled the blanket tighter over my head and forced it, dreamless sleep would return.

It did not. The child cried louder as I drifted in and out of sleep. The clamminess of the mildewed blanket, in my disturbed dreams, changed into the damp dirt walls of a cell and I slipped back in time to the place of waking nightmare.

The crying continued, turning from sobs to hiccups. Dahlia had once cried ceaselessly for two days. Sleepless and frantic, I had walked with her in my arms, step after step, till I fell into the soft bed of lavender outside the door, and we both slept like that, curled into perfume, our faces so close together we breathed in each other's breath.

The dilapidated wildness of Lee's house challenged me as I moved from room to room over bare, creaking floors, through cold patches where drafts merged. I had slept only for an hour or two and dizziness made my steps uncertain, but my nose finally caught the scent of coffee, and I followed it into the kitchen, where the young nanny sat with Lee's boy, trying to feed him.

"He doesn't like oatmeal," she said.

"No," he said, glaring at me. I poured a cup of coffee and fled.

Lee found me later sitting under the same tree that had sheltered us during our carousing of the night before. Wilmington Man, that long and ancient figure cut into the hillside, strode in his before-the-world-was-born way, taunting. I have always been here, he seemed to be saying. I always will be here, long after you are moldering dust.

Lee wore her battered combat boots, unlaced so that they

thumped with each step, and a military jacket over her white sleeping gown. The morning light was not kind—she looked tired.

"I hope the evening didn't upset you," she said, sitting next to me. "It does get out of hand sometimes. I admit, I encourage it to. There are days when the only thing that makes me want to be sober is Anthony."

We sat in what passed for companionable silence, listening for what we no longer heard: B17s overhead, the shrill screams of falling bombs, rifle shots. The morning was absolutely still.

I thought, then, maybe I would tell her about Dahlia. How I, too, was in love with my child, and that child was missing, that I had come to London looking for her, and hadn't yet found her.

"It has taken so long to get used to the silence," Lee said, standing. "I never thought I'd miss the noise. I never thought peace would be so hard to return to."

"It's not so peaceful yet in France," I said, remembering the jail cell in Lyon.

"I find it difficult to speak with people these days," Lee continued. "Especially old friends I haven't seen in a while. God knows what life has been like for them. And what question could be asked that isn't absolutely banal in its stupidity? For instance, tell me, Nora, was the war hard for you? Isn't that the most banal question you've ever heard?"

There was a little coffee still in the bottom, but it had gone cold and cloudy. I splashed the remains onto the stone at my feet. "Two years ago, I would have saved that bit for the next morning, and been glad to have it."

"I once saved a chocolate bar for a couple months, carrying it around just in case. By the time I decided to eat it, it was crawling with bugs. Such waste."

She wasn't referring to the hoarded chocolate bar. Waste. War, the carnage, the revenge and retribution. Giving birth to a child, then having her disappear.

I had been numb when I agreed to come here, but seeing Lee with her husband and child had stirred up such pain in me I wanted only to go back to Grasse.

"What time do the boats run? Would Roland give me a lift to the ferry?"

"Stay another day, why don't you?"

I sat looking down at Wilmington Man, who had been striding the hill through all the long and ancient ages. What did he think of us, the shortness of our lives, the silliness of our passions?

From inside the house, music jumped out at us, loud as an alarm. "Kiss me once, and kiss me twice and kiss me once again, it's been a long, long time." Laughter, shuffling feet. Dark-haired Roland came out of the house carrying a cup of coffee. In semishadow he looked a little like a taller version of Man Ray. It occurred to me that the men Lee had been most serious about had been physical opposites of her fair-haired, blue-eyed father. Roland saw us and waved but veered off in a different direction, leaving me still alone with Lee. The sun was halfway up the sky, burning off the chill and the damp.

"I remember the first time I saw you in Paris," she said, leaning back and looking hard at me through narrowed eyes. "At the Jockey. You were so pretty. I thought, 'That boy doesn't deserve her.' I even thought you might challenge me for Man. He was quite taken with you, you know."

"I remember it, too," I said. I had stood outside the Jockey with Jamie, thinking what a grand city Paris would be for raising a child.

"God, I miss the Jockey," Lee said. I could hear the other guests of Farley Farm laughing, dancing inside the cold, drafty house.

Nine o'clock in the morning, and they sounded half-drunk already. "We had fun there, didn't we?" Lee gazed out on Wilmington Man. "Time to chat," she said.

I was exhausted and in such deep emotional pain I no longer trusted words. Lee could tell her stories. I could listen. And then I would go home. Home. An empty house.

"So, Lee, tell me about your war. I heard you followed all the rules, as usual."

Lee laughed, loudly, immoderately, the laugh I remembered from Paris when she could make a whole room turn and look at the loud American and then they would smile, too, because she was so beautiful. "You heard about my little problem with the army. I suppose everyone has. It makes a good story. Can you imagine someone, even a general, telling me to stay behind the lines with the other women? I hadn't gone through the red tape and paperwork of becoming a bona fide war correspondent to stay behind with the gals. I got to some of the battlefields even before some of our advance boys." This was the Lee I remembered.

"And they found you there, already bivouacked and looking pretty."

Lee reached into the pocket of her fatigues and pulled out a small bottle. She poured a generous helping into the remains of her coffee. Her hands were trembling. "Remember that day we went out early to take photographs, and you told me the story of Atlas and his brother, what's his name?"

"Gadeirus," I said.

"Gadeirus. You were always the brainy one."

"And you were the brave one."

"Well, that's what my war felt like. Twin brothers, fighting each other, because part of me knew what it would be like, terrifying, yet

I couldn't stop. Once I started taking photographs of it, I kept pushing myself forward. Some things, I'll never forget. Maybe I should just show you. Want to see some photos?"

I followed her up a back staircase out of the kitchen, to an upstairs room with a single window, filled with cardboard boxes, dust so thick in the air it was like a blanket.

"This will be a darkroom, at some distant time," Lee said, sitting on the floor. I sat opposite her, my back against a stack of boxes. "I've been keeping busy."

Downstairs, there were shouts in the kitchen, laughter. Other risers up and in search of coffee, but Lee and I had emptied the pot.

Lee reached over to the box closest to her and took out the envelope on top of the pile. She untied the brown string and fanned out the photos, selecting one the way a magician takes a card from the deck. It was a view of the Eiffel Tower, banal enough in its own way, already seen on a thousand postcards, except Lee had captured it on a foggy winter morning. The tower, seen in the distance, was barely visible, ghostly. Instead, the eye went to the four statues guarding the steps of the Palais de Chaillot, black, frozen figures larger than the man walking beneath them, also black, with a black umbrella over his head to keep off the drizzle.

"I took this in 'forty-four, after the liberation," she said. "Those statues, the snow, the beauty of the city and the insignificance of everything else. Thank God for General von Choltitz."

Hitler had had his soldiers mine every bridge and major landmark of the city. The day the Germans were forced out, Paris was to be burned to the ground. But one of his own generals, von Choltitz, the last commander of occupied Paris, had refused to obey the command. There was already talk of giving von Choltitz (a German!) the *Légion d'Honneur* in gratitude.

Lee slid out a different photo. "That's the balcony outside my room in the Hôtel Scribe in Paris." Against the black scrolling ironwork of the balcony, half-buried in snow, were bottles of champagne and hoarded jerry cans of fuel.

"One of the jerry cans is filled with wine. Never know when any wine cellar is going to give out. Be prepared. My war motto," Lee said.

The next photo made me catch my breath. Montparnasse. The street where Jamie and I had lived. The memory of a fragrance, a combination of sweet coal smoke, vanilla from the pâtisserie on the corner, cat urine, and eucalyptus, all combined into the scent that had once said "home" to me.

I pointed to a fourth-floor attic window with a little wrought iron grille. I had kept our half bottle of milk on the sill. In the winter it froze, and Jamie and I would chip at it and float chunks of frozen cream in our coffee. I said, "If I leaned far enough out the window, I could see Notre-Dame-des-Champs."

Lee searched through the pile of photos. "This." She picked up a photo I recognized of two women, one wearing a black mask and eye shield, the other holding an air raid warden's whistle. They looked directly into the camera, two pretty woman in war gear sitting on the steps of an air raid shelter. "The Blitz," she said. "I took this for *Vogue*. Great fashion shoot, isn't it? It helped convince the editors I could cover more than skirt lengths."

"Who's this?" I picked up a second photo, of Lee playing solitaire, Roland on one side, another man in uniform on the other.

"Dave Scherman. Another war correspondent. We traveled together during the war. Sometimes he lived with me and Roland in Hampstead."

You could tell by his expression, his posture, that Dave Scherman was in love with Lee.

"Sweet boy, and very talented," Lee said. "When he first visited Roland, he thought all the Picassos and Magrittes on the wall of our London house were copies. Roland and his art collection have become real bigwigs, you know. He's head of the Institute of Contemporary Arts in London. He'll be traveling back and forth quite a lot. Too bad. I think I prefer it here now." Lee grew pensive again. Her voice trailed off into a whisper.

"What's this one?"

Lee tapped her cigarette ash onto the bare wooden floor. "Henry Moore. The sculptor. During the Blitz he used to go to the underground shelters and sketch people. Nice suit, isn't it? He dresses well. Ah, this one. Funny, isn't it? Davy in a helmet and gas mask under a sun umbrella. He liked to mug a bit for the camera."

The next photograph was of a surgery in a field hospital in Normandy, a man unconscious on a stretcher as a surgeon inserted a breathing tube. Next, a photo of a bomb bursting over Saint-Malo, the black cloud reaching up into the sky.

Lee picked out more photos in the order in which she remembered taking them, and all humor disappeared from the work as she, traveling with the army, pushed east, deeper and deeper into the ravaged landscape. A photo from Cologne showing a dead German soldier, his hands blown away. The daughter of the burgomaster of Leipzig, back arched in death on the leather sofa on which she had killed herself.

And then, the photos Lee took at Dachau after the camp had been liberated by the American GIs, dead bodies piled like firewood.

"Dave was with me," Lee said. "I thought I had seen the worst during the battles, but when we got to the camp, I couldn't believe it. How much worse the worst really was, the smell of hundreds, thousands, of decaying bodies. I thought I'd never wash that smell away. I still have nightmares about it. I dream I'm getting dressed up for a fashion shoot, but when I look down, I'm wearing those striped pajamas the prisoners wore and both my feet have turned blue with gangrene."

Lee was shaking so violently she dropped her cigarette. It landed on a photo and where the glowing tip touched the paper, a little ring of blue turned into a circle with minuscule flames. I slapped it out with my hands. Lee only watched.

"God, Roland would never forgive me if I burned the house down," she said.

As if on cue, we heard Roland calling for Lee. "Where are you?" he shouted. And then, in a lower voice, barely audible, "Damn." A few moments later we heard him calling from the front of the house, and then his voice faded away.

Lee smiled. "He's swell, isn't he? He came to fetch me from Paris after the liberation. I was having a little trouble maneuvering on my own by then. So he came for me, all knight on his white horse, and carried me back to England. Even kicked his girlfriend out of the flat so we could be alone together."

She lit another cigarette and picked up another photo from the pile on the floor. "Want to see more?"

"Yes."

"My favorite." The world's favorite, in fact: Lee having a good soap-down in Hitler's bathtub. The famous, beautiful Lee Miller had crossed Germany with the American army and stayed in his abandoned apartment in Munich when the Führer's death was announced.

As filthy as the soldiers with whom she marched and badly wanting a bath, Lee had arranged a few props in the tiled bathroom—a statue of Venus, her combat boots, a photo of Hitler—then filled the tub and climbed in.

"I stank that day." Lee exhaled a perfect circle of smoke up toward the ceiling. "We all did. When I saw that bathtub, I couldn't think of a better way to wash off the stench than to use the butcher's own tub."

There was a strange look on Lee's face in the photo. Her eyes were looking up to the corner, as if watching someone the viewer could not see. You couldn't help but wonder whom or what she was thinking of, who that unseen person was. So many of us had that expression during the war—the look of someone who didn't know the whereabouts, or condition, of a beloved. Natalia had worn it constantly in Switzerland.

"Were you thinking of Roland?" I asked her.

"Actually, I was thinking how boring Hitler's little apartment in Munich was. My God, his bedroom was upholstered in chintz. Except for all the linens and crystal monogrammed with 'AH' you'd think you were in a traveling salesman's home. I went to Eva Braun's house on Wasserburgerstrasse and had a nap in her bed, thinking how happy I was she was dead."

The final photo in this series: Hitler's house in Berchtesgaden, burning, a solitary male figure in the foreground watching. The photo seemed out of focus at first till I realized it was the rising intense heat of the flames that had set the air all astir. It was a photo of hell.

"That's it." Lee gathered up the photos and stuffed them back in the envelope. "That's what Mommy did during the war. I think soon I will be finished with photography. After taking these photos . . ."

We both stared out the small single window for a while. Time seemed to move back and forth from childhood to Paris to the war, and back to childhood. I felt like that little girl looking up the tree at Lee, waving down at me from the top, except that little girl had seen the future and was already haunted by nightmares of the evil yet to come.

We sat silently, not touching, both looking out the window, smoking cigarette after cigarette. Dahlia's name was on my lips—I was about to tell Lee about my child when Lee emptied her flask in one more long gulp and stood.

"Roland may have cooked up a few eggs," Lee said. "Better grab a couple. Eat while you have the chance, that's the rule."

# CHAPTER TWENTY

The record player was still on when we went back downstairs, now an old Jolson tune, and we could hear the two young women in the stove room, speaking in low tones so that only a word or two stood out as we passed them—Arnold, Normandy. I knew they were speaking of one more lost young man.

Roland stood in front of the ancient stove, frying eggs.

"Morning, Nora. Some breakfast?" He gave me a smile over his shoulder and flipped the eggs in the pan, showing off. "Hope your hangover isn't as bad as mine."

"I could use an aspirin, if you have any."

"If we have any . . ." Roland smirked in Lee's direction. "You're looking at the queen of contacts. Lee even had aspirins in her kit when she was at the eastern front, didn't you? What can we get you? A duchy in Romania? An ancient papyrus? An audience with the queen, to go with the aspirin?"

She blew him a kiss, but made a face behind his back when he returned his attention to the stove and the eggs.

And then, they did what most married couples do, began

talking about things I knew nothing about, part dismissive, part show-off, presenting their lives to this almost-stranger in the kitchen. I sipped my coffee, ate the eggs Roland put in front of me even though I wasn't hungry, and pretended I wasn't there.

From somewhere high upstairs, I heard a child's scream, a shout, a thud. Anthony was throwing things. When she was two, Dahlia threw everything she could get her hands on, anything she was strong enough to lift. She broke cups and plates and powder compacts and perfume bottles, laughing joyfully all the while.

"Bet you look forward to the sun," Roland was saying to Lee. "The warmth. Looks like it's going to rain again this afternoon."

"Mostly the fruit," Lee said. "Sicilian oranges. Can't wait. Did I tell you, Nora, I'm doing a photo shoot in Sicily next week? 'Traveling at Ease,' they're calling it. I'll have to learn how to say 'Don't look at the camera' in Italian. I can already say it in French, German, Arabic, and Romanian."

"There'll be the usual pretty young models in two-piece bathing suits and shorts, soaking up the sun," Roland added. There was an edge to his voice that made me put my cup down and look at Lee.

"He's always on the lookout for a new mistress," Lee said. "Be careful he doesn't ask you to apply for the position, Nora. He's greedier for women than Man was." Roland, still at the stove frying more eggs for himself, having fed Lee and myself, said nothing.

I went back outdoors, slamming the screen door behind me. Lee's comment about Roland's infidelity had broken open old scars, had reminded me of all the broken promises between Jamie and myself. But it was too late to catch the ferry. I'd have to stay another day.

Farley Farm had a library, as did all good English country houses, and even a few books that hadn't been burned as fuel, as well as some newer novels Lee had purchased in London and brought with her. I found a well-thumbed copy of *Rebecca* by Daphne du Maurier and walked out onto the flat Sussex landscape for a quiet day of reading, apart from the others. I took some rolls and butter and a half-empty bottle of cognac.

It was a fifteen-minute walk over the downs to get far enough from the house to achieve privacy, to find a place in the rolling green hills where I could neither see the farm nor be seen by the others. The vast openness of the landscape was another kind of loss and sorrow.

When you have lost someone, horizons change. You look, and force yourself to see her, top of the head, face, shoulders, torso, legs, appearing incrementally over the rise. But she never does.

Finally, I crested one hill and discovered a large boulder, too big to have been removed through those centuries of taming the very ground, and crouched against it, my sweater bundled up as a pillow, my face turned to the sun, now playing hide-and-seek in accumulating clouds.

Chirps sounded in the turf around me and protective mother birds, angered by my intrusion, hopped and stared me down with their round yellow eyes. A new season of the living yelled at me to go away. I sat perfectly still, and soon the morning returned to silence.

I opened *Rebecca* and read that glorious first sentence: *"Last night I dreamt I went to Manderley again."* But soon my thoughts wandered as aimlessly as the turf-grazing sheep. Lee and Roland. Little Anthony. Jamie. Pablo. Where was Man Ray? Lee hadn't mentioned him yet. Wise not to mention a lover in front of a husband, of course, but every time I saw Lee, I expected to see Man behind her. That was how it had been in Paris, Lee and Man, inseparable. Until she met Aziz.

The last thought before sleep claimed me: Dahlia, sixteen years old, just beginning that breathtaking change from child to woman, beautiful beyond words, the perfect blend of her mother and father. I tried to breathe shallowly to avoid the pain of her loss, but there was no avoiding it. The grief twisted inside me like a caged beast.

When I slept, I dreamed of damp cells and the double lightning-strike insignia of the SS flashing over the southern French hills—and the fields of lavender, the olive orchards.

Pablo found me several hours later, asleep on the turf with the sheep grazing around me, the emptied bottle still in my hand, the novel spread open to the first page. When I awoke, he was sitting next to me, a sketchbook on his lap, charcoal in hand.

"God, what boring animals sheep are. You don't mind," he said, a statement, not a question. "I drew you when you were sleeping."

"I probably owed you that much for having said no, in Paris," I said, sitting up. "I didn't think you would remember that." The afternoon had changed during my sleep; the air was heavy with the rain to come and the sun was completely hidden, no more hide-and-seek.

"You made such a contrast with Lee," he said. "It would have been an interesting exercise, a newer version of *Les deux amies*." In that painting, one of the figures had been of Madeleine, an early lover. Did that mean Lee had been one of his lovers?

Pablo gave me the notepad so I could see the sketch. He had drawn me as an odalisque, arms over my head in a circle, legs twisted to one side, eyes shut but with a suggestion of movement behind them. A dreaming odalisque.

"You have given me longer legs. Thank you."

"I gave you the legs you should have been born with." He smelled pleasantly of pipe smoke. "Or perhaps not. Not all women should be tall, like our Lee."

Our Lee. Of course they, too, had been lovers.

Pablo looked out over the gentle green hills, green as far as the eye could see with stone fences and white sheep, recently shorn so they appeared vulnerable and oddly shaped, all that tight white wool cut close to the skin.

Pablo had aged. We all had. But perhaps he had aged best, no belly paunch, no shaking hands, no visible scars or loss of limb; only two long furrows making commas from his nose to his jaw suggested his age. He had gone bald on top, and to compensate had cut the rest of his white hair quite short, so that his head looked like a handsome, perfectly shaped egg. Gone was the famous forelock. I remembered how he had tugged it at, repeatedly, that evening I first met him and his wife, Olga.

He signed the drawing, tore it from his pad, and gave it to me. "Keep it," he said. "Don't sell it."

"I wouldn't!"

"No. I mean if you need money, don't sell it to anyone but me. I will buy it back from you." That was how Pablo made gifts. He would give a drawing and then buy it back for a very good price. He was generous, and clever. That tactic helped keep his prices high, under his control. Pablo was very, very rich by then. He bought houses with two or three paintings.

"Thanks." I slipped it between the pages of the novel. A few years before, I would have jumped at my good fortune. But now that the war was over and Dahlia had disappeared, my only need, to find her, was not redeemable by mere wealth.

"So you survived," he said.

"Yes. When it got too dangerous, I went to Switzerland."

"I sent Olga and my son to Switzerland."

"But you stayed."

"Of course."

Pablo and his Paris studio, I had learned after the war, had become symbols of the resistance. He tilted his head up to the sun, then squinted down at me. "During the war all I could think about was food. I painted it over and over, fish, bowls of fruit, pigeons. Have you ever tried to eat a pigeon? The meat is black as a crow's."

"Man told me Hemingway used to eat crows, when he didn't have money for a meal."

"Man said a lot of things, not all of it true or important. Do you still live in Grasse?"

So he did remember.

"Yes. I went home, back to Poughkeepsie, once. But I went back to Grasse, and after the Germans invaded . . ." After 1940, no one traveled except to flee or escape.

"You stayed in the south. Safer there." He nodded. "The Germans used to come to my studio in Paris, you know, looking for Jews, asking me if I was Jewish. They liked culture. That was how they described it. *Kultur.* And I would give them postcard reproductions of *Guernica*, and they would thank me. Idiots."

I thought of his painting *Guernica*, full of screaming women's heads, dying horses, body parts. In the upper left there was an oval like an eye, but the eye's pupil has been replaced by a lightbulb, like those used to torture prisoners, to nearly blind them and sleep-deprive them. I had thought of that painting often while in jail in Lyon.

"Hard years. But I got some good work done. I, too, survived." Pablo leaned back and studied the sky, tilting his head so that his Adam's apple jutted out, sharp and dangerous looking.

"Where is Man?" I asked. "I didn't think I should mention him in front of Roland."

"If money is the root of all evil, then jealousy is the root of all emotion. Where would art be without it? But in this marriage, the shoe is on the other foot. Lee is jealous of Roland. He insists on certain rights, including the right to roam and keep a mistress." Pablo puffed on his pipe and made a face at the sheep grazing steadily closer, oblivious to us.

Pablo would know something about that, the keeping of mistresses.

"Man," he said, speaking without mirth, "is in California, with rich people and moviemakers. The women are very pretty, but I think he doesn't like it there. He is famous here, in England and France, not in California. But he had the sense to leave Paris before the deportations began, the trains to the camps."

"Good thing," I said. Man, with his Semitic features, his outspokenness, would have been spotted instantly, and we knew what had happened to those Jews who had stayed. They had been rounded up into a sports stadium, the Vel d'Hiver, and from there taken to the camps.

"Madame Hughes?" he asked.

This was a ritual we all went through after the war, checking lists, finding out who had survived, what had happened to whom.

"Quietly, in her sleep. A year after she lost her son, Nicky." That pain again, always coming when I thought I was dead to emotion. Nicky in the sunny Nice morning, pulling my toes to wake me up.

"She must have been quite old. Is it good to see Lee again?" Pablo asked. "You were close friends, weren't you?"

"When you are twenty and in Paris for the first time, I think there is no such thing as a close friend. I was all eyes and ears, all sensation, so busy taking everything in, there was little to give out."

There had been so much to experience, so much that gave enchantment to a life transformed, the steep narrow cobbled streets that Jamie and I slid down on icy winter days, the ornate Bishops' Fountain of St. Sulpice where we held hands and talked about the future, the bookstalls near Notre-Dame where we bought French schoolbooks to improve our grammar.

Pablo laughed. "That was how I was, my first years in Paris, that young boy from Andalusia. Paris was where everything happened, everything was new. Home was boring. Nothing changed. Paris was the magnet, the center. Was it like that for you?"

"At my home, things did change, but for the worse."

"A death," he guessed. "Children are more moved by death than adults, even when they don't show it. A sibling? Mother or father? Maybe the first love."

"My father."

He took a pouch of tobacco from his pocket, and a packet of papers, and rolled a cigarette.

"I think it will rain," he said, striking a match. I inhaled, noting the smell of ozone in the air, the sulfur of his match.

He leaned back on his elbow and stared up again at the glooming sky where the blue-tinged clouds bumped into one another. We seemed to have run out of conversation.

"How are Olga, Paulo, and Marie-Thérèse?" I asked.

He exhaled smoke through his nostrils and didn't reply for a long enough time that I knew I had made an error. He finally answered in a neutral voice. "They are well, I assume. I haven't seen Olga and Paulo in a while. I have a daughter now, Maya, with

Marie-Thérèse. But tell me, how does Lee seem to you?" Pablo turned those piercing black eyes on me.

"Happy," I said. "Because of the child. Because of Roland." That was the polite answer, of course. One day with Lee and Roland and I could see the chinks in the wall of their marriage.

"Roland thinks she is fragile. Emotional. She saw terrible things in the war and afterwards." Pablo puffed a perfect smoke ring.

"The camps."

"And the battles. She went where women hadn't gone before, and I think she will pay the price for a long time."

I thought of her hand in the tearoom, tapping, incessantly tapping on the table. She was drinking even more than I remembered.

"She took too many chances, went too far," Pablo said. "Her nerves are ruined. She destroyed herself, not for her art, but to prove something. I don't know what."

In my mind's eye I saw Lee, the little girl, climbing to the top of the tree. After the rape, she had climbed even higher. The rape. I thought of Dahlia and Bonner, and had to put my head into my hands so that Pablo would not see my face. The whispering wind quickened and the whole field became alive with an invisible destroying hand.

"The world has changed, you see it," Pablo said. "We change with it. When we move from a state in which we believe, know, we could die at any minute, to a new state where we see long, sometimes boring years ahead of us, that changes us dramatically. Matadors don't live long after they retire from the ring. The ennui kills them. I wonder if Lee will become bored with motherhood."

Pablo did not ask about my child. Had he forgotten I left Paris pregnant?

The first drops of rain began to fall. Pablo rose to his feet with a stiff, pained movement. Sciatica, I thought. Omar had a touch of it as well. Pablo tucked his sketchbook into his shirt, offered me his hand, and we ran over the fields, back to Farley Farm.

When I went into my room to dry my hair, Lee was there, sitting on the bed and holding the new green dress in her hands.

"It's gorgeous," she said. "Will you wear it tonight? We'll have a dress-up affair."

I took it from her and put it back on its hanger. "It was silly of me to bring it."

"Not at all. I still love a chance to dress up. Combat boots and a fatigue jacket do get old. I'll do your hair for you. Just like old times."

Had she done my hair in the old times? Not that I could remember. The notion had a sisterly ring to it and such familiar intimacy had never existed between us. Memories were often faulty. Did Lee remember events that had never happened, or was I disremembering something that had?

God, I was so tired, so full of questions for which there were no answers. "I have a—," I started to say. I was going to tell her about Dahlia.

Before I could finish the sentence, lightning streaked the sky. Thunder boomed and rattled the windowpanes.

Lee turned pale. We were an entire generation that would jump at loud noises for many years after the war.

"I'd better go check the windows," Lee said, jumping up. "I used to love thunderstorms, back in Poughkeepsie. Dad and I would watch them on the back porch, huddled under an old blanket. One year a gardener planted a vine on the porch, and Dad had to tear it down so we could see the sky. I'll tell Roland dinner will be formal, and see if I can scare up a tablecloth."

. . . . . . . . . . . . . . . . . . . . . . . . . . . . . . .

The rest of the day passed slowly with a constant murmuring of low voices, the occasional burst of music when someone thought to put a disc on the phonograph. We moved from room to room, window to window, glowering back at the glowering sky, carrying candles with us because the day turned dark long before sunset came.

Farley Farm felt haunted to me. So many presences of people who weren't really there: Jamie, Man, my father, whom I hadn't thought about so much for years. Being with Lee again, remembering her father, put me in mind of my own, how he smelled of peat moss and soap, the grime under his nails, his puzzled smile, as if life was something incomprehensible to him.

He would take discarded houseplants—geraniums, Christmas poinsettia, African violets—from the Miller trash and bring them back to life in our house, so that my mother complained of living in a jungle. He had been so pleased with the trumpet vine he planted in front of Mr. Miller's back porch that when he found it torn up, he brought a piece of root back home for our own small porch. Every summer after that, we had to duck through a fountain of orange flowers to get in the house.

Chicken again for dinner, but that night Lee cooked and instead of Roland's simple roast she served a casserole of chicken and potatoes in a red wine sauce, with a side dish of pureed spinach and pickled onions.

"I've taken up cooking," Lee announced, putting the platter on the table with a grand flourish. "This is the new me, the domestic little housewife." She gloated a bit as she served us, giving that satisfied smile, that slight tilt of the head to the side.

Roland blew her a kiss from his end of the table and pulled out my chair for me, formal as if we were at the Ritz, though water dripped into a pan in a corner of the room from a ceiling leak. Rain beat against the windows.

We all sat around the rickety table, dressed to the nines. I wasn't the only one who had tucked evening clothes into her valise. Lee wore a colorful silk caftan, very exotic looking and lovely. She had been photographed in it when she was pregnant with baby Anthony, she announced, and had gotten used to the comfort of a loose dress.

The two girls, Lisa and Carmen, wore similar dresses, wasp-waisted and cut very low in front. Lesley wore her good gray suit with a fresh blouse. Pablo wore a shirt instead of his usual sailor jersey.

"To a bevy of beauties," Roland said, raising his glass. Lisa and Carmen giggled with pleasure, and again there was that strange sensation that the past sixteen years and all their events had never happened. I was young and in Paris, awed by my surroundings, by my acquaintances.

The moment passed, and I was older, cold with English damp, aching for a lost child. We picked up our knives and forks. I pretended to eat.

"You went for a walk with Pablo today," Lisa said with a little pout.

"No. I went alone for a walk."

"You didn't come back alone."

Pablo leaned back in his chair and folded his arms over his chest, smiling. He liked to be fought over, liked to be the center of attention. That was what Paris had felt like: all those famous people or people about to become famous, each a sun demanding that the other planets orbit around him. There had been noisy collisions.

I concentrated on my plate, trying to stay out of the way of so many egos. That was how I had survived in Paris, until I was no longer a survivor: kept out of the way, remained invisible, didn't draw attention to myself.

"You are like a barn cat," Pablo had said to me once, early during the time in Paris. "Staying near enough to people to get their scraps, the safety of their homes, but not letting them get close to you."

"More chicken, Nora?" Roland asked, offering to serve me. "We bought two, today. Everyone can have seconds."

"Oh, poor little chickens," said Lisa. "I'll have more, thanks."

And, of course, we drank. Bottles and bottles of wine, and when the food was gone, brandy, sitting in front of the stove, each of us in a different stage of inebriation, leaning against one another for warmth, legs spread out or crossed tailor-style. We looked like a group of refugees who hadn't had time to change into practical clothing.

Lisa wound up the gramophone again and did a strange dance by herself, singing along to "Stormy Weather." Pablo watched, his eyes moving back and forth, drawing her with the pencil of his imagination. Lee and Roland cuddled together, he whispering into her ear, she looking occasionally toward the stairs, obviously thinking about the nursery at the top of them, and Anthony in his bed, sleeping.

Carmen leaned against Pablo, offering herself, trying to make herself irresistible. While Roland made the names of artists, Pablo made the names of models. I was back in the world where everybody wanted something, where all friendships, all loves, were part of an unspoken business arrangement, and even a world war hadn't changed that.

"So, who are you, really?" Carmen asked, catching me watching her.

"A fair enough question," Roland said. "More from our mystery guest."

"She's an old acquaintance of mine," Lee said.

"That's hardly enough for an identity," Roland said, and Lee blinked at the reprimand.

"I think she's a pianist. Look at her hands. Someone about to have a recital in Marseille or somewhere else in the south," Pablo teased. I held up my hands. They were brown and slightly freckled, too small to reach even a single octave.

"I think she's someone's ex-wife. A retired artist's model with a good divorce settlement," Carmen guessed.

"No," said Lee. "She's not wearing a diamond bracelet. All ex-wives have diamond bracelets." She held up her own, an extravagant gift from Aziz, and it seemed to me that Roland put a little space between himself and his wife, and that Lee made a surreptitious movement of her own to close that gap.

Well, if they wanted a game, I would give them one. "All wrong. But I'll give you a hint. Carmen, your perfume is Evening in Paris. And Lisa, you have borrowed Carmen's perfume."

"Have you? I never said you could!" Carmen shrieked, then remembered Pablo next to her and decided for a calmer approach. "You might ask, next time," she said sweetly.

"A nose," Roland guessed quietly.

"No. But I do work in the perfume industry." Each house had one nose, the person who created new fragrances, and they were trained from childhood. I had started too late, and was a foreigner, so that highest position had been impossible for me. But I had composed a few private commissions, one for Natalia that had smelled of Russian tea, one for Madame LaRosa that smelled of the salt and moss fragrance of Normandy.

"And do you make private perfumes for the rich and famous?" Carmen yawned.

"No. Not for the rich and famous. Only a couple of friends."

The stove in Lee's drawing room made a strange hissing sound. The rain had stopped, but the wind had picked up and the house moaned and shivered around us.

"I'll get more wood," Roland said. "Maybe there's a wet piece in there. Lee, I've told you not to chuck in damp wood." He had been frowning ever since Lee had held up her diamond bracelet for show.

"You loaded the stove, my sweet. Not me," Lee said, and the atmosphere changed from friendly to something more hostile. Pablo gave me a knowing look.

"So how do you and Lee know each other, then?" Carmen asked. "She's so . . ." Even dense, flirtatious Carmen had the sense not to finish that sentence, but it finished itself in my head. She was so beautiful. So famous. And I was a nobody.

"We are very old friends," Lee said, pouring more wine into her mug. "From Paris, before the war. And way before that, Poughkeepsie. At one time we even shared a lover."

Lee smirked when she said it, intending to give that little pinprick to Roland, who had just come into the room, his arms full of wood.

But I was the one most injured by that casual remark. And Jamie. Caught in her wake, her games, her predatory sexuality. He had suffered because of Lee.

Blame was a comforting emotion, and I wanted comfort. If it hadn't been for Lee, somehow Dahlia would never have disappeared. I would have had a family with Jamie, the three of us safe and together. Not true, perhaps, but at that moment I didn't care about the truth.

"We go way back, Lee," I said, locking eyes with her. She stopped smiling and her head tilted to one side. I was ready to pay her back for her betrayal, first of me, and then of Jamie.

"I was there one day when you came home from Vassar Hospital."

She froze. Her eyes opened wider. Carefully, she put her mug on the floor, her gaze never leaving mine, her mouth opening slightly.

We stared at each other for what felt like hours and I watched as shock flickered across her face. Did I imagine it, or did those famous lips silently voice the word "please"? She was frightened that I would tell, would make her own sad history part of the silly game we were playing.

"Hospital?" Carmen asked. "Were you ill as a child, Lee?"

"Poor thing," said Lisa, no sympathy in her voice. They both leaned forward, eager for gossip.

Roland poked at the logs in the woodstove, his face flushed with heat or emotion, I couldn't tell which. Surely she had told Roland, her husband.

"Tell them," Lee said, lighting a cigarette. "Tell them of my illness, Nora. Now is your chance, if you want revenge."

Roland put down the poker, closed the door of the stove, and came and sat next to her. Protectively, lovingly. So, he knew.

"Yes, tell," insisted Carmen, leaning forward. In the end, it was the look on Carmen's face, a predatory, vulpine glance, that changed the outcome of that moment. Lee did not make friends easily, especially with other women, who resented her beauty, her power, her almost masculine freedom. Carmen was no friend.

And much as I resented what had passed between Lee and myself, that look of casual indifference on her face when I found Lee and Jamie in bed together, I was not her enemy.

"Whooping cough," I lied, as if I were bored with the conversation, with the evening. "She was sick for weeks. Months."

"Is that all?" Lisa was plainly disappointed. "Who goes to the hospital for whooping cough?"

"Apparently I did. I don't remember. I think I hear Anthony crying. Back in a minute." Lee rose to go upstairs. She paused and put a hand on my shoulder when she passed behind me.

"Poughkeepsie must have been a complete bore," said Carmen. "Imagine growing up in such a place. I'll have some more wine, too, Roland."

"Where did you grow up?" I asked, not really interested but sensing that things needed to be said. The air had grown too thick and menacing.

"Los Angeles. City of Angels. I'm going back for a screen test soon. For a new Bette Davis movie, *All About Mary.*" Carmen lit a cigarette, posing like a girl in a commercial, head thrown back, hand suggestively placed in front of her mouth, fingers stroking the lighter.

"It's *All About Eve*, not *Mary*," corrected Lisa, downing the contents of her glass.

Pablo was looking at me curiously, black eyes under thick brows moving back and forth over my face. He knew the whooping cough had been a lie and was trying to discern the truth simply from my expression. I had seen him look that way in his studio in Paris before the war, when he stood in front of one of his paintings still searching for its truth.

Lisa rose, put a record on the phonograph, and danced a tango by herself, purposely tripping over her own feet to make us laugh.

Roland came over and poured more wine into my glass, his face a mask. "Thank you," he mouthed silently.

Thank you for not telling that Lee had been raped as a child, that she had been a victim. We lived in a time that made it dangerous to be a victim. Dahlia had learned firsthand what it meant to be a victim.

"I'm tired," I said. "I'm going to bed."

# CHAPTER TWENTY-ONE

"Not my daughter!" were the first words in my head when I woke up, arguing again with Nicholas, and it hurt all over again. I was confused, as I had been my first morning at Farley Farm, and the words rang with too many meanings, too many lost daughters and grieving mothers. Perhaps those were the words Lee's mother had used when she first heard what had happened to her daughter, that rape at seven.

I sat up in bed and looked out the window, over the picture-book landscape of Farley Farm, the velvety green and brown South Downs dotted with yellow flowers, the kind of landscape where happy endings are implied. I had stopped believing in them. Last night I had almost announced Lee's childhood rape to the house party, to those silly vain women who, you could see it in their eyes, would love to somehow get a claw into the very famous, beautiful Lee Miller; and to the editor, Lesley, with her hooded, all-seeing eyes, wheels always turning in her head, looking for a good gossipy story.

Almost. I had stopped in time. I think that even when I'd found

Lee in Jamie's arms, I could not have screamed the news of her rape to the world. There is destruction beyond destruction, the ground-into-dust annihilation of image, and Lee lived by her image. I couldn't do it. There had already been too much destruction.

It was still early—dawn was no more than a hint of gray in the eastern sky—so I hoped to be alone with my first cup of coffee. But Lee was already up and about. I saw her out the kitchen window in her fatigues and wellies, pacing and counting, perhaps planning a vegetable garden. When did she sleep?

When she saw me, she stopped counting, came into the kitchen, and poured two cups of coffee.

"Your mother used to bring you out to the farm. We played together."

"Yes."

"You never said anything. Not when we met in the bookstore in Poughkeepsie, not all that time in Paris we were together."

"No."

Lee went and stood at the window, her back to me. "So few people know about it. The rape. The more people who know, the more I am forced to remember it, to think of it."

Dahlia had said almost the exact thing when she begged me not to go to the police.

"You want to forget, but of course you can't," Lee said, lost in her own thoughts. "You just keep running away from it. And it's always there, in front of you, waiting around the corner to take you by surprise, and it's never even a damn surprise. Have you heard about the rapes? Women being raped by the thousands, all over Europe. France. Germany. Romania. The final act of war, the beginning of peace. Rape."

Lee came and sat at the table opposite me. It was a good table, thick scrubbed oak, the kind of table that lasts for centuries. "I think," she said, rubbing her hand over the table to brush away crumbs, "you are the only person who knew me both in Poughkeepsie and Paris, who knows what happened. And you kept quiet all these years."

Her voice was neutral, flat, as if her reaction were somewhere she couldn't reach, a dark corner. "You know everything about me, and I know nothing about you, I think."

Lee stopped flicking her hand back and forth over the table. She looked at me in a way she rarely did, the way she rarely looked at anyone or anything, seriously, unmasked, open. "When I saw you, there, outside of Harrods, I thought it was just the war that made you look like that," she said. "Devastated. Walking, but not really with the living. Then I thought maybe you were still angry about Jamie. But it's something else."

"I have a daughter, Lee. A child."

"Is that why you left Paris? Jamie's? If I had known . . ."

"Would anything have happened differently?"

She thought. Lee was many things, but never a coward, so she answered honestly. "Probably not," she admitted. "I was drunk the first time. So was Jamie. And you know the problems I was having with Man, his possessiveness, my need to be free, not owned."

I closed my eyes and thought back to that night, Jamie holding Lee in his arms, her little smile of satisfaction and something else. Power. Her power over men—and she had tremendous power—was part of her revenge for what had happened to her when she was seven.

Forgiveness is a kind of perfume, made of many different essences and materials, not just one. The *départ* is the memory of the wound, a bitter woody smell. The top note is anger and hurt, the smell of roses picked just past their prime, when they have opened too fully and already begun to drop their petals. The middle note is regret, an amber scent of time unable to move backward or forward. But the bottom note of forgiveness is understanding, and that smells of fresh air and a hint of lemon, astringent and healing.

"I don't know where my daughter is, Lee. She had disappeared."

I told her, the whole story, because telling stories is part of forgiving. It is the only way to move forward, even if the story moves back. So I told her about the early years in Grasse, Dahlia's childhood, Natalia, Nicky. The rape. When I told her about the rape, she put her hand to her mouth. Her eyes narrowed to slits. I told her about the jail cell in Lyon and coming home to my empty house, about the months of searching in Grasse, Nice, Paris, and London, how I thought Dahlia might have been following the path of the stories I had told her about me and Jamie.

But I hadn't found my child.

Outside the window over her sink we could see Roland and Anthony sitting in the dirt, playing with a kitten who arched her back with pleasure and figure-eighted in and out of Roland's feet.

Lee didn't speak. She rose from the table and dribbled some red wine left from the night before into the stew she had been preparing. She upended the bottle and drank the rest.

"I haven't heard from my daughter, or about her, Lee. She's disappeared." Outside, Roland picked up the kitten and scratched it behind the ears. We'd had a cat once, a marmalade tiger who followed Dahlia the way a puppy would have.

"I'll have to see about that," Lee said, distracted, throwing a pinch of salt into the pot. "God, things got screwed up, didn't they? Or maybe they just keep going round and round in circles. If anything happened to Anthony . . . I'll ask around. See if there's a trail of any sort."

She said it so carelessly, so lightly.

Lee's country house party played croquet that afternoon, a drunken match filled with quickly emptying wine bottles and language that would never have been allowed in the croquet games of our childhood. Roland was good at it, and when he knocked Lee's ball away from the wicket for the fourth time in a row, she threw her mallet, not exactly at his head, but close enough that we decided to think of a game that didn't involve potentially harmful objects.

She was pretty drunk by then, and so was I. When the others went in to play gin rummy, we opted to stay outside, in the fresh air. We were talked out by then and Lee had fallen into a black mood of sullen silence.

"Don't take it personally," Roland told me. "I've learned not to. It's going to take time for her to recover."

The next morning, when Roland rose early to take me to the first ferry, Lee didn't come with me.

"Still sleeping," he said. "Or sleeping it off, however you want to look at it."

Just like the old days. I left England certain that Lee had already forgotten or dismissed me and my daughter.

It was very late when I arrived back home. The Channel crossing had been rough, the trains had all been jam-packed and behind schedule, the stations impossible to navigate because of the crowds of people. The waiting rooms and platforms had been filled with a stench of sweat and beer and bandages, once in a while an oasis of a floral scent on a well-dressed woman.

France had been like this since the liberation of Paris. It was as if the war had frozen us in place, and now, unfrozen, there was a great need, desire, for the freedom of movement.

Freedom to be home, to be reunited with loved ones, to go somewhere new and without memories. Some of the travelers were men whose faces were still frozen with secrets that must not be said. Some travelers had been prisoners of war. Some had been liberated from the death camps in Germany and wore ill-fitting, foreign-looking clothes provided by the Quakers. The wounded, the traumatized, the almost-dead, moved among us like waking ghosts, searching for a familiar place, somewhere, perhaps, where they had been happy, or at least safe.

I scanned the faces, hoping that if I looked hard enough, long enough, I would see her bright eyes looking back at me from the crowd.

Would she be on a ferry going from Dover to Calais? Perhaps on the train to Paris, or perhaps on the night train south from Paris? God knew where she had landed. Some of the wounded, the starved, were young girls Dahlia's age. Their faces were the most painful to search, looking for familiar features. War should happen to men or at least grown-ups, not children.

I found one girl with a resemblance to Dahlia: the black hair, the brown eyes from my side, the thick brows and high cheekbones from her father. But it wasn't Dahlia. She caught me staring at her in the Gare de Lyon and pointed at me, whispering with her friends.

My house was dark, but as soon as I went in—no key was needed; I never locked my door, in case Dahlia might make her way back home—there was a strong fragrance of flowers.

Omar had placed a vase of roses in the sitting room, to welcome me. I sat in the dark, inhaling their perfume, trying not to feel anything. I fell asleep there, on the old chintz sofa, my traveling case at my feet, unpacked. One of the street cats pushed the door open sometime in the night and came and slept next to me. I woke to its purr, and to the sound of knocking on the ajar door. Who knocked in this neighborhood?

It was a deliveryman, all uniform and smiles, with a case of champagne. From Lee. The card said only "Thank you." A gift for my silence, for the lie about whooping cough.

I stored the champagne in the small space under the cellar stairs where Nicky had told me to wall in his best bottles of wine to hide them from the Germans. After the war I bartered them for potatoes, eggs, pieces of cheese. Food somehow was even scarcer and more costly after the war than during it.

The champagne stored, I washed, dressed in one of Natalia's old flowered housedresses, and unpacked, knowing that I had to get through the day, just as I had gotten through the other days since Dahlia's disappearance. I hung the green dress behind my bedroom door, where, each time I went to sleep at night, it would remind me of my folly. Green, the color of lost hope. In the kitchen, Natalia's little kitchen where I still used the chipped and cracked china she had brought decades before, I put chickpeas to soak. I had no appetite, but I had to keep going, and that required food. I swept the floors, dusted the bookcases with Dahlia's old schoolbooks in them.

I moved through the day like a sleepwalker, rousing only when the pickers started their procession through the town, pushing and pulling carts laden with the first baskets of tea roses for the factories. They had started picking at four in the morning. I went to the open window of my bedroom, as did all the other housewives of Grasse, and inhaled deeply: first, there was a hint of aggressive clove, and then came that haunting sweet smoothness that lingers in the back of the throat that is the hallmark of the tea rose, and then an aftertaste of citrus. Meandering through the notes were myriad little grace notes of moss, pine, and pepper.

So many different scents from one plant, so many memories with each one: clove for my mother, the back-of-the-throat sweetness for Dahlia, citrus for my father, who had liked bootleg gin flavored with lemon.

Scents are like people—they are never just one thing, but a constantly changing variable. Unreliable. Attar of roses made from flowers picked from the north field of Hervé's property in 1942 had a different fragrance from the same roses, the same location, picked in 1939. That's why some recipes for fragrances were thirty pages long and were constantly being rewritten, to compensate for the unreliability of scent.

That evening, Omar came to visit just as the sun was beginning to set. I had already prepared our meal: the chickpea stew, sweet mint tea, a bowl of oranges.

Omar, like me, was a foreigner in town. To live in a place where you have not been born is to be always out of place, even when it is your choice. We chose dislocation, the surrealist angles where edges didn't quite match up.

He had come to town two years ago, raising eyebrows among the women of the town with his waving sandy hair, blue eyes, and tall, slender form. Omar was one of those searching for ghosts. His brother had come from Algeria to southern France to work in 1942, but during the great disappearing he, too, had disappeared into a German forced-labor camp, and never come back. Before that, Omar's wife had died. He was alone, like me.

Omar towered over most of the men, and because he was a man of few words, the town, in that way that small towns have, soon had an unspoken agreement that although he was Algerian, he was a man to be respected. He bought a café from an older man looking to retire, and Omar spent his days there, sitting in a chair in the sun playing chess or reading.

We had been friends since the day six months before, when I came home from Lyon to find my daughter disappeared, the day I collapsed in the street outside Madame LaRosa's empty house. He had caught me in midfall and helped me back to Natalia's house. He had brought me a cup of tea and sat there, silent, watching. Omar knew when to talk and when to be silent. And he understood that in the ways that mattered, I was already a dead woman, incapable of caring for anything other than a missing daughter. I lived in the underworld of Dahlia's disappearance. Omar and I had a trusting friendship and nothing more. We were both too filled with loss to want anything else.

"Good journey to London?" he asked now, stepping through my doorway.

Simple questions are the most difficult to answer. Good. What made a journey good? The food? The travel arrangements? The company? Or perhaps, finding a lost daughter was the only way a journey could be defined as good.

"Not good or bad," I decided. "Just useless."

"You stayed longer than you planned. There must have been a reason."

"I ran into an old . . ." I hesitated. "Friend," I finished. How else to describe Lee? With all there was between us, *acquaintance* didn't quite work as a definition, nor did *enemy*. "She invited me to her home for the weekend. I went."

"Good." Omar smiled into his teacup.

"Don't gloat. I have not been miraculously healed of all pain.

No problem has been solved. I ate more than usual, and drank too much. That's all it meant."

"Good," he said again. "I didn't know you were looking for miracles, Nora."

"I'm not. Not anymore. I think, Omar, I am never going to see Dahlia again."

"That is a bitter thought."

"But true."

"Maybe it is too soon to give up completely."

"I can't live with hope anymore—it is worse than pain. Come on, supper is ready. Let's eat."

I pushed my food around the plate and watched Omar dip his bread into the stewed chickpeas, Algerian-style. No, I corrected myself. Not Algerian. That word was so large as to be meaningless to Omar. He was a Berber, a Kabyle, born in the mountains guarding the Berber desert, and his race was so ancient they were there centuries before even the Arabs arrived. Omar told me once that a scientist who traced peoples thought the Kabyle people were of Celtic stock, part of that wandering diaspora that also took root in Spain and Turkey, so that there were Spaniards and Turks with red hair and green eyes, just as Omar had sandy hair and blue eyes.

Widowed, brotherless, he had his own grief, and that was what brought us together, and kept us together, in an undefined relationship, neither brother and sister nor lovers, just two friends who had lost too much and could sit together in comfortable silence when there was nothing left to say.

We were silent while he ate and he was good-mannered enough not to press me to eat. But afterward, when we carried the tea and cups out to the tiny patio, he wanted to talk.

"I will tell you of Grasse in your absence," he said. "And you will tell me of London."

Night birds sang in the ancient olive grove on the terrace beneath us. I could see lanterns lit in houses, candles shining through windows, and in the greater distance a few headlights from cars climbing up and down the steep road connecting Grasse and Nice. The night was mild. Soon would come the heat. Dahlia had loved the heat.

"London was cold and wet," I said.

My next-door neighbor, Madame Orieux, was quarreling loudly with her husband. Her shrill reprimands pierced the quiet, and his dull, soft *"Non, non"* of denial was like the call of a dove. They fought often, and she always won.

"And who was the friend you met?" Omar asked, speaking very quietly, since the Orieux house was only yards away from my terrace and all her windows were open.

"A woman. Lee Miller."

"The photographer? I know her work." Omar sipped his tea and coughed a warning that we were outside, we could hear the quarrel. Madame Orieux stopped her shouting and windows slammed shut. "A copy of British *Vogue* ended up in the café last month. Lee Miller's photographs of the lovely people of St. Moritz are in it."

"The beautiful people, that's what they are called," I corrected.

"Lovely, beautiful. But they are not. The women wear too much makeup and they are built like boys." Omar poured more tea and sipped it thoughtfully. "So, you met this old friend, Lee Miller. Where did you go?"

"First, to a tearoom. We ate éclairs. Then, she asked me to spend the weekend at her country house."

"And you did."

"And I did. Why, I don't know."

"Do you not?" Omar reached over and took my hand. "So much has been lost it is good to find something again for a change."

I hadn't wanted to find Lee. I had wanted to find my daughter. The visit with Lee at Farley Farm had been a detour, that was all. But I found myself smiling, pleased that Lee had survived.

"Tell me what has happened in Grasse since I left," I said. "How is Fatima?" Fatima was his housekeeper. She was also a wonderful seamstress and a great fan of Coco Chanel, able to imitate her styles without patterns, though using much humbler fabrics and without using the glass pearls and beads. It was not unusual, in Grasse, to see women pickers in the fields wearing what, from a distance, looked like Chanel jackets.

I hadn't had the heart to tell Fatima when the great Chanel had been accused of being a collaborator and rescued from her own ignoble trial and possible imprisonment by her friend Winston Churchill.

"Fatima is well. She will come tomorrow and visit you. The first tea roses have been picked. Madame Guiard gave birth to a baby boy. I finished *La peste*. You should read it, Nora, it is quite good. Camus has created a fable about the German occupation. Did you see any soldiers in the north, when you were traveling?"

"Almost none. It is as if a street sweeper has pushed them down the rain gutter and washed them away."

Omar leaned back in his chair and thoughtfully steepled his fingertips together in front of his face. "Grasse is already busy with the season's work. I told you, the tea roses are already blooming. Don't worry, my friend." He reached over and took my hand, gave it a little squeeze of reassurance. "You are safe. Tell me, who else was there, at this house in the country in England?"

"Two silly young women from California, a journalist from everywhere, and Pablo Picasso."

Omar had been tilting back in his wicker chair, gently rocking it back and forth. He stopped. "The artist," he said quietly.

"Yes. That Pablo. I knew him years before, in Paris."

Omar laughed. "And you never thought to mention this? Next, you will tell me that Princess Elizabeth was Dahlia's godmother or that . . ." He struggled, considered. "Or that Albert Camus sends you letters."

"No. None of those things is true. But yes, I knew Pablo Picasso in Paris. He even did me a favor, once. He sent me to Grasse."

"Then I hope to thank him someday." Omar reached over and patted my hand. "I must tell you. André Bonner is gone."

"Gone?" I couldn't even say his name.

"Yes. He took all the money from his father's till and left in the middle of the night."

After Dahlia's disappearance, the police had finally questioned the butcher's son. He had denied everything, and his father had repeated the story that they had been together at home the night of Dahlia's rape. But after his false accusations about me, after Dahlia's disappearance, the entire town had turned against him. "Nazi lover" had been painted on the door of his house.

We sat in silence after that, Omar probably thinking of strategies for tomorrow's chess game with Monsieur Hubert, who was a formidable player. I tried to think of nothing, not of Lee or Jamie or Nicky or Natalia, or even Dahlia. And the harder I tried not to think of them, the more they crowded around me so that soon I was having trouble breathing. Where was my daughter?

# CHAPTER TWENTY-TWO

After that trip to London, that meeting with Lee, I resumed living, which was not the same as enjoying life. I woke and drank coffee, I went to my work. I came home, I ate a little. I sat in my chair and listened to the radio, and then I went to bed to sleep just enough to have strength to repeat the process the next day.

Sometimes I woke in the middle of the night and thought I heard the floorboards creaking outside the door of Natalia's bedroom, or the gentle breathing of Dahlia in the room next to mine, and I would have to suffer, all over again, the first pains of learning I was alone. Sometimes I thought about the panther in the zoological gardens in Paris, and wondered if he had survived the war. I hadn't stopped to see him, when I was searching for my daughter. The thought of his hard yellow gaze undid the little courage I had left.

I worked daily in the enfleurage room, pressing petal after petal of jasmine into trays of fat, where the flower essence would transfer itself from petal to fat. The petals had to be changed dozens of times during the next twenty-four hours to really saturate the fat with the odor. Then, the pomade would be washed in alcohol, and the alcohol itself allowed to evaporate. The "absolute" would be the end result, the powerful essence of fragrance that would be used, drop by drop, in the most expensive perfumes.

Slowly, the perfume industry came back to life after the war, despite a shortage of labor, despite the difficulties of obtaining supplies, despite still-irregular shipping. Perfume is not a thing aside from the rest of life. Love enters through the eyes, but joy first enters through the nose and celebration requires perfume. Many of the perfume manufacturers had celebrated the end of the war by passing samples to the American GIs, to thank them and to remind them they had girls and wives back home waiting to see them again. New perfumes had been named for the day that Paris was liberated, and one perfumer tied thousands of small bottles of his perfume to miniature green and white parachutes and dropped them over Paris.

Perfume was part of the celebration of victory for some, survival for others.

So, we were busy. Dozens of us would work at a time in the enfleurage and still rooms, filling the perfumed air with chatter, so that sometimes when I would smell a certain fragrance, it would remind me that Celestine's daughter had had the mumps when I pressed the jasmine petals, or that Anne-Marie had celebrated the birth of her first grandchild that day. Perfume itself was a form of memory, of a day, a certain soil, a particular flower in bloom. In the enfleurage room, we pressed memories into more memories.

Sometimes I would be asked to go to the director's office to translate a letter or business order sent to or from New York, and history would be repeated. I could see that eventually I would leave the factory for the office, for better pay and the things that money brought—new cushions for the sofa, rugs to replace the ones that had been taken, perhaps a car to replace the one I had given up.

But there was no pleasure in those expectations. Not without Dahlia.

And then one day in August I received a letter from Pablo Picasso. "Come see me," he said. "Day after tomorrow. I have news for you. Good news."

Omar had brought me the letter from the post office, and waited as I tore it open and read it.

"Ah," he said. He could see it in my face. "Don't be afraid to hope, Nora."

"He says there is good news."

"Then you must believe him."

"I can't. Because if it is not news of Dahlia, good news of Dahlia, I think I will not survive it." And then I felt selfish because he had lost his brother and his wife and yet he comforted me.

Omar should have been a photographer or an artist. He read people better than Man Ray had, even better than Pablo did. "It is all right, Nora. Your hope will not harm me. I take pleasure in any good news my friend receives."

The next day I rose early. I borrowed Omar's ancient Citroën and motored down through the hills, refusing to allow myself to feel hope and optimism. It was a fool's errand, I told myself repeatedly. He had some useless message from Lee, an invitation to a party or some nonsense. Do not feel hope, I commanded myself, much in the same way during the war I had commanded myself not to feel hungry, or afraid. Feel nothing or at least as little as possible. That was the safest path.

It was a fine summer day, hazy with heat and sun that made the scent of wild thyme and lavender rise up like a kind of hope and prayer.

By late morning, following Pablo's directions, I had reached Vallauris, a small seaside town of whitewashed houses and rocky hillsides dotted with silvery gray olive trees. People were sitting at the crowded tables set up on the beach, and children with sand pails and little shovels ran back and forth, shouting with delight.

I stopped at one of the red-and-white-striped-awning cafés for a coffee and sat remembering the times I had taken Dahlia to swim in the bay of Cannes, usually at la Napoule, a smaller and less expensive place than Cannes. The little town and beach there were presided over by an ancient castle guaranteed to fascinate any young girl. During the war the castle's owner, a rich American named Marie Clews, had stayed and worked as a maid for the Germans who had taken over her castle, so that she could remain there, close to her husband's grave.

Don't think of graves, I warned myself.

I finished my coffee, got back into Omar's car, and found the street leading to Pablo's villa, la Galloise.

It was a ramshackle little house, not very pretty or even well maintained, but lovingly situated in a sunny space on the hillside, with ocean views and silvery olive trees off to the side.

A pretty dark-haired young woman with a baby in her arms and a raw-kneed boy clinging to her legs opened the door to my knock.

"You must be Nora," she said. "He told me you would be coming." She did not sound pleased to see me, but any woman with two children under the age of three has the right to seem annoyed and preoccupied by a stranger on her doorstep.

"I'm Françoise. Come in."

Lee had told me about her, briefly: Pablo's new lover, the reason he had grown silent when I asked after Marie-Thérèse and Olga. Françoise Gilot had been studying law in Paris when she met Pablo in a restaurant. During the war she had quit her studies to become a painter and Pablo's mistress. She was less than half his age.

"I said, come in." Françoise was lovely and plainly impatient. She looked over my shoulder before taking me by the hand and pulling me into the house. "Last year Olga came and plagued us. She still won't give him a divorce, you know. Catholic. She stood in front of the house calling me names. God knows what the villagers think. Can you believe it? I keep checking to make certain she isn't back. Coffee?"

She thrust her head back out the door and looked left and right before slamming it shut.

"No, thank you." The house was cool and smelled of last night's dinner of scampi. Françoise was a different kind of housekeeper from Pablo's wife, Olga, and the little villa showed obvious signs of busy occupation—toys on the floor, a milk bowl for a kitten in the corner, a perch with an owl on it, blinking at me and twisting his head almost in a circle in that strange owl fashion. Gauzy curtains fluttered in the breeze, showing cobwebs attached to the underside.

Françoise stepped over a pile of wet beach towels and led me into the kitchen.

"So you are Nora Tours," she said, sitting down, balancing the baby on her knees so she could tousle the little boy's hair. He had a long forelock, just as Pablo had once had. "I know one of your perfumes. What was it called? Oh, yes. Panther. Almost all amber, with just hints of rose and thyme."

I had made that one before the war, for a niece of Madame LaRosa, as a birthday present.

"How did you come across it?" I asked, sitting down opposite her. "Only a few bottles were ever made, a single small batch."

"My father was a perfumer. He got it from somewhere. Friend of a friend. Are you still making perfumes?" Françoise took a biscuit from an opened wrapper and broke it in pieces for the boy, who looked up at her with Pablo's dark, expressive eyes.

"Haven't composed any in a while."

"I ran away from home, you know. My father wouldn't let me give up law to become an artist. I never see him anymore. For this." She laughed.

"I ran away, too. From Poughkeepsie. And then from Paris."

"I know. Pablo told me. Are you sure you don't want a cup of coffee? Maybe something stronger?"

"No. Please, why did he send for me?"

Françoise grew serious. She kissed the top of her baby's head, inhaling that rich smell of infancy, and a wave of brown hair fell over her face. "I'm supposed to prepare you," she said, brushing the hair back. "Oh, God. Look at your face. Here." She took a bottle of whiskey from the tray on the table and poured me a glass.

"It's good news, Nora. Lee found your daughter. Actually, her friend Davy Scherman found her. He's researching a book on Paris and Lee told him to ask everywhere, to scour the streets, ask favors of all their contacts, for her friend's missing daughter."

"I looked in Paris," I said. "Everywhere. Asked at all the centers, all the offices tracking people, all the hostels and rooming houses."

"I'll bet you didn't look in this place—a Dominican convent outside of Paris. The nuns had taken her in. Someone had found her begging outside of Notre-Dame."

I drank the whiskey but refused a second shot when Françoise offered the bottle. The baby on her lap began to pull on her long hair. Françoise patiently untangled his fists.

I had so many questions. Why had Dahlia gone to Paris? Why had she left? What had she planned to do? Why hadn't she come home to me? But the questions could wait.

"Where is she?" I asked.

"Down at the studio, with Pablo. She arrived the day before."

It seemed a century before I could react, before I could breathe, or see, or smell the little vase of wild lavender and roses on the table. A century of nothing passed, and then a moment of everything arrived.

"Dahlia is here?"

"I told you. In the studio. She knows you're coming. She seems to be in good shape. A little thin, a little dirty when she first arrived, but she cleaned up nicely. Pretty girl." Did I imagine it, or was there a hint of jealousy in Françoise's voice? "There's a letter here for you from Lee." Françoise took an envelope from a pile of unopened mail and handed it to me.

My hand was surprisingly steady as I took the envelope and opened it as carefully as I pulled petals from rosebuds in the factory workroom. I recognized Lee's bold handwriting.

> Dear Nora,
> Contacts can be useful. Davy and I used all of them, in the army and the diplomatic service, and of course, finally it was a fishmonger who supplied fish for the American ambassador who told Davy where the child was. She had been sent out to buy fish for dinner and he noticed her, a girl from the south. No one in that place had seen her before.

The other children the nuns had sheltered during the war had all gone home or found new ones and he wondered who the stranger was. I have found your daughter, Nora. She wouldn't tell Davy why she wouldn't go back home to you and he decided not to force her, to use an intermediary for the reunion. Remember being sixteen and being dragged back home? At least, I do.

I remember more than you think. I knew all along you had been that childhood friend, the one who pulled me off the porch to play. A couple of times in Paris I almost said something. But I didn't want to talk about it. Some memories, the more you talk about them, the stronger they become. Remember that when you speak with your daughter.

So, this is a very belated thank-you. If I had gone back into the house that day, instead of being pulled off the porch by you, I might never have been able to come out again. The favor is returned. Have to go. Anthony is screaming for attention.

Keep in touch this time.

Lee

I stood. "Where is the studio?"

"Follow the path down the hill. It will lead you right there. The studio is an old perfume factory."

I could feel Françoise's eyes on me as I found the path and began the gentle climb back down the hill. Then I heard the door shut and Françoise went back to her life, her children, as I walked to my child. Nothing mattered but that. Dahlia would be at the end of this journey.

Each footstep on that rocky patch made the world new. Put your foot down, and light separates from darkness. Another step and the water separates from the land. Birds fly overhead on the fourth step. Dahlia is here. Dahlia is here. Dahlia is here became the rhythm of my steps and nothing mattered except that. The sun was high and hot on my shoulders and it seemed I had never felt such a wonderful warmth before. The light itself was a kind of home and everything else was just an address.

# EPILOGUE
# SILLAGE

After the *départ*, after the surprise of the top note, the reassurance of the middle note, the longing of the bottom notes, there is *sillage*, the wake that is left when a woman wearing perfume leaves the room. *Sillage* is the closest thing to a molecular memory, the closest thing to permanence in the impermanent life of fragrance, for it is *sillage* that imprints on the mind to create the final, lasting impression. It is the closing of the perfume's story.

—Notebooks of N. Tours

## August 4, 1977

I am just going out the door for a picnic at Upton Lake with Dahlia and her three children when the postman arrives, carrying a letter from Roland Penrose. I haven't heard from him in years and I know without opening it what the letter will say. I take the mail and go back inside to the coolness of the kitchen in Dahlia's summerhouse.

Lee has died.

She was seventy, a bit young to die, I think, since, I, too, am now seventy. But considering all the risks she took, all she went through, perhaps it was a good span for her. She could so easily have died a violent death any number of times, but instead she died at home after a long slow illness, with her husband at her side.

Lee, that beautiful, radiant, damaged child. The drop-dead gorgeous model. The brave and talented photographer. The woman who found my lost child. Gone. After that weekend at Farley Farm when she showed me those photographs of the war and war's aftermath, Lee mostly photographed her family and friends, turning away from the crueler, uglier things that destroy, that kill or at least leave lasting scars.

I refold the letter and close my eyes, seeing that little girl in her white dress on her porch.

"Are you okay, Momma?" Dahlia comes in and sees the look on my face. She is in early middle age, but when I see her, I still see the girl sitting at the potting wheel in Pablo's studio in Vallauris, her face smeared with clay, her eyes wide with delight mixed with fear, the girl who stood hesitantly and came to me, older, sadder because that is what time does to us.

My daughter, who had once been lost to me, but was found by Lee. *After they took you away, André came to the house.* The hesitation lasted only a second. She ran to my opened arms. *He broke the window next to the side door and forced himself in. He told me I would never see you again. That you had been shot as a traitor. That it was my fault because I had told. So I ran away. I was afraid of him. I thought you were dead.*

We slept in Pablo's studio that night. Françoise gave us pillows and blankets and supper. Dahlia curled in my arms, a child again. The next day, we went home to Grasse.

"Lee Miller has died," I say, putting the letter in my pocket.

"Oh." Dahlia takes the car keys from the hook by the door and jangles them, an expression of indifference on her lovely face. She met Lee once, in 1955 in New York, where Lee had exhibited in the Family of Man show in the Museum of Modern Art. Dahlia was still a college student then, just beginning her final year. Lee had taken Dahlia's hand and winked at me. The three of us did not talk about 1949, about the six months of Dahlia's disappearance or what had happened to her before that.

But I knew that Dahlia still had the occasional nightmare, as did Lee. The past does not die. It just acquires more shadows, blurs a bit like a fading photograph.

Lee Miller's final photographic essay for *Vogue* had been published two years before that night in New York: a humorous guide for home entertaining that poked fun at the Soviet system of work camps. She had photographed Roland and a whole regiment of famous artists shelling peas, clipping the grass, watering the garden at Farley Farm. And then Lee had put away her cameras. I think she got tired of shadows, of tones of gray. I think the images she had taken as a war correspondent never faded in her imagination, and whenever she held a camera and looked through the viewfinder, she was seeing unspeakable things.

Lee channeled her famous energy and determination into cooking, of all things. I think that was how she finally found a measure of peace, through the simple act of preparing food and placing it before friends and family. She became quite good at it, a gourmet.

"Well, are you ready? Tad says he wants to drive." Tad is Dahlia's oldest son and he looks much like his father, Thaddeaus, tall and blond and a little too serious. Like his father, he wants to be a physician. Dahlia's second son, William, thinks only about football and Dahlia already worries that he will be aimless, unambitious.

Her daughter, ten-year-old Adele, is a beauty. All anyone asks is that she smile. The sun comes out and all is right with the world when Adele smiles. Adele plans to become a photojournalist. Jamie gives her a new camera almost every Christmas.

Dahlia herself is a professor of French literature at New York University. As soon as she was old enough, as soon as she was able, she returned to the United States and studied here, not in Paris, agreeing to spend her summers with me in Nice as long as I agreed to spend Christmas with her in New York. Omar doesn't like New York. Too cold. He stays in France when I make my visits, sits over his chessboard and answers the business phone when someone calls to commission a perfume. I have composed perfumes for several movie stars (more of Lee's contacts), for the wife of a Nobel Prize winner, for several department stores that want a name brand.

Omar and I live in Cannes for most of the year, close enough to my beloved lavender fields and olive groves, but far enough away from Grasse and that sad history there so that we could start fresh with each other.

Shortly after Lee found my daughter for me, Dahlia met her father, and her father's wife, Clara. We have created a livable peace for all of us, though when I visit, I still catch Mrs. Sloane looking at me as if she would rather I disappeared back to France and never bothered them again. Jamie adores his daughter by me, and Dahlia, an only child for so long, enjoys the company of her half sister and half brother, her nieces and nephews. It is a family filled with tension and sometimes ill will and much too much regret. But we are bound together. Dahlia and I move back and forth, by plane now, not ship, and home is always in front of us or just behind us, except for the home we carry inside that is more than mere place.

Now that Lee is gone, part of my home is also gone. I think of her that day in front of the panther's cage in Paris, smoking cigarette after cigarette, musing about love and what is given up in its name. Beautiful Lee Miller. The little girl, Lee. The radiant young woman enchanting all of Paris. The exhausted mother, the bickering wife. The model, the photographer, the trailblazing female war correspondent. They were all Lee.

Roland sent an old photograph along with the letter telling of her death. Lee and Man, me and Jamie, sitting outdoors at the Dôme in strangely old-fashioned clothing, looking young and hopeful, and all of us, in one way or another, wildly in love, in Paris. It's a good photo. I wonder who took it? A stranger? Perhaps Aziz was there, or Julien? Doesn't really matter anymore. There was a moment when anything was possible and the photograph proves it. Photos are a visual *sillage*, what remains when all else has left.

"Come on, Momma!" Dahlia yells. "The motor's running."

# ABOUT THE AUTHOR

In addition to several other novels as well as short fiction and creative nonfiction, **Jeanne Mackin** is the author of *The Cornell Book of Herbs and Edible Flowers* and coeditor of *The Norton Book of Love.* She is the recipient of a creative writing fellowship from the American Antiquarian Society and her journalism has won awards from the Council for the Advancement and Support of Education, in Washington, D.C. She teaches creative writing at Goddard College in Vermont and lives with her husband, artist Steve Poleskie, in upstate New York.

CONNECT ONLINE

jeannemackin.com
facebook.com/jeannemackinauthor
twitter.com/jeannemackin1

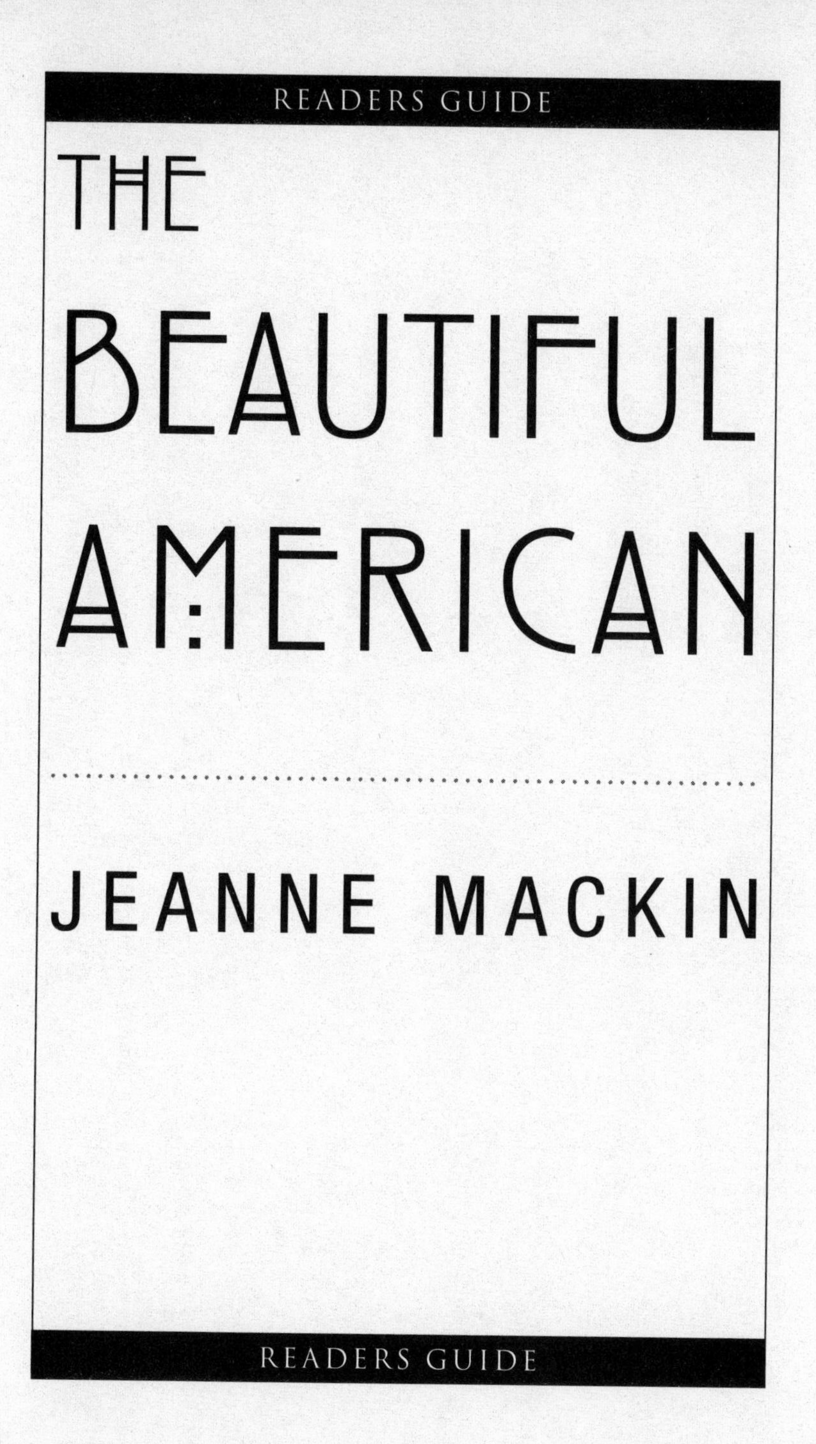
READERS GUIDE
THE
BEAUTIFUL
AMERICAN
JEANNE MACKIN
READERS GUIDE

# A CONVERSATION WITH JEANNE MACKIN

*Q. What inspired you to write this novel?*

A. Lee Miller was such a fabulous woman: beautiful, intelligent, brave, talented. Who could resist? Many people, myself included, read historical fiction because they want to learn about previous times and people, and it seemed the right time to bring Lee to the attention of readers. Her life was such a compendium of major events: the beginnings of photography as an art form, the Great Depression, World War II; her life seemed wide open for a fictional treatment. She was stunningly beautiful and yet she wasn't content to be merely beautiful; she went on to create her own art. Her photographs are bold and subtle and sometimes ahead of their time. She made surrealist photos, as did Man Ray, but you can also see the beginnings of minimalism in her advertising work. And her war photos . . . those speak for themselves. What bravery they required. I wrote about Lee Miller because I wanted to learn about her, to think about her, and I thought others would find her fascinating as well.

*Q. Why did you choose a fictional woman as your main character and make Lee Miller a secondary character?*

A. I needed a character who could be in a relationship with Lee during many decades and in many settings, from Poughkeepsie to Paris to London. I invented Nora as a counterpart to Lee, almost an alter ego. Lee is wealthy; Nora is lower middle class. Lee is bold and somewhat reckless; Nora prefers the sidelines. The two women learn from each other, and perhaps that is what a lasting friendship offers. In real life, I think Lee was closer to men than women, so I gave her Nora as a kind of gift, the friend she may not have had.

*Q. Several recent novels portray the American expat community in Paris during the 1920s, but your novel begins as the '20s was concluding and goes all the way to post–World War II Europe. Why did you want to cover this longer period?*

A. I wanted to show the full arc of Lee's life, not just a section of it. As I worked on this novel, I saw that it became a story about consequences, cause and effect—this happens because that happened earlier—and sometimes it takes years, decades, for those sequences to manifest in a life. It was also important for me to show historical connections, almost a kind of inevitability in the way history unfolded, from the recklessness of the Roaring Twenties to the Great Depression, to the war that resulted from the poverty and unemployment the Depression created.

*Q. Since readers may not be familiar with Lee Miller, can you tell us more about her popularity as a model and in what regard her photography was held then, and today? Can you tell us more about the childhood rape that haunted her? Do we know what medical treatment she received and what mysterious ill health dogged her for the rest of her life? What happened to her in her later years?*

A. Lee's father was a freethinker and he encouraged his only daughter to be equally freethinking. He encouraged Lee to pose for photographs, to learn to be comfortable in her body rather than be ashamed of it. I think that allowed Lee to heal as much as anyone can heal from the violence of rape. Because she was unbound by convention, and was startlingly, impossibly beautiful, modeling also made sense for her as a way to leave Poughkeepsie and live on a larger stage. Photographers as well as artists loved having her pose for them. You can see it in the photos of her: she treats her body like a medium as well as a message. She was unwittingly set up for scandal on some occasions, though. In one early modeling job she thought she was merely modeling an evening gown, but in fact the photo was used to advertise menstruation pads: it was the first ad to do so, and people were horrified that something so private was made public. Lee let the uproar die down, and went on modeling.

It's difficult to know how many people actually knew about the rape. For the novel, I imagined it as a closely kept family secret. Small-town gossip could be especially devastating then, and memories could be so long.

The treatment for the gonorrhea Lee caught during the

rape—this was before penicillin and other antibiotics—was gruesome to read about: acid douches, antiseptic sitz baths, catheters, swabs of the cervix with more acids, done in the hospital by staff and at home by Lee's mother. The child would have had to let her body be completely taken over by the process, no modesty allowed. In a way, it must have been a reliving of the rape every time she was treated. No wonder her father encouraged her to separate feelings from physical acts. And because the treatment was only moderately successful at best, for years after—perhaps for the rest of her life—she would have been dogged by the aftereffects of the disease, the debilitating fatigue and fevers.

After the war, after those images Lee took of the concentration camps and the general devastation, she eventually stopped taking photographs of anything other than family and friends. She turned to cooking and became well-known as a gourmet cook. She loved feeding people and Lee and Roland were famous for their hospitality. After Lee died, her son discovered crates of her photographs and journals, and they became the basis both of his wonderful biography about his mother, *The Lives of Lee Miller*, and the Lee Miller Archive at Farley House.

*Q. Why was it important to you that Nora's daughter should also become a victim of rape? What parallels between the two women did you want to explore?*

A. More attention is being paid to the relationship between war and rape. Women's bodies become so much collateral damage, a kind of territory to be "occupied." We've seen this over and over again in current political upheavals. Historians are also beginning to research wartime rape and document its prevalence during previous wars. *Savage Continent* by Keith Lowe (St. Martin's Press, 2012) is an eye-opening book about the raping in Europe during and immediately after World War II, and what happened to the children of those rapes.

Dahlia is not raped by a soldier, but I still see her as a victim of the war; her rapist is empowered by the chaos of war. With so many men fighting at the front or surreptitiously in the resistance, or in prisoner camps, entire villages and towns were left more or less at the mercy of the men who stayed behind. And because there was such poverty and hunger, many women, housewives and schoolgirls as well, prostituted themselves just to keep food on the table. When sex becomes a commodity, lines are blurred between willing and not willing. The police were concerned with war crimes and keeping order; tracking down rapists wasn't always a priority, even when the rapes were reported. In war everyone suffers, not just the soldiers.

Dahlia is older than Lee was when her rape occurs. Even in fiction, I couldn't bear the thought of forcing such violence upon a very young child; bad enough that it happens to Dahlia in her teens. I thought it important that there be that parallel with Lee, though, to show that rape isn't limited to certain times or ages. It is Lee's suffering, repeated in her daughter's life, that forces Nora to learn how to forgive.

*Q. Can you tell us more about what happened to Man Ray after Lee left his life? Is his art as well regarded today as it was in the 1920s?*

A. Man Ray created one of the most recognizable images of modern art: that photo of a nude Kiki de Montparnasse with the fret holes of a cello painted on her back, making the woman's body an instrument. That image will endure because, first, it is very beautiful and memorable, and second, because it is such an important statement about how men often objectify women. Man Ray was not a feminist in any sense of the word, but his images are important, often startling statements. Then, too, the violence of some of his images was a precursor of the violence to come in the war. His art was playful, but also in touch with something mysterious. I don't think you can know twentieth-century art without knowing his art.

Lee and Man became and remained great friends after their affair ended. I think Lee was one of those people with whom others just couldn't stay angry. Eventually Man did move back to Paris and continued to live and work there.

*Q. I loved learning about perfume. Is Grasse still the perfume capital of France? Have artificial scents improved since the 1940s?*

A. I revisited Grasse when I was working on this novel. It's such a beautiful place, one of my favorite French towns. And yes, they still think of themselves as the perfume capital, and with reason. They are still surrounded by fields of lavender and have several museums of perfume history.

Whether the artificial scents have improved or not is a matter of opinion. Certainly many essences are easier and cheaper to replicate, so good perfume is more affordable. What I found fascinating is that plants, like wines, have vintages and will vary from year to year, depending on the soil, weather, and other growing conditions. Fragrance formulas have to be continuously reworked to maintain consistency so that, say, Chanel No. 5 made in 2014 smells like the Chanel No. 5 made in 2001.

*Q. You make postwar France sound almost as dangerous as during the war. Can you tell us more about reprisals imposed on ordinary people for aiding and abetting the enemy in Occupied France?*

A. People tend to think the war ended when peace was declared. In fact, the hunger, the rationing, the shortages, the upheavals, lasted for years after. The violence lasted as well, not in the form of battles but in retribution. Estimates vary, but in France alone hundreds of people may have been shot by snipers or knifed in the dark by people wanting revenge, especially against those thought or known to have been collaborators. This included women who had slept with enemy soldiers, and in dozens of towns women had their heads shaved; many were stripped naked and marched through the streets. Men felt emasculated by the war and the Vichy government; they reclaimed their manhood by punishing women and assassinating the collaborators. Thousands of people were put on trial for the crime of collaboration or simply for being insufficiently patriotic. Pétain himself was sentenced to life in prison. The Europeans had to rebuild their relationships, their towns, their countries, and this took time.

*Q. Can you tell us a little about your background as a writer? Have particular writers influenced your work?*

A. When I was a kid, I read indiscriminately. Everything. My parents didn't look over my shoulder at the titles, and my father even joked that I read books by the pound. He used to read Victorian poems out loud in the evenings: "The Face upon the Floor," "Curfew Must Not Ring Tonight," "The Raven," "Only a Bird in a Gilded Cage" . . . those great old story poems. I went to Catholic school, and the nuns raised a few eyebrows over some of the books I chose to do book reports on. My grandmother's house had a small library full of the classics: Zane Grey, the Tarzan books, some weird and wonderful books about Victorian spiritualism. I would curl up there for hours at a time. I was, and remain, totally impressed that my grandparents, who raised ten kids in a small house, kept a room just for books and reading. I've read everything by Daphne du Maurier and Anya Seton, Dickens and Hawthorne. Popular authors like Romain Gary and Paul Gallico were a major influence when I was first mapping my way through my own fiction. I like the great storytellers, the narrative writers. Must be because of those great Victorian poems.

*Q. You live in a rural area of upstate New York. What role, if any, does geography play in your writing life?*

A. Geography helps form character, doesn't it? Our families, our historical settings, our inherent nature and personality, and then the world immediately around us, our geography, make us who we are, I think. I grew up in the country, at the edge of a small town, and I can't imagine what my childhood would have been like without trees big enough to climb, mud puddles up to my shins, robins' nests in the bushes, and snowdrifts up to my waist. My childhood made me a daydreamer, able to get lost in my own thoughts and be quite content with my own company—key ingredients for a writer. My writing room, now, is on the second floor with windows all around and trees outside the windows, kind of like being in a big treehouse.

*Q. Where do you keep the pile of books you hope to read soon, and what titles are in it?*

A. I love this question! I do have piles of books all over the house. Ask my husband, who patiently goes around and places bookmarks in them for me, since I'm usually reading four or five simultaneously and I tend to leave them open, like huge butterflies, on top of all the furniture. My reading right now includes research for the next novel: histories, biographies, memoirs. Research is a great adventure for me. Pleasure reading at the moment is *The Discovery of Middle Earth* by Graham Robb, about the ancient Celts. I regularly reread two titles that are masterpieces of historical fiction: *The Wide Sargasso Sea* by Jean Rhys, and *The Passion* by Jeanette Winterson. My book group just finished the *Old Filth* trilogy by Jane Gardam and we were all delighted by it. I'm still reading books by the pound.

# QUESTIONS FOR DISCUSSION

1. What did you most enjoy about the novel? What do you think you will remember about it many months from now?

2. When Nora and Lee play together as children, Lee is the more daring. During your own childhood, were you more like Nora or Lee? Discuss the dangerous risks that Lee takes during the novel. Does she pay a price for her boldness? Is great risk-taking necessary for great achievement?

3. If the friendship between Nora and Lee lies at the heart of the novel, what kind of friendship is it? How does it evolve over time? Discuss the ways in which they each betray the other, yet also save each other.

4. In the author's portrayal of ardent young love between Nora and Jamie, what details make their romance come alive for you? Why do you think Jamie betrays Nora? Is Nora right or wrong in not telling him about her pregnancy? Compare the Nora/Jamie

relationship with the Lee/Man Ray relationship. Is one love more "true" than the other?

5. Discuss how Lee's childhood rape might have shaped her adult attitude toward sex and emotional intimacy. What other factors might have also contributed to her unconventional beliefs? Do you consider her behavior liberated or pathological?

6. Like the main character in Woody Allen's movie *Midnight in Paris*, do you wish you could have lived in Paris in the 1920s? Do you consider our own time inferior to the past, and if so, in what ways?

7. Discuss the mother/child relationships in the novel—Nora and her mother, Nora and Dahlia, and Lee and Anthony. How is Natalia also a mother to Nora? Who among them is the "good" mother?

8. Jamie never finds artistic recognition for his photography and ends up back in Poughkeepsie taking pictures of local events. Does he consider himself a failure? Do you? Discuss the role that changing taste plays in keeping him from success. Do you know an artist of any kind whose work is currently out of favor but who is perhaps worthy of recognition?

9. As a model, Lee seems to be aware of how photographs objectify her beauty and turn her into something that isn't fully real or female. Discuss how she and Man Ray explore this idea in their art and in their life together (for example, at Lee's party). At

the end of the novel, are there indications that Lee has moved beyond this subject?

10. Lee describes photographing the Nazi death camps and taking a bath in Hitler's bathtub. What do you think the bath signifies for her?

11. What does the panther in the Paris zoo represent for Nora?

12. Do you have a signature scent? Would Nora think it suits you?